OUR FATHER

Marilyn French

OUR FATHER
a novel

BCA

LONDON   NEW YORK   SYDNEY   TORONTO

This edition published 1994
by BCA by arrangement with
Hamish Hamilton
CN 6624

Copyright © Belles-Lettres, Inc., 1994

Printed in England by Clays Ltd, St Ives plc

To my coven sisters

E. M. Broner
Carol Jenkins
Gloria Steinem

With love and gratitude

Part I

The Sisters

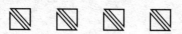

1

"Women can hurt you just as much as men!" Ronnie muttered fiercely from the shadowed window seat. The others sat around the fireless hearth in lamplight that glittered the golden threads in Mary's blouse, a gold chain at Elizabeth's neck, the gold of Alex's hair. Gold: his gift to them.

The phones had stopped ringing. Elizabeth took all the important calls. Wanted to be sure she was the one who spoke to the president, the secretary of state, the president of West Germany. She let Mary take the personal ones. They didn't let Alex take any of them. That Elizabeth: mean mouth, skinny, the eldest. Acted like a big important person. Guess she is. Secretary of the treasury or something. But Mary is just as snotty. What's her excuse. She's good-looking but she's getting fat. All she ever did was get married, I think. Married a lot of rich men. Legal prostitution. Alex is meek and mild compared to them. Ditzy little housewife. How did she get into this family? Hah! How did I?

No one responded to her. Alex turned around to look at her, lingeringly, but turned back without speaking. Ronnie abruptly swiveled to face the window. Dark out. She could see only a swathe of lawn and the dark mass of trees that concealed the house from the road a third of a mile away. Bare limbs ghastly stretching into darkness: November. Thanks to the goddess for evergreens — no sounds, not even car lights penetrated them. Few cars traveled this back road anyway. Road looked as if it traversed just old forest but was really lined with mansions.

Have to get out of here. Should leave, don't belong here, they don't want me here.

The telephone rang. Mrs. Browning entered.

"The governor," she whispered to Elizabeth, who leapt up and left the room.

What *is* the girl on about? Mary wondered. Was that outburst because of what I said about men? From the look of her, how would she know? God knows *I* have the right to comment on men: who's had more experience with them? Besides, Father *is* a tyrant and a baby at the same time, it *was* stupid and childish of him to go on using salt when he knew he had high blood pressure. They *are* all little boys, they never grow up. All my husbands were boys with toys: Don and his hateful motorcycle, Paul and his plane, Harold and his Rolls, Alberto — well, he played with women. And I got stuck with all the kids.

Strange girl, her face a fist, flushed, dim in her dark corner, tacky jeans and sweatshirt, sneakers and heavy socks, feet up on the window seat, looks like a dyke for godsake, does she know how she looks? Does she care?

Funny Elizabeth hasn't closed the drapes, she always does, shutting out the darkness, nothing else, nothing out there but trees. Never was. House in a void, emptiness, emptiness . . .

Stop.

Good heavens, those drapes look tacky and faded. When was I here last? Summer party, his eightieth birthday. Two years ago. Things weren't seedy then, that I noticed anyway. Window seat cushion is tatty, needs recovering, brocade faded, frayed cording. Father has let things slip. But did he ever pay attention to such things? I wonder who did. Housekeeper maybe. No one here but that woman . . . perhaps she didn't comprehend keeping up appearances but he should have. Surely some of his friends visited. Unless he outlived them all. Eighty-two: not so old, men like him live into their nineties, a hundred. They are so well taken care of all their lives long. They never take risks. Don.

*   *   *

Elizabeth returned, a self-satisfied smile on her face.

"The governor is deeply worried."

She sat down, giving Ronnie a sharp glance. She had already noted and filed away the fact that the girl was mad in some way uncategorizable at the moment but still noticeably insane. Probably we are too. But at least we put up a front. Maybe Alex is sane, middle-class housewife type, never thinks further than the next bridge party. Only way to stay sane, ride the current, let yourself be borne along. Still, you read about all those house-wives on tranqs. But Alex is stupid, best protection against madness. Of course, Mary's stupid too. Only brilliant when it comes to advancing herself through men. All driven mad, no help for it. Our Father. Father, oh Daddy Daddy. Our father which art not yet and perhaps never will be in heaven. But who knows, if the one up there made up the rules we follow down here, he may approve of him. In His will is our peace.

I wonder if his will is in his desk.

What do you suppose Ronnie meant by that? Alex wondered, her eyes flitting from object to object in the room, strange room, yet I must have been in it many times before. Barely remember. My curse, no memory. Of course it's probably been redecorated since then. A few glimmering images from long ago — I remember that Georgian side table, I think. Was she criticizing Mary for criticizing Father? But Mary was really expressing rage about some other man, I think. She's been married more than once, I think. Sad, divorce. That's probably what Ronnie is saying too, she's upset with some woman, some woman hurt her, her mother dying maybe, maybe us, sitting here so coolly when Father may be dying. But we're sitting in the quiet of shock, it seems to me. Not uncaring. Are we? Espe-cially me, summoned to the perhaps deathbed of my father when I never knew him living, can barely remember except for that day I came up here with Stevie, so terrible, but maybe it was because I never came to see him all those years, never even sent him a card or anything. But he never called me either. Ever.

But there were different times, weren't there? Don't I remember him crowing out with a great grin, Where's my little Alexandra, where's my girl? Hugs, whiskered cheeks, smell of tobacco, lap, I'm sitting on Daddy's lap. Didn't that happen?

*   *   *

Summoned by Ronnie, the sisters had arrived almost together Friday evening around six, Mary on the five o'clock shuttle from New York, Elizabeth on the four o'clock plane from Washington, Alex from Wilmington
half an hour later. The car was waiting at Logan to drive them out to
Lincoln — *crawl* really — through rush-hour Boston traffic. Ronnie met
them at the front door.

"Why is *she* here?" Mary whispered to Elizabeth in the upstairs hall.
"Why was she here when it happened? Has she been living here?"

Elizabeth shrugged ignorance.

"Do you think she expects something? Do you think he might have
said something?"

"No," Elizabeth said sharply.

"She *definitely* must expect something," Mary persisted, "or she
wouldn't be hanging around."

Alex, overhearing, interrupted. "Is it Ronnie you mean? Why
shouldn't she be here? Doesn't she live here? Isn't her mother the housekeeper?" The others looked at her scornfully and turned away without
answering. Alex watched them retreating from her and slumped.

Two unfamiliar women served them dinner. The sisters spoke only
desultorily over the meal: Elizabeth and Mary, the two elders, set the tone
and they would never discuss serious matters with servants walking in
and out. But now they were gathered in the drawing room, alone.

Elizabeth was speaking, saying her name sharply: "Ronnie?" Slowly,
she turned her face back to them.

"When exactly," she asked again, "did it happen? How is it you were
here?"

"I've been living here for the past four months. My mother was sick."
Ronnie turned her face away from them again.

"Isn't your mother Noradia, the housekeeper?" Mary asked. "Where
is she?"

"She died," Ronnie told the window.

"Oh!" A collective breath or just Alex? Then silence. Alex turned in
her chair, her face warm in the lamplight. "I'm so sorry, Ronnie. We didn't,
I didn't know. I'm so sorry."

"I *wondered* where she was," Mary defended herself.

Alex stood and walked toward the window seat, perched on its edge beside Ronnie and put her hand on Ronnie's arm. "You must be devastated," she said warmly. "First your mother, then — this." Ronnie sat rigid, staring into Alex's face, which gleamed into hers.

"What did she die of?" Alex asked solicitously.

Elizabeth's deep voice overrode Alex's light one: "When did she die?"

"What's today?"

"Friday," said Elizabeth.

Ronnie thought. "Tuesday." The word emerged strangled. "She died on Tuesday," she repeated.

"What was it?" Alex repeated.

"Cancer."

"Oh dear." Alex patted Ronnie's arm. Ronnie quietly moved her arm away, but Alex refused to take offense. "Had she been sick long?"

"A while."

"Can you talk about it?"

Ronnie's voice was truculent, her words an attack. "She started to feel sick about six months ago I guess and had an exploratory at Mass. General in June. It was breast cancer but it had spread all through her body. She wanted to die at home. Here," she amended bitterly. "We buried her yesterday."

"God!" Alex breathed. "She was so young!" She hesitated. "Wasn't she?"

How would you know anything about her? Ronnie thought, gazing at her with scorn. And why pretend you care? "She had a hard life. If any of you understands what that means," she said flatly. "She was fifty-four."

"Fifty-four!" breathed Alex.

"Here?" Mary asked in surprise. "You buried her *here?* In Lincoln?"

"In Boston. Where my grandmother is buried." Friendly company in the grave at least if not on earth. "Your father insisted I come back to Lincoln with him. He said it would be more *convenient*" (Mary and Elizabeth raised their heads at the word) "for me to come back and clean out her room. He wanted her things out of here."

Mary frowned. "Who are the servants now?"

"Mrs. Browning — the older one with the gray hair — she cooks and runs the house. He hired her when Momma got sick. Teresa is the one with the thick body. She's worked here for years, comes in days. You've seen her before." Or would have if you ever noticed such trivial things as the help.

"How kind of you to stay here and nurse your mother!" Alex gushed.

Ronnie glared at her.

"So what happened?" Elizabeth continued.

"He said I should come back with him and pack up her things and he'd send the car back to Boston so I wouldn't have to come all the way out here again and lug her things back on the bus." Lug her things: a half-dozen shabby dresses, a few photographs, a broken comb.

"He might have waited. Given you time to recover," Mary said with sweet condescension.

Ronnie shrugged. "What's the difference? I didn't want to come back to this house again."

"So Father had his stroke right after your mother died," Elizabeth said thoughtfully.

"Right after her funeral. The funeral was at eleven-thirty. We didn't get back here until almost two. Heavy traffic. He was used to eating lunch at twelve-thirty and he'd gotten very rigid — more than I remember, any-way. He was hungry and irritable, he snapped at Mrs. Browning. He had a drink while she fixed his omelet, a bourbon and water. He was in a terrible mood.

"I ate with him while I was here."

Mary looked meaningfully at Elizabeth. Ronnie noticed. "He ordered me to," she announced angrily. "Not that he enjoyed my company. He hardly spoke to me. But he seemed to want company."

Elizabeth nodded. "Please go on," she said.

"He ate like he was starving but he kept grumping, the soup was watery, the omelet was dry . . . I don't know, mine wasn't. Weren't. But he gulped everything down, he gobbled four pieces of toast, then he turned to me to say something, sneer something about my mother, I don't know what, and all of a sudden he jerked in his chair and yelled 'My head!' He grabbed his head and collapsed. I thought he was dead."

The emotionless recital held them transfixed, knowing the man.

"And you . . ." Elizabeth continued to lead the interrogation.

"I called 911. The ambulance took him to the hospital in Concord. I told them who he was and they called the head neurosurgeon. He wasn't there, but a staff neurosurgeon came down almost immediately to work with the emergency room specialist. They tended to him right away, gave him steroids, took him up for a CT scan. When they took him away, I called you."

"Had he been sick?" Elizabeth asked.

Ronnie shrugged. "Not that I knew. He took medicine for his blood pressure . . ."

"Propranolol," Elizabeth amended.

"How do you know that?" Mary wondered.

"I saw him taking it last time we were here. I asked what it was," Elizabeth explained shortly, then returned to the interrogation. "How did you get our numbers?"

Ronnie studied her grimly. "They were in his little notebook, the one he kept in his jacket pocket. They gave it to me when they admitted him. They gave me his things."

"YOU?" Mary exclaimed. "They should have held them for us."

"He had *my* telephone number in his book?" Alex asked, amazed.

Ronnie stared at the floor. "They're on the table in the front hall," she said in a metallic voice. "Wallet, keys, notebook, glasses, handkerchief. I don't know how much money is in the wallet," she spat. "I didn't look."

Silence.

"She was *with* him, Mary," Alex offered apologetically.

Ronnie's head jerked up. She glared at Alex and swung the glare on Mary. "They assumed I was related to him," she said in her tough little voice.

Elizabeth stood abruptly. "The drapes should be closed." She walked to the front windows and pulled the drapery cord hard, then walked to the window seat and stood there, a demand. Alex rose and went back to her chair by the fireplace. Ronnie sat unmoving.

"Do you mind?"

"Why not leave them open? No one can see in."

"Drapes should be closed at night!" Elizabeth's voice rose shrilly.

Ronnie looked at her without expression.

"Will you move!" Elizabeth shrieked.

Ronnie stood and moved away. Elizabeth tugged the cord brutally, the drapes flew shut over the window seat. She walked away and Ronnie sat down again, pulling her legs up onto the seat, leaning back against the wall.

Elizabeth returned to her chair by the cold fireplace. Her voice was as calm as it had been before the drape closing. "I only hope Hollis has a power of attorney. If not, we'll really be hobbled. There'll be decisions to make while he's in this coma — about his stocks, this house, other properties. And it's possible he won't regain consciousness."

"I suppose you expect us to give *you* that," Mary snapped.

Elizabeth gazed coolly at Mary. "If he has prepared a power of attorney, he has probably given it to Hollis. It doesn't matter who has it as long as someone has it. In any case, I am the best qualified to do the job. And I am the eldest."

"You're certainly the best qualified to cheat us."

"That's absurd. Whatever I do will be recorded. The records will be open. Unless we make the right moves, the estate can lose value. We'll all lose."

"Assuming you're all in his will," Ronnie shot in.

All three turned and looked at her.

The fourth time the telephone rang — "Margaret Thatcher," Elizabeth murmured when she returned, "deeply concerned" — Ronnie got up and left the room. "About time," Mary muttered. Must speak to Elizabeth about her: do we have to let her stay?

"Cointreau," she told Alex and settled back in the armchair, slipping off her heels and tucking her feet up alongside her. She accepted the small glass with a slight smile and turned to Elizabeth. "Well! At last we can catch up with each other. It's been so long! I haven't seen you since Father's birthday two years ago! You look thinner."

"Probably." Elizabeth sipped her Perrier.

"How have you been?"

"Not great. Clare died."

Mary sat up. "Oh, Lizzie! When?"

"This spring. You know I hate to be called Lizzie."

"God! Sorry! Oh god! Why didn't you let me know? I would have come to the funeral, at least stood there with you!"

"I didn't go to the funeral. His children arranged it, held it in Ohio, where his parents are buried, where one of his sons lives now. Old family house. Town he grew up in. They didn't welcome his Washington friends."

"Oh you must have felt terrible! You should have called! You could have come to New York and stayed with me for a while."

"What for?"

"I do know what it is to lose the man you love."

Injured dignity incarnate, thought Elizabeth. "Several times over," she said harshly.

Mary's fair skin mottled with pink.

Elizabeth relented. "Actually, the best cure for me when I'm upset is work. I just stayed home and worked on my book."

Mary studied her rings.

No one asked about the book.

"I feel odd one out," Alex said with a tight laugh. "Is it all right — I mean, may I ask — who was Clare?"

Lips tight, Elizabeth said, "Clare McCormick. The economist. A great economist. On the Council of Economic Advisers. The top government economic advisory body," she explained at Alex's blank look. "Consultant to the Federal Reserve and the OMB."

Alex looked stupid.

"The Office of Management and Budget. A government agency that sets the country's economic policies."

Alex had the look of a seventh-grader trying hard to memorize a Latin declension.

"You do know that I am an assistant secretary of the treasury, don't you? We just don't count the money, Alex, we set the nation's economic policy."

She doesn't know that I don't even know what that means. What is an economic policy anyway? Don't ask. "And you and Clare were married?" she said sympathetically.

"They were . . . very good friends," Mary explained.

"My best friend in the world," Elizabeth murmured.

"I'm so sorry," Alex breathed. "What did he die of?"

"Pneumonia."

"Oh," Alex said mournfully. "How old was he?"

"Pneumonia?!" Mary exclaimed doubtfully.

"Seventy," Elizabeth said. "A young seventy." She lighted a cigarette. "It's what happens in middle age, people start dying," she said brusquely. "We can expect to hear news like that daily. Death and sickness, loss on all sides. That's all we have to look forward to."

"Oh, Elizabeth, you're always so negative!" Mary snapped. "I definitely don't feel that all I have to look forward to is death and loss!"

"No, you're probably looking forward to another husband."

"I certainly am. And why not! You're just as nasty as ever!"

A long silence fouled the air like musty cigar smoke.

Alex stood abruptly. "Another drink, anyone?" she chirped, walking to the small sideboard and refilling her wineglass. She turned, began tentatively, "Do you remember me at all? I mean, I remember you both, but very — vaguely — I guess. You seemed so grown up to me. I remember your wedding," she said to Mary. "So grand! The striped tent and the men all in cutaways and crystal stemware on the tables and all the flowers, flowers everywhere! You had six maids of honor and six ushers. You were so beautiful, like a movie star, I thought you were a goddess!"

Mary sat silent. Elizabeth went to England, left me here alone. Desolate. "Yes," she said finally. "That was 1955. I married Harry Burnside. You were my flower girl. You wore pale pink and carried pink lilac flown in from Canada."

Faraway voice, remembering. "Nineteen fifty-five: I would have been seven, eight that Christmas. I still have that dress, anyway Mom has it in the attic, I saw it a few years ago when I went up to look for a steamer trunk for Stevie when he was going to camp. But I don't remember Harry."

"He died. In 1960."

"I remember he was much older than you."

Elizabeth grinned nastily. "Same age as her daddy."

Mary shot her a look but Alex was staring upward, remembering something, exclaiming, "Didn't you marry somebody famous? I remember my mother reading about you out loud from the papers one day. Much later."

"Probably Alberto. Alberto di Cenci. That made all the papers. He was famous for being gorgeous, rich, and a playboy, nothing else. He never *did* anything!"

"He *really* got famous," Elizabeth drawled, "when he left you for Nina Newton."

"The movie star?" Alex exclaimed excitedly. "I remember her! I've seen her old movies on TV." She glanced at Mary's face. "She must be very old by now," she added quickly.

"She must be very dead by now the way she hit the booze and drugs," Mary snapped. "She lived on a cocaine circuit even then. Cocaine was the drug of choice for high society for decades."

"For the Eurotrash set, anyway," Elizabeth added primly.

"You were well out of that, then," Alex said warmly.

Elizabeth smirked at Mary. The room was silent.

Alex tried again. "Oh, I envied you both — so beautiful and grown up and you had each other and this wonderful house. You" — she turned to Mary — "used to come to Father's house in Georgetown, but you" — she turned to Elizabeth — "never did. Why was that?"

"My mother was dead," Mary said shortly. "I had no place else to go on school holidays. I had to stay with Father — at Georgetown at Christmas and Thanksgiving and Easter, and here summers."

Alex frowned, pushing her memory. "Did you have a white room? All white?"

Mary nodded.

"But *you* never came there?" she asked Elizabeth.

"My mother was divorced from Father, she was alive, she still is. I lived with her. He had custody of me summers, so every summer I had to come to Lincoln. The rest of the time I lived with my mother in Boston," she said emotionlessly.

"Oh!" Alex breathed out deeply, as if these bits of knowledge appeased some hunger. Her voice reached out to them, heated, urgent. "My mother — Amelia — you knew her, didn't you? Yes. Well, she remarried, a sweet guy but they never had children of their own. I think Charlie was . . . well, I know she would have liked to so I guess he couldn't. I mean, it couldn't have been her. Could it. I mean, she'd had me."

"Oh, right," Elizabeth said in a mocking voice. "I mean, right on, I mean."

It went right past Alex. "And I used to wish, oh, I wanted sisters so badly, I thought about you two all the time. I'd think about where you were and what you were doing, I'd beg my mother to invite you to visit us. But she'd always have some excuse: you were grown up and far away, you had children of your own to take care of" — she addressed Mary — "or you were living in France or Switzerland." She turned to Elizabeth. "You had some important government job and couldn't leave." She paused. "I used to wonder how she knew about you but somehow I never got to ask questions about you beyond that. She'd always hug me or try to distract me. I came to recognize this tactic," Alex laughed.

The others gazed at her.

"Fuck sisters," Elizabeth said. "Consider yourself lucky. You had a mother who hugged you."

"Consider yourself lucky you had a mother," Mary said coldly.

Alex lay in bed, the drapes and curtains pulled open, looking out at stars. I finally find them, am finally in the same house with them and I might just as well be in Newark, Delaware. Her eyes filled. Would it have been different if I'd found them years ago, if they'd visited me, if I were allowed to visit them? Why weren't we? Of course, they're so much older, and with different mothers. . . . Oh, why do I care so much about them when they don't care about me at all?

Oh they didn't want to talk or maybe they didn't want to talk to me it's just like Mom, why won't anyone tell me when there's so much I want to know, need to know, why do I need to? but I do, I do, I want to know everything about them, him, their lives. My family. They are my family, aren't they? Alex put her hand over her heart, which seemed to hurt, and rubbed it gently. I wonder if it's really in your heart that you feel things. There are people in the world who think feelings reside in their stomachs or their livers. Do we feel things in our hearts just because we've been told that's where we feel? Who was it told me that if a chimpanzee suffers a terrible loss, like its mother dies or something, when it dies and they cut it open, they find lesions on its heart? Could that be true?

Pain suffused her body, and she turned on her side.

Back here again. Haven't slept in this house since I was nine. Twenty-seven years ago. Glorious then, the trees a mist of green, the gardens glowing, the house so luxurious, so much room. The Georgetown house was more crowded. I think. The Baltimore house sure was, she smiled. This house looks different now, like grade school if you go back after you're grown up, corridor walls crowd in on you, things that looked huge then look dwindled, little. Am I remembering wrong? Idealizing? Elizabeth was so tall and she knew everything, sometimes she read to me or pretended to play tennis with me. A few times the three of us went for walks, Mary was so fun, teasing, playing tag, she taught me to swim. Mommy would have lemonade and cookies served on the screened porch every afternoon for all of us. Sometimes Daddy would come too and sit with us, hold me on his lap, stroke my hair. I remember that! He did do that! And he bought me a puppy, called it Charlie Chaplin, then everything seemed to stop all of a sudden. We went to live with Grandma and Grandpa. I remember Momma's lips tight, Grandma and Grandpa so pale, hardly speaking. Everyone treating me as if I was sick. Then later Momma married Charlie . . . we went on living in the little rowhouse in Baltimore.

Yes, fits I had. Some kind of fits. Maybe I was sick. Maybe that's why Momma won't tell me. Maybe I have some congenital incurable disease that won't show up for another year or two. Some horrible degenerative thing that will wither my limbs, make my hair fall out, something that runs in Father's family that he didn't tell her and that was why. . . . Oh that's crazy. The others are healthy enough and they're not young. Elizabeth is in her fifties.

Eighteen years since I last saw Father. Suppose he never speaks again or hears or is conscious again I'll never be able to tell him . . . he'll never tell me . . . I'll never find out. Did he hate me? Why did he abandon me? He didn't abandon them. Mom could tell me, why won't she? Why is there this empty place in my memory? Maybe there's nothing to tell. That would be worst of all. Nothing happened at all. Just a couple splitting up. But Momma's so sweet, why would anyone want to leave her? He was a runaround, I guess, but he never married again after Momma. But it was Noradia, the housekeeper, he was sleeping with her, that's what all the business was about with Ronnie. She must be his child, look at her eyes, her mouth. But Noradia can't have been responsible for their splitting, was she even here then?

Something happened. No one will tell me.

They despise me, why do they despise me?

She tossed in the bed.

They don't want me here, I won't stay, I'll go home as soon as I can. She turned onto her other side, burrowed into the mattress, tried to sleep. It must have been the starlight that bothered her, that seemed to penetrate her closed lids. It was not moonlight, the moon was gone, sunk on the other side of the house. The insides of her eyelids were punctured by tiny brilliant lights.

Elizabeth removed her contact lenses by feel, not looking in the mirror. She laid them in a tiny box, and poured liquid over them. Then she undressed systematically, carefully avoiding the mirror. Does Ronnie know something? Is it possible he left everything to her mother? Noradia could have worked on him these last years, he was totally dependent on her. She had to hate us, she must have wanted to see her daughter taken care of. She could have got him to change the will and told Ronnie. Her face when she said that. Triumphant.

She stripped slowly, peeling away the layers that disguised the thinness of her body — jacket, sweater, belt, silk blouse, chemise, skirt, pantyhose, underpants — and stepped into the hot shower.

Never, she decided, as the hot needles hit her flesh. He was an Upton, Uptons value blood. Only blood and the name. For generations. Stephen Upton: the name passed from father to son. We were not sons. She paused in her washing, then decided: no. He never even acknowledged her. She has his eyes, like me, but she has his mouth too, the only one of us with his mouth, his eyes and mouth in a round brownskinned peasant-face stocky-body *chicana*. Shameful. He had to see, had to know everyone could see, treated her like the servant's daughter she was while looking into his own eyes. Did he care?

She slid into a terry robe, put a towel around her head and padded barefoot into the bedroom, her bedroom, kept for her all these years. She lighted a cigarette. She had not slept in it in what . . . two years. His eightieth birthday. Maybe he was lonely, hard to imagine, he who never needed anyone. He was only in his fifties when Noradia first came to work here, still in the cabinet, he could easily have married again, then or even later, lots of men do, marry women twenty thirty years younger. God knows he dated every eligible society broad going, his name always in the columns linked with some glamorous Washington hostess or other. But he said he hated women. Spat the words, said he'd had it with marriage after Amelia. Wonder why he left her. Alex doesn't know either. Bothers her. Well that's one problem I don't have.

She rubbed her head vigorously with the towel, then combed out her thin hair, still without looking into a mirror. Probably got worn down by desire hate need revenge, god the passions marriage generates, Mother so bitter still, forty years later is it forty, it's 1984, no, fifty, Jesus! And still gets that look on her face when she talks about him, hatred unto death even after death, she'll never be reconciled, well who can blame her after all. I'm lucky I never got into that morass, just as well.

Still even if you don't get married, if you have affairs, any relationship, one way or another you get worn down. Her eyes smarted, she wiped her hand across them and caught sight of her face in the mirror, her father's face, long narrow nose of a hawk. If he had married again, he might have had another child, another legitimate sibling. Estate split four ways instead of three. If it had been a boy we'd be disinherited, we'd get a nice little annuity. For sure. Better this way. But his eyes in that little thug: shameful.

By-blow, that's what they call them. As if a man did something with his left hand, swatted a fly, by-blow, meaningless. Does she think she's entitled to make decisions with us, be part of the family council? Why is she here? Of course, she came for her mother: Noradia dies, Father has a stroke or whatever he had. Maybe he loved her. He was dependent on her. Same thing. Her eyes burned again and this time she did not touch them, lying back against the pillow of the still made-up bed. A single tear ran down her left cheek.

Have to search his study, his papers, the will must be around somewhere, in the safe maybe, do I know the combination? Did I ever know it? Where would he keep it? Too tired to look tonight: got home so late last night, then had to pack, of course an eight-thirty meeting this morning. Seeing Mary again. . . . Always exhausting seeing her having to listen to her. And that Alex, my god, she's even worse than Mary: incredible.

Tomorrow I'll do a thorough search.

I would have liked to talk this over with Clare. He'd have said, "All these bits and pieces, darling, how can I sort them out? Love and desire and hate and jealousy and need and dependency, just words. They tear into a fabric that's like spiderweb in delicacy and strength — you know the African proverb — a spider's web can halt a lion — well, it halts me, darling." He would have laughed and made us fresh martinis and kissed me on the forehead and said "Let's talk about what we're going to say at the Council tomorrow," and we would have gotten off on that, both excited, laying down a game plan, and then, *then* he could talk about manipulation and dependency and psychological tactics. Then he could talk about power. And when he left I would feel high on all of it sailing on it tactics and strategies plugging into other people's weaknesses vulnerabilities got to keep your own hidden and by the time I got into bed I would have forgotten my own. Kept me high. Clare.

Mary folded her silk blouse slowly, over and over, until it was a tube, then let go and a swathe of white silk shot with gold fell across her knees. Hard to be in this room, in this house. Hard to be with Elizabeth. That stupid gushing Alex. Unbearable. And the little bastard. Does she expect us to treat her as an equal? With her manners? Feet up on the cushion with her shoes on, *sneakers,* for heaven's sake, drinking Coke out of a *can.* Walks like a boy, dresses like a boy, that might be forgivable but she looks like a *poor* boy, dirty jeans, ragged sweatshirt. If she came to the dinner table dressed like that, no wonder Father didn't speak to her. Surprised he didn't lay down the law. That morning I ran downstairs in my pajamas, ran to Mama, something had happened, what was it? I must have cut or banged myself, I was crying. Father stormed: Uptons do not appear downstairs in their nightwear or bathrobes! He was so stern I cried harder and Mama had Nanny carry me back upstairs. Which nanny was that? Nanny Annie, I loved her, I called her Annie Nanny, how I cried when she left. . . . Got married. "Annie is going to get married and have a little girl just like Mary!" she said. Another Mary supplanting me! I was horrified, I just screamed louder. No, it must have been Nanny Gudge because she scolded *"Pas en déshabillé!"* Nanny Gudge always spoke French, why Mama liked her even though she used to slap me.

The house will have to be sold, none of us can afford to keep it up, it's from another age, needs a regiment of servants to maintain it, half closed up as it is, only our bedrooms open. Who'd buy it though, who'd want it? stuck out here in Lincoln, miles from anywhere. Suppose we can't sell! Everything shabby, the dining room chandelier is filthy, Noradia really wasn't doing her job, maybe she'd been sick longer than they knew, well she could have said something, should have, he could have gotten someone else, I suppose that's what she was afraid of, being tossed out sick on her ear in her old age, the tennis court cracked and grassy, the pool a scummy bog. Maybe someone will want it because it's the house of a great man. But he could hang on for months. Years.

She rose and finished undressing. She did not look in the mirror until she had slipped the satin nightgown over her head. Then she moved in close, studied her image, moved back, lifted her chin. She took her beauty for granted, examining her face as a workman might his tools. She slipped her feet into high-heeled satin mules, teetered into the bathroom and began her nightly regimen. Brush, floss, Water Pik, face makeup remover, eye makeup remover, cleansing cream, toner, night cream, neck cream, eye cream, hand cream. She brushed her hair, still dark and glossy with a little help from Antoine. The face is still good, she thought, unconsciously raising her neck to view it again. Even without makeup. Still beautiful. That little eye job had helped enormously. Only the body . . . Still, men like voluptuous women, whatever the fashions.

She walked totteringly back to the bedroom, surveyed it, sighed. All white: the only way she could really rest. Hotels she'd stay at often had kept a room like that for her through all her husbands, *vôtre chambre*, Mme Burnside, Mme di Cenci, Mme Armonk. Didn't travel much with Don. At home, her bed and chaise were heaped with lace-covered pillows, the lace bedcover, the cloth on the little table, everything white. White furniture. Handmade lace curtains like the ones here, no machine-made abortions for her.

The sheets were not pulled down.

New housekeeper, not properly trained, Ronnie would not know how to train her of course but the maid wasn't new Ronnie said she'd been here for years, *she* should know better. Mary peeled the coverlet off the bed and dropped it on the floor. Let the maid — what was her name? — pick it up off the floor in the morning, maybe she'll get the message. She folded the sheet back and slid her body in between the clean cool sheets and sighed as her skin opened up, each pore drank in the coolness, sighed in pleasure, cool white satin on her body, cool white cotton around it, if it was, yes, she felt the sheet between her fingers, he still had percale sheets, that woman hadn't converted him to polyester even if she preferred not to iron.

Her face felt hot and her heart banged loudly as the recollection hit her, horrible, horrible, ironing her own blouse before she came. Horrible. Had to get some money. Immediately.

2

"I refuse to go to the hospital with her," Mary whispered hotly to Elizabeth in the upstairs hall. "I definitely will not!"

But at quarter to eleven on Saturday morning, all four women piled together into Stephen's limousine for the short trip to the hospital and trooped together to intensive care. They were met by the neurologist, who was so impressed by them, he nearly bowed as he introduced himself, shook hands (dropped Elizabeth's cold hand as if it were an ice cube), Dr. Stamp, Arlen Stamp, he was breathless meeting them, especially Mary. (The face holds, she thought.) His eyes simply passed over Ronnie; he ignored her utterly. Had he heard rumors?

He was slick, deferential, but could offer no prognosis. No way of knowing, he said. Stephen had suffered a hemorrhagic stroke, a hypertensive brain hemorrhage in the left frontal lobe, not unusual in a man his age with high blood pressure, an extravasation of blood from a ruptured artery that had totally destroyed part of his brain, how much they could not tell. The brain was still full of blood, once it subsided they'd have a better idea of the damage. They had given him intravenous steroids, were keeping him in the ICU and giving him medication to bring the pressure down, monitoring his blood and heart rate.

"We will of course deal appropriately with any swings in either of those parameters," he concluded. Glancing at their faces to see if they were properly impressed, he was uneasy: unreadable women these were. He moved to diplomacy: of course they were doing everything they could, such a great man, wasn't he? Focusing mainly on Mary, the doctor proclaimed pompously, as if he were telling her something she did not know, that Stephen Upton had been a distinguished adviser to every Republican president and to the party since Hoover left office. The whole town of Lincoln was proud he lived there, they must be desolate about the illness of such a father, such a wise good man. He would do everything he could to restore him to them.

"We're sure you will, but we'd like a second opinion, if you don't mind," Elizabeth said in a tone of voice that made it clear she would do it whether he minded or not.

"Of course! Of course! Dr. Roper, chief at the General — which is *the* Harvard hospital, you know — is the big name in this field. Shall I call him for you or will you do it yourself?"

"We'll call him, thank you." After checking first, Elizabeth thought. "What about his personal physician, Dr. Biddle?"

"Yes, the young lady" — he glanced at Ronnie for the first time — "suggested we call him yesterday, and he came down and looked at your father. He took care of your mother, is that right?" he asked Ronnie, who nodded.

So everybody knew, Mary thought.

"Yes, surely we're happy to have all the cooperation we can get," he said in a strained voice, and led them to the old man's room. Stephen lay, a white distorted lump in the bed, his face askew, a mask over his nose, an IV attached to his forearm, another inserted in his neck above the collarbone, a catheter attached to his nether parts and dripping into a bag hanging on the side of the bed. Mary gasped when she saw him, tears filled those great brown eyes, the doctor was moved, he edged closer to her, he put his hand on her arm. But she ignored him, grabbing the old man's hand, "Father! Oh, Daddy! It's your little Mary! Mary Mary quite contrary!" she cried, but the hand did not respond, the eye did not open. Elizabeth too looked distraught, but she did not touch him. Alex's voice dwindled as she spoke, ending in a whisper, murmured, "Hello, Father, it's Alex. . . ." Ronnie said nothing.

They stood beside him as over a corpse for some minutes, then the doctor led them out. Elizabeth asked a few detailed questions about medication and nursing, then they left. They piled back into the limo. They did not speak.

Elizabeth stared out the limo window. Horrible: *him* so helpless. How he would have hated us standing there looking down on him, he never let anyone look down on him if he could help it, always stood when he spoke. He was taller than we of course, taller than lots of men too, but he always liked to stand when he spoke to someone. If he had to sit, he looked for a chair with a high seat, he sat high anyway, long from the waist up. The quiet forceful voice, the stillness of his body, no superfluous gestures, for years I copied him not to be like Mother, always with a hand on her hair or fiddling with her rings or waving her hands around. I wanted to command attention the way he did, learned how to do it too, Clare said I had it down, but not the same, they don't listen to me the same way, it's different. They *liked* listening, looking up to him, elder statesman. They don't like listening to me.

"Father would have hated us standing around looking down on him," Elizabeth said into the silence.

"Yes. And with his mouth open like that, and his face drooping . . . !" Alex rushed on, "*Anyone* would hate that, it's so demeaning! I only hope he doesn't remember his condition when he comes to." Poor thing, poor man. Feeling oozed around her heart. Why can't I think of him as my father?

No one responded.

No one ever responds to me.

Elizabeth and Mary sat side by side in the back seat; the two younger women sat facing them in the jump seats beside the bar.

Mary turned to Elizabeth. "Did you get an impression of what the doctor really thought the prognosis was?"

Elizabeth shook her head.

Alex said brightly, "David's father, Sam, had a stroke and was in a coma for about forty-eight hours, but he recovered and is fine now, really, he can even speak and walk now. Of course, it took a few years."

Silence.

"It's true," she answered her own objection, "he was a lot younger than Father."

"How old?" Mary wanted to know.

She spoke to me! "In his sixties, sixty-one or -two. Sam's sixty-seven now, he can even drive again! He drove himself and my mother-in-law to Stevie's high school graduation a year ago."

"Our father never drove himself anywhere," Elizabeth said brusquely.

Ronnie took pity on Alex. "Who's Stevie?"

Alex smiled on her gratefully, poured words out. "My son. He's almost nineteen, he'll be nineteen next month, the day after Christmas, I had both my children right after Christmas, which is really amazing because I was born on Christmas Day myself. He graduated from high school last year, he's in college now," she beamed, "at Lehigh, to be an engineer, his father's a chemist, David, my husband, he works for Du Pont, has all his life, well, since he's worked," she giggled nervously.

Three pairs of eyes stared at her fascinated.

Damn them, she thought and plunged on. "My daughter Amelia, we call her Melly, she's named after my mother, it was *so* confusing because Mom was around so much and David calls *her* Amelia, so we just started calling Amelia, my daughter Amelia, Melly. She's seventeen, she'll be eighteen three days after Christmas, she's in college too, they're both in college!"

She searched their faces for the confirmation she was used to receiving from women, smiles and nods, yes the children are adorable and we love them, yours must be especially darling since you're so lovely, and how wonderful they are good children, safe in college where they should be, where we want them to be, the messages women send, little sighs and murmurs, smiles, a hand reached out. Nothing. Ronnie's impassive Indian face was turned toward her; Elizabeth and Mary stared at her as if they were observing a foreign species.

Still she couldn't stop. "My children were born exactly a year apart, we didn't plan that, it just happened, you know in those days birth control wasn't so reliable, I was using one of those vaginal creams, but . . ." She blushed, stopped, then jump-started again. "I named Stephen for Father and of course for David's grandfather Schmiel, but he was dead and Father was never around so there was no confusion, he didn't need a nickname, I mean, he never visited or anything. Father. But he was so cute we just fell into calling him Stevie, not Stephen. Did anyone ever call you by a nickname?"

Now they were looking at her as if she came from another planet. She burst out, "I named him for Father because I thought it might please him!"

The eyes of both Elizabeth and Mary flickered simultaneously, as if a puppeteer controlled their heads. A little smile tipped Elizabeth's thin mouth. "But it didn't did it?"

"Not really," Alex admitted, flushing. *So now some little kike has my name.* That visit, the only visit she had ever made after Momma took her away, eighteen years ago, bearing in her arms her offering to him, her seven-month-old rosebud baby son. With David, who did not hear that — fortunately. Who therefore did not understand when she announced they were leaving immediately, although they had just arrived. Long trip up from Delaware by car and she wanted to turn right around and go back? He was fascinated by Father, the great man, famous father, you mean your father is Stephen Upton?! *The* Stephen Upton? What do you mean you don't know him? You haven't seen your own father since you were *nine?!* Unthinkable to someone from so tight a family as David's. A little embarrassing, his reaction to the house, my god what is this place, it's not a house, it's a mansion! Must have thirty forty rooms, set in a park! Geez, Alex, every bedroom has its own bath! Too bad she hadn't grown up here instead of that little Baltimore row house! All the advantages. On the other hand, he was glad she hadn't, she never would have married *him!* Laughing, full of pleasure. So naive. So am I, I guess.

She hadn't told him, but still he repacked the car, silent, puzzled, knowing that if she demanded it, there had to be a good reason. And never asked why again after that day. David. Who let it alone and didn't complain when Stevie cried all the long trip back. And never again asked why they never visited her father or asked him to visit them. He must have wondered. Her heart oozed again, love for David, the dear, the good, her husband, the father of her children. My husband, she repeated mentally, my dear husband. Why can't I feel that?

She caught herself up, breathed deeply, turned toward Mary. "You have children too, don't you? I know you had a darling baby boy, just a few months old, you brought him to Lincoln one Fourth of July party, years ago when I was still a girl. When we lived with Father. I think your husband was there too . . ."

"Yes," Mary said abruptly. "I have three."

"Oh, how wonderful!" Alex gushed.

Elizabeth grimaced. "What's wonderful about being a fertile cow?" She lighted a cigarette.

Mary fanned her handbag, waving away Elizabeth's smoke. "What's wonderful, Elizabeth, is that some people have love in their lives."

Ronnie watched them, a smile playing around the edges of her mouth.

Alex's hands were tightly clasped in her lap. She cleared her throat. "How old are they?"

"Twenty-eight, twenty-two, and twenty."

"Boys or girls?"

"The two eldest are boys. The youngest is a girl."

"Oh, they're really grown up, aren't they!" she gushed. Like pulling teeth. What do I have to do to get them to talk to me?

"Quite grown," Mary said coldly. She turned to the window. "*That's* wonderful too. No more nannies to contend with."

"What are their names?" Alex asked, leaning forward, her face alight, eager.

"The boys are Martin and Bertie. They're *both* lawyers. Tiresome profession. The girl is Marie-Laure. Beyond using the pill, she has not yet decided to grow up. She's at school. Bennington. My alma mater."

"Your alma mater?" Elizabeth sneered.

Mary bristled. "I went to Bennington!"

As Elizabeth prepared a sarcastic comment, Alex swooped in, interrupting. "And they're like us, aren't they!" she exclaimed in unaccountable joy.

Elizabeth and Mary looked at her. "Well, we all have different mothers," she answered their glances miserably. "They all have different fathers, don't they?"

"No. Harold is Martin's father. Alberto is Bertie's and Marie-Laure's father." Not that he ever laid eyes on her. "Two fathers, not three." Mary fanned smoke away.

Elizabeth put out her cigarette and stared straight ahead. Alex flushed. She tugged dark glasses out of her purse and put them on. She turned to the window. Stupid. I'm stupid. Damn. Damn. Damn.

After lunch, they lingered at the glass table in the sun room facing the garden, ruin really — overgrown, ratty anyway in November, the saddest month, Mary thought, because there were still signs of what had been, a few brilliant leaves clinging to dead-looking branches, women clinging onto men who had turned toward death. What made them do that? Patches of vermilion and gold chrysanthemums among the brown stalky mess. When I was a girl, the garden was a wonder, blooming by season, waves of color tended by an army of groundskeepers. Her heart felt stopped in her chest. Was it possible? Could he have gone through everything, was he broke? Was that why everything was so seedy?

"Why is everything so tawdry!" she exploded. "Why isn't the garden cared for, the house!" She turned almost tearfully to Elizabeth.

Elizabeth's mouth set. "We have to find out. We need to have a meeting." She looked pointedly at Ronnie.

"He *couldn't* be broke!" Mary cried. "He bought IBM stock in the fifties!"

Ronnie did not even try to hide her grin.

Elizabeth turned to her. "If you will excuse us . . ."

Ronnie looked at her, uncomprehending.

"We need to have a family meeting," Elizabeth said, staring at her. Ronnie paled.

"Ronnie is family," Alex objected.

"No she's not."

"She's his daughter, we all know that. She's his daughter as much as we are. Even more, really." She appealed to Mary. "You went away to school when you were seven. You lived mostly with your mother," she told Elizabeth, "and I never saw Father after I was nine." Except that one time . . .

"What does that have to do with anything?" Elizabeth asked curtly.

"Well, after he *retired,* he lived here, didn't he! So Ronnie saw him every day. None of us ever saw him every day after we were very little!" she announced, as if she had provided conclusive proof of something.

Elizabeth stared a question at her.

"Well, she saw more of him . . . was around him more . . . than we were. I mean, she *lived* here all her life! So when he came to stay in the summer, she was here. And then he retired and he sold the Georgetown house and came here, didn't he? Isn't that what you said?" she asked Mary.

"No," Elizabeth asserted authoritatively. "He sold the Georgetown house when he left the cabinet. When Kennedy was elected and a new administration came in. But he went on practicing law — in New York — until he retired. *Then* he moved here permanently."

"So from the time he retired, he lived here in the same house with Ronnie." She turned to Ronnie. "When did he retire?"

"At seventy," Elizabeth said sharply before Ronnie could answer. "In 1972."

"How old were you then?" Alex continued addressing Ronnie.

"Thirteen," she mumbled.

"You see! From the time she was thirteen she saw him every day of her life until . . . when did you leave?"

"Fourteen," Ronnie said, with a little grin.

"Fourteen! You left home at fourteen! Where did you go?"

Ronnie thought about that for a moment. "To live with an aunt in Boston," she said finally.

"This is all nonsense," Elizabeth interrupted, "and it's irrelevant. Exposure, even if she had it, is not legal right. Ronnie has no legally recognized relation to our father. She has no legal right to any claim on the estate. So she is extraneous to this meeting."

"But morally, she has a voice," Alex protested. "I mean, aren't we going to decide what to do about him? And doesn't she have as much a right to discuss that as we do? She surely knows him better than I do. You can say exposure is not legal right but who has a right to a thing, the person who knows it or the person who has some formal connection to it? Morally, I mean. I don't care about the estate. Besides, maybe she does have a legal claim. Maybe she could sue the estate."

Mary glared at Alex. "Let's not give people ideas!"

Ronnie stood up so suddenly her chair fell over. She didn't pick it up. She leaned across the table on her hands and spat, "Legal! That's what you all are, aren't you! Letter of the law! Well it's on your side and you can have it! I don't want anything from him! Or you! I despise you all, nothing but a bunch of spoiled princesses! You" — she swung to face Elizabeth — "work for the most corrupt mindless government this country ever had, you support those fascist pigs in Washington, just the way he did! And you!" — she swung toward Mary — "are nothing but a high-class prostitute, something my mother never was, you have gall looking down on her! And you!" — she turned to Alex — "are a patronizing hypocrite, a stupid middle-class liberal! Count me out!" She darted from the room, slammed the door behind her, leaving the glass panes rattling.

Elizabeth and Mary sat impassively, but Alex, pale, glared at them. "How could you talk about her that way! In front of her! That was cruel, mean, it was horrible! You're . . . terrible! She's our sister!"

"Half sister," Elizabeth corrected.

"Illegitimate. A bastard," Mary corrected.

"We're all half sisters. She's a human being," Alex said wonderingly. "With feelings."

"I haven't noticed any except jealousy and resentment," spat Elizabeth.

"Oh, knock it off, Alex," Mary said contemptuously, adding, "She wasn't exactly affectionate toward you."

Alex examined their faces. "You really don't feel anything? For her, about her? Do you ever think what her life must have been like here? A servant's child, and you know how he was about . . . minorities. And living in Lincoln, little brown girl in a white school, lily-white neighborhood? What's wrong with you?"

"Oh, I feel something!" Mary exclaimed. "Every time I look into her baby blues. Father's eyes. How did she get them? Blue is recessive — she couldn't have blue eyes unless she had a blue gene from somewhere else too. Her mother wasn't the only whore in the family. Probably a whole long line of them."

"You're hardly in a position to call any other woman a whore," Elizabeth said coldly.

"What's that supposed to mean?"

"Just because you marry them . . ."

"WHAT?"

"One after the other — how many, four? You're an expert at fucking for pay, just like a prostitute. As Ronnie so accurately said. Sexual service in exchange for cash. Had to be sexual services you provided, you never had anything else to offer."

Mary's pale face blotched blood-red. "I didn't marry Don for money! Or . . . any of them! I loved them! But you don't know anything about love, you frigid cow, you're probably still a virgin! I don't believe that Clare ever got it up in his life! He had about as much sexuality as a dead mackerel!" Her eyes were wet.

"You bitch!" Elizabeth whispered.

Alex gaped at them. Mary swung on her. "Don't sit there with your mouth open catching flies, Alex, you simpering little creep."

Alex closed her mouth, but her face was frozen in shock. "Why?" she cried tremulously. "Why such hate?"

"Why not?" Mary exploded. "You hear how she talks to me! And was she ever a sister to me? When I needed her, growing up in this house? I loved her so much, I have a loving nature! But she treated me like dirt, beneath her, she was much too good for me! The big brain," she brayed, whirling to face Elizabeth. "And you had a mother to go home to, I had to stay here. . . ."

"My mother was a world-class bitch," Elizabeth spat, "so don't try to pretend that I had it easy. She bounced me back here to him like a tennis ball. If I'm a responsible member of society and not a parasite like you, it isn't because I had such a wonderful life. I formed myself. I made myself into what I am. By willpower and brains."

"And Father's help," Mary said venomously. "He got you your first job. He never did anything for me."

"What could anyone do for you? You didn't even finish college. All you could think about was getting in bed with some man with deep pockets. Anyway, you were his favorite, he doted on you."

"DOTED!" Mary shrieked. "He was never home! He worked all the time. We were lucky if he was home on Thanksgiving or Christmas. The most he ever took off was a month in the summer, and he didn't even do that during the war. He never spent any time with me, not even after my mother died. Right after she died, I was shipped off to school, like he was punishing me! I was seven. Seven! I grew up with a nanny and a housekeeper. I needed you!" she sobbed.

"You were not my responsibility. I had my own problems, something you never noticed."

But Mary's head rested on the table, she was sobbing. Alex's face twisted, her hand hovered over Mary's head, but she did not touch her, did not speak. She gazed mutely at Elizabeth.

Elizabeth lighted a cigarette and turned to the window.

It played itself back in Elizabeth's mind, her younger self, brokenhearted, weeping, "I don't want to go!"

"You have to go," Mother said, exhaling smoke, "whether you like it or not. I want you under his nose like a bad smell, constantly. You have to be if you're going to get anything from that bastard. He'd love to forget you exist."

She reached for her Manhattan, bangles jingling on her arm. "And you have to get something from him. I have nothing to give you. My alimony supports us but that's all it does and it ends when I die or if I should remarry, so just watch your p's and q's, young lady. You don't do what I say, I might just marry Mike O'Brien, the car mechanic my parents wanted me to marry when I was eighteen. He's a widower now with eight kids so you'd have lots of brothers and sisters, you'd just love that, wouldn't you, spoiled little princess that you are, that he's made you! Expecting the house to be cleaned around you, meals served. And if I do, you can just forget college — you can go out to work as a secretary, the way I did."

She lighted one cigarette from the tip of another. "I want you there every summer, any holiday he invites you to, and you'll be obedient and polite, you hear me? You be a good little daughter and don't you let him forget that you exist. I won't have him treating you the way he treated me!"

"Please don't make me go, Mother," Elizabeth wept. "I hate it there. I'll clean my room! I'll wash the dinner dishes! I'll go to college on a scholarship."

But Mother couldn't hear her anymore, she was off in that place she went, repeating to herself that same old monologue, only seeming to talk to Elizabeth.

"He threw me out the way men throw out whores, when he knew I was a virgin, a good Catholic girl, when I met him. How he wooed me then! He'd come up behind me in the office and kiss the back of my neck and stick a rose in front of my face. He wanted to see me every night, a moment apart was too much, he said, he liked to sit in his office so he could see me all day long. He'd follow me when I went to the ladies' room. The ladies' room! The girls all teased me about him, standing outside the ladies' waiting for me. Said he was jealous, couldn't bear for me to be out of his sight. Well, I had some looks I guess, I had great hair, red like yours but thick and curly not thin and limp like yours. But I thought I was ugly because I had freckles. At least you didn't get them. He was so handsome then, tall and slender and dark with those gorgeous blue eyes and a hawk nose, such a strong face! So manly! How could I resist? I tried, I told him it was a sin! But when he pulled me toward him, oh he was so forceful, and I resisted but he wouldn't take no for an answer. . . .

"I felt like some little servant girl in the hands of her master. He said that. He said, You are my servant, my slave, and you will do what I want. I laughed, I thought he was playing. But I did it, god I practically swooned in his arms, he had me, he knew it. After that he'd look at me across the office like Clark Gable, that kind of all-knowing look, you know, the one that says you belong to me. Until I found out I was pregnant. Five weeks of bliss I had in my life. Then he didn't want to know me. Said he wasn't the first. He saw the blood, it was so difficult the first time trying to get it in! I was so stupid, I thought he was just still jealous, I couldn't believe he'd stopped loving me after all that passion. . . .

"So I insisted on marriage. And I won. The battle. And lost the war. You were three years old, he stuck it out for three years, he was never home, we never went anywhere together not even on Christmas. He went to his family alone, he said he couldn't take home an Irish slavey. I took you to my parents, I cried the whole day. Then he threw me out, you were there, you know what happened. Settlement conditional on a promise to shut up. He framed me and no law stopped him, all the laws in the world are on the side of the Stephen Uptons of this world."

As if awakening, she blinked, looked around the room, looked over and saw her daughter. "He will *not* treat you the same way. You may not like it, but it's your good I'm thinking of. You'll thank me someday. You'll need to make your own way in the world, the way you are."

How could anyone define the way I was when I was twelve? Pale, scrawny, too smart, Grandpa Callahan said. I never understood how a person could be too smart. Stuck here in this house with him every summer, him always calling for his baby, where's my Mary? Mary had him, she had a nanny, she had a mother, but still she was always whining, always being coddled, spoiled. Until the accident and then she was always just crying, wanted *me* to be her mother.

By sixteen, I was brilliant but they kept watching me, waiting for the falloff. I wouldn't give them the satisfaction of falling into a stupor like other girls at that age. At eighteen, still too thin and smart. Too smart. Father surveying me with those cold eyes, head to toe, dull thin red hair, glasses, my body skinny, shapeless, a stick, you could see him thinking it: "With charm like yours, you'll have to be educated." Surveying my grades at the end of my first semester at Smith, nodding: "If you keep it up, I'll send you to graduate school. If you can get in!" he exploded, laughing. A female economics major at the London School of Economics in 1953. Such dreams I had of the school founded by Beatrice Webb. Brutal. But it made me grow up. And at least it was London, far away from here, from her, from him. And my tutor: Clare! O brave new world! For a while, I thought I might be happy after all.

Poor marymiggypiggy, I suppose it isn't her fault she's stupid. If she just didn't vaunt it so, only love matters, everything else is a substitute, preening herself that summer we went rowing on the lake, Clare I had just realized, thirty-one years old and such a fucking fool, I wanted to die, I researched dying, tranquilizers, booze, slit wrists. I even thought of driving into a tree like Mary's mother. I always scorned her for that, but it took more courage than I had anyway. In the end I was chickenhearted. A coward in the end. So I'm still here living out my life day after day. I deserve my life.

And Mary had just married the gorgeous Alberto, playboy prince of the world, had brought him here to the Fourth of July party to parade him before the family and Father. And me. Of course, Father snorted at him, parasite pansy wop, he called him, the gorgeous guinea. Might as well be a woman, he said. Both of them gorgeous, she in a floaty white dress, he in a trim white suit, she voluptuous, pale skin and dark hair, she had on a floppy straw hat. I worked the oars, while she leaned back against the green-striped cushion, preening, "I know everything about love!" Everything about love! I wanted to hit her, smash her with that oar. I could have told her a few things about love she never imagined.

Well whatever she knows about love is probably not much use to her anymore, what is she, forty-five, forty-six? No, I'm fifty-three, she's five years younger, she's forty-eight. Getting along. She's still a beauty though, the doctor was knocked out by her, maybe a little help from her local plastic surgeon. Acts terrified. Seems to be desperate for money. And she's always lived like a queen; apartments on Fifth or Park, houses in Paris or Capri, lodges in Maine, country estates in Virginia, villas in Vail or Gstaad, what money those men had! Staffs of servants, limousines to take her shopping, she still doesn't know how to drive. Immobilized by money. One even had his own airplane I think. Which one was that? Paul. Lived it up, all those rich husbands.

While I was making do with a little apartment in Washington. Still, I was working. Always a joy, even when it gets mucked up by the politicians.

Harry Burnside left Mary a bundle when he died. But then they sued — his children from his first two marriages. Still, she got millions, I read. Got a huge settlement from Alberto too when he took off with that movie star, I had to laugh, I wanted to mail her an anonymous card: how did the woman who knows everything about love manage to lose the world's greatest lover? The next guy was richer than the two of them rolled together, Paul, the one with the airplane. Of course, she left him for that crazy Don, who probably didn't have much. Left a man with an airplane for one with a motorcycle: hah! Still, how could she be broke? She'd have to have gone through all Harry's money and Alberto's. Couldn't have: she may be dumb but not that dumb.

She turned back and tamped out her cigarette. She glanced down at the table, where Mary still lay, her head on her arms, quieter now, sniffling. Alex fetched some tissues and slipped them into Mary's hand. She sat up and blew her nose. Nothing ladylike about that snort.

Elizabeth gazed at her calmly. Mary looked back over the tissue. "I know you hate me," she said in a quiet hoarse voice. "You've always been jealous of me. You think Father likes me better than he likes you."

"He does. Pretty vacuity, he likes in women. Like your mother." She turned to Alex. "And yours. I've long since accepted that. Pretty vacuity entertains him. But you can't love without respect and he *respects* me."

"My mother is not a pretty, vacuous person," Alex said. "She may not have your education, Elizabeth, or your kind of brains. But she has kindness."

Elizabeth raised her eyebrows. "Learning to fight back, are we? Might as well, you'll get no pity here."

"And *your* mother?" Mary shot back.

Elizabeth was ready. "That was my mother's great flaw: she *seemed* a pretty bubblehead because she was so young. But soon enough her true intelligence appeared. That's why he got rid of her so viciously."

"He got rid of her because she trapped him into marriage," Mary argued.

"What do you know about it? What do you know about anything?"

"Aaaaaagh!" Alex cried, putting her hands on her temples. "Is all we're going to do fight? Don't we have anything in common? We're *sisters*! We share a bloodline, genes, some history, whatever you want to call it! Can't we talk peacefully?"

Elizabeth and Mary looked at her.

"You're right," Elizabeth conceded, but continued before Alex, sighing in gratitude and relief, could speak again. "There are decisions to take, and we need to be able to speak civilly." She tapped her pencil end on the glass tabletop. "We have to decide what to do. He could stay in a coma for weeks, maybe months. I have an important job, I can't be away for weeks and months. On the other hand, he could come out of it at any time. What I propose is that we take turns — each of us stay a week, so someone's here to visit him every day, and to signal the others if any major change occurs."

"So one person would be here alone, in this house alone," Mary said, frowning. "Including Ronnie?"

Elizabeth shrugged.

The door burst open and Mrs. Browning rushed in. "Ma'am" — she swung her head from one to the others — "Miss Upton" — she settled on Elizabeth — "there's people here from the papers and the TV. Reporters. Out front. A whole bunch of them with cameras and all. They're asking about Mr. Upton. What do you want me to tell them?"

"We'll see them, Mrs. Browning. Tell them we'll have a statement in fifteen minutes. Maybe you could prepare some coffee for them."

"Oh. Yes. I can do that." The woman bustled out bursting with the importance of the event.

"Close the door after you, Mrs. Browning."

As soon as the door shut, Mary wailed, "I can't see anyone in my condition! My eyes must be red, I'm a mess!"

"You're fine. You'll look like the loving daughter. We have to appear together, worried, the Upton girls, remember? His queens, weeping for him. I'll draw up a statement that says nothing, says we can't predict what will happen, we are hoping for the best, grieving. . . ."

"And praying," Alex murmured.

Two heads turned to her. Again the wrong thing.

They look pretty good for a bunch of over-the-hill broads, the reporter thought, standing there together in front of the gray stone house that looked like it belonged in a BBC film, only one of them still young, thirties probably, blonde and slim, pretty. The dark one gorgeous, really stacked, if a bit short in the leg. Even the old one with silvery hair didn't look bad — slim, elegant, grand, a power in Treasury. Famous when they were young, magazine pieces on family parties featuring "the three Massachusetts graces," one just a kid then, all different mothers, the old man a real swordsman. Don't look anything like each other except the blonde and the old one have his eyes, unmistakable eyes, proof of fatherhood if I ever saw it, ice-blue. Real patrician, upholder of tradition, his class. The dark one has dark eyes, warm, she looks like she belongs on satin sheets with an ostrich boa around her. Big big big knockers. They all look sad, as if they really cared. Blonde one pale as a ghost, dark one even looks like she'd been crying. Old man in his eighties and they still cared.

The reporter was impressed.

The eldest sister took the microphone.

"Our father" — she paused and looked at the other two — "would want us to thank you for coming, for being concerned. He has had a stroke and is receiving the best of care in Emerson Hospital."

"Any plans to move him to Boston?" a voice called out.

"Not at present." Coooold. This lady did not like being interrupted. "We are anticipating his swift recovery. Since he is presently in a coma, my sisters and I would appreciate your not disturbing hospital personnel. If you will leave your cards, we will inform you of any change in his condition."

She seemed to be finished but the photographers did not put their cameras down. They were waiting for something.

"Has the president called?"

"Yes, the president was kind enough to call this morning to convey his hopes for our father's full and swift recovery." She waited too. Immovable, not a twitch. Erect as a soldier, completely in control. A real bitch. The dark one was fooling with her hankie, pulling in her tummy. The blonde one looked dead. Dead white. Tragic. Amazing. Eighty-year-old man.

"Anyone else call?" someone yelled.

She held up an envelope. Prepared. She read them off in order of protocol, heads of state of foreign countries, American cabinet ministers, senators, agency heads, an Episcopalian bishop, a slew of Republican mayors, movie stars. Rewards of greatness: a bunch of telephone calls. Still, it must make them proud. Stephen Cabot Upton, Big Daddy. No sons. Must have killed him. Not even a by-blow according to the grapevine although seemed there was talk of a nigger daughter years ago. Not here today. Probably buried away in Podunk, Mississippi, bought off with a nice little annuity. Keeping her mouth shut for dear life.

The crowd of reporters and cameramen — and one camerawoman — shuffled uneasily. Waiting. Wanted something.

"Do you have someone advising you?" yelled Bill Dwyer from the *Globe*. Yeah.

"I beg your pardon?" Voice swooped up. First time her cool cracked.

"I mean, a lawyer or somebody?" A man, he meant. Who's taking care of you all, who's telling you what to do. Hah, bet that gets her. But it was true, they looked naked there in front of that house if you could call it a house, mansion, castle. Old family, goes all the way back to fuckin Plymouth Rock or something. Old old money. They couldn't possibly manage all that, three women by themselves. Relicts.

"We are of course in contact with our father's lawyers and physicians," she said, "who will provide whatever advice we may need." Not that we do need any, fella. "If that is all, gentlemen . . ." — she noticed Ann Canning from the *Newton Times* — "and ladies, we will leave you. I trust Mrs. Browning has provided you all with some coffee to warm you on this chilly damp day. Good day and thank you for coming." She turned, the others followed her into the house, walked like ladies, no hip swaying, no small talk, heads high on proud necks. She's good, boy, professional, Washington-trained. Knew how to say nothing and make you write it down. Still, there's something real in this family: they all looked really sad.

3

Ronnie watched from an upstairs window, concealed by a lace curtain. Mary's room. She had no business there, no business outside either, what would those reporters do if they knew she was inside the house, bastard kid, not white, they'd surround her with microphones, she could TELL ALL. Get headlines in the *National Enquirer,* maybe even the *Globe.* She couldn't hear them but Elizabeth was probably doing the talking, smooth and in control, flawless performance surely. They were finished now, had turned, were walking like royalty back into the house. Ronnie dropped the curtain edge and darted from the room, softly closing the door behind her, house with closed doors, not like Rosa's, no doors ever shut there except when Rosa and Enriqué fucked.

Illegitimate, it was illegitimate for her to be in Mary's room, in anybody's room but her own, in the front sitting room, the drawing room, the dining room, the sun room, the library, Momma shooing her out, whispering, "Inside, Ronalda," even when he wasn't there. But in later years she'd plump herself down in the window seat and read and tell Momma to leave her alone. And Momma would sigh and wipe her hands on her apron as if they were wet. But only when he wasn't there. And the truth was, she was never comfortable, she just did it to do it. She couldn't relax there, only in her own room or Momma's, or the kitchen when it was Momma's kitchen.

House she'd grown up in, hidden in the kitchen, her room and Momma's, servants' quarters. She'd loved it best outdoors, in the woods or trailing around behind the groundskeepers or the gardener. At eight she'd plastered her room with pictures of movie stars, astronauts, basketball players, the Beatles, Jacques Cousteau. She'd pasted autumn leaves on the wall where her dresser stood, behind the mirror, along the moldings, wall covered with redyellowgoldorange. It might be a prison cell but it was hers, she'd do what she liked. Momma wondered at her but left her alone as long as she didn't forget the cardinal rule: the house was *their* property even if they were almost never in it. When any of them was there, no noise, no running, no laughing, no playing in the front and only very quiet playing in the back. Any sign that a child was buried in the back rooms of the castle endangered their survival, Momma said, or implied. Probably right too, he would have thrown them out without a thought. He had probably loved Noradia but he didn't recognize that. He could have tossed his own heart on the trash heap and never noticed. What kind of man was that?

After I left, he was here all the time, retired, she with him, silent, standing beside him, sí Cabot, but she only called him that when they were alone. Waiting to serve, bowing her head ecstatic in her submission. Anticipated his needs, watching his face to see if he liked the soup, the roast. Her god. First came as a chambermaid, watched the cook for years and learned to cook Anglo. Her intelligence his gain, her brain his property. She saved him money: once the girls were gone, he fired the cook and just kept her and some dayworkers. She tried to expand her repertoire when I got old enough to read, had me read the recipes to her out of the cookbooks he'd bought her. By the time I left, she had them by heart. Illiterate people have wonderful memories.

Ronnie made it down the back stairs and into her room without anyone seeing her. She plunked down on her bed. Have to do something. Should go someplace, get away from here. No money, no place to go, damned dissertation to finish. Ideal if I could just stay here and work on it. My home. In your dreams, girl.

The sisters were in the kitchen, she could hear them talking. Never set foot in the kitchen in the old days. Arguing? Discussing: tea or cocoa? They were ordering both and tea cakes, did Mrs. Browning have any tea cakes? Linzer torte and brownies, wonderful, serve them in the sun room please. Mary's voice, so commanding with servants. Looks like she's had plenty of tea cake in her time.

Need to get a job. But with a job, it would be hard to finish the dissertation. Maybe BU would give me a grant. Six months' work should do it. Should read some of the books I brought with me, barely opened these past months. Sitting with Momma. Wiping her poor forehead, cleaning her poor bottom. Why did I drag out this pile of tomes? Prove something to Him? But He never saw them, wouldn't be interested if He had, would never ask "What are you doing these days, Ronnie?" Would He have been impressed if He knew? Had I hoped? Should read, she thought, and was overcome with weariness. Her body moved itself toward the door of her room and through it into the hallway leading to the kitchen, and her mouth opened and asked Mrs. Browning if she'd put an extra cup on the tray, and she floated into the sun room where her sisters sat.

"Hollis will be here at six," Elizabeth was saying, but stopped when Ronnie entered.

"Are you going to join us for tea? How nice! Sit here by me, Ronnie," Alex said, patting the chair — stupid, it was the only empty chair at the table, still, it was nice of her. She at least tried to be cordial. Probably shouldn't have called her a hypocrite. Maybe she means it. Who knows. Ronnie tried to smile at her, but her mouth couldn't. Wouldn't. Mouth just twisted. Alex patted her hand. Ronnie stared at her dumbly probably looked like some goddamn dumb wetback. Elizabeth and Mary watched in stiff silence. Frozen faces. Hate.

"You know, I didn't grow up in this house," Alex said warmly, now rubbing Ronnie's hand, "and I never got to know you."

Jesus Christ, she talks to me as if I was six years old. Fucking patronizing hypocrite.

"Tell me about yourself and your mother. I did meet your mother I think and I saw you, you were a girl, a teenager. When I visited our father. Eighteen years ago. With my baby," she faltered.

No one spoke as Mrs. Browning came in with the tray and poured tea. Alex had cocoa and exclaimed, thanking Mrs. Browning for putting whipped cream on top.

Yes. I remember her standing in the front sitting room wearing a beige dress I thought was silk, holding the baby out to him, smiling, "We named him Stephen." He was tamping his pipe, he grinned and muttered something and walked over to his favorite chair to sit down and smoke. She dropped the baby in a chair, and whirled around real fast as if she was going to run out the door and saw me in the hall. Saw me. I took off like a bat, hid in the woods behind the garage. I wasn't supposed to be seen. I expected his wrath to descend, lightning bolt, ejecting us from paradise. I pictured Momma weeping, wiping her face on her apron. But when no one came, and I calmed down, safe behind the garage, I said out loud: silk. I had seen the word but could only guess what silk looked like. Silly, there's plenty of silk in this house, but I didn't know it then. But I thought her dress was silk: I wasn't sure.

Pink, she and the baby both pink and smiling. Heir and heiress to paradise, allowed to walk around and sit in all the rooms. Baby's pee even dampened the gold chair in the sitting room, Momma said afterward. But after poor Momma unpacked their bags, hung all their things up, they packed up again and left an hour after they arrived. Problems in paradise?

"You didn't stay long," Ronnie said provocatively.

"No," Alex smiled. "We couldn't. My husband had to get back. He's a chemist. We just came for the day. We just wanted to introduce our son to Father."

Never lie to a servant, idiot. Servants know better. Alex turned her lying face away from Ronnie and sipped her cocoa. But she was indefatigable. "Tell me about your poor mother," she began again. "Was she sick long?"

Six months. I already told you. Diagnosed and damned last May. Ronnie's voice emerged gravelly: "I don't know how long she was sick. Maybe for a long time but without telling anybody. Sometime this spring she went to see Dr. Biddle. He said she had to have an exploratory operation. She called me to tell me. I met her at Mass. General for the biopsy. When they opened her up . . . they found it was all over her body. Everywhere. It was too late for chemo. He didn't go into Boston, to the hospital with her. He sent her in the limo."

The sisters gazed at her, expressionless.

Why am I telling them all this? Why am I letting them see? But she went on, in spite of herself. "The doctors called him here and he called her and then he spoke to me. . . ."

"*He* asked to speak to *you?*" Mary interrupted.

"Yes. She knew she was going to die. She wanted to come back here, she wanted to die here." Ronnie's voice cracked. She sipped her tea. She wondered if she should take up smoking. "May I bum a cigarette?" she asked Elizabeth, who slid her pack across the table. Ronnie lighted one, inhaled. It burned her throat. Cauterization. She resumed. "He told me he wouldn't let her come back unless I came and took care of her. So I did."

"That was very kind of you," Alex said, laying her hand over Ronnie's.

Ronnie stiffened. "I wasn't being kind. I loved her."

Alex flushed.

"I guess in your family, you don't know anything about love!"

"I love my mother," Alex said. "I'm just stupid. I mean, I don't express myself well. I express myself stupidly."

"Patronizing is what you are."

"I'm sorry. I didn't mean to belittle you. I meant you were a good daughter. I meant, your act testified to love."

Ronnie shrugged. "Forget it. I'm sorry too. Sorry I barged into your tea party." Her eyes skimmed the two silent sisters, she got up and left the room, closing the glass door quietly.

Elizabeth studied the papers spread out on the desk. Hard to know what to think, things were scattered as if he didn't want anyone to be able to make sense of them. He didn't trust anyone. All she had been able to find were accounts on an interest in a resort in Nevada, a condo complex in the Bahamas, two apartment houses in Boston, stock in IBM and six other blue chips, he seemed to have plenty but nothing really recent here, must be in the safe. No will. In the safe too, probably. If only I knew how to open it. He must have kept a record of the combination, he was old, he wouldn't have trusted his memory. She pulled out the desk drawers again, searching for a card, anything with combination numbers jotted on it. She riffled through the papers in an unlocked metal strongbox. Nothing. She sighed, lighted a cigarette.

He might have cut us all out. It's possible. He might have had a change of heart. Summoned every summer, Christmas, to a family get-together, but not last year. Why was that? He was old and alone, with only that woman. But he wouldn't have left much to her if anything. What a bastard he is: he didn't even go to the hospital with her. Proper of course. Wouldn't do to be associated with her, a servant after all. Still.

He might have left everything to Harvard. Maybe he hated us for being girls.

Smoke drifted into her eyes, burning them to tears. Why would he hate us? We were his children. It was just the way he treated us. He would have treated a son hatefully too, would have made his life a misery, belittling, resentful, competitive. Still, he would have left a son everything, made him executor, left us small bequests. The way his mind worked. Works. As it is, no saying what he did.

She swung around in his huge desk chair to face the window behind her. Liked a window behind his desk, light behind him, blind the appellant, halo him.

Graybrown November trees grass, gray light fading.

Day's end, year's end, end of an era. When I go it will be the end of an era, he said at his last birthday, his face rigid as a robot's, staring glaring at us, his hand cradling the bowl of a brandy snifter. Who could tell what he felt or why? If he dies this year, 1984, symbolic. End of an era. End of his branch of the family too, he didn't say but thought. His brothers had sons with sons, Uptons still walked upon the earth but not of his getting except me but girls don't count. No, he meant the new men were not men of distinction, character. All punies now. Different breed, he said. End of an era. End of the Republic. Slimy moneygrubbers appealing to the mob in a world of television and computers, Jews and Arabs and Japs and Chinks and godknowswho taking over the world. Not English gentlemen no matter how many generations removed from the seat of empire. Lords of the earth recognizable by their good shoes and tweeds. Japs can buy those too. Come on, ever see a Jap in tweeds? Hah. England a third world country now, yellow people taking over the world.

You never saw that I am like you, Father.

After sipping it, Hollis Whitehead set down his drink. "So your best bet is to petition for a conservatorship," he concluded. "He was stubborn, your father, I tried to get him to give me a power of attorney for just such an eventuality. You know, we old men have to think ahead, expect things like this, I did it myself five years ago, gave my son a power of attorney conditional on my being put out of action, of course Cab didn't have a . . . a, anyone in practice with him the way my son is with me, but I warned him years ago, when he retired. . . ." Deciding to stop before he stepped even deeper in the elephant shit, he sat back and sipped his Manhattan.

"How long will it take?" Elizabeth asked.

"A month. Six weeks. If there's no problem."

"What do you mean, what kind of problem?" Mary leaned her full bosom toward him, tilting her head up so it seemed he was above her even sitting down. Had to do it, Elizabeth thought, had to seduce every man she met. Even a dried-up old coot like Hollis Whitehead. One of the reasons I hate her. The way she always tilts her head just a little when she speaks to a man, exposing her neck. Just like a wolf losing a fight exposes his vulnerable spot, statement of defeat. Don't attack me, I submit. Then he feels safe, relaxes, expands, takes her over. And she begins to take control over *him* through *his* weakness — which he is completely unaware of. Mary a master at that. Age-old game, way of the world. I was better off out of it.

He leaned toward her smiling warmly. "Well, for instance, Mary, my dear, a family conflict. If one of you were to oppose the petitioner, for instance."

Mary sat back, biting her lower lip. She must be thinking. I wonder if her lips move when she reads. She looks at him like a six-year-old, in utter credulity, Elizabeth thought.

"What happens in the meantime? What about the bills that need paying right away?" Elizabeth threw in.

"I don't imagine there's much that can't wait a month or six weeks," he said dismissively.

"Mrs. Browning and the gardener/chauffeur are paid by the month," she said, "but the dayworkers are paid by the week."

"Ah, well, can you cover them yourself for the time being? You can repay yourself later."

Mary looked aghast.

"Did he make a will?" Elizabeth prodded.

"Yes. It's in my office safe." He shut his lips.

"I see." She thought. "Will you draw up a petition for us?"

"Sure, if you know which one of you is making the application."

Elizabeth looked at Mary and Alex, then back at the lawyer. "I will make it."

"That all right with you two?"

They nodded. "Okay. Well, if that's all, I'll be getting along." He pulled his body slowly from the chair as if it hurt. "Good to see you all again. Really sorry about the occasion, though. Cab and I have been friends since the war: we were both in Washington together. I was just starting out then, a young lawyer. He was my mentor, he taught me the D.C. ropes. I've known Cab for almost fifty years," he concluded solemnly.

The three sisters ushered him to the door. "I'll drop in on him tomorrow," the lawyer said, patting Alex, kissing Mary's cheek, shaking Elizabeth's hand.

They returned to the sitting room, where the drapes were drawn and where, tonight, in honor of Hollis, a fire was burning in the hearth. Mary sat on the sofa opposite it, fanning herself. Alex refreshed their drinks at the sideboard bar, then sat beside Mary. Elizabeth sat in an armchair near the hearth.

Nothing warms her blood, Mary thought. She can sit by the fire but she's still frigid. Iceberg. Always like that. Please play with me Lizzie, oh Lizzie, can we play ball dolls pretend will you teach me to swim please Lizzie.

"So you're taking over," Mary accused her.

"I am the only one of us who is qualified to handle financial matters, after all." She sipped her Perrier (Perrier!) and lighted a cigarette. Mary glared.

"You don't seem to understand my work," Elizabeth exploded. "I travel around the world for the government, working out economic agreements and policies that will benefit this country. I went to Egypt last week and was met at the airport by two three-star generals in a limousine! I meet with the highest-ranking economic officials of every country I visit, often with the head of state! Whereas you, I daresay, cannot even balance a checkbook." She looked meaningfully at Mary. "Do you really want to pay Father's bills? I'll be paying the servants out of my own pocket."

Mary studied her rings.

"I mean, if you want to be conservator, just tell me. I'll call Hollis in the morning and tell him to draw it in your name. It's a lot of work for nothing, and I'm not about to take it on if you are going to pout and sulk about it afterwards. I don't need that."

"Oh I wouldn't think of standing in your way, Elizabeth," Mary snarled. "I know what happens to people who stand in your way. You just cut them out."

"And I know how you whine and sulk!"

"Even Father said you were a bitch," Mary cried.

Elizabeth whirled. "And he called you a cunt!" she screamed. "I was right there at the breakfast table, I heard him!" Summer before she left for college, long dark hair in a pageboy, pouty lips ruby-red, begging, Daddy, please let me take driving lessons and buy me a car, any little car, an MG maybe, so I can get home to see you. Father smiled his sneer: "Any time you want to come home, I'll send the chauffeur with the limo." Mary's face fell, she whirled out of the room. He puffed on his pipe, watched her go. Cunt, he muttered. Was it because of her mother, because of the way Laura died that he wouldn't let her drive? But why "cunt"?

Mary screamed, "He *loved* me!"

Elizabeth saw the tears in Mary's eyes. Palpable hit. "He *respected* me," she smiled coldly.

Mrs. Browning came in and announced dinner.

Elizabeth prepared for bed automatically, but her mind was racing. Oh god why did I have to come back here, why does she have to be here, remembering everything, it's like drowning in a wave. All these years, I managed to forget. Why Jesus Christ why should I hate her so much? She's nothing, means nothing to me. My life has gone on, she's stuck where she was. I have accomplished something, have even a degree of fame, the book maybe someday, soon, yes. All she has is three kids after four husbands. Typical woman, life in her cunt and uterus.

Did I really have to make her cry.

Oh Christ, she cries at the drop of a hat. Always did.

Alex sitting there looking white staring at us, well so what, who cares what she thinks or feels. Stupid housewife like her mother, Amelia.

Amelia, slender, young, long honey-colored hair, plain clothes, nothing like Mary's mother, Laura. Must have been hard for her, stuck up here all summer with Stephen's daughters, her own baby, Alex, only about six months old. That day she laid her hand on my knee, me sitting in the sun room reading, face looking up to me just the way Alex looks up at people, will you be my friend, Elizabeth?

Why on earth would I want to befriend my father's third wife, only four years older than I?

I already have a mother, several sisters, and aunts, none of whom love me very much. What in hell do I need with you? But my insides were crying, can you help me? Save me? Made me hate her — she was just a stupid woman, what could she do. "Sure," I said, in a tone that meant don't be ridiculous. She smiled a little, turned away. She was trying to embrace me, help me, I guess, but what could she do. And she was Father's wife. I was relieved he married her but jealous jealous.

Mother asking about them all, I probably know more about Stephen's life than anyone, watching all those years, Mother's spy on all his later wives. With each new wife: what does she look like, how tall, what color hair? God she was splenetic about Laura, society girl, dark and slender, beautiful to Mother's pretty, her family rich and old like his. How she crowed when Laura had Mary, another girl! Hah! She didn't give him a son either! Maybe it's his fault! He wouldn't have thrown me out the way he did if I'd had a son, believe you me Elizabeth Upton. Five I was. What did she think she was saying to me? Didn't notice, didn't care, driven by hate, I a mere weapon in her war against him, against her own boozing heavy-handed father, little Irish Catholic girl never got no respect. I wrecked her life, and my being a girl compounded the ruin. Oh god. . . .

I would lie in bed figuring out ways I could redeem myself. When I grow up, I'll be rich and famous and take care of Mother. I'll buy her a big house on Beacon Street and a long car and pay a man to drive it. That will make her smile. She'll be happy. She'll love me then.

But after all the golden Laura killed herself in a drunken accident, suicide if I ever saw one, spoiled brat angry at him for never being around, for working day and night for the War Effort. Laura a selfish little princess, Mother had that right, she paid little attention to Mary, cared about her ladies, her admirers, her cocktails, her fittings. She would stroke Mary's head, kiss it, call her sweet names — on her way out. I knew that. Still I hated Mary for having her, having even that much sweetness in her life. Mary hardly knew her. Raised by nannies. For Mary, her mother was a yearning. Me too: Lizzie please play with me.

The baby's heart yearned after me.

But Father always made so much of her, looking around for her, crying Where's my Mary? Where's my baby?

Heah I are, Daddy! Leaping into his arms. He always caught her, hugged her, kissed her. Me a bad smell hanging in the air, one people were used to, barely noticed. He built the playhouse for her. Gave her everything she asked for. I had to fight to go to private school. He never held me when I was little. . . .

Mother's fault.

But if Laura made her crazy Amelia really threw her, hah! Amelia was ordinary, not upper-class, didn't even go to college, Stephen forty-four to her nineteen. Mother's teeth clenched when I told her (how I enjoyed that) (yes, but you ached for her too) Amelia'd been a secretary in his office like Mother. I didn't tell her the rest. That Amelia was a sweet kid, that he seemed to love her and she him. The soft way they looked at each other, the way she laid her hand over his so lightly, careful not to disturb, just to touch. Holding her breath. And he sitting back, a glint in his eye with no cruelty in it, all pleasure. But Mother triumphed when Amelia had Alex, another daughter. So much crowing about girls, you'd think people were glad to have them. Hah!

What happened there? Was Mother right: her sin was having another daughter and no sons? Suddenly Amelia was gone, taking Alex with her, never came back. Did Father summon them to the July Fourth party the way he did us? Did he not ask or did Amelia not allow her to go? Did he pay her alimony? Child support? What was the deal? I was long gone myself, no longer had to report to Mother. Mother lost some of her interest in me when I had nothing more to tell her about him. Still calling herself Mrs. Upton, Mrs. *Catherine* Upton, no claim to the Stephen Cabot part anymore, dressing in Chanel suits and necklaces but the suits were ready-made, the necklaces *faux* as they say, smoking, drinking Manhattans, living in that Back Bay apartment, playing bridge, going to any party she was invited to, woman alone not all that acceptable, not many invitations, trying to keep up her standing with her lady friends. Scorned her family, the boozing old man, the worn-down old woman. Why not? Her father in that three-decker in Somerville couldn't lay eyes on her without starting to rail, here's Mrs. Highhorse. We only went there at Easter and Thanksgiving and Christmas. That was enough. Her brothers and sisters resented her too. And me.

I astonished her, I think, ambitious as she'd been herself. The most she could aim for was a good marriage — which meant marriage to money. I was in another solar system. "London School of Economics: what's that? Why in the name of all that's holy do you want to be an economist, what do they do?" Looked at me as if I came from another planet. Still does. Seventy-four, voice grating with whiskey and cigarettes, still good-looking, still as bitchy as ever, saying she's determined to outlive him so she can inherit something from the bastard. Reconciled to me in her way: "You may be a frigid bitch but maybe you were smart after all not to marry and have kids. At least you never went through what I went through." Wentthroughwentthrough.

And I escaped?

Mary woke in terror, wet, got her bearings: Lincoln, Father's house, Father not here. She pulled herself up, looked around the room, then rose and went into the bathroom. Dripping, she was. She dropped her nightgown to the floor, turned on the shower and pulled a plastic cap over her head, then stepped inside. Lincoln, Father's house, Father not here. He's in a coma. Same old nightmare: car over embankment, Father driving, me in flames. Don. She started to cry and let herself sob, no one could hear her over the shower. When would it end? Cry Mary baby poor Mary. Oh god Don, how could you? How could you die, how could you leave me, how could you? When you knew how I loved loved loved . . .

After some minutes, her sobbing abated, and she turned off the shower and stepped out, wrapping the bath sheet around her. She dried herself vigorously, walking back to the bedroom. She felt her bed sheets: still damp. She drew back the blankets to let the sheets air, then went and sat on the chaise near the window. Her purse was lying on the floor nearby and she dragged it over and took out a cloisonné box and some cigarette papers. She opened the box, pulled out a lump of hash and crumbled some inside a paper. She took a cigarette from an open package, broke it and sprinkled the tobacco over the hash. She rolled it up, licked the ends, and twisted them tightly. She lighted it. Ah.

When she had smoked it down to a tiny nub, she put the roach back into the box. Have to find a connection here. Probably have to go to Boston. Aldo might know. Ronnie probably knows lots of sources. Can't ask her.

Why am I so upset? Elizabeth, Elizabeth's fault. So full of hate, so hateful. And I loved her so much, needed her, no mother to speak of, Laura always off at some do, luncheon, tea, cocktails, whatever. Led in to say good night before she went out for the evening, in my nightgown, my hair brushed, oh my pretty girl, my adorable girl. She smelled of powder, perfume, stroking her dresses to feel silk, taffeta, velvet, wool soft as velvet. Good night Mama, have a good time.

Sometimes she had a funny smell, sometimes Daddy did too, strong and sour, funny talking, words drawn out heeeer's my liille giiirl, Mommy's baaaby. . . .

Only thirty when she died, papers full of pictures of her, Laura Upton, society matron dead in automobile crash. Nanny hid the newspaper but I saw it, I could read, I was seven. "DEATH IN ACCIDENT" it said. Nanny Gudge's mouth tight when she told me, holding me on her lap, Mommy won't be coming back anymore she's gone to heaven to live with the angels, she's an angel now looking down at you protecting you, Maudie across the room making the bed, the way she looked at Maudie her eyes a warning when Maudie said "I'm not surprised." How come I remember that when I didn't understand. Aunt Pru sweeping in from Boston in a felt hat with a feather and a carved jade ring, Uncle Samuel behind her like a thinner shadow, she grabbing me, poor child, and Daddy so angry crying his face red and white, his eyes red. He had the funny smell. Aunt Pru scolded him, she wasn't afraid of him, her baby brother.

She'll have to go away to school, he told Uncle Samuel, I can't be here to look after her there's a war on I'm needed State Department works day and night, had my bags packed shipped off to Miss Peabody's.

Everyone I've ever loved has abandoned me.

But at least at Peabrain's there were other girls, friends — Amy, Caroline, Elena, Catherine, all unwanted children. Happier there, children to play with be with. But lonely in the summers, long lonely summers at Lincoln, all those years. Only Elizabeth here and she hated me, always hated me. Well, most of the time. When she didn't — the day we got cook to fix us a picnic lunch and sneaked off, all the way down to the brook. We played let's pretend, Elizabeth was Rosalind and I was Celia, that was Shakespeare she said.

Amy married a French count, Catherine turned bohemian and opened an art gallery in New York, Elena dead of a drug overdose at thirty, Caroline lives in Boston now, married again, like me divorced four times well I was only divorced twice, widowed twice. Widow. Relict.

She got up and pulled the quilt from her bed, returned to the chaise and wrapped herself in it. She lay back staring out at the sky, really black here in the country never saw it that way in New York, like the sky over Vail or Gstaad but no stars tonight just the blackness, clouds like smoke, like pale light.

Oh Lizzie probably couldn't help it, given the way things were. Her mother thrown out to make way for mine, she thrown out to make way for me. She was always alone here, always, hanging about in corners, pale, holding a book, looking at us with those pale cold eyes, me and my momma and my nanny and my maids, I a cute little baby, where's my little girl, Daddy's home and he wants his Mary! Barely spoke to her, she tall and gangly and charmless. Alone always. What else could she feel, she was only a kid.

But I loved her. Couldn't she feel that? She hated me for loving her, what's the matter with her?

You'd think she would have told her mother she didn't want to come here! Why would anyone want to be where they clearly weren't wanted? And she's not a kid now. She's a hateful adult. I should just shrug her off, what does she matter? I will. I'll simply ignore her, she doesn't matter, she isn't important to me. She doesn't matter, she's insignificant. Forget her. Jealous bitter dried-up old maid. I'll bet she's never had an orgasm in her life.

4

A rabbit darted soundlessly across the path into the underbrush. Terrified, little heart racing, afraid of me the way I was afraid in England. Held myself stiff and superior when Clare took me up to Oxford to meet his friends. Why was I so terrified? They all seemed so brilliant, that Oxbridge accent and scathing British wit, I didn't don't have it, couldn't keep up my end. My jokes come out heavy, sarcastic, nasty. Jokes of a child nourished on hate. Elizabeth trod heavily on the forest mast.

Oh, why do I keep thinking about those days, being a child, all that? Ever since I got here. Spent my life burying it. Transcending it. It's being here with Mary, feeling the way I so often felt in those years. Same hate and jealousy even without Father around to put us in our place, terrify us. Your mother does not educate you socially, Elizabeth, but of course how could she, shanty-Irish that she is. Uptons do not use salad forks for their fish or fish forks for their meat; they do not chew with mouths open, drink until they have finished chewing, pick up a dropped napkin, blow their noses at the dinner table, speak about personal matters in front of servants, make requests of servants who expect to receive orders, hold a piece of bread in the palm of their hand while they butter it, eat with their forearm upon the table, slurp soup. They do not show themselves outside their rooms in their dressing gowns or attend to personal hygiene in public; no Upton woman would ever think of combing her hair or refreshing her lipstick in a public place, much less try to fix a flaw like a hanging slip in the front hall of the house as I saw you doing last week! Uptons avoid slang and Upton women never never never use words like "damn" or "shit" and I don't want to hear them cross your lips again young woman.

Another age. Gone but not lamented.

Upton women are gracious, they defer to men at all times, they remember their lineage. Your ancestors were ministers, one the greatest preacher of his day, held the Colony in the palm of his hand. Your great-great-grandfather was governor of this state, your great-grandfather was majority leader of the Senate, your father, miss, is more powerful than the secretary of state. . . .

Men in limousines came and went, all superimportant. Whispers and Secret Service men. Library door closed for hours, the butler — we had a butler then, I'd forgotten — knocking with his white-gloved hands, carrying in trays of booze, a Secret Service man sitting on a hard chair in the hall. Another outside the French door to the garden, sitting in the hot sun on a folding chair. But I eavesdropped from the toilet off the play-room. Mary never found that out — not interested, probably. Long arguments for or against bombing railroad lines leading to some camps or other, must have been the Holocaust. Father against it, he carried the day. Was it after the end of World War II that I heard Father argue that we should drop an atomic bomb on the Soviet Union? Me maybe fourteen, fifteen. He was yelling that Bertrand Russell and John von Neumann were both urging preventive nuclear strikes against the Soviet Union. Goddamn Reds have nuclear weapons, Father growled. Better to get rid of the commies before they corrupted the whole goddamned world. Commies powerful in Germany before Hitler, could arise again. Strong movement in China. Did they want to see that here?

Made sense I suppose. Look what's happened. Soviets, Eastern bloc, China, Africa, spreading to Central America, South America if we hadn't got rid of Allende. . . .

Still, that seemed a drastic step. . . .

I wonder if he supported Hitler. In 1939, say, or earlier.

Later Russell turned into a Red himself. Father hated him. And I heard that when von Neumann was dying, he spent his nights screaming in uncontrollable terror.

What goes around comes around.

That's all over now, everything over now. Father's dying, and the CIA reports I've seen show the Soviet Union collapsing from the inside. We've won. I suppose I should include myself on the winning side. Capitalism has won. Still there are things I don't agree with, things I can't seem to work into the theory, things Clare never dealt with, did he think about them? I need him now, I need him to talk to.

I don't know why I'm so . . . Father isn't here and his demands aren't important anymore are they. Only Mary's here and Alex. The way it was most summers, Father down in Washington, Mary here, then Alex, little towhead. Sends my mind back, not my mind, my mood, feel childlike somehow, as if all the years I've lived since are part of a movie and this is real, I'm home again. My adult life only a movie. I walked in these woods day after day when I lived here. Walked in them before I went to England that first time, so frightened so determined my teeth clenched with it like Mother, I would would would. Would what? Show him. Escape. From Mother. From him. From my sense of not having any place. Would make a place for myself. Would end my helplessness.

But how could I do it there? Those Brits, that British wit superior and light, life an amusing absurdity. Intimidating. I acted even more superior than they, hoping they couldn't see. Terrified I'd be discovered stupid after all. Maybe underneath the manner, they're frightened and shy too. What do such people say when they're in pain? The manner proclaims they never are. A clever quip tossed off as they slit their wrist, a jest as they tip themselves off the edge of the balcony.

LSE another kettle of fish, full of wogs and pinkos, everyone buzzing about the famous American who decamped with his tail between his legs in 'fifty-three to escape McCarthy. Who knew it would be a goddamned pinko refuge! Except for Clare, thank god. So much prestige it had. Econometrics department completely ignored women. Male professors preferred men, even wogs. A lot of those Muslims, Africans, Indians, presidents or prime ministers of their countries now. Last year I sat on silk cushions drinking tea in porcelain cups, chatting about old times with my friend Sayyid the president of Iman. He's forgotten that I didn't speak to him then. Remembers LSE fondly, yet it was an unhappy time: strange how that is. Laughed about the smell of the place, the eternally boiling cabbage. All day every day. Disgusting food. Toilet paper read "London Country Council" on one side, "Now wash your hands please" on the other. Sayyid had never seen toilet paper before, thought it was reading matter. We each had a desk in a graduate reading room and whenever the Queen Mother visited we had to open our lockers for her. They gave us a brush to remove the dust from books brought from the stacks, dust of ages.

My flat in Hampstead, not so fashionable then. Top floor, little gable windows, gas ring to cook on, heater took shillings. Always cold and damp.

A gaggle of girls, but not in economics: three of us in the class, two dropped out the first year, one pregnant, one a nervous breakdown. I determined I *would* get through, wouldn't let them destroy me. Clare got me through. Different kind of intelligence, kind I understood, tying things together. Sitting in his study, a fire always going the room so damp, piled with books and papers, served me tea or sherry, talked, just talked for hours. We loved each other's minds. Both American.

We both saw money as a concept, a convention: a human agreement to value something inherently valueless. One of the Trobriand Islands, what was its name, Kiriwana, Kiriwina, they value banana leaves. Women tie them into whisk broom shapes, the men raise pigs, things with real value, of course the women do the work. But the women get even: only they can bind the banana leaves and the men will give anything for them, use them to unbind the living from the dead in burial rites. Treasured bundles, sign of wealth: utterly worthless really. I laughed, snorted my contempt for such stupid people! Primitives! How his eyes lighted up, he loved cutting me down: "It *is* amusing, but consider, Elizabeth, if you will for a moment, how creatures from outer space might view our reverence for gold or diamonds or paper money for that matter — which can't feed or warm us or in any way keep us alive. Yet for which we fight, even kill. You may find Kwakiutls or New Guineans absurd for sacrificing to throw big-man feasts to gain prestige but the good ole boys at Virginia, where I got my undergraduate degree, drank themselves sick for the same purpose. And it is not unknown for adults considered perfectly rational to bankrupt themselves buying houses, cars, paintings, for the same purpose. Consider that one of the most valuable — and expensive — substances in the western world is plutonium — which is utterly lethal. A tiny ball of it can kill an entire city."

Sent me off silent with thought.

Diamonds just bits of rock, gold just bits of metal. Even the real things people want — fancy clothes and cars, fancy houses — are just icing. Entire world system artificial, a game of let's pretend, great states mounted on paper. But when currency collapses, so do real human lives. Real life built on nothing. Nothing comes from nothing: Shakespeare was that? *King Lear?* Not true. Everything comes from nothing, from a word, from declaring that this is good, that is valuable. He found it brilliant, a magnificent artifice: man recreating the world through words and money. He crowed about it, the triumph of man's will over matter.

Never discussed what has real value. What does? Food water sleep. Love? Is there such a thing? Or is "love" just another word for power? Mary: I know everything about love. But what she calls love gets her money. What she calls love is power.

Elizabeth kicked through dead leaves. The sun, pale, still low in the sky, spilled faint light on the forest floor through a stand of leafless maples and oaks, where she stopped for a moment to warm herself in the pale light. So quiet. No one up yet, no coffee made even. I don't mind making it myself.

Mother trying to keep up appearances, pretending we had help, scurrying around the apartment, was it Edith Wharton's mother said, "Drawing rooms are *always* tidy." Whenever it was her turn to entertain her lady friends she'd pretend she was a lady of leisure. Lucky she got to keep the wedding presents, the silver tea set, the Rosenthal crystal.

Actually, I think she got decent alimony. Just not enough to keep her on Beacon Street. So important to her to be part of that wealthy crowd. Why she fell in love with him. No, be fair to the bitch. It was also the old name, the status, the class. She grew up in a three-decker in Somerville, eight children in a three-bedroom flat, laundry hanging on the lines out the back porch. Yelling Friday nights when the men got paid and boozed up, her father always waving his belt at one of them. Her mother old at forty, hardly any teeth left in her mouth and a front one black. Mother had ambitions or anyway dreams. Paltry as they were: "If you are bright and accomplished, Elizabeth, someday you may marry a Big Man." Well it was the 1930s after all.

Lost her family really when she married Father. His turned its back on her, but not on him. Father's mother — did I meet her when I was a baby? — refused to go to the wedding of her son to a Catholic. And Mother's lout of a father, Jack Callahan, hated mother for marrying a man who thought himself too good to set foot in his house. "She married out of the faith," he'd yell when Grandma tried to defend her — as if he cared about religion. He hated me for being Father's child; Father hated me for being hers. Father hated Mother for forcing him to marry her; Mother hated Father for forcing divorce on her. My legacy: hate. What a family. Callahan kids with bruises and bad memories grew up to beat their own kids. Mother couldn't stand it after a while, stopped going to Somerville. Both dead now, li'l' ole Gramps and Granny. Sweet dreams.

Her dreams: I became their instrument. All I ever was to her? Even now? Still, that's more than I was to Father. And to Clare?

Clare loved me. I know that. I'm sure of it.

Mary loved me too. Why couldn't I love her?

She walked on, hands in her pockets, kicking leaves, raising leaf-dust, making noise, swsh swsh. How it sounded when I was little, when I was here at Thanksgiving, Christmas. Long walks by myself, get out of that house.

Had to get out, my innards aflame with envy. Envy hurts, it screams, burns. Mary and Laura and all the attention they got, the cousins too. My aunts and uncles — *his* brothers and sisters and in-laws. All of them looked at me coldly, seeing my lower-class Catholic mother, one step re-moved from a prostitute, me one step removed from a whore's bastard. What would they have thought if they ever met Ronnie! Hah! Mary such a spoiled brat, used to being waited on hand and foot. Expected everything, expected everyone to love her. She had all that love and still she clung to me, always seeking me out, Lizabit, play with me, Lizabit, I color with you. Sometimes I'd give in, go swimming with her or play hide-and-seek in the woods. Not much fun with only two of us and she so little, five to my ten, seven to my twelve . . . I stopped then. Not a child anymore. No other children ever here until Alex. Alex born when I was sixteen, already planning my getaway, to get out for good. Took me another few years. No children visited regularly. Aside from family parties, the only visitors men in limousines, no children with them, imagine a limo with a sign in its window "Caution: Baby on Board." Hah!

But what did I care, I didn't get along very well with kids anyway. Nothing mattered but using my mind, thinking. Finding my intellectual equals. Certainly didn't find them here — Mary, what a joke! Father understood politics and money but what he had wasn't really intelligence, oh he's smart enough I guess, but not like Clare. What he was was known, part of the inner circle, accepted by the right people, into inside conversation for years, privy to the secret springs that drive a state: street smarts à la Constitution Avenue.

But Clare! God I was so excited, stimulated, oh god the desire that surged in my gut! Something I'd never felt before. Me twenty-one to his forty. Sitting in his study while he talked, so easily, all of it in his head, never needed a note. His blond forelock falling in his face, tying a capitalist cash economy to the philosophers, to Hobbes and Hume and Adam Smith of course and then Darwin and Herbert Spencer, to painters, writers, capitalism creating art forms, the novel, family forms changed by removing production from the home. To Marx, who really understood capitalism, its potential.

Clare so golden, so beautiful and brilliant and passionate, Ellen so sour, I couldn't understand it, how could she not love being married to him? How I envied her. She wasn't jealous of me, looked at me with contempt another stupid little protégée as if she knew something I didn't. Well, she did didn't she. But I could never stop adoring him. Even now. She's still alive I hear, living in a cottage in the Cotswolds, doing her vapid watercolors. While he in a cold cold grave lies. . . .

Will Father die unscathed, with nothing said between us, not the one thing or the other? If I asked him straight out how he felt about me, he'd probably laugh. But if he didn't love me why did he say he did, well of course I suppose in that situation he would. But that didn't have to happen. Was it love? Could anything I did hurt him, make him suffer? Is that the definition of love, putting yourself in a position where someone can hurt you? Once in a while a glint in his eye I thought might be pleasure in me, in my brains. I thought he liked me that day I went to him in

Washington and told him I wanted him to get Clare a job in the government commensurate with his stature and not the puny little job he'd been offered, *or else*. I'd prepared myself, I was tough. He was amused. That day he saw his own flesh and blood. I probably couldn't have damaged him no matter what I did. He must have known that but he did it anyway. But said "I don't want to see you here again."

Still, even after that I kept getting summonses from his secretary, family get-together at the Lincoln house, July 4. Be there. His brothers and sisters and their families, all the cousins, famous friends, all the bedrooms opened, a huge staff in those days. A hundred people milling around, he courtly, showing off: my daughters Elizabeth, Mary, and Alexandra, their mothers named them after queens and I'm sure you can see why. Oh he was good, so gracious. Mary with the husband of the moment, children. I took Clare a couple of times: what did they think? Father respected Clare, they spoke the same language somehow. But Father never again spoke to me privately, personally. Only that cordial public persona, what a master he was, fooled everyone. I never mastered it. Only men can really get away with it: the world is my oyster. Women are the pearls.

Fewer parties after Amelia left. But some. And he still called me, Mary too. But never Alex. What did Amelia do to him that he cut off her child so completely? God knows he hated my mother but he still called me. Had me called.

His eightieth birthday the president came for an hour. Helicopter on the front lawn. Photo op, the *Globe, People*. Grand old man, distinguished elder statesman. He still looked fine, as if he might live forever. Arms around his grandsons. Children not mine. I end with me: she goes on. My work my immortality. I'd like to see her write a book on capitalism as the triumph of Man the Creator, everything from nothing. Clare's ideas extended, deepened. If I ever finish it. No heart since he died.

Loved reading sections to him sprawled on the couch in my apartment Sunday mornings, a Bloody Mary in one hand, cigarette in the other, those eyebrows raised, always ready to make some witty supercilious remark. He'd wake me up after his morning jog, make brunch with me sitting there drinking coffee in my robe, an Upton no-no. He'd make omelets or eggs benedict, hollandaise sauce from scratch. Always impressed me. Or bring bagels and cream cheese. A ritual. Lying around the sunlit living room reading the *Washington Post* and the *New York Times*. Happy. Always scoffed at me doing the *Times* crossword puzzle — "such a middlebrow hobby, Liz" — but he loved knowing an answer when I asked. Careful to ask about the clues he would know: Greek letters, quotations from poetry, geography. River in east Borneo. How did he know things like that? Then I'd read a new section out loud, him listening with his whole self, his body intent, face gleaming. Cared about my work, wanted it to be great. Didn't care to do it himself. His fame established among the cognoscenti. His immortality guaranteed. The man who showed Keynes was wrong.

But now, 1984, Orwell's year of the apocalypse, something new happening, recession 1981–82, well they're to be expected, necessary purgations of waste, of course they hit the poor first, that's par for the course, that's not what's frightening me, it's the new systems, new approaches, make me old-fashioned, global markets, global accounting, transnationals moving to countries without labor laws, junk bonds, hostile takeovers, last year Siegel saved Martin Marietta from Bendix, something new is being unleashed exploding the way Clare felt something new had exploded in the fifteenth century, thirst for something, powerful drive trampling down everything in its way, things that deserved to die anyway of course, can't hold Man back. One of the great purges necessary for the survival of the fittest, catharsis that cleanses the economy, purges wasteful lazy workers, methods. Can't concentrate on the misery, have to look at the big picture, future of the human race.

A church bell clanged eight times in the distance, each note trembling on the air: Sunday morning. Stomach pursed up, she headed back toward the house, then slowed in a patch of sunlight: I could take a leave of absence! I could work on it here! Fly home, pack up disks, books, files. Have to have them sent, too much to carry. That would take days. Maybe drive, take the Alfa, no one here uses it.

Her mind stopped. An image seeped into it like ink on soft paper, an October day in New England, Elizabeth driving Clare's Porsche, he sitting beside her sulking because she refused to hear a Brandenburg Concerto one more time, she'd put on a tape of Bill Evans playing "I Was Up with the Lark Today," the music lilting with an easy joy, driving down a road tree-lined like a *chemin cru* in Normandy, a tunnel of scarlet, orange, crimson, shades of gold, the red maples coloring in a corkscrew pattern, around and around, shading from orange to vermilion to maroon, he beside her smiling after all, she steeped in contentment, thinking that whatever the cost, it was worth it.

Was it?

There was no change in the old man's condition, said Dr. Stamp. The sisters understood that he came to the intensive care ward especially to see them at eleven Sunday morning, that he made his rounds early, before eight, and often did not come in at all on Sundays. Elizabeth also understood that he did not want them to move the great man from this little local hospital to Boston: if there were television cameras or journalists, he wanted them to focus on him. The sisters were content, Mary especially let him know she appreciated the personal care Father was receiving here.

Elizabeth had called Dr. Biddle to ask him to recommend a neurologist, and he had named the same Professor Roper at Harvard. But she told Dr. Stamp they had taken *his* recommendation and that Dr. Roper would be arriving tomorrow afternoon around four. Would that be convenient? He was pleased (such a grande dame), he left the room almost bowing, walking backward.

Such are the rewards of fame and wealth. Ronnie smirked.

The sisters stood around the old man's bed and studied him for ten minutes, then left.

In the car afterward, Alex said tentatively, "Do you think it's true that people in comas can hear what is said around them? I mean, I read that someplace. Do you think it's true? Do you think we should talk to him, say who we are and tell him we are hoping he recovers soon, and that we are thinking and praying" — she saw their looks — "well, anyway, say something to let him know we are there and we care?"

The other three gazed at her.

"Do we?" Ronnie grinned.

Alex charged on. "Or we could play tapes. You know, calming music. They have these tapes of the ocean, waves breaking, gulls, the roar of the crashing surf. They might calm him if he's upset. And he's probably upset, you know, being unable to speak and everything. You know?" She studied their faces, desperately seeking response.

No one looked at her.

"What would you say to him?" Mary asked after a time. "You hardly know him."

"I know," Alex worried. "That's why . . ."

"He was no father to you. He left you when you were — how old?"

"No, *we* left. Mom and I, we left suddenly. In the middle of the afternoon. It was right before my tenth birthday, I remember because I was sick on my tenth birthday so I missed my birthday *and* Christmas, all at once! I don't know with what, something funny, a fit of some kind. It wasn't epilepsy," she added quickly. "I don't think. At least, I haven't had a fit in years. Since I've been grown."

"Okay," Mary said in irritation, "so he threw you out. In any case, you don't know him."

"He did love your mother," Elizabeth mused.

Alex's entire body yearned toward Elizabeth, her glance a plea. "Did he?"

"Didn't he summon you to family parties?" Elizabeth asked.

"I don't know. . . . I don't know. Mom never said."

"Well, it is strange," Elizabeth said. "He may not have been an attentive father but he was proprietary: he wanted his daughters to appear at ceremonial occasions; he wanted to show them off."

Alex's eyes misted. "I can't tell you how I longed for him — longed for my father. Of course," she added swiftly, "I don't mean Charlie wasn't wonderful. But of course, Mom didn't marry him until a few years later. And I didn't understand why I didn't have my old father and why Charlie was my father now. I do envy you having a father," she said timidly to Elizabeth.

"He was no father to me," Elizabeth snapped.

"He was no father to anybody," Mary said sadly.

"He fathered you more than he did me," Elizabeth barked.

"That was only because he hated your mother. *That* was the problem," Mary said coldly. "He didn't hate *you.*"

"But you said" — Alex appealed to Elizabeth — "that he loved mine. So why didn't he ever come to see me?"

"Don't ask me to explain him!"

Ronnie, mute, gazed thoughtfully at them. Didn't seem to do them any good, being princesses in paradise. What miserable women. My friends in Roxbury are better off. Oh come off it, Ronnie, don't get sucked into buying the capitalist myth that the rich are unhappier than you and me. Propaganda, don't believe it not for a minute. These women are just a particularly wretched bunch, rotten like Him.

And me? I'm of Him too, like it or not. But no exposure, no fathering. I didn't even realize He was my Father until that day I looked in the mirror and saw His eyes. I must have been ten, eleven. He was there, the family there for the Fourth, I helped Momma serve, I carried food to the long table in the tent, helped clear away, I was little but quick and neat and strong. Elizabeth was with a man with funny blond hair, looked dyed, curled, something. Suddenly saw Elizabeth had the old man's eyes and looked at Him, He was talking to some senator. That night I saw them in my face. They were what made me look so different from Momma, her round face, high cheekbones, simple clean noble face color of sunlight. Her face an ancient face but still young, uncorrupted. No hard tight lines of greed, hard folds of mendacity from smiling against the grain.

Still I'll never forgive her.

I knew she loved Him, knew it long before that, knew it forever. Bent toward Him, her head a little bowed, *sí señor, sí Cabot* if I wasn't around.

Furious as I was, I couldn't challenge her that night, she was exhausted, next day too, poor feet all swollen, calves swollen almost to the knee. When the family went to bed, I made her sit in the kitchen, I filled a basin with warm water and Epsom salts and made her soak them, I fixed a plate of their leftovers for her but she was too tired to eat. Then everyone went home, but He stayed on, stayed for weeks, demanding something every minute, up the stairs down the stairs, tray in the morning, Noradia, draw my bath, press my trousers, prepare tea sandwiches and cakes for this afternoon, Mr. Saltonstall coming to tea, homemade soup for lunch every day of His life, crab salad, omelets, fillet of sole with fresh asparagus, all that work for one person, then dinner as well, three courses when He was alone, five if company, Momma in the kitchen humming, she didn't mind, she seemed to enjoy it, *why didn't she mind?* Ronnie felt rage rising, felt her face flush.

The car pulled up in front of the house and stopped. Getting out,

Elizabeth announced, "Meeting after lunch. You too, Ronnie." Ronnie stared at her with fury.

Elizabeth waited until Teresa had cleared the table before she launched the meeting, ran it just as if it were some formal Washington affair, all she needed was a gavel for fuck's sake. How dare she summon me. Does she think she can order me around?

"We'd know better where we stand if we could find the will," Elizabeth continued. "My guess is it's in the safe but I don't know the combination."

"I don't see what difference it makes whether we find it or not," Alex said. "I mean, what would we do if he left us money that we wouldn't do if he didn't?"

"You think we'd hang around here visiting him every day, acting the loving daughters, if he's cut us out and left everything to Harvard?" Mary spat at her.

Alex looked bewildered.

"Or to your sons," Elizabeth said to Mary.

She paled. "Oh god." She rolled her rings. "He *could* do something like that."

"Well surely they'd share it with their dear loving mother," Elizabeth sneered.

"Oh god." Mary was too distraught to retaliate. "We have to find out!" she burst out.

"We can't. Hollis made it clear he won't tell us. The only way we can find out is by finding the will. And we can't do that unless we can get into the safe."

"Hire a safecracker," Ronnie joked.

"Know one?" Elizabeth asked coolly.

Ronnie flushed.

"Aren't we entitled to something by law? Being his daughters?"

"Not if he specifically cuts us out."

Mary considered. "We definitely haven't been the most attentive daughters."

"He won't cut us out entirely," Elizabeth asserted. "We're his blood. But he may leave us small annuities. We're girls after all, expected to find husbands to support us." She turned to Ronnie. "Your attitude suggests you don't expect to be acknowledged in his will."

Ronnie gave her a long cold look.

"So why are you hanging around?" Mary wanted to know.

Ronnie looked at her with hate.

"For the same reason I am," Alex said quietly.

All of them looked at her. She looked steadily at them.

"To get to know you. All of you."

"For heaven's sake, why?" asked Elizabeth after a pause.

Have to have something to do, can't just sit in my room, can't be around them much, why am I staying here, what am I doing? Ronnie picked up and put down one book, leaflet, packet of papers after another. Organize my research data, start to write the goddamned dissertation. Read the material I didn't get to last year. Make up a schedule for myself, stop wandering around this house like a lost child. Could she be right? Am I staying to get to know them? Why? What do I want from them? Elizabeth always in His study, Mary lounging in the sun room reading, Alex out walking for hours, walked all the way into town to get a library card, plenty of books here, mostly unread. Otherwise hides in her room like me, no place to go, all these rooms and no place to go. Drawing room with that stiff French furniture, can't relax there, why did He call it the drawing room? Out of a nineteenth-century novel: what in hell's a drawing room? No one ever drew there that I saw. Sitting room, anyone could walk in, see you there. So what? I am a member of this family, Alex says so, I can go anywhere now.

Or is it for Him after all that we're here, something we want from Him. Acknowledgment?

I HEREBY DECREE THAT RONALDA VELEZ IS MY NATURAL DAUGHTER, A LOVE CHILD, BECAUSE I LOVED HER MOTHER, THAT DEAR SOUL WHO TOOK SUCH GOOD CARE OF ME UNTIL SHE BECAME MORTALLY ILL, WHO CARED MORE ABOUT ME THAN SHE DID ABOUT THAT DAUGHTER WHO HAS THEREBY BEEN DOUBLY DISPOSSESSED.

Ridiculous. Will never happen.

I could clean out Momma's room, get rid of her things, such as they are. Take them to a church or some charity. Even a poor woman would probably turn up her nose at them.

Her eyes filled. Can't.

She sat on the narrow bed and leaned back against the headboard. Servant's room in the kitchen wing, narrow, shabby, but with a window facing the overgrown kitchen garden. Bed, dresser, hard-backed chair. But at least it has a desk, well table really. "Momma, I need a desk! I have to have someplace to do homework, we have to write a Paper, Momma, a Paper! When I work at the kitchen table, everything gets spots on it! It's important, Momma!" Her homework on lined paper, food-stained, other kids typed theirs by seventh grade on nice neat clean white paper without lines. Couldn't tell her, couldn't ask for a typewriter; make her feel bad. Always tried not to make her feel bad. But then I'd burst out in fury at her at some stupid inconsequential thing. Sudden spurt of rage. Way she looked at me, dark brown eyes, she'd shake her head so sadly, sometimes she'd just open her arms while I was screaming at her, and I'd throw myself into them and she'd hold me and we'd both cry. She loved me. Momma loved me. It wasn't that she loved Him more, it was just that He had all the power. But did He or did she give it to Him?

She poked around until she found something, a table in the barn, old pine thing long ago discarded but beautiful, she was so happy. "Ronalda, look!" Something she could give me. Now it holds the computer. I wish I could keep it. Nothing mine in this house, not even the desk I used for years. They'd probably let me keep it, they wouldn't want it, but I'd have to ask them, be a beggar at their door. Couldn't.

Funny, you can know that money isn't the thing, that love is what matters, know that you were loved by your mother at least and that they weren't anyway it seems they weren't, Elizabeth and Mary. But it doesn't help, nothing helps. I hate them, hate hate hate them. And I can't bear to think that maybe I love them, want to love them, I love my hate, I want to keep it. Why I wonder. Did *their* father love Momma? Could He love? Did He see how beautiful she was inside? Surely wasn't her clothes attracted Him or her shape. Simple face, no makeup. But maybe that's what drew Him after all His society women, secretaries, call girls, all decked out in designer suits and necklaces, dyed, painted, high-heeled, mannered. She might have been a relief, someone He could despise openly, treat like a servant and she accepted it.

This house. His. Grand spaces, light pouring over the shining floors, wonderful old carpets, the elegant tables, paintings . . .

Momma had to wax those floors, vacuum the rugs, dust the tables, the picture frames, clean the chandeliers, ammonia and water with newspapers, Ronalda, that is the best cleaner for glass. Remember. Remember that so that when you grow up and become a servant like me, you will have skills I had to learn. That's what she meant even if she never said it: my future a given. Our color. An unchanging unchangeable prison we carry with us wherever we go. Servants even in the country her parents came from, Mexico. No way to go home to a different kind of place.

The gardens used to be so beautiful, catch your breath in April, the forsythia and the hyacinths and daffodils, then tulips and lilac, then the wisteria, and then May oh god everything burst out, the rhododendrons and azaleas like flame, lavender orange pink cerise and the roses the old-fashioned ones with a scent like poetry, and then the peonies and the clematis. I thought I wanted to be a gardener, gardener in paradise. Asked Momma to ask Him. I was twelve, after all. Tony used to bring his son to help him with the lawn, little Tony, he wasn't much older than me. Lots of women gardened, I used to see them in front of their houses when Momma and I drove into town to do the marketing, wearing lovely straw hats, kneeling on mats, gloves on their hands. I hid behind the door when she went in to ask Him. A GIRL gardener! He exploded, laughing. What next! Tell her to study dusting and she has a deal!

Is that all He wanted for me.

Well, suppose He'd said yes. Work for Him the rest of my life like Momma, servant in His house. Live the rest of my life in this room or maybe Aldo's apartment over the garage. Take care of the car and supervise the gardening. Summoned for praise or reproach, head bowed, yes sir. Like Momma.

Wish I could keep that desk.

I was never able to say anything to her. Not then, not later, not even the times she came to see me in Boston after I left. Couldn't. She loved Him, the only one in her life besides me. For her the most important thing was to love, not to be loved. Besides, she never knew. If she had . . .? Maybe He was kind to her when they were alone. Never *really* looked at her that I saw, but He must have, must have.

She never had anything but us, Him and me. No, long ago she had her parents, her sisters and brothers, they loved each other, she had happy memories. Happy memories!!! A childhood in workers' camps among rusted-out cars and broken crockery, her momma and poppa and all the kids moving from farm to farm California living in shanties no toilet or bath, crates for furniture, one stained mattress on the floor for all of them. All of them had to work even the kids to earn enough to carry them through off-seasons. But what she remembered most was the light at dawn as they set off for the fields, dew still on the leaves, holding her momma's hand, or carried on her poppa's shoulders, the family together.

Brother, sister, poppa dead of TB, another brother dead from violence, other sisters went to Los Angeles to find jobs as maids, what a joke. How could they be maids, they had never had houses, washing machines dishwashers vacuum cleaners coffeemakers Cuisinarts. Had to learn everything, everything terrifyingly new, threatening. But Momma did.

My momma with her momma, my *abuelita,* the grandma I never knew, two women alone in a hostile world, who had always lived so closely with their kin. Took two years to work their way across the country, often hungry. Picked their way to Vermont and when the last apple was packed, Grandma got them on a bus to Boston, the postcard clutched in her hand with an address where Momma's aunt, Abuela's sister Imelda, had gone with her man years before. But Imelda was gone from the address on the card saved over all the years, a card neither of them could read and Imelda couldn't have written. Who wrote it? Who read it to them?

Ronnie's throat felt tight and she got up and walked the length of the room.

Forget all that, all over, done with, I'm not doomed like them, I have a chance. Her gaze fell on the disconnected computer, the piles of books and papers on the desk.

Lazy wetback.

Well, how could I do anything, she silently shrieked at herself, when she was dying, when she was in such pain, when I tried to be with her every moment! I finished the coursework, didn't I? In a tough discipline! I did the research!

She fell into the chair at the desk and gazed out at the brown ruined kitchen garden. It hadn't been tended since Momma fell ill, but a few straggly lettuces still struggled for life, a couple of tomato plants had reseeded themselves and sent up leggy shoots.

Every spring, the gardener turned the ground over for Momma and she planted the hot peppers and herbs she couldn't buy here and pole beans and tomatoes and squash and eggplant. Up every morning early, out there with her small golden hands working in the soil, pressing and pulling, treating the plants as if they were her children.

She was happy here. Only she missed her momma. Grave in Boston, too far away for her to tend. Together now.

What happened? She only got sick last spring. Maybe she was sick before that, couldn't attend to things. Because everything has gone to pieces, all the gardens are a wreck, He still had the groundsmen working, how come? As if when she stopped overseeing things, they fell apart. As if she was the soul of a house she could never own. All His money and power couldn't keep things together.

Maybe it takes love to keep things together.

Hah! Where do you find that?

Where could Momma find it, twenty-six years old, her own mother dead, alone alone alone in the world, friendless world for her. Getting this job a fluke for her.

She never tired of talking about the man in a uniform who came for her in a limousine! Her shabby coat, belongings in shopping bags. Servant shortage or she never would have got such a job. The driver told her to sit in the back and she held on to the handgrip in terror, sure someone would come and rip her out of this car in which she did not belong. They drove to this town, all white the trees iced the snow still over the fields not like Boston where it had turned to stained slush. And the houses so big, so many trees, she hadn't imagined houses like this, farmhouses were sometimes big but not like these houses.

And then her first sight of the house! And then inside! All those rooms, all that furniture, so grand, so elegant, so rich. She even had her own room up on the third floor, closed now, a whole floor of servants' bedrooms, little cells with one shared bath. Thing is, it was better than what she was used to. She was working in a palace. Housemaid to an Anglo god. Must have terrified her: what did she know about polishing silver and crystal? Treating antique walnut and rosewood? She tiptoed around the rooms terrified of breaking scratching soiling something. He had a full staff then, she could already speak English, she listened, watched the cook. Each thing she learned made her proud of herself: mastering skills, acquiring knowledge. Well she had hadn't she: how to clean crystal chandeliers, get stains out of Persian carpets. How many people know such things? She learned so well that when He reduced the staff He promoted her to housekeeper and cook. On call twenty-four hours a day six days a week, two hundred dollars a month plus room and board. Almost never anyone here anymore except Him for a few weeks in the summer. All the wives dead or gone, the children elsewhere. Only the July Fourth party. Maybe He was fucking her from the beginning, why He kept her on, promoted her.

I was born in April 1959. AprilMarchFebruaryJanuaryDecember-NovemberOctoberSeptemberAugust yes, August 1958, in the summer when he was here alone, that's when. Maybe started earlier. She came in the snow, after Christmas JanuaryFebruary probably, 1956. I know how it was, had to be. Some night, late, He in bed, calls her on the intercom, Noradia bring me a brandy, she young and smooth and simple climbs the stairs approaches nervously carrying blown glass on a silver tray, come here, sit down. Do you like me? Oh, *sí señor*. Fervently. Loved a disgusting old man, over fifty already, wrinkled skin white as a dead fish, head half bald, that hawk nose. All he had was money. Power. Is that what you loved him for Momma? Because he was the *señor*? Droit du seigneur. The women of your family had to know all about that. Still, how could you stand those hands on your smooth golden body?

Fury gushed around her heart and Ronnie rose and paced but it was a joke pacing in that room, three steps one way, three back. She fell into the chair again, put her head in her hands.

I hate you Momma, she whispered weeping, I hate, hate, hate you!

5

Sunday it rained off and on all afternoon, the sky a thick gray gruel. The sisters could not settle. Elizabeth plonked herself in Father's study to examine his papers and put what she had in some coherent arrangement, but kept waking startled from minddrift, finding herself leaning back in his high-backed desk chair facing the window and the bleak chilly November day. Her eyes seemed to burn all the time, and she had put on eyeglasses instead of her contact lenses. But the bone-framed glasses annoyed her too and she regularly removed and wiped them clean, rubbing the sides of her nose and the spot they touched behind her ears. Occasionally, laying the glasses on the desk, she would get up and wander into the kitchen for some coffee, or to the toilet to wash her face, or to the sitting room where Mary was reading, some stupid romance probably. Mary always wrapped her books in tooled leather covers. Pretentious way to conceal her trash. Unspeaking, Elizabeth would stand by the front windows and look out at the rain.

Then she'd return and begin to search the room, already searched thoroughly several times. The need to find the will was sharp in her chest like the stays in those corselets worn in the fifties. . . . Mary would remember, what were they called, merry widows? So thin we were, but we encased ourselves in those iron maidens, and sometimes the stays broke through the fabric. Metal or bone, they poked at, dug into the skin, they hurt. Happened to me once at a tea dance with some Princeton boys. By the time I got back to my room, the skin over my ribs was cut and bloody under my breasts, my ostensible breasts, as Mary called them. She was five years younger but twice my size, there at least. So proud of that. Funny. So much feeling about the size of breasts. Never understood. Still, I was trying in those days to be a girl, to be like other girls. Deep red lipstick, pale eyebrows, high heels.

She always said I was jealous of her looks but I never tried to compete with her, knew I couldn't. Didn't even want to. It wasn't looks I wanted. . . .

She slammed a file drawer in exasperation. Why am I doing this! I have searched this room five times over! Why am I so intent on finding the will? She flopped in the desk chair and her head fell onto the desk. Oh, god because I want it, I want to be his heir, I want to see the words typed on the paper, I want to hear my name read out: "and to my daughter Elizabeth . . . my dear daughter Elizabeth" . . . I could even accept "my dear daughters Elizabeth and Mary" . . .

I need to hear it.

But I don't need the money. In itself.

Knock it off, Upton, you'd love to have millions.

What would I do with them?

Feel rich. Buy a country house. Buy a Porsche like Clare's. You loved driving that car.

But you're dreaming of money like winning a lottery. You don't need it.

I need it I need it.

Don't tell me you believe in symbols: Money equals love. If he loves us, he will leave us his estate? My father's house. My father's estate.

What I really want is to see my name listed as executor, as he would have named a son.

She raised her head. Oh, god, what if he didn't! She bit her lower lip, eyes alarmed, upper body stiff and erect. It would be unbearable if he had not entrusted *her* — an assistant secretary of the treasury — with that job, if he had consigned her along with his other daughters to the keeping of some man. Unbearable.

Mary had had Browning build a fire in the sitting room. It was a large room for one person to sit in, large even for four or five, but it was more comfortable than the stiff formal drawing room and had a wider fireplace. She nestled in a big armchair wearing a soft sweatsuit, a cashmere confection. As she read, she sipped herbal tea, which the housekeeper replenished every hour. But she kept drifting off and would come to staring at the fire remembering her mother sitting in this chair in a white dress, laughing, holding out a pale graceful delicate arm encircled with diamonds, reaching for the cocktail glass the butler handed her. A party it must have been, me carried down for a good-night kiss.

She glanced down at her own pale delicate wrist lying across the book and started, shuddered in horror to see tiny brown hairs rising out of her arm. "Arms that are braceleted and white and bare / (But in the lamplight, downed with light brown hair!)" Ugh! Disgusting.

She rose, stretched, walked through the front hall, peered into the empty dining room, walked down the hall past the billiards room and into Father's study. She studied the books on the shelves, ignoring Elizabeth at the desk.

"Not much there you'd be interested in," Elizabeth said nastily.

"No," Mary murmured absently.

"Mostly history and politics. Law. Not many novels and *no romances*," Elizabeth goaded her.

"Yes," Mary said, drifting out.

Alex found lots of old rain gear in the mudroom behind the kitchen. She took a raincoat and hat and short dirty boots that fit her and went for a walk. She walked for hours, welcoming the cool rain on her face, her mind drifting murkily, all paths leading into an opacity heavier and less penetrable than the weather. Twice as she walked, her entire body jerked the way it might jerk in a bad dream — a sudden, electric, terrifying spasm. It seemed to pierce her entire body. Then it would pass. Am I going crazy? Pushing the thought away, she kept walking.

*   *   *

Ronnie hooked up her computer, transferred her research data from floppy disks to the hard, and made up a schedule. Then she collapsed on the bed, lay there spread-eagled, staring at the ceiling. It was cracked and discolored, probably hadn't been repainted since she first entered that room as an infant, a few months old. Noradia had told her the room's history once when she was around fourteen after she railed against Stephen. Momma explained that Stephen had had the huge old kitchens renovated and subdivided after Ronnie was born, so Noradia and her baby could have rooms on the first floor. Momma's face shone as she told Ronnie of His kindness, His pity for her at having to climb all the way to the third floor several times a day. Ronnie shot back that He'd probably done it so she wouldn't carry a baby with her as she moved around the house working. Noradia sighed, laid her hands gently on Ronnie's cheeks, looked at her with that sweet face full of sorrow but radiant. Said, "Ronalda, Ronalda, to be happy in life you must love."

"Love what!" she'd cried, "anything that comes down the pike? Love evil, love the devil, is that what you're telling me?" She leapt up, crazy with rage, danced around the kitchen with it, jumping up and down: "Love a rapist, a murderer, a massacrer, a marauder, is that what you're saying?" Frightening her mother, who sat back heavily, pale, staring at her, murmuring "Ronalda, Ronalda" and twisting her fingers.

The next day I shoved some clothes in a backpack and took off, hitchhiked into Boston. She must have been frozen with fear, not knowing where I was, whether I was alive, if I'd been kidnapped or just run off. He summoned the police for her after two days, but it was hopeless, they couldn't trace me and what the hell, just a wetback kid, His servant's kid. Different if it had been *His* kid. Almost a year I let her wait here in torment. Poor Momma, how I made her suffer, I wanted her to suffer, I didn't care.

But you deserved it, Momma. You did.

She leapt up from the bed, wandered to the desk, the closet, the door, wandered out, met Alex coming in from the mudroom with wet hair, eyes glazed, not even a smile, no word. She just passed by.

Restless, each of them except Ronnie, who never changed for dinner, went up early to change her clothes, and simply by chance each meandered down again and peered into the dining room around six. Table not even set yet. Meeting in the hall, they made their way into the sitting room, seeking something, feeling a need for something. The fire was low but still burning.

"Shall we have cocktails before dinner?" Alex asked brightly. The others agreed with varying degrees of sullenness. "I'll pour them!" she chirped. Elizabeth had a Perrier, Mary a vermouth cassis, Ronnie a cola; Alex had white wine. "Isn't this nice?" she smiled, snuggling into a big armchair. "It seems so much homier with a fire, doesn't it?"

No one responded.

Ronnie added some logs to the fire, piling them on their ends as if she were building a tepee.

Mary frowned at this unorthodox method. "Browning takes care of the fire. She doesn't do it that way."

"*Mrs.* Browning has enough to do getting dinner," Ronnie said dismissively. The fire flared brilliantly. She wiped her soiled hands on the sides of her jeans, then perched on the footstool beside the fireplace, watching over it as if it were a baby in a cradle.

"Oh, there's just nothing homier than a fire!" Alex cried joyously.

Elizabeth rolled her eyes, Mary eyed her.

"It's true!" she protested, laughing. "Say it isn't true!"

They smiled. Grudgingly.

Alex leaned back expansively in her chair. "This is such a beautiful house. Has it always been in the Upton family?"

Mary looked at Elizabeth. "You're the family historian, Lizzie."

Elizabeth frowned. "No, it came from Margaret Linden, who married Abner Upton in 1868. She was our great-great-grandmother and the only heir to the Linden fortune, one son having died in his youth, the other during the Civil War. Lincoln has an interesting history. One Squaw Sachem sold the six square miles that became Lincoln to English settlers in exchange for some hatchets, hoes, knives, cloth, and clothing. In 1636, Thomas Flint settled Concord farm and Flint's Pond, which became the town center of Lincoln — which was incorporated separately in 1754. On April 19, 1775, Paul Revere was captured here. It was always a town of mavericks, people who insisted on their own religion, their own ways. It was just a little farm town until the twentieth century, when the railroad was extended, and people began to build summer homes here. It's still a maverick town, really. The first Linden house burned down; this one dates back to the 1780s, the old part, Father's study. The house was added to and added to over the years, the last time after Margaret married Abner. And of course it's been modernized since. Inside.

"The Uptons have lived in Louisburg Square for generations. Worth got that house of course, he was the older brother. Old man Upton didn't believe in total primogeniture but Worth got the lion's share — the house on the ocean in Manchester, most of the money. Father got this house and a goodly chunk of stocks. Prudence got mainly jewelry, some of it very valuable. No real estate, but the old man bought her a house in Back Bay when she married Samuel — Grandfather Upton was still alive then. Father was the youngest child. He would probably have inherited more from his mother if he hadn't scandalized her by marrying a Catholic — my mother — then divorcing her. He's had to make his own way to some degree. Far more than Worth did."

"He had to make his way with only a few measly millions?" Ronnie jeered.

"Less than that," Elizabeth said coldly. "You may scoff, but it takes effort and talent to build a fortune, even when you start with a million dollars."

"Of course! Even when most people were earning twenty dollars a week or less."

Elizabeth threw her a look of disgust.

"My mother decorated this house when she married Father," Mary said dreamily. "It hasn't been redone since her time." Over forty years: looks it.

"Well, she did a beautiful job!" Alex cried. "So tell me: what has everyone decided to do! Is everyone going to stay?"

Elizabeth lighted a cigarette. "Well, if I'm going to be conservator, I guess I'll have to. I made some phone calls yesterday. I can probably get leave, although it's a bad time: we are involved in major negotiations with Chile, there's a chance of new constraints on trade with South Africa," she said self-importantly. "But I've already drawn up the guidelines and I've overseen most of the background work. My staff can draft the reports and express mail them to me for approval. I can work with them over the phone."

They were silent, comparing Elizabeth's life with their own.

Tuesday night Women's Club, Wednesday the shelter, Thursday the hospital. David plays golf every weekend, the kids gone most afternoons and weekends: I am a useless person, thought Alex.

Nothing but boredom and unpaid bills waiting for me, thought Mary. How long will it be before the girls realize how long it's been since I picked up the lunch check? How long will my old clothes see me through? I'll end like some nineteenth-century spinster, replacing the collar and cuffs of the old black dress worn shiny.

I have important work to do too, Ronnie thought fiercely. I just have to get going on it. But if I leave here, I'll have to get a job to live. Then how will I finish the dissertation? If I stay, I live free. Is that corruption?

"So," Elizabeth continued, "I've decided to work on my book while I'm confined here. I thought I'd take the Alfa and drive down to Washington tomorrow and vote while I'm there. You know Tuesday's Election Day — maybe you all want to fly home and," she grinned, "make sure the right man wins. I'll get my computer and files and bring them back."

"Oh! Election Day!" Alex murmured.

I can vote in Massachusetts, you snotty cow, Ronnie thought. And will, to cancel out yours.

"Election Day," Mary repeated vaguely. "But surely there's no question but that Reagan will win, is there?"

"None," Elizabeth announced.

Mary said lazily, "I think Alex is right about — it's probably good for Father for us to visit every day. So I'll stay for a while. Even though it's a real bore here."

Alex clapped her hands like a child. "Oh, I'm so glad! So happy! I really want to get to know you," she said. "My mom's retired, she's taking care of the kids and David while I'm here. And I just called them, and they're all fine and she says she's happy to stay on, it gives her something to do. And David . . . well, David believes family always comes first, he wants me to do everything I can to help Father. And the kids . . . well, I think they barely notice I'm gone. Such an indispensable mother I am!" she mocked herself. "So I can stay!" she crowed. "And you too, I hope," she said to Ronnie, who was staring at the fire.

Mary's face stiffened. "I'm sorry but I have to say that as far as I'm concerned, Ronnie definitely has no right to be here. Neither Elizabeth nor I has invited her and I don't think you have the right to invite her."

Alex frowned questioningly. "Why?"

"You left Father when you were ten and never saw him again!"

"He's still my father," Alex argued quietly, "*and* Ronnie's. What do you say, Elizabeth?"

Mary screamed, "Don't ask *her*! *I'm* saying she can't stay! *I'm* saying it, *me*! I'm saying I don't want her here! She's the bastard child of a colored servant! As far as we're concerned she has no relation to him — or us! And you he repudiated! He never invited you to the family parties! Only Elizabeth and me! He threw your mother out! A little nobody, a secretary, a nothing!"

"So was my mother," Elizabeth inserted coldly.

Mary whirled on her. "And look how he treated you!"

"Are you saying you are the only legitimate daughter?" Elizabeth laughed.

Mary sealed her lips and sat back.

Ronnie watched them, fascinated. And herself: how come I'm not storming out of the room? she wondered.

"Well, all right, Alex can stay but Ronnie can't!" Mary burst out finally.

Without rancor, Elizabeth said, "Because her mother lacked a marriage license? He lived with Noradia longer than any of our mothers."

Ronnie gaped at her.

"She was a servant! Not even white!"

"My children are Jewish — I converted when I married David. And two of yours had an Italian father," Alex said firmly. "And Noradia probably gave him more comfort than any of our mothers."

"Alberto was an aristocrat!"

"Oh, please," Elizabeth cut in, "save us your snobbery. You were always such a snob. The only thing you learned at Peabrain Academy."

"Miss Peabody's was the finest girls' school in Virginia!" Mary protested. "You talk about snobbery, there's no bigger snob than you! Always boasting about Concord Academy, Smith College, that fancy London Economics College!"

"London School of Economics!" Elizabeth blasted.

Mary charged on. "Who's the snob around here! Of course with a background like yours, you insist social distinctions are snobbish! Your mother's family was nothing but shanty Irish from Chelsea."

"Somerville," Elizabeth said.

"She was a little tramp who trapped him into marriage."

Elizabeth turned white. "My mother was no tramp, but your mother was a lush who committed suicide in a drunken car crash hushed up by family money!"

"She was not! It was the other driver's fault! Father told me!"

"What other driver, you idiot! She drove into a tree! Spoiled brat princess pissed off at Father because he was working day and night in the War Effort. He had it hushed up, but it was suicide! How would you know anything about it, you were only seven! But I was twelve, I heard the servants, the aunts and uncles talking. Everyone knew but you!"

"You bitch! You bitch!" Mary sobbed.

"She was a drunk! Don't tell me you don't remember her drinking. If I saw it, just spending summers with her, even a stupid cow like you must have seen it living with her! She was falling-down drunk half the day and she stank of booze all the time!"

Mary wiped away tears, glaring at Elizabeth. "My mother was a lady, she was sweet, gentle, everyone loved her. Yours — even you call her a world-class bitch! A cheap tramp! You call *me* names! Father even *caught* her with another man, there were photographs! Aunt Pru told me!"

Elizabeth spoke slowly, coldly. "You stupid fucking cunt, you silly cow bitch, you asshole. That was a setup. Don't you know Father yet?" She stood up and walked to the bar set up on the sideboard. Leaning against the wall, she poured Perrier into her glass. She stood there looking down at it.

Mary was sniffling. The others watched white-faced.

"My mother never looked at another man," Elizabeth said after a time. "Even after the divorce. Said once was enough. I think she hated men after Father. When Father lived with us we were living in a brownstone on Beacon Street. I don't think he was there very much. I don't remember him but I was very little. I don't know where he spent his time. Mother said he was either fucking some secretary or sucking up to some man who could advance his career. 'Fuck or suck, everything he does rhymes with luck,' she said. The setup — I was only two and a half when it happened. But I remember it. One night, I was asleep in my crib but I heard terrible noises, pounding, shouting, Mother screaming. I was big enough to climb out of the crib and I ran out of my room, there was a man in the upstairs hall holding a camera with a flashbulb that kept going off. It was blinding, I was terrified, I didn't understand what was happening. Mother was screaming, her nightgown half off, her breast flopping out, she was pounding another man on the chest, yelling at him, screaming.

"The flashbulb kept flaring, while the other man posed with his arms around Mother. He was naked. Mother got away, she ran for the phone and the naked man grabbed her, knocked her down, she screamed. The man with the camera held her down while the other one threw clothes on, then they left, ran down the stairs and out the front door. Mother was crying, muttering, she kept saying 'That bastard, that bastard.'

"Her arms and back were black-and-blue for weeks afterwards. The house hadn't been broken into, they had a key. Father didn't come home that night. He never came home again. I didn't understand what had happened until years later. He had set her up, he hired the guys. Mother said, 'He always wins.' "

The room was silent.

Mary chewed her lower lip. "Well, she shouldn't have forced him to marry her," she said finally.

Elizabeth whirled. "For Christ's sake, Mary, even a world-class bitch was an innocent girl once. She was only twenty, she was a good Catholic girl, she didn't believe in abortion, she loved him, she thought he loved her. She would not be bought off by the family. By her standards, she was behaving honorably. They offered her fifty thousand dollars! They offered to send her to Switzerland! But she thought the family hated her because she was Catholic, but that Father loved her and that's what mattered. That's the story he gave her — said he couldn't buck his family or they'd cut him off."

"She threatened him! Pru told me!"

"I didn't say she was a saint. She threatened to sue him for breach of promise. And he did get her to bed by promising to marry her. That was true. She thought she was pressuring the family, not Father. She convinced herself he wanted what she wanted."

Mary argued, "But the threat means she recognized that he didn't love her. And she still insisted on marriage. She was some nervy bitch, going up against a family as powerful as Father's. That doesn't sound like an innocent girl to me."

Elizabeth walked slowly back to her chair, sat, threw her head back. "She was very religious," she said wearily. "The conviction of righteousness can give an innocent girl courage. He should have known better than to dally with someone so religious but I think her piety was a challenge to him, goaded him. That's the way he is after all," she said bitterly. "He always wants what's forbidden."

Mary was silent.

"Is she still religious?" Alex asked.

"No. She says if God could let what happened to her happen, he isn't worth worshiping."

"So what happened?"

Elizabeth shrugged. "The family arranged an annulment. He didn't want a divorce, he wanted a career in public service and in those days — 1934 — divorce wrecked people. The family paid people off, the church, the courts, to get it on some spurious grounds, they didn't have real grounds for annulment. They had a baby for godsake. It broke her heart, she didn't believe in divorce and for her it was divorce, no matter what it was called. But she had no choice, felt she didn't, anyway. She crumpled because of the pictures — he had these pictures proving she had committed adultery. He threatened divorce cutting her off with nothing. She didn't realize until afterwards that he didn't want a divorce any more than she did.

"If she'd accept an annulment, he promised her a decent allowance for the rest of her life and a bequest in his will if he died first." Which he may. "So she gave him the annulment to get the allowance, so she could support me the only way she could. Decently. She couldn't have earned enough to keep us both in any comfort." So childbirth does make cowards of us all — women anyway. Hostages to fortune. "She knew when she was beaten."

Ronnie got up and put more logs on the fire. They watched, listened to the crackle.

"You spent every summer in this house," Alex said wonderingly. "What did that feel like, living with him knowing that? Was it awful for you?"

"I didn't know the details until later . . . until I was grown."

"At least he wanted you here," Alex said longingly.

"He didn't. Mother insisted he have custody of me summers. She wanted me to have . . ." Her voice clouded.

"She wanted you to get his money!" Mary brayed.

Elizabeth looked at her wearily. "Yes. Get something from him, contacts, entrée to his world, education at least. And she was a bitch, is a bitch, she's impossible, a hateful woman. . . . But part of it, I can hear it between the lines when she talks . . . she wanted me to have a father, a male parent, some kind of . . . Her own family disinherited her — metaphorically — they had no money — when she turned up pregnant without a wedding ring. Her father called her a whore, me a bastard, because she didn't marry a Catholic. He hated me for being Stephen's child, he saw him in me."

"The eyes," Alex murmured.

Elizabeth shrugged. "Whatever."

"Oh, it's more than the eyes. Look at the chin. And the carriage. Elizabeth is the most like Father," Mary said.

The women appraised each other. "Except Ronnie," Alex said.

They studied Ronnie.

"She's so short," said Elizabeth.

"She's *brown!*" Mary cried, outraged.

"She has his eyes, his chin, his mouth," Alex argued.

"So do you. Have his eyes," Mary said to Alex.

"Do you know I never knew that until I visited here eighteen years ago," Alex exclaimed. "I didn't remember what he looked like and Mom didn't have any pictures of him, not even a wedding picture." She paused. "I could never understand that."

"There were plenty of pictures in the papers when he married her," said Elizabeth. "You could have checked a newspaper morgue."

"I guess." Alex leaned forward, her voice fervent. "What do you think happened with my mother? Do you remember what she was like then?"

"I only read about their wedding in the papers. Heaven forfend that Father would tell *me* what he was doing," Elizabeth said sarcastically. "I was at school, the new term had just started at Concord so it must have been fall, I must have been . . ." — she calculated — "fifteen. Nineteen forty-six, I guess, soon after the war ended."

"Yes. I was born on Christmas Day, 1947," Alex said urgently.

She's doing a jigsaw puzzle on which her life depends and has just fitted in a piece, Ronnie thought.

"I was at Concord. I picked up the paper one night and there was Father — right on the front page. Walking down the steps of some church with this young woman with a headline, 'CABINET MEMBER WEDS SECRETARY.' I had to read well into the first paragraph to find out that her name was Amelia."

Alex leaned farther forward. "But you knew her later on, didn't you?"

"I told you he loved her! What do you want from me?"

Alex stared at her. "Please."

Elizabeth gave her a long sober gaze. She stood up and walked to the bar, poured scotch into a glass halfway up.

"Please," Alex begged. She was almost whimpering.

"I remember the first summer they spent up here. He was still working in Washington, they lived in Georgetown, in the same house he'd lived in with Laura. Mary's mother. She — your mother — was very pretty — she looked like you, same golden hair but her face was softer, not so . . . fierce," she concluded in surprise. "And she transmitted . . . a great sweetness. It enveloped him. His face changed when he looked at her, he softened. He was always touching her, putting his hand on her arm or her back or stroking her face. And she'd look up at him so adoringly. It made me sick." She sipped her scotch. "I hated her."

Alex stared at her. "Why?"

Elizabeth considered. "She'd been a loved child. Like Mary. You could see it. Loved children expect everyone to love them and they do. They radiate that expectation, it's self-fulfilling. They get love everywhere. I wasn't loved. By anyone."

Ronnie studied Elizabeth.

"I *wasn't* a loved child," Mary muttered. "I just *appeared* to be a loved child."

"I'm sorry, Elizabeth," Alex said sadly.

Elizabeth flared, "Don't feel sorry for me! I'm okay, I've done just fine, I'm doing fine."

Alex ignored this. Relentless as a hunting dog on the scent, she turned to Mary. "Do you remember her? The way she was then, the way he was? Do you remember me?"

"I was ten in 1946, at Peabody School. Father was living in the Georgetown house, my mother's house, she'd furnished it, decorated it. . . . I went there holidays. I was probably there the Christmas after they got married, Father and Amelia, maybe Thanksgiving too, I don't remember. . . . I don't really remember her then. Maybe they went away on a honeymoon?"

"I don't know." Alex kept staring, concentrating on Mary, who shifted uncomfortably.

"It was so many years ago!" Mary protested. "I remember your mother was pretty, very pretty. Pretty hair. I was just a girl, taken up by my own affairs, *you* know. There were always so many parties at the holidays. I had my own room, my books, my radio, my phonograph, I had a huge record collection, and my own maid."

"I remember your room," Alex breathed, her eyes shut. "It was all white."

"She's spent her adult life trying to recover her virginity," Elizabeth snorted.

"She was only ten," Alex demurred, gently. "She *was* a virgin."

They were all silent.

"Your room was white," Alex recalled, leaning forward as if her posture alone could exert pressure, could extract whatever it was she wanted.

Mary sank back. "Yes," she said quietly. "I was upset and Father was trying to calm me down. He let me redecorate my room. He let me make it all white. The housekeeper helped me, called in decorators, took me shopping. . . ."

"Why were you upset?"

Mary's body stilled utterly. "Your mother . . ."

Alex's posture was a pressure.

Mary threw out a hand. "I don't *know!* I *don't* know! Maybe I was jealous. Maybe I felt he was betraying my mother."

Alex sagged.

Mary sat up angrily. "What do you want from me! They were in their own world! I can't remember! Yes, I guess he loved her, if that's what you're asking."

Alex prodded. "And what about me?"

"You like mainly white food too," Elizabeth murmured, chuckling with pleasure. "Fish, potatoes, cauliflower, cake, cake, cake . . ."

"SHUT UP, ELIZABETH!" Alex cried, silencing all of them. She stood suddenly, went to the bar and poured wine into her glass without offering anything to anyone else.

"What about here," she began again, "do you remember her here?"

"Jesus Christ, you're impossible!" Mary cried. "Your mother is alive, why don't you ask her whatever it is you want to know!"

"I want to know what you remember." Patient but tense.

Mary sighed. "Look, she was nice to me but she was only a kid herself, nineteen or twenty, she couldn't help. But she was kind — to both of us." She turned to Elizabeth. "Remember? She went swimming with us and played checkers with me and every afternoon she'd gather us for lemonade and cookies on the porch." Her face soft, she turned to Elizabeth. "Remember, Lizzie?"

Elizabeth shrugged.

"But after you were born," Mary continued, "she was busy, I didn't see so much of her or if I did she had you in her arms or was nursing you or something."

Alex cried out in pain, "Do you remember *me*?"

The sisters stared at her.

"She was always fussing over you, talking to you, holding you, carrying you around. You had hardly any hair, just fuzz, golden fuzz. Like a halo. You were a good kid, though, you weren't a brat," Mary conceded.

"All kids are cute, aren't they?" Elizabeth snarled.

Alex glared at Elizabeth.

"Look, I went to England to graduate school when I was twenty-one. You were still only five or six. I didn't come back for four years and then I got a job in Washington and lived there. I never lived here again, I just came for the family parties and after a while you weren't at them. I saw very little of you after you were five or six. And I never paid that much attention to you. Little children bore me."

Mary studied her rings, recalling. "You went to England after the Fourth of July party in 1953. Father had been made under secretary that spring. How old were you then?" she asked Alex.

She counted back. "Summer of 'fifty-three I would have been five. Six that Christmas."

"I went away to college in 'fifty-four and got married the next June. I never lived here again either."

Alex subsided.

"What are you trying to figure out?" Mary challenged her.

"I don't know exactly. What happened. Why we left. How he felt."

"How he felt *about you*," Elizabeth corrected her.

"Yes." Faint voice. "I guess so."

"What does your mother say?"

"She doesn't want to . . . she won't talk about it. She just says they weren't getting along and she decided to leave. That's all she'll say. But . . ."

"But?" Mary picked it up.

Alex shrugged. "I don't know."

"She remarried, didn't she?"

Alex smiled, shifted into another gear. "Yes. Charlie really was my father. He and my grandfather, they played with me, took me places — the playground, the zoo, ice skating, the circus. They were great. Charlie's dead now. Gramp too of course. Mom really misses them. Between Charlie and me and her parents, she was filled up, she didn't need any other life so she didn't make a lot of friends or anything. She has no one now."

She has you, she waited for them to say. She has your children, your nice family, she waited to hear.

"Your childhood was probably a hell of a lot more pleasant than ours," is what Elizabeth did say finally, "so don't envy us Father. There was nothing enviable about our childhoods, however it may seem."

"It's just . . . you wonder why your father doesn't care about you," Alex said, her voice thickening. "You wonder if you did something — or *were* something — that made him abandon you."

They sat in silence watching the fire wane and die. No one got up to poke it back to life.

After dinner, exhausted, they watched TV in the playroom. As they separated to go to bed, Alex stopped them. "Ronnie's staying," she said. "I want her to." No one argued, not even Ronnie.

Stupid cow, feeling sorry for herself because Father abandoned her. Doesn't know how lucky she is. All that love her family lavished on her for no reason, just given. All the luck of who you're born to. Jesus loves me that I know cause the Bible tells me so. Hah! Enough to make you want to go to church. Not the way Mother's religion tells it. That bitch, even though she'd left the church she sent me to a fucking church school because she couldn't get Father to spring for private school. Hell and damnation, sin all over the place. The damned nuns: the Catholic way to brush your teeth, the Catholic way to fucking sit and walk. No patent leather shoes because they reflected up your skirt. Until I complained to Father about my education. Heard the word Catholic and in a fury had me transferred to Concord. Mother gloated, she'd gotten him to pay for it without begging. Didn't matter what it cost me. Made me complicit in her games.

Father never did anything until he was forced. When Mary suddenly refused to eat red meat, poking around at the food on her plate, pushing the meat aside, trying to dam up the juices, keep them from running into her potatoes, crying if the juices stained her potatoes. Ate nothing stained by blood. Father shouted at her to eat it, sent her from the table when she got hysterical. She never became a vegetarian, she became a blancomaniac! Hah! Took Father years to give in.

We're all peculiar in this family. Look at Alex. I thought she was so normal. But she's indefatigable, a driving pushy little thing, she wouldn't let Mary off the hook, me either. Is our family abnormal well of course it is how could it not be, so are the Callahans, what a heritage I have, Grandpa Callahan always drunk or getting there, always brawling his arm always raised ready to hit, Grandma always cowering, the sons skinny and pale and scared-looking but full of bravado the daughters always trying to make nice act cheerful how ludicrous what a bunch except Mother, she had spirit, you have to hand it to her, she didn't let them dominate her.

Maybe that's what being a society lady meant to her, a way out. Every day puts on a suit or a silk dress, red red lipstick, eye makeup, blonded hair, high heels, sits there in that apartment working her wrinkled upper lip, waiting for the phone to ring. "My dear! So glad you called, yes, me too, so busy, mad isn't it? Oh how nice, I'd love to come, I do have another party that afternoon, they pressed me so I promised, but perhaps I could stop in afterwards. . . ." Then sit around all afternoon and show up late. SEE: I AM WANTED.

Still she's better off than her sisters, worn out by forty with six, eight kids and husbands who know what it is to raise a hand to a woman. Just like dear old dad. Without a pot to piss in except Geraldine, who married a man with enterprise, five-truck fleet, lords it over all of them. Hah! The things that make people proud.

Better not to marry. Helena, the nun, at least has peace and quiet in her life. And the brothers are losers, replications of the old man. Wouldn't mind seeing them all, actually. See how they are now, how life has carved their faces. But they would probably look at me with pity, a dried-up spinster, ugly duckling. . . .

Mother's maybe a little proud of me. My daughter, a career woman, assistant secretary of the treasury, very important, works in Washington like her father did, you know, years ago. An economist, travels around the world arranging economic policy. She is met at the airport by three-star generals in a limousine she meets regularly with heads of state drinking perfumed tea from delicate porcelain cups. . . .

Elizabeth lay on a pyre, aflame. From forehead to toes her body burned in shame.

The things that make people proud . . .

What have I become.

She sat up, pulled herself out of bed and walked across the room. In the dark, she found her cigarettes on the dresser, lighted one, stood there inhaling deeply.

She made me come here, summer after summer, year after year. No matter how I begged.

Someday I'll tell her.

She walked to the window, pulled the drapes open, stared out. At nothing. Blackness.

Nothing.

Wouldn't you think this pain would end someday?

6

Monday morning early, before the others were up, Elizabeth was off, taking the Alfa. She left a note: "Packing the car, I saw some bicycles in the back of the garage. They need to be cleaned up and oiled but Aldo can get them in shape. ECU."

"What's ECU?" Alex asked Mary.

"Her initials, of course, what do you think. Elizabeth Catherine Upton. Her mother's name is Catherine." Mary moved away from Alex with a petulant jerk. "I like that! She takes the car and leaves us the bicycles."

"She said she was going to. Anyway, I thought you couldn't drive," Alex said. "She signs notes with her *initials?*" she asked Ronnie.

"You think we correspond?" Ronnie snapped.

"No but both of you drive, don't you?" Mary said. "Suppose I want to go into Boston, I'll need Aldo to drive me, and you won't be able to get around."

Alex and Ronnie looked at each other. "You're concerned about *us,* Mary?" Ronnie asked.

"I just don't want any arguments if I need the limo."

She got no arguments. After the three of them visited Stephen in the morning, Ronnie and Alex vanished. Mary had to face the gray overcast day alone in the house. When she finally went in search of Aldo to ask him to drive her into town, she found Alex in the garage, pumping air into the tires of a bicycle. Aldo drove her to Concord, where she wandered through a few shops. She found a bookstore and in a move that would have surprised Elizabeth aimed not for the romances but for the poetry. She bought a volume of Anne Sexton and a notebook covered in Italian paper swirled with crimson, silver, and turquoise. On the way home, she stopped at the DeCordova Museum, but it was closed. Of course, Monday.

Disheartened, she entered the dim silent house. So big, so empty. Such a bleak feeling it had this house. Memories like a bad smell lingering. Would the Georgetown house feel this way?

A sudden clatter above her startled her. No one came when she called, so she climbed the stairs to the second story. The door to the third floor was open: she peered up the attic staircase. "Somebody up there?"

Ronnie called down that she, Mrs. Browning and Teresa were doing something — what, Mary couldn't make out, didn't care. She ran back downstairs and stood at the foot of the stairs, her head pounding with fury. I want my tea! And *she* has the help helping her; *she!* when she's the help herself! Or should be! Mary felt like Saint Sebastian, as if arrows were shooting into her body at every point. She wanted to pound her feet and screech.

Why am I so exasperated? What is the matter with me!

Petulant baby, Lizzie always said.

Well, I'll do it myself!

She marched into the kitchen, filled the kettle, found the tea canisters and chose Lapsang souchong. It took a little time, but she found the tea set and laid cup, saucer, and sugar bowl on a tray. She found a lemon in the fridge, cut off some slices and arranged them on a little matching plate. As she worked, she watched herself with some surprise. It didn't feel humiliating, why was that? Doing chores in her own apartment always corroded her with shame; she scurried, hid, terrified that someone might see her, that she might see herself in so humiliating a position. She did not do chores! But today it did not feel shameful, it felt — all right. It even made her feel strong.

And while there were many ordinary things she did not know how to do — cook or bake, for instance, wield a hammer or screw driver or drive a car — she found she knew exactly how to make tea, knew to pour boiling water into the teapot to warm it, then pour it out and add three teaspoons of tea, pour in water freshly brought to the boil. She wondered how she knew to do these things. She covered the pot with a cozy, set it on the tray along with a smaller pot of hot water, and carried the tray into the sun room. Letting the tea steep for a few minutes, she picked up the book she had left lying there and began to read. After a time, she poured tea into the cup, added sugar, lemon, stirred, sipped the hot liquid. Perfect.

I did that! I made that!

She sat back, her finger holding her place in the book. The sun room was bright even on this overcast day. A stream of quiet contentment rippled over her. The little playhouse out behind the old tennis courts, Daddy had it built for me, I had little chairs and a little bed and a table and a little china tea set. I pretended to make tea — Eloise showed me how, she was our housekeeper then, she was nice to me, she felt sorry for me because my mother died — but Eloise really made the tea and brought it out, weak tea heavily laced with milk, all prepared. I poured it out for my dolls, chatting away, Yes, Mrs. Carruthers, what do you think, Mrs. Bradford?

Then Lizzie . . . She shuddered and returned to her book, Sylvia Plath's *Ariel*.

It took her an hour to finish, and she closed it thoughtfully. I've read it so often, I wonder why I brought this one. Just what I happened to pick up or is it symbolic? *Daddy, Daddy, you bastard, I'm through.* I'm not though, am I, I'm still here waiting for him to decide to be or not to be. *He* may be through though. Him and his fat black heart.

I never could talk to you.
The tongue stuck in my jaw.
It stuck in a barb wire snare.

You wonder what happened to Sylvia Plath to make her write things like that. It feels as if her life was like mine, but it wasn't, was it. No one else had a life like mine, something wrong with me, about me, my nature. Father said so, said it was me. She wasn't like me, she was smart, she went to Smith like Elizabeth, went to school in England too, Cambridge.

Married a poet. And killed herself. Over him it seemed. I'd never do that: no man worth it. I don't think I'd do that. Would I?

I wanted to die after Don.

Maybe over her daddy, really. What about her mother? My mama a suicide Elizabeth says. A lush. Did I always know that?

Stop!

She stood, stretched, walked to the window, gazed out at the trees, most of their leaves gone now. Bare ruined choirs where late the sweet birds sang. Me, grieving over goldengrove unleaving.

Things are easier with Elizabeth gone. Less pressure in the house, everyone feels relaxed, you can tell. Alex is stupid and vapid and one can ignore Ronnie. Boring though. Elizabeth at least keeps you on your toes.

First, are you our sort of a person?
Do you wear
A glass eye, false teeth or a crutch?

Elizabeth my sort of a person. Alex not.

Stop reading Plath for a while. Maybe I'll read my new Sexton, but damn, she knocked herself off too. Should have thought of that before I bought the book. What else did I bring? Merwin, McClatchy, Berryman's *Dream Songs*, Adrienne Rich, lovely poet but I can't take that feminism. Stupid: like accusing the gods for the way things are. Have to accept reality, work around it if you are to get what you want. Everyone wants power. Men have it. Women at a disadvantage, pregnancy, raising kids. That's nature, a fact of life. The feminists would like to eradicate that but how? Women have to get power any way they can. Elizabeth's way or mine. We understand power. The other two are out of the running. They're ordinary. Cows. Elizabeth and I are extraordinary, saved from the common fate of women.

Mary rose and wandered into her father's library and scanned the shelves. Nothing here I'd want to read. Wait, look: all of Trollope: better than nothing. She slid out *Barchester Towers*. Haven't read this in years.

She gazed out at the gray landscape in the fading light and the irritation she had felt earlier overflowed. AGHH! BORING! Boring day! She wanted to do something violent.

She carried the book up to her room and searched for her exercise tape. No one was in the playroom, she could use the television in there, plenty of room for stretching. Damn. Didn't bring it. Meant to. She pondered. Could watch a soap. But suppose someone came in. I can just see Ronnie's face if she caught me sitting there watching *As the World Turns* or a game show.

She eyed the chaise. Didn't sleep well last night, did I. She lay down on it, pulling a white alpaca throw over her legs, and fell into an immediate deep sleep tumultuous with nightmare. She didn't wake until nearly five, which meant she had to dress for dinner in a rush. Didn't matter that much, she thought. No one here for dinner but women.

In spite of wasting most of the day in sleep, she continued to feel irritable and unrested. So it was even more annoying that the other two were so cheerful when she entered the sitting room around six, Alex rosy-cheeked and blabbing ad nauseam about the joys of bicycling and Elizabeth's thoughtfulness in suggesting it, Ronnie also pink-faced and complacent-looking, pleased with herself, why, Mary couldn't fathom. Maybe everyone was happy because Elizabeth was not here.

Alex finally wound down at the dinner table. "Elizabeth is really wonderful," she announced.

Mary raised one eyebrow.

Alex pointed her fork at her (good god what manners! she was as bad as Ronnie!) and crowed, "You too! That's what she does! The both of you so tough and hard but underneath you're a couple of pussycats."

"The two of you," Mary said sourly.

"Excuse me?"

"Either 'the two of you' or 'both of you,' but *never* 'the both of you.' "

Ignoring this, Alex gushed to Ronnie, "Don't you think so? Pussycats. Just a pair of hurt babies."

"Maybe. But hurt babies grow into people who hurt babies," Ronnie said, her mouth twisted.

"Oh Ronnie!" Alex exclaimed, "you're the biggest pussycat of all!"

"Alex, sometimes I think you live in cloud-cuckoo-land," Ronnie said with disgust.

"Call it what you want," she said. "But where I live is a real place."

Ronnie rolled her eyes. Can't bother with this conversation: too stupid. Mary yawned, covering her mouth. Tired.

"Anything on television tonight?" she asked.

While the other two watched some old movie, Ronnie lay on her bed reading, marking the journal with a yellow highlighter. She stretched her head back on the pillow, a broad smile on her face. I did it. Got organized. Got going. She glanced with satisfaction at the computer, all hooked up and loaded with files, the old bookcase she'd dragged down from the attic today and cleaned with lemon oil, her journals filed in it by category. They'd had to move her chest of drawers out of the room to fit the bookcase in, but that was all right, they'd put it in Momma's room, so crowded now you can hardly walk in it. But no one does unless Momma's spirit . . . how I wish . . .

Just give her one last hug, kiss her soft cheek again.

Don't lie to yourself Ronalda. You want to accuse her.

No. Never did never will. Decided that long ago. Forget it.

Have to clean up her room, air it out, so dusty, Teresa didn't even want to go in there, smell of death, she says. Get rid of her clothes. Poor clothes. A few photographs stuck in the frame around the mirror. Me at six months, two years, grade-school graduation. Aldo took that one, I wonder who took the others. Momma didn't have a camera. What to do with that goddamned crucifix over her bed. Looks like gold, wonder where she got it. Maybe Him. Maybe the nuns will take it, give it to some poor kid they want to brainwash. Can't just stick it in the trash, she loved it. Should have put it in her coffin with her.

Think about that tomorra, Scarlett.

Meanwhile: tomorrow she would take the train to Boston and vote. She could pick up her stuff from Linda's while she was there. Then spend some time at the BU library, buy some reference books she needed at hand, more floppy disks, soft-tipped pens, a disk file box. Still had a little cash left from her fellowship last year, one benefit of poverty: you learn how to live frugally. But what would she do when that was gone?

She leapt up and pulled open her backpack, fished for her wallet, opened the secret compartment, pulled out some folded bills. Tight roll: she counted: two hundred thirty-six dollars. Not very much.

Don't think about it now. You'll find a way to survive. You survived six months on the streets of Boston at fourteen, didn't you? Without hooking. Stealing stuff, getting free food at shelters, churches, sleeping in the T, in the library until they kicked you out, at the laundromat. Rosa at the laundromat eyeing me. "I seen you here before, no? How old you are?" Like an accusation. I was scared. But she didn't look like anyone official in that old skirt, scuffed bent shoes. Big big big bag of laundry, she could barely manage it, "The washing machine, she broke," it made sense she needed me to help her. She needed help, four little kids, only two in school, Enriqué working two jobs, she doing piecework on the sewing machine. Promised me meals, a bed, shared of course, and once in a while a dollar for spending money, and all I had to do was watch the kids when I got home from school, do the dinner dishes, bathe the kids, put them to bed, help with the laundry, give her a little freedom so she could do that fucking sewing for two cents an hour or whatever she got. It was better than the street. Poor people's version of the au pair.

Insisted I go to school. I didn't really mind, just had to give her a hard time. Bitter angry runaway. I didn't make it easy for her. Saved my life. Seven people in five rooms. Disgusting rooms, ceilings cracked, plaster corroding, roaches and sometimes rats. Better only than the street. Pushed me all the way to the school, two months late, registered me as her niece, wept, "My sister, she die!" It worked: all Latinos look alike even though they were PR, not *chicano*. They were a lot like Momma, though, always stroking, but *they* were noisy, laughed a lot. Momma crept around this house like a mouse and hardly ever laughed. When she did, covered her mouth like a Japanese woman to muffle the sound. They liked to touch each other, especially babies. When she had Joey, she let even Lidia and Téo hold him, fondle him, play with him. Even the boys changed his diapers. Nice. Nice there.

Mrs. Jenkins knew something was off, knew Rosa wasn't really my aunt, knew I wasn't PR. She wasn't even Latino, she was African, but observant. Thoughtful. Cared, even after all those years of teaching. Saw something in me. Saved me. Still there in Roxbury, working against despair, saving a few kids, losing most, she said when I went back to see her. "Graduate school, Ronnie! You're in graduate school!?" Hugged me like I was her daughter. Well I am. Hers and Rosa's. Gave me more than Momma ever did. Carrie Jenkins gave me a sense of my own strength, of other possibilities. . . . I didn't have to be a servant.

No! She sat up in excitement, mind whirring with possibilities, body eager to move instantly. Not reference books, they're so expensive. Buy a modem, plug into a data base. That's what I should do. Then sat back smiling at herself. Funny how you come to take things for granted, like having the money to buy a modem, which I may not even have, who knows, I don't know what they cost. But I do know I can get a research grant that will cover it, I know it. Know things other little *chicanas* don't. Makes all the difference: gives you confidence.

Carrie Jenkins did that for me.

How easily you get used to having everything done for you, food put on the table, house cleaned, bed linens changed, Teresa even does mine. Never cold, the way it was at Rosa's some nights. Always a spare blanket if you need it, always something to eat in the fridge, car to drive you into town. Do I dare to ask Aldo to drive me to Boston? Will he be outraged? Mary will be. I don't care. It's not as if He was here.

It's nice having these things except you come to expect them.

Will I get spoiled, like them?

It will be hard to give them up.

She pondered. Maybe I should try not to get used to luxury. Maybe I should hitch to town and take the train to Cambridge instead of asking Aldo. Or take the bus. Don't buy books, use the library. Go over to BU, find Professor Madrick, he'll help me get a research assistant's card. But then I'd have to go into Boston a couple of times a week.

Don't want to.

Why? What holds you here? When you have so many friends in Boston? Yeah, suppose I ran into Sarah walking down the street holding hands with Becky. No, she wouldn't walk in public holding hands, she wants to stay closeted. Be great though if she looked worn out, old, dried-up. Whereas I am looking pretty good, well, better, I have to recognize that, even though Momma's death was such a drain, I look better than in years, I lost all that weight, I look rested, my eyes are clear, why is that when I hate these women, fucking *sisters,* hate this house. Decent food, probably, and enough sleep. Fresh air.

She let the journal fall from her hands, her arms hang limp at her sides. She held her body stiff, like one at a seance, waiting for the ghost to speak, for revelation. What was here in this house, what was it she felt here? Momma, unable to rest? Trying to tell me something? She had no words for her sense that she was living at the hot molten core of her being and that if she left now, it would harden and cool and she would never never never find out.

What?

Having completed her evening regimen, Mary noted with satisfaction that the lace bedcover had been removed and the sheets turned down. That little talking-to she'd given Browning had been effective. These days you simply had to keep after servants or they took advantage of you, provided perfunctory service, always in a hurry to run back to the idiot box, don't want to miss the latest episode of their favorite soap. Of course, she had been known to watch them herself, but that was different after all, she was the one *paying* for service. . . .

She slipped a satin peignoir over her nightgown, pulled open the drapes — which she had instructed Browning to close at night, as they had been when she was a child — and carried her handbag over to the chaise. She pulled out her box of hash and rolled a joint. Getting low, have to do something soon. Have to cash a check. Maybe Elizabeth would advance her some cash. . . .

She inhaled deeply and leaned back against the chaise arm, put her feet up, gazed out into the blackness. Moon gone but lots of stars tonight. Have to do something about this feeling, can't stand it, all squooshy inside, everything felt wrong. It was so *unjust!* She wanted to shriek with it, suddenly understood people who scrawled messages on sheets and hung them out their windows, INJUSTICE! UNFAIR!

How could they talk to her the way they did, talk about her the way they did, call her names. Prostitute, whore, that other word! When she had never, not once in her life, had sex outside of marriage, she never fooled around even though god knows there were plenty of chances even now, men still desired her. When she was young, she had been the belle of every ball.

True, she loved to flirt, but it was just fun, she never ever went further.

So how could they . . . ?

Well of course, that one's a lesbian, bitter, she couldn't ever get a man, just look at her, well her face is pretty enough I guess, striking, those blue eyes and that brown skin, she could be pretty if she had even a rudimentary understanding of cosmetics but not an iota of charm what man would want that and the way she dresses . . . And Elizabeth a dried-up spinster, probably still a virgin that Clare didn't look like he had a working instrument, and he was the only one, the only one she ever brought home anyway. Bitter jealous shrew. Jealous of my looks, my style, the way men crumple at the sight of me, look at that Dr. Stamp, look at Hollis. Even Aldo watches me longingly, he thinks I don't notice of course I'd never let on I do, a servant. Even that reporter in the brown jacket, his eyes were hanging out of their sockets looking at my chest. *That's* power, real power for a woman, bringing men to their knees, making them do whatever you want. Everyone knows that. Men may rule the world but women rule men.

Besides, a woman needs a man. It's obvious, women were made for marriage and children and you have to have a man for that, someone to support you. A woman needs an *escort!* Otherwise she could never go anywhere at night, never travel except on those hideous tours, buses filled with dried-up old women all desperate for a man. Without a man, you live all alone like Elizabeth, lonely old age.

. . . .

Well, I won't be alone long! I just need to get on my feet, a few hundred thou would put things in order. If Father hadn't fallen ill, I was going to come up and ask him. If he dies, I should be all right. Alberto's fault, the bastard. Then Don but that had to be, could not not be. . . .

It isn't true I married for money. So UNFAIR! Lizzie should know, I wrote her. Still corresponded in those days, well I did anyway, and she wrote once in a while, wrote that time to crow, so proud of herself getting into that fancy English school. Oh how I cried when she went away, I was brokenhearted, it was awful when she wasn't here, worse, even though Amelia was here with Alex. I needed her so, she must have known, I wrote her. Please don't go and leave me, Lizzie! She never even answered. Came home for the Fourth of July party and then left, never came back, never. Left me alone here.

So of course as soon as I could I got married, what else could I do? He would never have let me live someplace else on my own, he wouldn't have given me the money, besides I would have been terrified, I didn't know how to do anything, manage a household, servants. And Harry was so sweet, fatherly, well he was the same age as Father, but that didn't matter to me I told him it made me love him more, so sweet, he took care of me better than Father ever did, gave me my own charge accounts and didn't quibble about the bills like Father, gave me a household allowance, never questioned the amounts, we ate well, he liked that. He even went with me to the fashion shows, liked to see me looking splendid. Holding me on his lap like a baby, well I was one really, wasn't I, only nineteen. Thought I was so grown up of course. Looked so grown up to myself in strapless gowns, my hair swept up, black stockings and high heels.

Harry was like a father to me, took care of everything, I didn't have to worry about anything except managing servants, he hired that housekeeper, Mrs. Brundage, because I was so young when my mother died. She taught me to arrange menus, oversee the housekeeping, talk to servants like a grown-up.

He was kind, patient, never got angry like Father, of course he was different with his children. But who can blame him, they were a terrible lot. Dealing with them wasn't much fun, many's the time they made me cry, they were older than I, it wasn't my fault Harry adored me. When they called me names I told Father, he bought me a Jag for a wedding present, threw that gigantic wedding, that stopped them. No poor little gold digger seduced their father. Harry pursued me, came at me the same Fourth of July party Elizabeth came to before she left. Serendipity. Father's best friend but he came after me anyway, that showed how much passion he had. Father embarrassed, tried to stop it. Said I'd elope if he didn't give me permission, embarrass him even more. Willful little vixen, he said. Looked at me with his eyes skewed up, sometimes when he did that I thought he hated me. In the end he gave in, gave me that beautiful wedding, the tents, three orchestras, a dance floor built out over the lawn, oysters and champagne — I looked so gorgeous then, picture still on my table. . . .

It wasn't my fault Harry died, he was fifty-eight after all, those kids of his saying I wore him out. Of course Father's still going at eighty-two. But that was absurd. We didn't even do it that much after the first year, once I got pregnant and then after I had Marty, he couldn't. . . . Sometimes I had the feeling he was seeing someone else but by then I didn't care. It's fun having someone crazy in love with you but sex was overrated it seemed to me. Really a bore.

Until Don.

But even if he was seeing someone else I had to stay married to him, I had a child, his son, true Marty was his fourth son, third family, he wasn't exactly thrilled. But I didn't care what he did on the side, I didn't want a divorce, I wanted to be a wife, I wanted to walk into parties with my husband, be *Mrs.* Somebody. I didn't want to be on my own like these young women today, to hear them talk you'd think it was fun to have to worry about money and how much you spend on clothes and have to find your own apartment and order your own telephone and pay all the bills by yourself and run things all by yourself. Worry about your cars, insurance, garages, repairs, chauffeurs. Just as well I can't afford them anymore. . . . Still I do miss it, hate taking cabs, surly drivers who can't speak English, who expect you to tell them how to get where you're going, hot smell of their bodies penetrating the cab, nauseating. . . .

When he died thank god it was at the Athletic Club playing squash not in another woman's bed, that would have been so humiliating. Humiliating as it was, his children suing as if he hadn't already given them huge annuities, so greedy, all that money he left me tied up for years, then most of it entailed to Martin, my son richer than I, really unfair that judge. How was I supposed to keep up the apartment and the house in Vail on three million dollars? How far does that go? Probably punishing me for marrying Alberto, my lawyer warned me to wait, judge's revenge, he had the hots for me that judge I saw it. But I couldn't wait, five years it took to settle, I was so lonely, stuck in that apartment with a baby, and Alberto was so gorgeous and a nobleman, so glamorous, he'd dated Rita Hayworth, Ava Gardner, and he wanted *me.* But he drained me dry that bastard, put hardly a penny into the kitty, and for all his ardor he was worse in bed than Harry, leaping on me from behind, humping me like a dog. Paid practically no attention when I gave him a son. Then humiliating me that way, all the papers full of it, Nina Newton and Alberto on the beach on the Riviera, both nearly naked, made me feel like an old stay-at-home, fat and pregnant and old, the two of them gold in the sun, their bodies still slim and muscular. . . .

Only twenty-eight and alone with three kids, well two and a half, Marty was eight, Bertie two, Marie-Laure about to be born. And nearly broke, that bastard lived it up at my expense, that was another irony, the papers full of this huge settlement I got from Alberto, not a penny of that did I ever see, he had nothing, Nina Newton supported him until she got tired of it and threw him out. He married the virgin daughter of some Italian industrialist who wanted to buy his little girl a title, all Alberto had to offer. Still he probably demanded she undergo a virginity test like Princess Diana.

I was getting old, a bit plump, had three kids to support and was nearly broke. I *had* to get back in circulation fast, find a husband, I had no choice. I disciplined myself. People think looks are an accident of birth, they don't know the work it takes. Went on a strict diet after I weaned Marie-Laure, lost twenty pounds. Exercised to get my skin looking good again. I had to marry the first eligible man who came along, lucky Paul wasn't repellent and he didn't mind that I had small children as long as he didn't have to have anything to do with them, made me sign a prenuptial agreement not to have any more not to claim more than — how much was it? — in case of divorce. God knows he was rich enough, if I had just waited for him to die I wouldn't have had to worry the rest of my life, but Jesus he's still alive, his own airplane, the château in the Loire Valley, the villa in Gstaad, one in Costa Rica, Capri. . . .

Oh that house on Capri. The only thing Paul had that I miss. Bougainvillea mounting the hills, cerise and lavender, orange, red, uncontainable flowers pouring out of the warm earth. Everything green, leaves on stone, gray stone roads, stone walls, white houses with red tile roofs. The villa surrounded by lilies and hibiscus, hidden by vines and tulip trees but from upstairs you could see water, the Bay of Naples the color of Don's eyes, water all around, as far as you could see. Donkey bells, old women in black trudging up the hillsides bent under their loads, the servants quiet, knew their place. Downstairs rooms cool and dark however hot the sun, white walls with sienna tile floors, I'd play Debussy, I could still play then, feel the music float out into the morning. Better when he wasn't there: he didn't like Debussy. Or Mozart or Beethoven or Bach. Complaining, do you have to play that muck? Only Chopin he liked. That was okay I suppose, I got so I could almost play the Ballades well.

Gone now. Fingers weak. So caught up with Don, grief, I never play. Maybe try to get it back.

Sex a duty. He liked it that way, liked me still and taut, liked to hurt me, twist my wrists, bite my breasts, hear me cry out. That look on his face afterwards, triumphant, scornful. Me something bought and paid for, owned.

She stood suddenly, the roach still between her fingertips, and stared at the window as if a ghost stood there.

Bought and paid for. That's what they mean.

She lowered herself slowly to the chaise.

But it's not fair! I gave it all up, oh what a pleasure to tell him I was leaving him, the look on his face, oooh! what a triumph, *my* triumph that time, you won't get a penny from me you know that, bitch.

I didn't care. Nothing mattered but Don, Don, my darling Don. The minute our eyes connected, electric, unbreakable connection, had to touch, had to hold each other. . . .

Anyway, I thought the prenuptial thingy said I was to get so many hundred thousand a year in case of divorce. I didn't realize that was only if *he* wanted the divorce. My lawyer didn't explain that. Men stick together. Cut me off with nothing.

I didn't care what it cost me. Then. Don't care now. Couldn't stand near Don without my blood rushing from my head, vacating fingertips, toes, lips, all pumping away flooding my heart. Couldn't speak. That first time, that party at the Swedish embassy: blue eyes piercing mine as if they'd discovered a miracle, finally found what they needed. Direct line to my heart and I thought, oh my god, this is it what I've wanted. Always. I wanted to walk into his arms but I didn't even know his name, he was just a man standing in a group at a cocktail party. Eyes the color of the sea, the bay, aquamarine, piercing, penetrating me, skin, bone, muscle, wanting me, wanting to take my bones in his hands, control my body. I would have let him break them, me. Take me. Do what you want with me.

Day we had a picnic in the Rockies, I still had my house in Vail then, Paul thought I'd gone out there alone, he didn't care, he was in Brussels doing one of his superimportant things. Don bought lunch in a picnic basket, wine and cheese and pâté and bread and grapes and apples and we drove out and spread a blanket and ate and made love in a wide gully full of wildflowers. And fell asleep with our arms entwined — never before had I done that — and when I woke up he was gone and I was terrified for a moment until I saw him it looked as if he were rising up out of the earth, he was coming back over the edge of the gully, had gone to pee probably. And he looked like a giant, huge, his arms thick-muscled shapely strong to work the earth, to work machines, to exert control, to work, to use on me, a Man's arms meant, built to hold me, embrace me, own me, Woman, lying there white and soft and silky and his, oh his, only his. Forever.

Mary wept, rubbing her clitoris in her intolerable need.

7

When Mary heard that Ronnie was planning to go to Boston after the hospital visit on Tuesday, she made some phone calls, then announced she would go too and that Aldo would drive them. Ronnie, surprised and relieved, then surprised at her own relief, puzzled over it: Do I really care that much? What they think, how they act to me? At the same time, she dreaded the drive there and back with the sister most hostile to her. Would it be a long silent ride, bristling with unspoken hate? Better to take the train. There's no possibility that we can talk to each other agreeably — she hates me, hates my color, my background, my bastardy, my existence. If I tried to be agreeable, would I be acting with admirable restraint or corrupt complicity? Would I be an Auntie Tom?

For the first quarter hour, Mary spoke only to Aldo, commenting on the changes in the landscape from her girlhood. Aldo, in tones of deep devotion, agreed readily with everything she said. Still the quiet hum of the heavy car was becoming unbearable and Mary was examining her hands, her white gloves in her lap, when Ronnie decided to plunge in.

"I notice you read a lot of poetry," she said.

Mary's body swelled subtly like a dried fruit dropped into water. "Yes. How . . . nice of you . . . to notice." She fanned herself with her purse. "Elizabeth thinks I'm a dunce. I guess I imagine everybody does."

"I saw you reading W. S. Merwin. I'm very fond of him too."

"Really!" Mary looked at Ronnie strangely. "Whom else do you like?"

They discussed favorites for a time, until Ronnie mentioned Adrienne Rich.

"Feminism seems to me so stupid," Mary said. "You can't fight nature after all. As long as women have the babies they will need protection."

"From who?"

"I beg your pardon?"

"Who do they need protection from?"

"Really, Ronnie, your grammar. . . ."

"Fuck my grammar, Mary. Why do women need protection? They wouldn't need protection if men didn't attack them, would they."

"They need support!"

"They wouldn't need support if men hadn't grabbed all the property and resources of the world, would they."

Mary gazed at her. "But that's the nature of the male, isn't it. To be predatory, aggressive."

"I can't believe nature created a species in which one sex systematically preys on the other."

Mary considered this, frowning. "But how else could it be? All through history . . ."

"History is men's version of what happened in the last five thousand years. They have every reason to tell the story to make it seem that their predation is a natural fact."

"You must be a feminist," Mary concluded.

"Damn straight."

"Well, I can't argue with you about the past. I don't know anything about it. All I know is women have to survive as they can, in any way they can. And the surest and safest way is to attach themselves to a man."

"Through marriage without possibility of divorce."

"Men just have to be forced to support their children. Of course then I . . . well, I just would have run away," she ended mysteriously.

"Or abortion?"

Mary shrugged. "Oh I don't care about that. But women and children need to be protected. It's terrible what's happening to all these single girls with babies and middle-aged women thrown out on the refuse heap. My friend Marge Germaine was fifty-two when her husband decided he wanted to marry a twenty-five-year-old chippie. He cut her off with nothing through some legal manipulations and now she's destitute. Her children have to support her." She shuddered. "Horrible!"

"At least her children *can* support her," Ronnie could not resist saying. "Unlike some."

"I suppose," Mary offered vaguely.

"For a nonfeminist, you have a very political view of marriage," Ronnie commented.

Mary dismissed this. "Anyone with brains knows that marriage is a political affair. *Life* is a political affair, for godsake," she added. "Feminists are *not* the only women with brains, you know."

"So I see," Ronnie smiled.

Mary's heart gave a little lurch. She smiled at the back of Aldo's head.

They dropped Ronnie at Boston University, then Aldo drove Mary to the Ritz, where she was meeting her old friend Christina for lunch.

Ronnie visited Professor Madrick at BU and arranged to get a research assistant's library card. The paper-work took forever and she didn't have time to eat lunch. She went to the polls, then hopped the T to Cambridge to shop at the Coop. Aldo was to pick her up in front of it at four-thirty.

Mary was pink-faced and happy with wine and companionship: "It was lovely to see Christina again, I haven't seen her in years! And oh but it's good to get out of the house! Such an oppressive house!"

"It is."

Mary looked at her in some surprise. "For you too?"

"Yes." What did she think, that luxury could make up for everything else?

Aldo then drove them to Ronnie's old apartment near Copley Square to pick up the belongings she had been storing there. The neighborhood was vibrant and shabby, the broad avenue lined with old brownstones transformed into cheap shops with apartments above them. Mary was appalled. "You lived here?"

Ronnie girded herself for attack. "Yes."

Mary peered out. "It looks frightening."

"It's not bad. It's alive."

Ronnie directed Aldo to her building.

"Here?" Mary cried, seeing the brownstone, the basement and first story given over to a tiny shop selling records and tapes, a travel agency, and a restaurant offering genuine Mexican tacos and enchiladas. Ronnie's stomach was tight waiting for the comment; her hand was on the car door. "I'll just run up. I won't be a minute."

Mary stared around as if she were in a foreign land. "You weren't frightened living here?"

"No. Why?" Ronnie was bewildered. "I've lived in much worse places."

Mary gazed at her. "May I come up with you?"

Ronnie stared back. "Why?"

"I could help you. You have things to carry down."

"I'll be glad to help her, Miss Upton," Aldo said, turning in his seat. He called all the sisters Miss Upton except Ronnie, whom he called Ronnie.

"I can do it alone, there's not that much. It's all right," Ronnie said, trying to escape.

"I'd like to see how you lived."

"It's just a grungy apartment."

"I've never seen a grungy apartment."

Ronnie shrugged. "If you like."

Aldo jumped out to open the door for Mary, a service he did not feel obliged to offer Ronnie. Ronnie pulled her face down into her jacket, keeping it bowed. She hoped no one she knew would see her emerging from a limousine, see the chauffeur opening the door for an exquisitely dressed woman in a sable coat and white kid gloves.

"You'll have to walk up three flights," Ronnie warned, still hoping to dissuade her.

"I'm not an invalid yet," Mary said, but she tottered on her high heels and was breathless by the second landing.

Linda answered the door, cried "Hi!" and hugged Ronnie, looked amazed at the woman Ronnie introduced as Mary Scott. "She drove me out here," she said without further explanation. Mary studied the large bright room furnished with odd pieces in varied stages of disintegration — a couch with wooden arms, the stuffing poking out of one of its cushions, a shaky table, an old standing lamp with a fringed shade, a couple of nondescript armchairs, a broad table holding books and papers with the remains of a meal pushed to one side, and an unmade bed.

"So, sit down!" Linda cried. "Want a Coke or something?"

"Thanks. We can't stay. They're driving me back to Lincoln."

"Oh." The girl seemed really disappointed, as if she actually *liked* Ronnie. Mary peered down the hall leading off the front room.

"Well, I've got your stuff all together here," Linda said, pointing to some plastic bags lined up against the wall.

"I really appreciate your keeping my stuff for me, Lin. How's the new roomie working out?"

"Pretty good," Linda said, nodding. "She pays her share on time and doesn't steal food. Can't ask much more," she laughed.

"I wonder . . . ," Mary began. Both stopped and looked at her. "May I use your toilet?"

"Sure." Linda led her through the room to the hall and pointed at a door.

Ronnie stood in shock. Mary using the toilet *here*? Mary the finicky, of the white rooms, the white food, the fastidious aversion to a whole host of contaminants? But her face revealed nothing as she chatted with Linda waiting for Mary to return.

Mary explored. She peered with fascination into a small dark kitchen with sink and stove from another age, as she entered the long narrow dark bathroom cluttered with the legion of toilet necessities of two young late-twentieth-century women. She of course would not sit upon that toilet or wash her hands in that sink; with her gloves on, she used her handkerchief to flush the unused toilet and run the tap. She crept out quietly trying to get a glimpse of the other room, its door partly closed. She pushed it lightly, to catch sight of a dim room furnished with a bed, a table that doubled as a desk, an old plush sofa, an armchair, and an assortment of old-fashioned but not antique lamps. Smaller and darker than the main room, it seemed to face an air shaft or alley.

"Thank you!" she announced, returning, and offered to help Ronnie carry some of her bags. Both women looked at her.

"It's okay, I'll make two trips," Ronnie said.

"It's okay, I'll help her," Linda said.

But Mary insisted, and was handed a light bag of clothes. Ronnie and Linda each grabbed four bags of clothes and books.

"I sort of hate to see your things go, Ron," Linda said as they descended the stairs. "It's like you're really leaving, you know, for good. You know how it is around here, people disappear. I'm afraid I'll never see you again. Promise you'll stay in touch?"

"Promise. I'll be coming in to use the library. I'll call you, we can have coffee or lunch or something."

"Great. Don't forget now." Linda kissed her good-bye, held her in an embrace while Aldo leapt out of the car, snatched the bag Mary was carrying and stowed it in the trunk, and helped Mary into the car. He stowed the rest of the bags as well, slammed the trunk lid, and got back into the car. Through her good-byes to Linda, Ronnie could sense his outrage that Mary had been pressed into service, and she got into the car with a sarcastic smile. Only then did Linda take in the car, the uniformed chauffeur, and her eyes popped. Ronnie waved good-bye, happy not to have to make any explanations.

"I'd of been glad to come up and help, Ronnie," Aldo growled. "You didn't have to ask Miss Upton."

"Don't be upset, Aldo," Mary purred. "I insisted." And she patted Ronnie's hand. With her gloves on.

Alex, having a lonely tea in the sun room, glanced up at an exhilarated-looking Ronnie, loaded down with clothes and books and brown bags marked THE COOP, as she vanished into her room without offering an explanation. Good to get out of the house, Alex decided. It's funny: home is so important to us, we sacrifice everything to buy a house or rent an apartment, to furnish it, fix it up just the way we want. Then we feel oppressed if we can't get out of it.

Me too.

Mary too seemed more cheerful than usual, after a large lunch at the Ritz with an old friend, and some strange trip into the wilderness (isn't that what she said?). Some joke or other that I didn't get, that's not unusual. Maybe she meant the polls: no, she couldn't vote, she said. New York. David said last night that he was voting, so I shouldn't feel too guilty about failing in my duty as a citizen this year. But the truth is, I don't really want to vote this year. I'm not so sure David's right about Reagan, I don't like the way things are going, so many more women at the shelter. . . . Still, I wouldn't want to cancel out his vote.

Maybe I should have gone with them today, but what would I do? Mary didn't want me with her at the Ritz, and Ronnie was too busy to worry about me. I could have just walked around, I guess. I've never been to Boston.

Oh, why didn't I go?

Nobody asked me.

By the time Elizabeth returned late Thursday afternoon, the sisters had been in residence in the house for a week, and had settled into habits as fixed as if they had lived there — together — all their lives. Everyone knew for instance that Ronnie would never be found in the house proper except at meals, but would be outdoors or in her bedroom. Everyone knew that Alex was given to long periods of solitude, walks into town, bicycle rides through the countryside and — Mary insisted (having one day when Aldo drove her through town seen Alex emerge from St. Joseph's) — visits to the Catholic church. Ronnie and Elizabeth received this shocking information with shrugs.

Elizabeth spent hours in the library either at her computer or lying on the couch reading some awful huge tome, a pencil stuck behind her ear, half-glasses perched on her nose, a pad at her hand. Why she had brought clothes back with her, Mary couldn't conceive, since she seemed to have been influenced by Ronnie and now wore nothing but old corduroy pants and saggy cashmere sweaters with sneakers. Running shoes, Marty called them. Elizabeth's slimness, it was true, invested these clothes with some kind of seedy elegance, but she was also given to early morning walks in the woods, on rainy days wearing an old poncho she had found in the mudroom. She rose at six and went to bed at eleven-thirty every day. Rigid as a post, Mary said.

Mary was the least fixed in her habits, the most restless. She read, lying in one chair or another, in whichever room was lighter and brighter — usually the sun room in the morning, the sitting room afternoons. Sometimes she scribbled in a notebook; Elizabeth laughed that Mary was writing love letters to herself. And one day she opened the great old Bosendorfer, which hadn't been touched in years, played a scale lightly, exclaimed in horror, and demanded Elizabeth call a tuner. It was in such bad shape that the tuner was not able to bring it to concert pitch and Mary complained.

"Oh the princess and the pea!" Elizabeth said irritably. "You'd think you had perfect pitch."

"I do," said Mary.

Still, she sat down every afternoon and stumbled through scales and exercises, causing doors to slam throughout the house.

But she daily complained of boredom and several times over the following days had Aldo drive her into Boston. She had searched her address book for the names of old school chums or friends who lived in the area and met them for lunch, a visit to an art gallery or the Gardner Museum or the Museum of Fine Arts, or a matinee, while Aldo contentedly waited for her in the car, reading his newspaper, knowing she was doing the proper thing for a lady and was therefore safe.

Without discussion, the sisters also adopted a division of labor. Elizabeth took care of business — dealt with the groundsmen and Aldo, called repair people when something broke, and paid the bills. Mary dealt with Mrs. Browning, supervising the menu and the marketing, and on occasion, instead of merely having her telephone, accompanied the housekeeper in the car (driven by Aldo) to Donelan's market or to Concord to make sure the items chosen were of the proper quality. But so much fish, chicken, turnip, potato, celeriac, and parsnip grew boring, and so much caviar (the only nonwhite food Mary favored) expensive, and Elizabeth assigned Alex to go along and supervise, with a side note to keep Mary within their budget. After protesting that after all, she allowed green food too, Mary only shrugged.

Alex spent most of her days outdoors, but after Teresa left at four, it was Alex who helped Mrs. Browning chop vegetables and clean salad greens, set the table. She helped clear the table after dinner and prepare the night's leftovers for soup for the next day's lunch. One Wednesday — Mrs. Browning's day off — she baked a pie.

Only Ronnie did nothing or so Elizabeth thought until one day she looked out the study window and saw Ronnie outdoors with Aldo putting up snow fencing. She mentioned this to Mary, who said she'd noticed Ronnie raking leaves earlier in the month. It appeared she worked outdoors every day, had helped rake up the rotting fallen apples, cover the sensitive plants for winter, and turn the mulch pile. This knowledge filled Elizabeth with a deep contentment. It was, she thought, as if they were living in a little convent, each contributing in her own way, enjoying the days passing in near silence, solitude, apart from the world. Their work gave them a sense of peaceable order, harmony that offset their angry comings-together.

And every day at eleven, the four of them were ready when Aldo pulled up to the front door to take them to the hospital. Every day they stood together at Stephen's bedside and gazed down at him, saying only "Hello, Father, how are you today?" Ronnie never said anything at all, and none of them ever touched him. Dr. Stamp always turned up to chat with them. After twenty minutes, they would leave.

Stephen had been in a coma for a week when the doctor met them without his usual smile, his sober look seeming to bear import. "After you visit your father, I'd like to speak to you," he said, and when they came out, he led them to the lounge. He explained that they had done several CT scans since Stephen's stroke to check on the dissolution of the hematoma and that there was some infarction of the brain.

Elizabeth lighted a cigarette. Mary batted her eyelids and tilted her head up to Dr. Stamp. "Could you explain that?" she asked like a sweet ignorant child.

"The brain tissue is damaged — has been destroyed. So that even if he does regain consciousness, the outlook is not . . . hopeful."

"You mean Father will be an idiot!" Mary cried.

The doctor smiled benignly at her. "Not exactly . . . but he may not be able to speak or move. I just wanted to warn you that the outlook is somewhat pessimistic. The longer he remains in coma, the less hope . . . I'm sorry."

"Oh," Mary said.

"Thank you," Elizabeth said, rising.

The others echoed her and left, no expression on their faces. Strange women, thought Dr. Stamp. Not what they seem, somehow. And why did they always bring that colored girl?

That day at lunch Mary announced she felt she had to repay her friends' hospitality and wanted to invite them to Lincoln to tea. Alex was delighted, Elizabeth groaned, and Ronnie looked appalled until Mary added that Ronnie would be excused — which somehow did not make Ronnie any happier.

But, Mary added without taking a breath, before they came, the house had to be made presentable. She opened a beautiful leather binder, displaying a pad covered with lists, and whirled into action. First, she demanded Elizabeth call an upholsterer to re-cover the window seat cushion within ten days (which no one could do of course, so Mary made a trip to Boston to buy fabric and Teresa made the cover). She herself called a dry cleaner to clean and rehang the drapes in the downstairs rooms. This could be done in a week for a premium price. She told the servants to wash all the lace curtains in the house, upstairs and down, *by hand* (they were handmade after all, she argued) and stretch them in the old way. Mrs. Browning and Teresa were dismayed: there were only two stretchers and forty panels of lace. It would take much longer than a week, they argued, trembling. Mary insisted. She pressed Aldo into service to help the women wash all the windows in the house, polish all the wood floors, clean the crystal chandeliers, shine all the silver. But to do all this in a week was almost impossible: Teresa began to talk about quitting and by Tuesday, Mrs. Browning with heavy sighs gave them canned soup and sandwiches for lunch.

"This is ridiculous, Mary," Elizabeth yelled. "You can't drive these people this way! All this for a bunch of silly women who won't even go upstairs?"

"It needs to be done!" Mary yelled back. "It hasn't been done for years!" Glaring at Ronnie, whose mother's fault this presumably was. "And they're not silly! How dare you call them silly! Francine is married to the richest importer in Boston, they have one of the finest pop art collections in the country! All the museums woo them! Christina is . . ."

"DON'T tell me who these broads are married to," Elizabeth cried, putting her hands over her ears. "I don't want to hear, I don't want to know!"

Mary stared at her uncomprehendingly.

Ronnie leaned back with a malicious smile. "She seems to think that being married to a rich man is not a guarantee of nonsilliness," she explained to Mary.

"Well then, I don't know what is!" Mary exclaimed in outrage. "To marry and stay married to a rich man takes more skill and cleverness than any other job I know!"

Ronnie burst out laughing; Alex smiled uncertainly; even Elizabeth grinned sidelong. When Mary let a small smile escape, all the sisters laughed out loud. It was edged with hysteria, but it was the first laugh they had ever shared.

"Mary," Elizabeth said more kindly, "it's just too much for the staff. It's inhuman, what you're asking."

"Well, then hire some extra people!"

"I'd be glad to help if . . . ," Alex began tentatively, "if that's all right with you. You seem to — people who live in houses like this seem to have strict rules about what you can and can't do, but I'd be glad to help. To have something to do."

"In fact, wasn't that you up on the step stool the other day wiping a globe of the chandelier?" Ronnie smilingly betrayed her.

She flushed. "Well, Teresa and Brownie were struggling so with the curtains. . . ."

"Brownie?!!!" Mary cried.

"That's her nickname," she said innocently.

"One doesn't call servants by nicknames, Alex," Mary scolded, then considered, weighing her options. "Well. I guess it's all right if you help," she decided. "Why not. We're living in a different age, aren't we. I don't know how to do these chores but I'll try to help too." She looked expectantly at Elizabeth.

"Don't look at me. It's your party."

"And *I'm* not even invited," Ronnie threw in, escaping from the lunch table.

"Well but Elizabeth, you have to get someone to help poor Browning. We can't be having canned soup and sandwiches for lunch!" Mary concluded.

Fifteen days after his stroke, two weeks after their arrival in Lincoln, on the morning of the Friday before the tea party, Alex cried out that Father's left eyelid was fluttering. They froze instantly, studying him. Nothing.

Saturday, she said his left hand moved. Again, they froze and concentrated on the hand. Nothing. Mary rolled her eyes at Elizabeth.

Sunday, Alex very calmly said, "I know you don't believe me but look at him! His eyelid fluttered!"

Ronnie said, "I saw it too."

Mary stared at Elizabeth. They gazed at the old man. Nothing. "I think housecleaning has affected your mind, Alex," Mary said, stalking out. Elizabeth followed her, leaving Alex and Ronnie to walk alone behind them. They contemplated each other.

"You saw it, didn't you? You weren't just humoring me?" Alex whispered.

"I saw it," Ronnie said. "They don't want to see it. They want him dead."

"Oh, surely not!"

"Why, surely not," Ronnie mocked, "Ms. Pollyanna?"

Alex punched her arm lightly, grimacing, then put her arm around her as they walked out. Elizabeth was talking to Father's ICU nurse, Edna Thompson.

"Certainly, Miss Upton." She fingered a card. "I'll call if there's any change at all."

Elizabeth hired two extra women from a temp agency so most of the work got done although Mrs. Browning confessed to Teresa in the kitchen that having Mary help was like taking on an extra job. "Like having your five-year-old help you," Teresa agreed, and they laughed comfortably. They were discomfited by this breach of decorum, but they also felt a grudging thrust of vengeance at the sight of Mary in cashmere twin set, miniskirt, pearls, and an apron, trying to remove a lace curtain from the stretcher, crying out as she stuck her finger on one of the needles that held them on. It was satisfying on a number of counts — not only did she suffer (you see what *we* go through?) but she would then go off to suck it and could do nothing until it stopped bleeding lest she stain the freshly washed lace, so she was out of their hair for minutes. Also, they were vindicated: it was impossible to wash and stretch forty lace panels in a week, and Mary finally agreed to leave the curtains in the upstairs rooms for later. But the satisfaction was undermined when Mary walked around the house exclaiming at the refound brightness and beauty of the place, as if she had worked this miracle single-handedly — except that she literally cried about the draperies that had returned from their cleaning with threadbare patches.

Two days before the party, with several lace panels remaining to be washed and much of the silver yet to be polished, Mary set to work drawing up and discarding menus, flustering Browning anew by demanding sandwiches of cucumber, watercress, and ham, smoked salmon on thin brown bread, artichoke bottoms with shrimp and mayonnaise, caviar with chopped egg, onion, and toast points, pound cake, lemon custard cake, midnight cake, all to be marketed for and prepared in two days.

But somehow this too was done and the three ladies — for ladies they unquestionably were — arrived together by limousine Monday afternoon promptly at four. Mary greeted them in a high-necked fitted flared-skirt wine wool Trigère adorned with a simple thick gold necklace; Alex wore the best dress she had brought, a pale blue silk shirtwaist (Mary had to admit it did make her eyes look brilliant). Elizabeth had to be dragged out of the study, but at least she had put on a well-cut black skirt and a white shirt, mannish but of heavy silk, cut full. The ladies, dressed more like Mary than the others, saw nothing at which to take offense, and embraced Mary and met Elizabeth with emphatic declarations (Such a long time, Lizzie! or I'm glad to meet you after all these years! I've heard so much about you!). They studied Alex unobtrusively and walked around the sitting and drawing rooms exclaiming at the beauty and wonderfulness of "these old houses."

Teresa served the tea at a tea table unused for decades, opened in the sitting room where the fading light gleamed on the new gold brocade cushion of the window seat and the newly cleaned but very old tapestry drapes, folded carefully to conceal worn spots. A fire burned high (but not as high as Ronnie's fires, Mary noted) in the fireplace, the lamps were lighted, the ladies chatted. They talked of children and dogs and vacations, reminisced about events at the Lincoln house years before, about their girlhoods. Everyone had had a friend or relative who had suffered a stroke and recovered, as they were sure Stephen would. Threading their conversation like a lively drone in a septet, Elizabeth noticed, was congratulation, praise. So lovely Mary was and Marie-Laure too, Christina had seen her only a few months ago when her own daughter had a party, Marie-Laure had come down from Bennington, so beautiful so charming. Elizabeth was elegant, and a friend of Mark Lipman, no? They knew him well — he had been in partnership with Christina's husband years ago.

And the secretary, such a fine man, so intelligent, like Elizabeth herself. Such an important job! And surely so difficult! How intelligent she must be.

Alex's credentials they researched almost immediately.

"Where are you from, Alex?" Eloise asked. "Wilmington, oh you must know the Mountjoys, of course you do, Caroline Mountjoy is just about your age! Really? But surely you know the Rosses, they live out at Glen Ross, another wonderful old house like this. No?"

No unkind word said, not even a look exchanged, but they all knew and with a wry smile, Elizabeth registered their knowing: NOT one of us. Dismissed as insignificant.

Bitches. Her heart heated in defense of Alex, she began to prepare her case.

But Alex seemed oblivious both to the meaning of their questions and their dismissal. It was as if she simply did not *feel* it. Truly dense, Mary thought, not unhappy with Alex's failure to pass muster. That loved-child syndrome, Elizabeth decided. Can't conceive of people not liking her, so doesn't ever feel rejected. Alex, expansive and happy with company (COMPANY!), listened to them and questioned them with such interest and warmth that despite her unworthiness, they allotted her a share of praise — lovely hair, her father's brilliant eyes. Warming even further in this female climate so familiar to her, Alex spoke more calmly, less compulsively than she did with her sisters, about her children, her husband (that poor David was clearly not in *their* husbands' league was acknowledged in the visitors' tight smiles), her house in Newark — pronounced New Ark — Delaware, her poor widowed mother who had no one. With a grateful smile, she breathed more deeply and evenly than she had in days as she accepted their assurances that her mother indeed had someone, she had Alex and her lovely children, she was not alone.

Women are the same everywhere, Alex thought. Even if they are rich.

Alex discovered they did volunteer work, like her. She worked with poor people, mainly women and children, hands-on work in a shelter. This did shock them a bit.

"You work in one of those places?" Christina frowned. "Isn't it — depressing? grimy? dangerous?"

"It's depressing and grimy," Alex admitted. "I never feel endangered.

You know" — she glanced at her sisters briefly — "I know it sounds sentimental. But every time I make a child laugh, help feed a baby, let a worn-out woman get some rest, take some of her burden — you know, people act as if these women are just parasites on the public the way they talk about welfare mothers. But these women are doing a hard job, they are working! They are raising children, and they don't get paid for it or even supported, they are destitute — well, I go home every Wednesday feeling so good, feeling I matter, that my life matters. . . ." She gave up.

The women stared at her soberly.

"I worked in a soup kitchen last winter," Francine offered. "So I have some idea what you mean."

"So many poor people," Eloise murmured. "The streets are full of them."

"I tend to stay out of the fray. Mainly I raise money for the hospital," Christina said quietly. "Maybe I should do more."

In fact, Alex proved to be the hit of the party, Elizabeth thought afterward. *She didn't need my defense. Her naiveté, her ignorance of their standards, their language, the way their minds worked, gave her an advantage with those supersubtle Venetians. They enjoyed her far more than Mary, whose constant references to Gstaad, Capri, Paris, to Alberto, long-past parties with the Duchess of Windsor and the Duke of Marlborough, gossip about Princess Di and Prince Charles recounted with a full measure of "definitelys" and "certainlys," only underscored how far she had slid from such glories. The women were clearly aware of her decline. Aware too of how tenuous their hold was on the things they insisted defined them. A knowledge they resisted. Willful blindness. I am superior, one of the elite. I am! Knowing they were a man away from Mary's situation. Most of them had nothing of their own — unless some man had died and left it to them. Of course, in this overblown economy, their men might soon be only a decimal point away from poverty. Hah! Her mouth twisted in scorn.*

God I can't stand the dictatorship of women's niceness. All that smiling, embracing, kisskiss, coocoo, cuckoo, that's what it makes you. Yet, as she walked back to the library she had come to think of as hers, Elizabeth found herself humming. She felt cheerful, her heart light. *Why should that be? It was unthinkable that that stupid conversation, all those nicenesses could have cheered her. It must be she was happy they had left.*

*   *   *

Ronnie, who was relieved to be excused from the tea party, did her part by remaining invisible and silent. Same old role she had always played in this house. But this time, a throng of questions buzzed around her head — what are the rules of this world? what do you wear? how do you act? are you allowed to sit with your legs up on the chair? are you allowed to say "fuck"? do you eat those little sandwiches with a fork? is holding out your pinky when you sip from a cup good manners or bad? do you sqeeze lemon into your tea with your fingers? do you have to wear white gloves to do it? where do I find white gloves in Lincoln? what happens if the gloves get wet when you squeeze the lemon? Reduced to giggles, she comforted herself at being excluded: she was happy not to have to sit for two hours listening to what she knew would be trivial snobbish superficialities, two hours in which she could get some work done.

Still, when she started to hear bustling in the kitchen, she got up from the computer and opened her door a fraction. Mrs. Browning was frantically telling Teresa how to hold and pass the silver sandwich tray. Through the open swinging kitchen door voices drifted from the sitting room. And something twisted in her stomach, twisted and hardened. She picked up a journal and lay on her bed but she could not concentrate.

Suppose I just wander in there, hello everybody, how do you do? I'm the bastard sister. Ronalda Velez my name, invisibility my game. Even Alex would be shocked much as she pretends to be tolerant. Takes the position that's easier for her, that doesn't strain her brain or her moral sense. At least the others have the guts to say what they mean. They're honest, the bitches. She reached for the sneering smile she always used when feelings like these overcame her, but it wouldn't come, her mouth only trembled. Instead, a blanket of feeling spread across her body, like a flush suffusing a face.

DON'T.

This feeling made her weak, made her mouth tremble, her eyes wet, her hands limp.

DON'T.

But she sank into the warm, liquid, mushy, comforting forbidden underwater realm. Poor Ronnie. Exiled then, exiled now, called a bastard — well she was wasn't she. Big-eyed little golden-brown child hidden in the kitchen, don't disturb The Man. Little brown person in a white world where brown people weren't considered people.

Remembering, she wept. And weeping made her feel as if she were blowing up into a soggy weakling.

For twenty-five years she had avoided self-pity. Sign of weakness. Made you weak. Have to be tough, tough it all out. But the stuff ran out of her uncontrollably, like pus, like pee.

I hidden, they in the light. The color of my skin makes me unwelcome at a tea party where six women sit making trivial conversation. "You are excused from the tea party, Ronnie," talking to me like an inferior, known certified *inferior*, Mary's superiority equally known and certified. Her birth certificate proves it. How can she go on believing that she and her ilk are superior and everyone else inferior? What gyrations must she go through to maintain such a delusion in the face of fact? Superior? She's better-looking than most, fatter than many, stupid or smart but she's accomplished nothing in her life and has no thought for anything but herself.

Don't do that. She's had kids. Stick to your principles: bearing children is the most important contribution anyone can make to society.

Yes but she didn't raise them herself. It wasn't that much of a contribution.

Don't do to her what she does to you. She sobbed aloud. No one needs a justification to be alive. No one! Remember that! Don't do to others what they do to you! Not looks or smarts or morals or strength or accomplishments or religion or color or sex or . . .

Why! She was crying softly, but aloud. Why would it be such a shocking invasion for me to eat the same sandwiches, drink the same tea, use the same cups as them! It isn't even the illegitimacy: if my mother had been some madcap bohemian British noblewoman who simply refused to marry, some Isadora Duncan type, some movie star, they'd parade me at their parties, crowing over their marvelous sister conceived on the wrong side of the blanket. It's class and color. Even if my mother was lower-class but white I'd be acceptable if I was educated, a bastard with a Ph.D. They wouldn't like it but they might pass me off with a joke: Father was such a roué! But there's no cloud without a silver lining, look we have this brilliant sister, a surprise we just discovered, she's getting a Ph.D. in ecology, isn't she wonderful?

Well, maybe they wouldn't. But they could.

Is that why you are getting a Ph.D.?

Of course, she's also a lesbian.

Ronnie laughed out loud.

Still, the feeling would not blow away, would not budge. The room shimmered in front of her eyes as she did something even more forbidden than pity herself, let herself imagine Elizabeth's arm lightly on her back, ushering her into the sitting room miraculously clothed in something acceptable, with a good haircut, introduced as the long-lost sister. Saw Mary rise, come across the room, kiss her cheek, dear Ronnie. Felt Alex embrace her, so glad you came. Sat in the warmth, the four of them together by the fire asking each other what their lives had been like, lamenting the sorrow each had suffered — and she now knew there had been plenty of sorrow even for them — holding each other in a shared embrace, weeping, saying we love you. Because you're my sister.

She sobbed out loud.

Love you. Because you are, not for anything you do or own or know.

Like Rosa's little ones, everyone loved simply for existing. I hadn't been there two days before they were crying out when I came home, running to me, clinging to me. I looked up at Rosa, astonished. She smiled, said, "Ronnie, that's the wonderful thing about babies. They love you. You don't have to *do* nothing, they just love you."

But not my real sisters.

The vision was unendurable and she sat up, wiped her cheeks hard with the back of her hand. She reached for a cigarette and lighted it, inhaled deeply.

Shit, you asshole, they don't even love each other and you expect them to love you! Elizabeth and Mary are full of hate and rage and Alex is full of bubbles. And it can't be one-way, you'd have to love them too, how do you feel about that? Be like loving Him. To be happy in life you must love, Momma said. Formula that's upheld every tyranny since the world began. Love God who torments you, love the king who takes your wheat, makes you build his wall, drags you into the army or makes you bear his child. Love him, celebrate him, honor his name.

Fuck'em all.

8

According to the schedule they had silently established, the four of them lunched together every day at twelve-thirty in the sun room, where they met again for tea at four. Before dinner at eight in the dining room, at about six or half past, they meandered into the sitting room for cocktails, although Mary insisted Elizabeth and Ronnie could not call what they drank *cocktails*. But on Monday evening, after the guests left about six, the three sisters sat on.

"There's no way we're going to eat dinner tonight," Alex moaned.

"No. I told Browning just to serve us some soup," Mary agreed.

Ronnie remained conspicuously absent until Alex went into her room and ordered her out, pulling at her arm until she joined them. Elizabeth, glancing at Ronnie's face as she entered the room, thought she was simmering with resentment about her exclusion from the tea party. As would I be.

"I've enjoyed today so much!" Alex cried. "It's just as much fun having sisters as I thought it would be! I'm so glad we're getting to know each other."

"To know us is not necessarily to love us," Mary said.

"The two may even be mutually exclusive," Elizabeth said.

Alex didn't seem to hear. "But Ronnie should have been with us today! You would have loved it, Ronnie," Alex went on, immune to Ronnie's look.

"I doubt that," was all she said. Quietly.

Alex stopped, suddenly, seemed to think. "We've never asked you. Never talked to you about . . . I mean, we all talk about our childhoods except you. And I would really like to know about your mother's relation to our father."

"That seems clear," Ronnie said dourly. The others laughed.

"Oh no!" Alex put her hands alongside her head. "I'm sorry sorry sorry, that was stupid, that wasn't what I meant!" She leaned toward Ronnie. "I mean," she said, "were you all happy when you were here alone?" She searched Ronnie's face, which remained impassive, then stared at the fire. "I used to picture him here summers with Elizabeth and Mary. And after I saw you, I wondered about him in, you know, this other life, this cozy little family no one really knew about, the three of you happy and content together. . . ."

"Sitting around the hacienda eating rice and beans?" Ronnie mocked her. "Stephen in a poncho strumming a guitar and smiling paternally at his little brown child?"

Alex flushed. "That isn't what I meant," she protested. "By the time he got involved with your mother, he was older, more settled maybe. Maybe he could be — I don't know — easier, more relaxed, comfortable — with a woman of . . ."

"The lower classes? Like the many emperors who preferred their concubines to their noble-born wives? The aristocrat unbending with his mistress?"

Elizabeth smiled meanly. Exactly what she meant, of course. Head full of stereotypes.

A little anger flared on Alex's face. "Well, is it impossible that the three of you lived . . . in some contentment, had some . . . understanding among yourselves?"

Ronnie sat back. "What, *Little House on the Prairie*? Are you kidding? There was a house and the man who owned it. He had a brownskinned servant who waited on him, served him, bowed and scraped to him, *sí señor, no señor*. And there was this little brown girl she kept hidden in the back of the house because she knew that if the girl made noise or showed herself or in any way bothered him, they'd both be sent packing. Except for an annual Fourth of July party when the servant and her daughter and all the other hired help worked like slaves for ten straight days, the house was empty and silent most of the time. The little girl learned her place — which was to be invisible even when there was no one to see her. The man never never spoke to her. Only after he retired, decided to become an old man, were there constant demands, Noradia draw my bath, Noradia bring me a brandy, Noradia find my glasses."

"And when you were staying here with him these last months? When your mother was sick? Couldn't he get beyond that then?"

Mother in bed, Mrs. Browning in the kitchen, Teresa cleaning upstairs: I didn't know where to go, how to behave, not a servant anymore but certainly not a resident either. Out of place helping them, out of place in the house. Stayed with Momma, read to her, talked to her, got her tea when she could drink it or water. Stomach edgy all the time. Both of us had a hard time keeping food down. Thought I had cancer too for a while. Why I lost all that weight.

Ronnie tipped the Coke can to her mouth, found it empty. She put it on the table and stared outward into space. "There must be something real to drink in this joint."

Elizabeth rose and walked to the bar against the side wall. "What would you like?"

"I don't know. What is there? What do people drink? I only know about beer and wine, and I hate beer and I don't want wine."

Elizabeth smiled at her. "Gin and tonic?"

"Fine."

Elizabeth made the drink in a tall glass and carried it across to Ronnie, who accepted it in silent amazement. Jesus, could she be gay?

She sipped, rolled the liquid around over her tongue and nodded at Elizabeth, almost smiling: "It's good!" She turned to Alex. "He had me eat with him but he didn't talk. The only thing he ever did was complain — 'This steak's tough' or 'This broccoli is not cooked enough,' something like that. Every afternoon he'd visit Momma for an hour. I'd go outdoors while he was with her, just walk around. Most days when I came back in, he'd bark at me like he was defying me to contradict him, 'She's better today' or 'She's getting her strength back.' As if she *could* recover, as if that really were a possibility. As if he didn't know she was dying."

Three pairs of eyes stared at the floor registering "He must have loved her."

"So when she died, he was furious, as if she'd betrayed him. . . . That's how he acted that day, the day he had the stroke. Enraged that she'd done something hostile to him, outraged at her malicious perversity."

"That's how I felt when Don died," Mary murmured.

They all looked at her.

"Your last husband?" Alex asked.

She nodded. "He was crazy about motorcycling, he had all kinds of motorcycles. He especially liked to ride in the mountains — I still had the Vail house then — and he'd go out into the passes . . . he hit something, a rock or something. Threw him. Flipped him. Broke his neck." She searched her purse for her hankie, wiped her nose, glared at Elizabeth. "It *wasn't* suicide! We were gloriously happy."

Maybe so, Elizabeth thought, but can't you open your mouth without sounding like a movie magazine?

Alex made a sound of lamentation. "When was that?"

"Two years ago . . . two years in June."

Mrs. Browning appeared, announcing dinner.

"We've all had so many losses," Alex said, turning to each of them as they rose and walked to the dining room. "You lost your mother, you lost Clare, you lost Don. . . ."

"I lost Charlie . . . and my grandparents. Of course, they were old, but I really missed them, you know, we lived with them all through my childhood. Always: until I got married. And Charlie was like my father. . . ."

"Don was only forty," Mary mourned, then tensed, waiting for Elizabeth to sneer, "Robbing the cradle, Mary?" But what she said was — harshly — "That's what it means to get old. That's what a survivor is: a person who can outlive losses."

Alex frowned. "But I'm not that old."

"You're not. You're only thirty-six. That's young," Mary said, dismissing her.

Alex rubbed her fine-boned hand across her pale forehead. "It isn't *really* young. Ronnie's only twenty-five, but she isn't *really* young. . . ."

"*Chicanas* have a hard life," Ronnie cracked.

"I mean, people didn't use to live much beyond forty. Most people. In the world." She turned to Elizabeth. "Isn't that true?"

"Before the industrial revolution," Elizabeth agreed.

"Oh Jesus, don't get her started on the industrial revolution!" Mary cried. "She'll talk your ear off, all this garbage about capitalism and industrialization as the salvation of the human race! Trying to impress Father and make me feel stupid. At the latter of which, at least," she said to Elizabeth, "you succeeded." She turned back to Alex. "Whereas it's clear to me that people lived far far more graciously in the old days before we had either."

"How do you know what I'd say about the industrial revolution?" Elizabeth asked, puzzled.

Mary shrugged. "For heaven's sake, for years you used to hold forth. Regularly. At the dinner table, to Father. Trying to get him to talk, to impress him. Don't you remember? After you came back from England, when you were working in Washington and came up here for the July vacation." She turned to Alex, smiling meanly. "You think Elizabeth's so grand and dignified, you should have seen her then. If she wasn't groveling, it was the closest thing to groveling I ever saw! We'd stay here for a few days after the Fourth of July party. Elizabeth kept trying to get Father to talk to her but he wouldn't, oh he would *not!*" Mary laughed. "As if he'd taken a vow not to have a conversation with you. What a hoosher he is!" Mary giggled, wiped her eyes, sipped wine, giggled again.

Alex stared at her soup. Ronnie watched with intense interest. Elizabeth turned a tight face to Alex.

"So what about people dying at forty?"

She smiled gratefully. "Just that I'm almost forty. The age most people died at. Before. And I feel . . . I often feel . . . I *know* . . . that I haven't really lived yet. Is that crazy?"

"Oh, my dear, you've never been in love!" Mary said grandly.

Elizabeth groaned.

Intent on her point, Mary paid no attention. "And don't tell me you're married. People can be married for years and not realize they've never really been in love. Not realize what love is, can be . . ."

"So, what, you're only alive when you're in love but you can spend most of your life not in love? So then what are you, dead?" Elizabeth mocked.

"*I* was," Mary announced dramatically. "I spent my life acting a part, performing. I was never fully alive until I fell in love!"

Alex pondered. "I love David," she said tentatively. "He's a lovely man, a good man."

"I don't mean that!" Mary flung her arm out, sweeping away all objections. Her rings glittered in the lamplight, diamond, ruby, sapphire. "I mean passion, the kind that sweeps you away, that makes everything else unimportant, the kind worth dying for!" Her uplifted face was radiant.

"The kind they sell in those romances you read," Elizabeth sneered.

Mary stopped and stared at her sister. "Elizabeth, I don't read romances. If you'd ever bothered to look, you'd see that I read mostly poetry. You think everyone in the world is stupid except Father and you and your Clare! Why don't you just step off your throne. It's flushing under your feet!"

To hide her grin, Ronnie dropped her fork and bent to pick it up. In her triumph at having shaken Elizabeth, Mary didn't even remark Ronnie's breach of manners.

Alex was elsewhere.

Totally self-involved, Ronnie thought.

She began talking, it seemed, to herself; her eyes were focused on nothing in the room. "You said my mother was a loved child. Well, I was too. I had my mother and my grandparents and Charlie and he was a wonderful man, so dear, so kind to me, as if I were his own child — but they all took care of me, they all loved me. I loved and was loved.

"Maybe" — she returned to the room, to Mary — "that's not the kind of love you mean. But when David and I were first married, I felt what I imagine you mean by passion. I felt. . . ." She broke off, laughing. "He used to tease me, accuse me of trying to possess him utterly, he liked it of course, that I wanted to touch him, hold him, all the time. I wanted to hold all of him in my hands all at one time, I told him I wished he were tiny so I could hold him in my palm, I wanted to own him, to gobble him up, his sweet mouth, his beautiful smooth golden skin."

Mary frowned. She had it wrong.

"And probably you're right," Alex went on unheeding, "during that time I did feel completely alive. But I still feel that way about him every once in a while. When I see him standing in front of the window in the back door in his plaid woolen shirt with the sleeves rolled up . . . with the light behind him, his profile is dark and clean and strong. . . . I want to go up to him and just . . . contain him, surround him, swallow him up. . . ."

"What *do* you do?" Ronnie was amused.

Alex was startled. "Oh! Well that depends. On what we have to do. I mean, if the kids have to be driven somewhere or I'm in the middle of baking a pie . . . well, then I just smile at him. But sometimes I go up to him."

"And?"

"I contain him, surround him, I swallow him whole!" Alex cried, laughing. They all laughed. Even Mary.

Alex sobered. "But that doesn't change the fact that all those years — I felt something was missing. I don't know what. I've always felt — I *think* I've always felt — that something vital was lacking in my life. And I think I imagined you all had it — well, Elizabeth and Mary, I didn't know about you, Ronnie. I thought of the two of you as if you were angels living in paradise — without the, I don't know, *constraints* I had."

"Constraints?" Elizabeth, cool.

Alex sat back. "In 1978, David got a promotion and to celebrate he took me to New York for New Year's Eve. We stayed in a nice hotel on the East Side and he took me to a fancy place for dinner and dancing and afterwards to a jazz club in the Village. And we were in a cab going back to our hotel, it must have been three or four in the morning, we were driving I remember up Sixth Avenue, and there on the street, in the middle of the street, was a young man in full evening dress, his arms out like wings, his white scarf flying out behind him, on a skateboard. And my heart stopped. And I knew that's what I had always wanted to do. I had always wanted to feel that free. And I knew I never had."

"And you never will. Because of male predation," Ronnie declaimed. "No woman can ever feel that free or act that free because the male of the human species preys on the female. The only species in which one sex systematically . . ."

Elizabeth interrupted. "What made you feel unfree? Did your parents keep you from doing things?"

"Oh, I suppose the things all parents keep their children from doing — playing in the traffic, you know. I don't know," Alex said vaguely. "I mean, they loved me — they kept telling me what a good girl I was — and I knew I was a good girl. . . ."

"But you felt that to keep their love, you had to go on being a good girl," Mary said. "Which meant obeying. Not playing in the traffic, not skateboarding on the boulevard."

"Maybe."

"Well, you're clearly still a good girl," Elizabeth said, with an amused smile that included Alex.

"Yes," Alex smiled back, sighing. "But I don't know if that's it." She faced Elizabeth, her face intense. "When you work, when you're doing economics, whatever it is you do, do you feel . . ." — she stopped again — "*alive?* The way Mary means?"

"Yes. Totally. I feel full. I feel in gear, like a powerful machine working at full capacity. Not a machine, really, because there's nothing mechanical about the way I feel. I'm using everything human in me — what I feel and think and want and don't want, body mind emotion, everything. . . ."

Alex attended closely. "What about you, Ronnie? What do you do when you're alone in your room?"

Thought you'd never ask. "Actually, I'm writing my dissertation."

They all stopped dead, staring at her.

Yeah. *That* knocked your socks off, huh? Didn't expect an educated wetback.

"In what?"

"Energy and the environment, ecology, really. Specializing in ecosystems, everything in the universe part of one system, everything keeps everything else going, everything contributes to continuing life. Plants, especially, I concentrate on."

"I'm impressed," Elizabeth announced.

Shit why does that feel so good. Ronnie lowered her gaze to hide the dampness of her eyes.

"Well so am I, Ronnie," Mary agreed hesitantly.

Alex gave Ronnie her yearning look. "And what is your dissertation about?"

"I did fieldwork in the Appalachians for a year, studied mosses and lichen. Now I'm writing up my conclusions."

"Mosses?" Alex said, wonderingly.

"Mosses are fascinating," Ronnie said defensively. "They are right at the crux between algae, which are completely dependent on an aquatic environment, and vascular plants, which live on dry land. And lichen is a symbiote — it's really two species from different kingdoms, one an algae, one a fungus. But it lives as a single plant, and neither part really survives without the other."

They stared at this sudden volubility in her, and remained silent when she finished, allowing her time to continue. But she didn't.

"So you'll have a Ph.D.?" Elizabeth asked. "When you're finished?"

"If it's accepted. If I pass my orals."

"You must feel you're doing something really important, something that matters. To everyone, to the whole world. That you're contributing to humanity," Alex exclaimed.

Ronnie shrugged. "It's probably not any more important than having children. And I'll never have children."

"Oh, how do you know!" Alex protested warmly, reaching across to pat her hand. "You're still a young woman, a girl, really, you're only in your twenties!"

"Because I'm a lesbian."

"Oh!!!" Hand pulled back swiftly.

Bingo.

Knew it, thought Mary.

"Any cow can have children," Elizabeth said. "Not everyone can write a dissertation."

Jesus, could she be gay? Ronnie wondered. Out loud she said, "I think having children is hard. Takes a lot out of you. Maybe not having them — although I guess that takes enough — but raising them."

Poor Momma's voice breaking when she heard my voice on the phone, shrieking, "Ronalda, Ronalda, I thought you dead." Sobbing, "Where you are, what you do, why you go, why you do this to me?"

"It *is* a bore," Mary said.

"What would *you* know about it?" Ronnie said fiercely. "You had servants to do all the work!" Rosa, worried about the boys all the time and then after all it was Tina who flipped out, coming home drugged and disheveled. Rosa working all day working all night sick with worry all the time, if it wasn't money it was the kids, if it was money it was *for* the kids.

"I nursed my babies!" Mary cried indignantly. "I didn't have them carried in to visit me at night before I went out and ignore them the rest of the time! *I* didn't send my children away to school at seven! I didn't raise them the way I was raised! I spent time with them, gave them attention, and sometimes it was very hard . . . you may not know but Alberto left me when I was pregnant with Marie-Laure. I had her all by myself. Completely alone!" She burst into tears.

Alex sighed, "Life is pain."

Elizabeth rolled her eyes.

Ronnie smirked.

Still, from that day onward, the climate was different among them: they were somehow calmer together, as if they had passed through a lock and sailed in slightly lower channels.

On foot or by bicycle, Alex visited Lincoln's three churches, having discovered there was no synagogue of any persuasion in this town. St. Anne's in-the-Fields, an Episcopal church, was really in the middle of fields two miles from the town center, across the road from the Codman House. It was the official church of the Upton family, although there was some question as to when the last Upton had attended any church. Despite seat cushions, (thin) pads on the kneeling benches, and a carpet down the center aisle, it was austere. Yet it appealed to Alex, and she attended a couple of services there, amused to find that they used pita bread for the communion wafers.

St. Joseph's, the Catholic church, a plain white frame structure, was very neat and clean, more like a classroom than a place of worship, she thought. Even its carved wood stations of the cross done in freestanding scenes without a frame and painted in muted pinks, browns, greens could not save it from a studious dryness, not at all what she associated with Catholicism. It was like a Knights of Columbus meeting hall, she thought, with its small round-arched windows and geometric stained glass, each window devoted to the memory of some man or other, all Irish. There was one woman listed, she noticed. But what most upset her about St. Joseph's was the warning in the parish newsletter: *"PLEASE! PLEASE! PLEASE! NO EATING IN THE CRYING ROOM."* What could that be, a crying room? Was there a place in this church where people went to cry? Did going there guarantee that tears would come? Maybe she should look for it. But instead, she scurried away on her bicycle and she returned to St. Joseph's only once more, to attend Mass.

Alex's favorite was the Unitarian church, called the White Church. Built in 1842 in Greek Revival style, it was small and wooden, with closed pews. Some were larger than others, and Alex wondered if they belonged to richer families or larger ones. The White Church was simple and clean and somehow piety was built into its very walls, into the single plain chandelier, the organ in the choir, the twelve-over-twelve windows, the Empire style burled-walnut altar.

Alex would stop in of a morning or an afternoon to sit and try to sense import in the quality of light, the look of the altar. She strained to hear voices she felt hid in the echoes, the hollow footfalls. She attended services there and at St. Joseph's and found herself drawn to the music, flowers, and incense of the Catholic church. But the only sermon that lingered in her memory was one delivered by the Episcopalian priest.

In time, however, she decided that a spot in the woods behind the house was the best place to do what she wanted to do. While she did not think of this as worship, she called the spot, a small clearing amid a patch of leafless maples and oaks where the sun broke through to the forest floor, her cathedral. She could come here every day: it was never locked, no one ever barred her way or questioned her presence, and there were even benches — a fallen log and the stump of a tree that had not fallen but been felled, so it was smooth and even.

Walking to her cathedral Tuesday morning around nine, she saw Ronnie bent over in the thick woods off the path. She picked her way toward her through clotted underbrush. A wheelbarrow stood in a small clearing, piled high with twigs.

"Hi! Whatcha doing?"

Ronnie raised herself, pink with exertion. She held some broken branches in her hand, a canvas bag hung over her shoulder. "Gathering wood. Broken twigs. For kindling." She dropped the branches in the wheelbarrow and wiped her hands on her jean legs. "Saves money. We use a lot of firewood these days."

"What's in the bag?"

"Mushrooms. See?" She walked toward Alex and slid the bag off her shoulder. She pulled it open and Alex peered in at huge ruffled fungi. "While I was in Appalachia my friend Lois taught me about mushrooms, how to tell the poisonous ones, which ones are edible. These are chanterelles. I get mostly these and cepes. We've been having them for lunch lately, haven't you noticed?"

"Oh! The mushroom omelets!"

"And mushroom risotto. And remember that delicious mushroom soup the other day?"

"That's wonderful!" Alex marveled.

"Where are you off to?"

"Just walking."

"I was just about to take a coffee break," Ronnie said, nodding toward a thermos lying in the wheelbarrow. "If there was someplace to sit down, I'd offer you a cup. I usually sit on the edge of the wheelbarrow, but it's precarious."

Alex considered. "I know a place where we can sit down."

"Lead the way." Ronnie went for the thermos and followed Alex back to the path and down it for a quarter of a mile to the sunlit clearing.

Smiling, Alex pointed to the stump. "Seats have been provided."

Ronnie sat on the log.

"You should take the stool. It's more comfortable."

"This is fine." Ronnie unscrewed the thermos and poured steaming coffee into the lid, passed it to Alex.

Ronnie tipped the thermos and sipped from its mouth. The lip was too thick for drinking from and some coffee ran down the side of her mouth. She wiped it with her jacket sleeve.

They sat unspeaking, hearing the busy silence of the forest, Ronnie studying the landscape.

"This your place?"

Alex nodded. They fell silent again.

"Ronnie?" Tentative voice. Waited until Ronnie looked up at her again. "What you said the other day — about it being important to raise children? Did you mean that?"

"Don't say what I don't mean." God you sound like a pompous ass. She tried to soften her tone. "Why do you ask?"

"Well, you know, I mean, everyone assumes they're going to get married and have children." She glanced at Ronnie, flushed, corrected herself. "I mean, *most* women think that. And most of us do. And then the children grow up and you wonder what your life was about. You know? Was that *it*? You know? They don't really even need me anymore and they're not even twenty. They hardly notice that I'm not there."

"I helped raise some children — my aunt's — in the inner city for a while. And the kids were great, adorable, sweet, terrific — but doing that job in that place with no money is pure hell. Maybe I'm idealizing — some people say I am — but even though there's worse poverty in Africa and India and Latin America I think people there're better off than people in cities here. Maybe in any industrial country. In cities you don't just have to worry about finding food for your kids, you have to worry about everything around them, the people, the drugs, the guns, the community. . . .

"And those mothers — the ones I know and I know a lot — are incredibly brave, good. All their thoughts are for those kids, keeping them alive, getting them through, getting them grown, trying to make the kids' lives better than their own. And I imagine it's like that even if you're better off. Hard."

Alex's face softened in sympathy. "It is hard. You never know if you're doing the best thing. What works with one doesn't work with the other. They're all different and need different things. But even after you go through all that, does it matter? Suppose the children die after all that? And whether they live or die can destroy you but it makes no difference to the world. There're so many people. What does it matter that we have kids, spend our lives raising them? On the grand scale."

"So what do you think is more important?"

Alex shrugged. "Almost anything."

"Making cars? Making airplanes? Making bombs that will kill someone's kids, maybe your own?"

"Well, when you put it that way. . . ."

"What job do you think is harder than raising kids?" Ronnie persisted. Rosa and Enriqué nearly coming to blows over what to do about Tina, experimenting with drugs at fourteen. Worried talks long into the night about Raoul drifting toward a gang at thirteen, ten-year-old Téo failing in school. Enriqué threatening the belt, Rosa begging, "Ronalda, speak to them, they'll listen to you!" Talking was like trying to blow out a forest fire.

Raoul dead now, Tina in the life, the family split apart.

— You wan me to do what you do, Mama? Sit at a fucking sewing machine all day?

— You watch your mouth when you talk to your mama, girl!

— What does she make, huh? Twenty, twenty-two dollars for a whole day's work? I can make two hundred dollars in a night.

— And that *cojones* takes it all off you, whore!

— Is he any different from you? Don you take Momma's money, don she use it to feed you? Where does all Mama's money go, huh? What does she see? Has she got boots like these, clothes like mine? Hah? It goes to you and the kids, the kids and you! You're the same as him!

Enriqué pale, driven beyond endurance, arm raised.

— Out of my house you whore, you no blood of mine! And don come back! We raised you decent!

Rosa weeping. Still a chance for Téo, maybe, but he'd always be slow. Lidia and Joey all right so far. Rosa wants to move. But where can *they* be safe? They wouldn't want to live in any neighborhood that would let them in, she thought grimly.

"It *is* hard," Alex repeated as if by rote. "You're never sure what's the best thing to do."

Ronnie smiled. Not interested in this conversation, this woman, her problems. Maybe she wasn't raised to the purple like Mary and Elizabeth but her life was a far cry from Momma's or Rosa's. Nice middle-class white couple, professional husband, two kids, two cars, house in the suburbs. Country club just for Du Pont employees, she said the other night, dinner, dancing, golf links. What is it, she's suddenly worried about her image — just a housewife?

Jesus Christ, what makes any life worthwhile? Does the great arch of nature care how we plague ourselves for meaning? Love, Momma said, loving makes life worthwhile.

Alex said, "I want you to know . . . I think of you as my sister. I'm *glad* you're my sister."

Ronnie studied the ground. "Well, I'm glad to have you as a sister too," she said tightly.

They smiled at each other ruefully.

"I feel like you . . . here. Maybe not otherwise, I'm not saying I've had your experience . . . but in this house."

Ronnie questioned her with her face.

"You know, I feel like I don't belong."

"Illegitimate."

"Yes."

Ronnie thought about that. "I guess."

"I love Elizabeth and Mary. You know, I knew them when I was a baby, I loved them then, adored them really the way a baby does, you know?"

Seeing them glamorous, dashing, in their full-skirted pastel summer dresses, full of confidence, talking to senators and presidents under the green-striped tent with a mouthful of canapé and a cocktail in one hand. I remember.

"And it would be hard for them to dislodge that love," Alex continued. "But" — Alex looked straight at her — "everyone in this house has a hard time loving. It's like they grudge any sign of love, as if they feel that if they give any away they won't have anything left, as if they secretly hug what shreds of it they feel they have to themselves like they were hoarding bread in a concentration camp. . . ." She dropped her eyes, let her arms fall limp ". . . Or a house of secrets."

Ronnie just stared at her.

Alex listened as Ronnie's light tread, crackling branches and leaves, faded: I can sit for a while, I'm dressed for the hospital, I don't have to change. Nice here this hour of morning, the sun still in the east. Oh I love the morning sun flaring down through the bare branches, god's fingers whenever I see it I feel so grateful I want to cry out hallelujah well of course we call it the grandeur of god when it's just a ball of hot gases burning, sending light through the universe. But it *feels* like some beneficent presence meant just for us and it does enable us to be — us, the plants, the animals, bugs, everything. So why shouldn't we worship it? But then we say it wants this or that as if it were sentient and we knew what it wanted, as if virtue, sin, redemption, were words we knew the meanings of as if lines were clearly drawn in space. Still they exist, don't they — virtue, sin. If not redemption. Or was that St. Anne's priest right in that wonderful sermon and redemption is the power to love. You can love because you are loved, Jesus loves you. You don't have to earn his love, you just have to be. He reaches out and embraces you simply because you are. So embarrassing, weeping like that in public, people around me looking at me. Maybe they thought I was a widow or had lost a child. . . .

She shuddered.

I am NOT going to lose a child.

Strange too: I don't believe all that business, Jesus, god, any god. Sam so upset that David doesn't go regularly to temple but David can't understand how he can go on believing after the Holocaust. I don't believe either: God the Father. Who needs a father like that? Yet that time in Jerusalem. Like my eyes opening, like something ancient calling me, pulling on my very flesh, some way of life, some other way to be. I tell David I pray but I think what I call praying is just thinking. Not like a real thinker, like Elizabeth, say, not like an intellectual.

Her mind entered the state she called praying — sensation and emotion wrapped in imagination. Scenes, words, characters popped up in it like jetsam carried by a flood, but the stream moved on its own and she never reached any conclusion, never even framed a question in words. She knew only that the periods of quiet solitude she called prayer were necessary to her existence.

I am loved and I love, I know that. If love is redemption, why isn't that enough?

Elizabeth's grim face as she pounded the table, Mary sobbing frighteningly, uncontrollably, Ronnie's dark resentment, eyes haunted with rage, pain they live in so much pain, I too with no cause. Useless suffering.

What religion is about? Suffering earns you brownie points with god, phah, what kind of god is that. That book David made me read when we were first dating, what was his name? Russian. Suffering alone redeems.

Why? How?

No.

All of us walking around smiling, bobbing, working, scurrying, catching buses, inside an acute pain, a nail in the flesh a need a hope a tragic loss a something that cannot can never be made right. What good is that? The only thing we share, the pain of living and of the knowledge of death. Move from childhood is the movement into the knowledge that pain is always with us. True loss of innocence. Never did have anything to do with sex. Only thing pain is good for is to help us to connect: weep for me sister for I am sore at heart you too I weep for you I feel your pain I feel mine you feel mine you feel yours know we are together in that if nothing else whatever the cause. We weep together if alone.

Air brushed her cheek, images flickered, slight bird sounds animal movement in the forest that forgot she was present, had adjusted to her utterly still silent body. Faces flickered, wrenched and gray, bodies missing limbs, dancing, dancing. The lines on people's faces are scarifications — deep straight scars, curled shallow scars, purple-red zigzags. Each set of hands traces the scars on another face, tenderly, strokes the crippled limbs, the stumps. Music playing, we are alone, together, together alone. We are therefore we suffer. Animals march into the room in pairs like into the ark, sheep elephants gazelles dogs anteaters ants scarified but less than the humans, biting and nuzzling each other, noisy, mooing and baahing, rank familiar comforting smell of living flesh and dung, all shitting on the floor and all hungry, always hungry.

She shuddered awake. I'm going crazy. I must go away.

9

"I'm ready to go," Alex called, putting her head out the front door where they stood waiting for her. "Just have to pee! Get in the car, I'll be right there." Mary tried to share her contempt for Alex's crude speech with Elizabeth but Elizabeth was gazing into space. After a few minutes, Alex hopped in the car where the others waited. "Sorry," she offered breathlessly as the car started up. "I was out in the woods and lost track of time."

"We need to stop for milk on the way back," Mary said.

"Can't Mrs. Browning telephone the market?"

"And ask them to deliver a quart of milk?"

"Can't Aldo get it later without holding us up?" Elizabeth protested. "I have work to do."

"I'll get it, on my bike," Alex offered.

Mary shrugged. "He'd have to make an extra trip. Use more gas. You're the one always on about saving money."

"We're not *that* broke," Elizabeth said.

"You said every penny counts when I wanted the beluga."

"There's a huge difference in price between beluga and sevruga caviar, Mary."

"But that's a difference that matters."

Elizabeth exploded. "Maybe you enjoy it, but I don't like stopping at Donelan's in a limousine. Do you mind?"

Mary arched her eyebrow. "Reverse snobbery?"

Elizabeth pulled out a cigarette and lighted it.

Mary fanned herself with her purse.

Alex wondered why her offer to pick up the milk had simply been ignored.

Ronnie grimaced. Their squabbles no longer fascinated her: it was no longer a surprise to discover signs of trouble in paradise. Clearly, the idea of paradise had been a delusion. Just had to find something to fight over, those two. Tedious, she thought, then discarded this as a Mary-word. And however she sounded, she didn't want to sound like Mary. She'd rather reek of the streets.

Funny. She'd almost liked Mary the other week. Shy but curious, wanted to see how I live. The other half, the *lower* half really. She lives like practically nobody. One percent? Less? And it seems like she can't afford to keep doing it. Maybe getting ready for her future? Never happen. Ronnie chewed on the inside of her lip.

But all of them were out of kilter today, surprising after the general harmony yesterday.

Today when Stephen's eyelid fluttered, all of them saw it. Mary cried out, "Father! Father! You're awake!" The others stood watching, silent, and all seemed deep in their own thoughts on the ride home. They did not stop for milk, but Aldo drove back to town after dropping them at the house.

"I would've gotten it," Alex said reproachfully to Mary.

"We need it for lunch," she said brusquely.

They spoke little at lunch. Some geese flew over honking, and they all looked out at the sky. Mary said it was late for geese. Ronnie agreed. Elizabeth remarked that she should call Hollis. The conservatorship hadn't come through yet and perhaps he should delay it if Father was going to wake up. No one responded. They had finished eating and Elizabeth had rolled her napkin and slid it back in its ring when Alex said, "Do you all realize that Thursday is Thanksgiving?"

They looked at her blankly.

"So what," Elizabeth said.

"Oh dear. That's why Browning asked for the day off," Mary said petulantly.

"Well, what are we planning to do?" Alex pushed.

They all shrugged, muttering that they didn't know.

"Well," she began brightly, "I was thinking we could cook a Thanksgiving dinner and take it to Father in the hospital!"

This earned her looks of disgust. Everyone left the table.

Later in the afternoon, hearing the loud banging on the piano, Ronnie wondered what was up Mary's butt, then hearing the door to the study slam shut, extended the question to Elizabeth. Are they upset that he's getting better? But why are they angry with each other? She wondered if anyone would show up at cocktail hour.

But they all wandered in, Mary with a tight angry mouth, Elizabeth looking distracted, as if she were not inside her body. She made an announcement: she was having a gin and tonic; Ronnie and Alex joined her. Mary stuck with her vermouth cassis.

"So what do you all think?" Alex began tensely.

"About what?" Mary asked sullenly.

"Thanksgiving!" Alex cried. "What we were talking about at lunch!"

"*I* for one — I don't care what the rest of you do — have no intention of eating in a hospital on Thanksgiving — or any other day," Mary announced. "Absolutely not!"

"We can't take our Thanksgiving dinner into the intensive care ward, the hospital wouldn't allow it," Elizabeth cried in scorn. "Father can't eat! They're feeding him intravenously, can't you two see that? It's a stupid idea! Really, I can't understand how both of you can be so stupid!"

Alex paled. "No, no, I knew that. Really. What it was — I was counting on his being awake by Thursday. And us having a celebration. I guess I'll have to go home after all," she added faintly.

"What, it's either dinner in the hospital or dinner in Newark," Ronnie laughed, "and Newark is worse? You're having such a wonderful time here?"

"It's just that my kids keep phoning, they're clamoring for me to come home — and David's getting antsy too, I've been away so long. So I told them we were going to celebrate Father's waking up. You see, I'm sure he'll be awake by then. I know it."

Mary drew a sharp breath.

Unheeding, Alex continued, "All along I've been telling them that I have to stay here, that it's vital to Father's well-being that we all visit him every day. I believe it is." She turned and glanced at each of them. "But I can't explain not coming home for Thanksgiving if we don't spend it with Father. It's such a joyful holiday in our house. The kids wouldn't understand. Or David."

"And you don't want to go home," Ronnie concluded. So was there trouble in that little middle-class heaven too? Didn't sound it, she always made things sound perfectly ordinary, perfectly happy. Build a heaven in hell's despite and it turns into hell. Wonderful irony.

Alex's face twisted. "It's not that . . . I can't explain . . . I feel . . . There's so much going on inside me these days. I need to let it happen and it won't happen if I go home, it will stop. And I need something . . . it feels as if something terrible will happen if I leave."

"To you? To your father? To your kids?" Ronnie asked with intense curiosity.

"To me."

"Thanksgiving was never one of my favorite holidays. Actually I hate all holidays except Mardi Gras," Mary said, "and that only in the old days." She grimaced. "Too . . . déclassé now."

"I just hate them all," Elizabeth said dourly. She and Mary looked at each other.

"I love Thanksgiving," Alex said, her voice very soft, "the family gets together. . . ."

"Precisely," Elizabeth muttered.

God how I hate Thanksgiving: Mary let in the thought she'd been shutting out all day. All the way out to Pound Ridge to Martin's house, sitting there eating a dried-up turkey with Marguerite so supercilious and bored-looking, those white eyelashes of hers how I hate them wouldn't you think her mother would have taught her to use mascara? and those brats, and Bertie acting like a silly fool, Marie-Laure sulking. No one else invites me anymore. Have to go to Martin's or sit alone in my apartment with no maid to cook for me. I couldn't go to a restaurant alone.

Call someone to escort me: Larry? Oh, it's too late. Everyone has plans by now.

"My children are dying to have me come, of course," she said, "but I must confess I find it trying being around babies — my grandchildren are still small. And Martin lives all the way out in the suburbs, such an awful trip." Have to beg him to drive all the way to the airport to pick me up. He hates doing chores, expects Marguerite to do everything for him. Just like his father. He'd do it, but with that martyred air, Yes Mother, get in the car Mother. Horrible. Or he'd send Bertie, who drives like a maniac.

Thanksgiving in Washington, Elizabeth thought with a sinking heart. Always welcome at the Bernsteins' but there's limited pleasure in sitting at the dinner table of somebody who works for you, everybody so excessively polite you could die from facecrack. Year the secretary invited me, now that was worthwhile. No invitation this year: wonder why. Am I on my way out? Could go to the Ethiopian restaurant in Georgetown. Or stay home, eat a frozen dinner. Could do that here. Save a trip.

"Actually, I don't want to break off my work at this point," Elizabeth said self-importantly. "I'd prefer to stay here and maintain the continuity. And of course, if Father is about to wake up, it's vital to be here," she added, looking at Alex.

I could have dinner with Rosa, Ronnie thought, she invited me last month. I forgot all about it. I have to call her, she's shy about calling here. Would be good to see them all. But Rosa has no room for me to sleep now the kids are grown. Lidia sleeps on a futon as it is. I have no place to stay. But I bet Linda'd let me sleep on her couch. She'd welcome me. If she's there. Maybe she'll go home too. Anyway, I could go, use her pad. Wouldn't want to be stuck here alone. Or with them if Alex left.

Alex's eyes were damp. "I want to stay with you," she said.

Three pairs of eyes met hers, held.

After a long silence, Mary said vaguely, "I suppose we could do something. Have a turkey or . . ." She gasped. "But I gave Teresa the day off too!" she recalled.

Elizabeth shrugged. "So we'll go out. What's the difference?"

"Restaurants are horrible on Thanksgiving!" Mary exclaimed petulantly. "Besides, don't you think it's a little late to get a reservation at one of the few decent restaurants around here?"

"Why don't *we* cook?" Alex asked, her voice brightening.

"That would be nice," Mary agreed, "but I can't cook. I *can* make tea."

"Neither can I," Elizabeth said. "But I'm willing to peel vegetables if someone gives me directions."

"Tea and peeled vegetables for dinner!" Ronnie brayed. "Wonderful! Well, hell, I can make beans and rice for dessert."

They all laughed. Together. The tension loosened.

So that was what it was all about: Thanksgiving.

Only Alex was biting her lip. "I guess I'll have to lie and *tell* them we're spending the day with Father."

Drawing up the menu proved fertile ground for disagreement.

"Quenelles for *Thanksgiving*, Mary! Only you would want that!" Alex laughed. "And I don't know how to make them."

"Beans and rice? Beans and rice? What *is* that? Yes, I know it's Mexican, but do you eat it *with* the turkey, *instead of* the turkey, or *after* the turkey? I mean, why do we have to have that at all?"

"Because I want it," Ronnie said. "We have to honor my traditions too. Like pricking our fingers and mingling our blood," she smiled.

Mary shuddered. "Suppose one of us had AIDS!"

"Well, if one of us does, it isn't likely to be Ronnie," Elizabeth quipped.

After much discussion, they decided on a traditional turkey with stuffing and cranberry sauce, guacamole to start, Mexican beans and rice, Mary's white puree, a salad, and a pumpkin pie from Alex. It was agreed that all of them together would market, that Alex and Ronnie would cook and Elizabeth and Mary would clean up, not just after the meal but after each stage of preparation — of the cranberry sauce, the pumpkin pie, the giblet stuffing. Mary was not enthusiastic about this idea, but since she had quashed eating in a restaurant, she had little choice.

They were high, even a touch giggly on the day itself, driving back from the hospital (no eye flutters that day), eager to get into action in the kitchen. Mary turned up the volume on the old stereo in the playroom so they could hear it in the kitchen and took charge of putting on records. The sisters commented on each selection — all of *The Well-Tempered Clav-*

ichord, played by Artur Schnabel ("Bor*ing,*" Ronnie yelled; Mary thought that set must date back to her mother's day); the Mozart Piano Concerto K. 467 ("Father must have seen *Elvira Madigan,*" Mary said sarcastically); two Beethoven piano sonatas ("Why do you think he bought those?"); Frank Sinatra ("Yuck," cried Ronnie, who also decided that Stephen had liked Ella Fitzgerald because she sang white bread music). Wayne Newton was unanimously booed off the turntable. "It's what he has," Mary apologized.

But when she put on some fifties big band records, Alex dropped the basting spoon and Ronnie stopped mashing avocado and they began to dance together in the modern style, without touching their partner. Elizabeth stopped wiping the stove and Mary dropped the dinner forks and they tried to fox-trot. But they quarreled almost immediately over who would lead.

"It isn't that I don't want to," Elizabeth expostulated, "I don't know how!"

"Well, neither do I!"

"I always had a problem dancing," Elizabeth recalled. "Boys always led and I never liked the way they did it. But I don't know how to lead."

Finally, "Let's dance their way," Mary suggested, and they did, all four of them dancing in a circle, alone yet together.

They did not stop until the record did, and began again when Mary put on another big band record. When that ended they were out of breath and returned to their chores. Then from the playroom, Mary cried out in pleasure, and put on Peggy Lee singing "Is That All There Is." They all stopped what they were doing, and simply listened.

Is that all there is,
Is that all there is,
If that's all there is, my friend,
Then let's keep dancing,
Let's break out the booze
And have a ball
If that's all
There is.

When it was over, "Play it again," they urged Mary. She put it on and returned to the kitchen, and the four sisters held each other around the waist and swayed with the music.

With the turkey roasting, the vegetables peeled, the table set, and the mess cleaned up as much as it could be, they decided to go for a walk. They put on heavy rough coats and wellies — there had been rain that morning and the ground was muddy — and headed for the woods. They spoke little, walking sometimes in single file, sometimes in pairs, sometimes in a row. Alex seemed to be in the lead and she headed straight for her cathedral, where they stood looking at the light seeping through the branches, the sun low in the western sky, wan and weak at this hour, lighting the cathedral with a soft hazy glow. When Alex stopped, they all did. She stood in silence, her arms akimbo, head high, looking straight ahead, like a priestess about to lead a ceremony.

"Today is a day for giving thanks," she said, "to whatever for whatever. I think it's important to take time to give thanks you know, to remember the good things in our lives that we forget about because they're familiar, you know like liking the way your body smells or the color of your eyes or the sound of your own voice or the way your living room looks in the afternoon light. I don't mean we should thank some big deal in the sky or anything, try to bribe some god by thanking him so he won't hurt us tomorrow, I don't mean we should burn innards or anything. But for ourselves. For what we have been given. For any beauty in our lives. You know?" she appealed to them. "Not in humility to something, but in gratitude." She gazed at them uncertainly. "Well," she shouted, "I like to do it." She looked up and out into the forest.

Elizabeth watched her, a sarcastic look on her face. Thanks for the memories? I used to hang out here too in the summers, I remember that stump. Came here when I couldn't bear things. Even then I didn't cry. Past it. Stone, I was. Wanted to be stone entirely, wanted not to feel ever again. A form of death.

Still, she thought, I'm alive. Not all of me, but some. Is that something to be grateful for? Would I rather be dead? I guess not — I didn't drive a car into a tree, didn't fill those prescriptions for pills and I'm not choosing to die at this moment anyway. Not really choosing to be alive either: that would mean letting myself feel it all, go back into it. Spent my life getting out. Too hard.

And when you think about it, I haven't done all that badly. Considering. Figure I'm a creature deformed, not from birth but from childhood handling. What can such a creature expect? I have a life that lets me use my mind the way I need to. That's the most important thing. Lucky I was born into an age when I wasn't married off at fourteen to spawn a brood of sniveling kids. And I live pretty well. I have my own apartment, my car, books and clothes and food I like. Which is more than about 90 percent of the human race presently living has. That's sheer luck too: luck of the draw of birth: century, continent, nation, section, sex, color, socioeconomic sector.

She paused. I'm glad I had Clare, however I had him for however long. But is that all there is, all I'm going to have now he's gone, now I'm utterly alone? I don't even have a friend. Even Mary has friends. Of a sort. She raised her head and looked around at her. The sisters stood communing with themselves. A wave of feeling surprised her: maybe I have them, she thought wonderingly.

Why are we letting Alex tell us what to do, Mary wondered, gazing unseeingly at trees. Who the hell does she think she is, a druid priestess or something? What do *I* have to give thanks for? Don's dead, I'm broke. My kids? I suppose I'm glad they're healthy, well-off, educated, all those things you're supposed to be happy about. I wish I liked them more. Aren't they supposed to be a joy to you in your old age? Not that I'm old of course.

Course I'm no joy to Father either. But that's different. That's *his* fault. I always loved him.

Her eyes dampened.

She looked up at the tallest branches of the trees, at the evergreens beyond this grove, fragrant and green. But oh, I am glad I had Don, that experience, at least once in my life if that's all I'm allowed, to feel that kind of love swelling the heart making it into a huge hot center warming the entire world, making it radiant. I loved the city because he was in it even when he was downtown and I wasn't going to see him that day. I loved certain songs because he whistled them, and all men because he was a

man, and hated any woman who might take him away from me. I loved
watching him eat, loved thinking about the food that went into his mouth,
nourishing him, enriching him, making him strong, and when he looked
up at me watching and broke into a smile I wanted to throw myself down
on the floor before him, worship, with my body I thee worship, oh Don, I
did. I even loved myself, loved my pale green silk suit, my soft heavy body,
my dark hair like a glowing halo he said, because he loved them. I loved
life because it let that happen — let me know what it felt to love and
miracle of miracles — let him love me back. How many have that?

The trees blurred.

But is that all there is?

Christ, Alex must be some kind of religious freak. And look at them —
Elizabeth has her head bowed and Mary is gazing up at the treetops with
tears in her eyes as if she were having an orgasmic experience with a god!
She probably is, knowing her. Although she's the kind of little seductress
who never has an orgasm in her life. Maybe they were taken to church as
little girls, are pious little goody-goodies at heart. Rosa always trying to get
me to go with them, her and the kids, Enriqué hardly went. Momma went
to St. Joseph's a few times, stopped. All those Irish faces staring at her.
Shee-it. I will be goddamned if I bow my head to any Big Daddy or even
any Big Mommy for that matter. Everyone I ever loved betrayed me, starting with Momma. Never had even one decent lover: every one of them let
me down. Even Julieta, and she was a sweetie, a real sweetie. She didn't
mean to. But Sarah, that was the worst blow. Liar, cheat, hypocrite. Tell me
you'll love me forever Ronnie and two weeks later she's shacking up with
somebody else. Women. As bad as men.

The only person I'm grateful to is myself. Whatever I am, I made
myself, did it all myself, turned a little terrified *chicana* on the run awed by
the Anglo world by Him into a self-possessed professional woman. Well
almost. No Big Momma or Big Poppa helped me. Rosa of course. And
Carrie Jenkins. But she said doing that was her own reward, she said
helping me come alive mentally kept her alive emotionally, my flowering
was her flowering, she said, kept her from entirely burning out as a
teacher. Rosa too whenever I thank her, she says I helped her as much as
she helped me. I couldn't save Raoul though, or Tina. But maybe Tina will

be all right someday, being a hooker isn't the end of life. Unless she gets AIDS, or killed. Or can't get off crack. Or gets pregnant.

Christ. It's all unbearable.

Still, I'm okay. Is it selfish to feel that?

I guess I'm thankful for whatever it is about our genes that makes us feel that way. Act that way. Grateful there are Rosas and Carries in the world. I'll try to be like them myself. Not sure I have the gift. Selfish. Seems to run in my family. Hallelujah, I've found common ground with my sisters! She smiled.

Alex closed her eyes, tried to feel the surround through her pores, smell it, hear it, merge with it. Her body trembled with images — Stevie at six, the skin of his cheeks fine as satin, how she loved to caress him. His brown eyes bigger then, trusting, adoring, Mommy, he called me then. Melly at eight, skinny long-legged, tearing out the door with her hockey stick, confident she would win. At ten, in her nightgown after her bath, glowing pink cheeks, her hair curled up and damp, hands over her ears. No Mommy, I don't want to hear about that stuff, we heard about it in Scouts, I have a book about it, I'll read it when I want to! Still a baby, not ready to hear about menstruation but the next year she was menstruating. Shocked she was, hated it. I no help.

Her hands ached with emptiness of them, her hands remembered wanting to hold them keep them safe forever. So vulnerable. But not hers any longer. Stevie still that translucent skin but dark hard little hairs beginning to poke through it, standing in the doorway laughing at her as she rapped out a series of commands about his behavior at the party; Melly, curled on the chintz-skirted window seat in her bedroom, her face downcast and thoughtful, upset about the plight of a school chum. Wouldn't tell me what happened to the girl. Could have been anything — pregnancy, rape, her father beat her, her mother an alcoholic, who knows? Wouldn't say, tried to work things out herself. Of course I never tell *her* anything serious either. Like my mother. Generations of silence.

I can't bear letting them go.

Love for them mixed with terror, knowing the vulnerability of flesh and spirit, seared her heart.

But they have left me. Are lost to me.

Then David stepped in and smiled at her and reached out his arms and she stepped into them and rested her head on his chest. Samuel and Lilian stood behind him, hovering, ready to protect him from any danger. All this she had, this richness, this connection, but it could be snatched away tomorrow. She could lose it. . . .

Then Mother smiled from across the room, looking like a woman never touched by mystery or wonder, like some sweet little middle-aged woman who was a secretary all her life, who had a happy marriage, a good daughter, grandchildren, a woman who has fulfilled all she set out to become. Yet she is full of mystery and she stands silent. I hate that. I hate her for that.

Terror. That's what Thanksgiving's really about, she decided, superstition. So you can thank fate: I'm grateful, I'm grateful! Look, I'm *saying* I'm grateful so don't take it away, take them away. Let me go on having them. Yet every minute someone died and left someone and if they live they're always changing. Melly gazing at her with those distant eyes (*who are you?*); Stevie treating her as if she was irrelevant. When once upon a time, she had been the sun that lighted their mornings, they stretched their little arms out to her from their cribs like tree branches to sunlight, their bodies reached to her like tides to the moon. Her love and care had been everything to them, kept them alive. When did that change?

And she too, changing. Her head on David's chest, his arms around her no longer made her feel safe, why was that? She no longer felt endangered, she felt strong. And David seemed different too, why was that? Always so steady, a stalwart bolster, with Sam and Lilian behind him. But they were old now, Sam a bit feeble since his stroke, Lilian worn out taking care of him those years. Can't protect David so much anymore. Need him now. And he didn't need support so much, he was stronger too, like her. But also weaker. Just a man, a human being, not a pillar. Sweet David.

And while the sunrise went on being glorious, sunset a moment when the world stood still, trees leafing, unleafing, gardens blooming and drying up, people being born and dying, the suffering went on and on. Eternally endures, only that endures. Two kinds of pain: that caused by nature and that caused by man. The first eternal. But not the second. So there was something worth doing. The only thing worth doing: ease the pain that could be eased: but how? A stupid woman like me.

Alex opened her eyes. The others were looking at her. No one spoke or moved for a moment, then they all turned and started back to the house. Without a word, without any sudden motion, they fell into a row and someone — could it really have been Ronnie? — put her arm around Alex, who embraced her and put her arm around Elizabeth, who embraced her and put her arm around Mary, who burst into song:

> Four little maids from school are we,
> Pert as a schoolgirl well can be,
> Filled to the brim with girlish glee
> Four little maids from school. . . .

The others did not know the lyrics, but chimed in on the refrain, "Four little maids from school," as Mary sang on. Laughing they went back to the house where they were greeted by the wonderful aroma of roasting turkey ("So much better than the taste," Elizabeth pointed out). Dinner preparations began in earnest, even the non-cooks pressed into service ("Mary, anyone can peel potatoes," Alex insisted, and Ronnie ordered Elizabeth to stir, stir, stir, that's all, stirring will reduce it). They were hungry and started to eat the guacamole in the kitchen as they worked, but when Mary heard the turkey had another hour to go, she insisted they abandon the kitchen and have a civilized cocktail hour in the sitting room.

Alex put the food on a low heat or in a warming oven, Ronnie built a fire, Mary carried the guacamole and corn chips into the sitting room, Elizabeth poured the wine. They all had wine this evening. They sat around the fire, glowing with pleasure in themselves.

Elizabeth leaned back in her chair, her glass in one hand, a cigarette in the other. "You know my first memory of this house? I was four, wearing a little white dress with a full skirt and a floppy white hat that fell down over my eyes, and a lot of people were here — I don't know who, I don't know what the occasion was. I remember what I was wearing because there's a photograph of me that day, with Father and Aunt Pru and Uncle Samuel behind me. And whoever it was, they all made a fuss over me, said how cute I was, smiled at me, laughed at me. I don't know why. Maybe I looked funny in the hat. But for years afterwards I remembered that day with joy. I kept waiting for it to happen again. It never did."

"I remember Mama taking me into the pool," Mary said in a soft thick voice. "I was about four, too. And she held me and moved her arms, showing me how to swim." She sipped her drink.

"And?" Elizabeth prompted her.

She shrugged. "Well, it's just that Mama never held me like that before. The day was radiated with joy for me." She caught Elizabeth's eye and grimaced. "Yes, I waited for it to happen again. For years. It didn't."

Alex remembered Father bringing home a puppy and saying his name was Charlie because he had a little dark mark over his mouth like Charlie Chaplin's mustache. And the puppy was so little he fit in the crook between Alex's head and shoulder, and sat there shaking while Alex stroked him, sensing his terror, trying to calm him. And Father watched her smiling, with love.

No, she admitted under questioning, she did not recall any other occasion on which Father had smiled at her with love. But surely if there was one occasion, there were others? At which Elizabeth announced with some portentousness that to them that had would be given. Always.

They had to prod Ronnie to admit that she had ever had a happy experience in this house, prod her with NEVER NEVER NEVER RONNIE?, to the point of laughter, until she dredged up something. She always helped Momma plant the peppers and cucumbers and lettuces and tomatoes — of course, she was just a baby and probably not really any help. Then one spring when she was about seven, she begged Momma for a garden of her own where she could grow flowers. And Momma didn't say yes or no, but she had Simpson — the head gardener then — dig up a patch about four by three and she bought some seeds — zinnias, marigolds, cosmos, and cornflowers, Ronnie remembered. And she gave the plot and the seeds to Ronnie. Ronnie read the directions and planted them all by herself and watered them every day and waited in great anxiety for them to sprout, afraid to weed them, unsure of what was weed, what flower. Only some of the seeds came up but when there were a few dozen blossoms, she picked them and carried them indoors.

"These are for you, Momma," she said, full of self-importance at being able to give her mother something. And Momma exclaimed at their beauty, their health, and kissed Ronnie and put the flowers in a glass with water on the kitchen table.

Yes, it happened again. Every year after that. But it was never as wonderful as that first time, when it was a miracle.

The discussion at the dinner table grew more animated with more wine. Even Mary had to admit there was a laughable amount of white food on the menu — turkey, rice, and a puree of potatoes, leeks, celeriac, and turnips. Mary decided beans were all right despite their redness. "They're a different red from meat. It's blood that's appalling," she concluded. By the end of the meal, they were all pink-faced with heat and food and wine and were talking together without fighting.

Then the telephone rang.

It was Edna Thompson. "Ms. Upton, you asked me to let you know if your father became more responsive. Well, I think he's waking up. He's sleeping right now, but he was awake for a while earlier and he was moving his left hand. You and your sisters have a real reason for Thanksgiving now!"

Elizabeth returned to the dining room. She stood at the head of the table and faced them: "Father's coming to."

They merely stared at her. Mary threw down her napkin. "Do we really have to clean up this mess? Can't we leave it for Browning to do tomorrow?"

"Let's," Elizabeth agreed tiredly.

Neither Alex nor Ronnie argued. They picked up their wine glasses and went into the sitting room. The fire was nearly dead.

"You feel like building that fire up again, Ron?" Elizabeth asked.

"Not really."

They sat in silence.

"What did you tell her?" Mary asked after a while.

"That we'd be in tomorrow at the usual time."

"So what does this mean to us?" Ronnie mused. "Each of us. Because it probably means something different to each of us."

"Depends. If he recovers completely. . . ." Elizabeth stopped. "Why then, we go back to where we came from and go on with our lives."

"But we're changed," Alex said. "We have each other now."

Elizabeth looked at Alex's thin clean profile, noble in the soft lamplight. "Yes. We do," she said softly.

Elizabeth loves me!

"Does that include me?" Mary asked in a tremulous voice.

Elizabeth looked at her intensely. "Of course, poor Mary."

Mary's mouth trembled, her eyes looked damp. "I feel . . . it's almost as if . . . we can't have each other *and* him. I don't know why I feel that."

"As he recovers — we dwindle," Ronnie said, puzzled.

"But maybe he won't recover completely," Alex said matter-of-factly, a tone none of them was used to in her. "You know, he was paralyzed on one side, he may remain so. And the part of the brain that controls his right side and language functions has sustained permanent damage. He probably won't be able to speak."

They all gazed at her in shock.

"I've been taking courses for the last few years — nothing very advanced, just basic medical knowledge. I wanted to help Lilian — my mother-in-law — after Sam had his stroke. And I thought it might help in my volunteer work," she explained.

"Well, you sound very . . . authoritative," Elizabeth said.

"Really?" She turned pink, trying not to smile in her delight.

"So what are the possibilities?" Elizabeth asked her.

Elizabeth asked me!

She ticked them off on her fingers. "He could recover completely, but the fact that he's been in a coma for almost three weeks makes that unlikely. He could regain the use of his left hand and leg and recover some function in his right side. Then he would probably go to a rehab center for therapy. But it's unlikely they would accept him if he remains totally paralyzed on his right side and without speech. So he would have to go to a nursing home for full-time care."

"Father in a nursing home!" Mary cried. "No!"

"He'd hate that," Elizabeth muttered.

"Yes. He'd probably die soon," Alex said calmly. Not adding: if that's what you want.

"We could take care of him," Ronnie said, "the way I took care of Momma. A nurse came once a day and I did everything else."

"That could mean taking care of him for years," Elizabeth said.

Silence.

"I could give up my apartment in New York," Mary offered finally. "I could move up here permanently."

"I'm not willing to give up the rest of my life to him," Ronnie said.

"Nor I," said Elizabeth.

"No," said Alex vaguely.

"Do you really want to spend years of your life taking care of a sick bitter old man? — because he will be bitter, you can be sure of that, Mare," Elizabeth said.

Mary considered.

Elizabeth stood up. "We can't decide anything tonight, we don't know what shape he's in. I'm going to bed."

Mary rose then and walked over to Elizabeth and held out her arms. Elizabeth stiffened, but allowed Mary to embrace her, and even put her hand up and patted her sister on the back. Mary warmly kissed her cheek, Elizabeth lightly kissed Mary's.

Faint kiss.

Alex hovered near them. Elizabeth saw her and opened her arm and Alex walked into it and embraced them both. The three of them stood that way for a moment, then Alex yelled, "Oh hell, come on, Ronnie!"

But Ronnie stood stiffly aside until Elizabeth reached out and grabbed her. Then Ronnie melted in and the four of them stood together in an embrace. Ronnie's eyes closed as if she were praying.

Part II

The Father

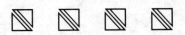

10

A sober Dr. Stamp met them Friday morning. "I hear Nurse Thompson called you," he said. "I have to admit that I was hoping he'd just drift off." He was leading them to Stephen's room in the ICU when he stopped. "Of course, life is life, after all. But Mr. Upton has clearly suffered a serious permanent deficit. You must be prepared for that. He isn't his old self. But he *is* awake, alive."

They looked at him, said nothing. He could not name what he felt in them, something strange, powerful, like the high tension you picked up in parents with desperately ill small children, in young lovers, newlyweds, people with intense connections, connections they feel are crucial to their survival. Were they that attached to him? At *their* ages, his age? Amazing. Whatever it was, it was something he decidedly did not want to be part of. He was a scientist, emotions were not his terrain. He stopped again and waved them ahead of him into the room. "I'll let you welcome him back to life alone," he said and returned down the hall.

Stephen was sitting up in bed. His eyes, huge and ice-cold, stared at them, took in the four of them, together. They froze in the doorway. Mary knew he *saw*.

Elizabeth stepped forward. "Hello, Father." She walked to him, bent and kissed his forehead.

Mary stepped forward, a nervous smile playing on her lips. "Oh, welcome back to life, Father," she gushed, "we're so glad you're awake! We've been coming every day ever since it happened, visiting you loyally, hoping for this moment!" She rushed to him, sat beside him on the bed, kissed his forehead, ruffled his hair, took his hand. "How do you feel?"

He frowned, gesturing with his left hand, and Mary dropped his right one and stood up. "Oh, I'm so sorry, Father, of course, that must be uncomfortable!"

He was staring at Alex and Ronnie, who remained where they were. Finally, Alex approached him shyly.

"Hello, Father, it's Alex. How are you?" She bent and kissed his forehead.

He stared at Ronnie. She nodded at him. "How ar'ya feeling?"

Was he glowering, or was that expression normal for someone in his condition?

Mary fussed with his bedcovers, folding the top sheet more neatly, smoothing it out. She cried out, "Oh, you need more water, poor baby!" and filled his glass. She looked wildly around for something else to do. "You haven't seen the flowers, Father, they don't allow them in here, but *thousands* of people have sent flowers, wonderful flowers! The president sent a huge bouquet, and the secretary of state, and" — she turned to Elizabeth — "who else, Lizzie?"

Elizabeth recited the list of names in strict order of protocol, as if she had memorized it.

"We sent them to other people, dear, people who don't get flowers, they don't allow them in intensive care you know. But as soon as they move you, we'll bring flowers to cheer you up, so that when you wake up the first thing you'll see are fresh flowers!"

He kept glowering.

"Can you talk, Father?" Elizabeth asked in a businesslike tone.

He glowered.

"If you can't, for the time being maybe we could set up a signal system. You could move your left hand once for yes, twice for no. Or nod your head. You can nod your head? Is there anything you'd like us to do?"

He did not move.

"Are you in any pain?" Alex asked timidly.

He shook his head from side to side.

"Are you happy to see us?" Mary whispered, an edge of whine in her voice.

No response.

"Would you like me to leave?" Ronnie asked coldly.

He glared directly at her.

"I'm outa here," she said to the others, and turned and left the room.

"Is that better, Father?" Mary pleaded.

The doctor knocked on the door frame and entered smiling. "Well, sir, how do you feel? Your lovely daughters have been in here every day for the last three weeks, good to see that, some coma patients get abandoned, a shame . . . helps a patient recover, I believe," he told Mary. "Studies seem to suggest that having visitors, being talked to, assist recovery even if the patient seems unaware." He turned to Stephen. "So you can thank your daughters for at least part of your recovery."

Stephen glared at him.

He moved to Stephen, and called to the nurse for information on pulse and blood pressure. The nurse ran in, crowding the small room, and Elizabeth said, "We'll wait outside, Dr. Stamp." She bent to kiss Stephen's head again. "Good-bye, Father, we'll be back tomorrow and if you can think of anything you want, figure out some way to tell us, okay?" she smiled.

Dutifully, Mary, then Alex, bent to kiss his forehead and say good-bye.

They ate lunch in a state of shock, hardly able to speak or look at each other, and after lunch, they avoided even the sight of each other, each going her own way as if the others did not exist. Elizabeth and Ronnie went to work in their studies; Alex went off on her bicycle; Mary had Aldo drive her to Concord and bought an exercise tape. She brought it back and played it on the VCR in the old playroom, exercising until she was soaked. Then she bathed and dressed for dinner and opened the piano and played for several hours. She was starting to sound pretty good, Ronnie noticed. Elizabeth didn't even slam her study door.

His study door.

Ronnie lay on her bed trying to read a pamphlet on Thallophyta, but she kept seeing the white ICU room, Stephen's face, her sisters' backs stiff with shock. One thing for Him to look that way at me — He never saw me as a daughter, never by glance, word, or deed acknowledged I was the fruit of His filthy sperm. Momma never spilled out the past until she was dying. Course I never asked till then. How she didn't realize she was pregnant until after Stephen had gone back to New York. How she pondered about what to do, a single woman, a servant without money, only a few hundred dollars she'd managed to save living rent-free in the Lincoln house. Abortion illegal then, but she had kept her Latino friends in Boston from her days cleaning offices, she still saw them on her days off, some of them married and with large families, working at home, some women who like her had risen and now cleaned houses instead of offices and so also had days off during the week instead of at weekends. They knew people who would do it for a couple of hundred dollars. She could get to Boston easily enough — she took the bus and then the T — amazing how she found her way around, illiterate as she was — and went to their houses and had tea and pastries. So she could get to an abortionist. But would she be able to come back the same day? Suppose she was sick, bleeding? Alone here except for Simpson. But the day maid might help her if she needed it.

It never occurred to her to tell him. He was the seigneur, such things not his problem.

She was twenty-eight years old, old for a Mexican woman to be single, childless. Wouldn't tell me if she was a virgin when she came here, refused, set her mouth. She loved Stephen, admired him profoundly, the rich powerful Anglo, one of the gods who ran the world. And who seemed to care about her. A relation such as they had would never happen to her again. She knew it. On the other hand, if she had the baby, he might well just throw her out.

"But I would have the little one, eh, Ronnie? I would have you. And no matter what, I can always work. And my *amigas,* one has a spare room, I could live there, work. So that was good."

She decided to go ahead and have the baby. Even though Upton groceries were mainly ordered over the telephone, word must have gotten out. What the local shopkeepers thought about the Upton housekeeper having a bulging belly, Noradia didn't know. Maybe thought Simpson was the father, or some guy she shacked up with in Boston on her day off.

Shocking, but no more than you can expect from people like that. Maybe some of them thought she had a husband somewhere. Her accent was so thick, they didn't try to hold long conversations with her. She went to Ronald Wanger, an elderly, kindly local GP long dead now, who didn't press for a father's name, didn't act as if she was scum. Named me after him. Better than after Him.

Stephen knew nothing. Even after He came up a few days before the July Fourth party, He didn't know. Noradia was thin again, kept the baby in the kitchen or her bedroom on the third floor in which he never set foot. Until the day He heard wailing, the day before the big party. Elizabeth and Mary already here, Pru and Samuel too, a slew of temporary servants around the house. Hit the intercom, summoned Noradia, thundered: there's a baby in this house! Whose! Whoever it is, I want her out of here! This house is not a baby-sitting agency!

"*Sí*, Cabot," she said, eyes down. "Is mine, Cabot."

Dumbfounded. Stared at her.

She kept looking down.

Finally: "When was it born?"

She looked up. "April, Cabot."

He counted back. "I see." He considered. "Boy?" Was there hope in His voice? Would it have been different if I was a boy?

"Is *niña, señor*. Girl. I try to keep quiet, *señor*." Did the fact that she was begging filter into her tone?

He nodded. "All right, Noradia. See that you do."

End of subject. It was never brought up again. He never asked to see me, never held me, and even when I was walking around, never looked at me. She didn't mind. She was so grateful that He let us stay, didn't throw us out, that He could not offend her. He must have looked at me once or twice when she wasn't around. Didn't like what He saw, presumably. Little brown baby with blue eyes and black hair.

So hardly surprising that He stared at me with malevolence. But the hatred He directed at His legitimate daughters! *Why*, she wondered, *why*? What had they ever done to Him, how could they have let Him down, betrayed Him, to deserve such hate? And why were they all so terrified of him? Because they were. Even Elizabeth!

*   *   *

By cocktail hour, the sisters had calmed but were irritable.

Mary attacked Ronnie for drinking cola — "You're an ecologist! What's the matter with you? How can you drink that awful stuff? Don't you know it can rot metal? You have to take care of yourself!"

In response, Elizabeth sneered at Mary's drinking habits: "Look at who's talking! The one who always has to have something sweet, just like a baby!"

Mary retorted, "At least I take the risk of imbibing alcohol. I don't sit there like a dried-up prune so terrified of losing control that I drink only water! And expensive water to boot! If you're going to drink water, why don't you take it from the tap? Talk about saving pennies!"

Later, when Ronnie bummed a cigarette from Elizabeth, Mary protested, "You must be a great environmentalist! How can you take up such a filthy disgusting habit!"

Even Alex seemed edgy and frequently stood up, moved about the room, poured herself more wine, looked out the window, sat down again. Finally she burst out, "Oh, Ronnie, build a fire, will you!" as if, without a fire, they would all perish.

Mary complained it was too hot for a fire, it was hot in here tonight, but Ronnie got up and crouched before the hearth. She leaned back on her heels. "Well, which is it? Fire or no?"

"FIRE!" Alex shouted. "Turn the damn heat down if you're too hot!"

Mary flinched, fell silent.

Ronnie piled up newspaper and kindling, set them alight, laid on a few small logs. When the fire flamed high, she stood up, wiped off her hands on the sides of her jeans, and turned around. "What in hell is the matter with all of you?"

Mary burst into tears. Elizabeth gazed into space. Alex looked at the floor and chewed her lower lip. "The old man really has you all corralled, doesn't he?"

"It was a shock," Elizabeth said.

"What? His recovering?"

"The way he looked."

"Fuck that. This ain't worry. You were terrified in there. You're still terrified. All of you. Even before we went in there, you were quaking."

"We were tense. Not knowing what we'd find," Mary said in a stiff formal voice edged with exasperation at Ronnie's denseness.

"*You* were terrified too," Alex accused Ronnie.

"I was not!" Ronnie yelled, but stiffened, trying to remember. "I don't think I was," she added.

"Why! Why, why, why!" Alex exploded. "I haven't seen him in eighteen years but he's my father, why should I be terrified!"

"Maybe because we betrayed him," Mary said.

They all stared at her. "How?" Alex cried.

"By making friends with each other. He knew it, he knew it the minute he looked at us."

"We're not allowed to make friends . . . ?" Ronnie wondered.

"No, of course not! Don't you see! He never allowed it." She put her head in her hands and moaned, a long deep moan of dread.

Elizabeth swung her head toward Mary. "You're right," she said slowly. "He set us against each other. Comparing us. He'd castigate me for not being charming and lovable like you. . . ."

Head in her hands, Mary seemed indifferent to what Elizabeth was saying.

"And he told you you were stupid — unlike me," Elizabeth continued. "My mother did the same thing. Always setting me up against you, then later, against Alex. I was either better or worse."

"Me! I was just a baby!"

Elizabeth shrugged. "Didn't matter."

"Why?" Ronnie asked in wonder.

They looked at each other. Elizabeth shrugged.

Mary raised her pale face; it looked lined, almost gray. "I don't know about your mother. But *he* did it because he had to be the *one*," she said. "Not just our center but the only one we had. If we liked each other, we might band together, might rebel against him, ally against him. He had to keep us at war with each other."

They considered that.

"That's very smart, Mary," Elizabeth said in a low voice. "Very smart."

It was a measure of Mary's distraction that she said dismissively, "Oh, about some things."

Ronnie's voice asked anxiously, "Do you think it was me? Me being there that set him off? That he thought we were together — friends?"

"That didn't help," Mary said dryly.

"And here I was saying we should take care of the old bastard so he shouldn't have to go to a nursing home," she mused.

Alex shuddered.

Ronnie took one of Elizabeth's cigarettes without asking. She glanced at Mary. "Can't help it. I'll stop as soon as I leave here. Promise."

They watched the fire.

"It's good to recognize that, though," Elizabeth said thoughtfully. "It changes things somehow." She looked at them. "Affects the way I feel about you all."

"Yes. When we're at each other's throats, we're doing just what he'd want us to do," Alex said. "We should support each other," she added a little pompously.

"How, when we hate each other," Ronnie said glumly.

"Not anymore," Alex argued. "I never hated any of you anyway. And I don't believe you hate me." She gazed at Mary and Elizabeth.

Mary looked at her appraisingly. "I never hated you, I just looked down on you."

Alex laughed. "I know you look down on me. But that's not hate."

"It's just — habit. A habit of mind. I'm trying to change it. You were so nice the day of the tea party. My friends liked you so much. I think they liked you better than me," she concluded with a little sorrow, a little indignation.

"But you like to think there is such a thing as superiority," Ronnie said nastily.

"Yes."

"And you had it because of your class."

"Yes."

"And color."

She nodded.

"And money."

Mary stared silently at the fire. "I've always believed that. I was taught that. It's hard to unlearn. Not in your head but . . . in habits of mind, you know? It's comforting, somehow."

"But doesn't it make you feel. . . ." — Alex paused — "separate? Alone?"

"Of course not!" Mary said haughtily. "I am part of a class, a group, there are others like me!"

They gazed at her. She kept staring at the fire. She sipped her drink. "But I have to admit — the day I went to Boston with you" — she turned to Ronnie — "and met your friend. Linda?"

Ronnie nodded.

"She really loves you, doesn't she. You could see it, she hugged you and offered help and if you were desperate, Ronnie, she'd take you in, give you a bed, wouldn't she? She'd even feed you."

"Sure."

"I don't have a single friend like that in the world," Mary said bitterly.

"I'd take you in, Mary," Alex said warmly.

"So would I," said Elizabeth.

Mary looked at them startled. Then she smiled and turned to Ronnie. "I notice you're not offering."

Ronnie laughed. "Mary, I don't have a bed to offer you and you wouldn't sleep on it if I did!"

Mary grimaced, smiling. "You're right." She got up and walked to the bar. "Does anyone want a refill?"

"A unique occasion!" Ronnie cried. "Mary's doing the serving! I'll have a Coke — no! I'll have a glass of wine!" They all wanted refills.

"But I'm not the only snob in this room," Mary defended herself, returning. "What about Elizabeth."

The three of them examined Elizabeth.

"What is this, retreat time?" she snapped. "A bunch of nuns preparing to flagellate themselves?"

"Elizabeth believes in the superiority of mind over body," Mary announced airily.

"Male over female," Ronnie shot in.

"That would be self-defeating, wouldn't it?" she asked coldly, lighting a cigarette.

"Maybe all snobbery is self-defeating," Alex offered timidly.

Elizabeth rolled her eyes. "Wisdom of the simpleton."

"That's not fair, Lizzie!" Mary protested. "Alex isn't a simpleton."

"Really?" Elizabeth swung her head around. "When did you start to believe that?"

Mary flushed.

Alex shook her head. "Oh, don't bother being embarrassed, Mary. I know you all look down on me. Think I'm stupid. I do myself. In some ways. There are ways though . . ." — she gazed off, dropping her eyes — "ways I trust myself. Trust what I feel. Like I knew I had to come here even though — I was full of dread about it. I mean, I was thrilled at finally getting to see you two again," she said, glancing at Elizabeth and Mary. "But . . . Father. I had a terrible experience with him eighteen years ago. I haven't been able to forget. Or forgive."

Mary raised her head. "What happened?"

"I never told anyone. Not Mom, not even David. I came up to introduce him to my first baby, to Stevie. Mom didn't want me to come, she really argued against it. But I challenged her to give me one good reason why and she backed down. I thought it might please him that I'd named my son for him. You know, maybe it would make up for whatever made him act as if I didn't exist all those years.

"David, my husband, is Jewish, his name is David Stein. I converted to Judaism when I married him, not because he asked me to, but for Sam and Lilian, it was so important to them that they have Jewish grandchildren, and they couldn't unless I converted. And I love them and I wanted them to be happy. I didn't care. I mean I feel something I guess you could call religious, but it isn't attached to any particular church. It isn't connected to anything, except maybe the outdoors, nature. . . . Anyway, Father knew nothing about that, but I guess he knew I'd married a Jew. He was okay when I called, he said I could come, he'd be here. It was July, David's vacation. And Father was polite when we arrived, he acted polite to David, he shook his hand, he patted his shoulder, said he was glad to meet his son-in-law even a few years late. Stevie was asleep in his car bed, so we carried him into the house but left him sleeping in it in the front hall, the foyer or whatever you call that big entryway. We didn't want to disturb him, he'd been so fussy the whole trip up.

"Then David went upstairs to wash up and Stevie began to fuss and I lifted him out of the car bed and carried him in . . . in here . . ." — she looked around — "and handed him to Father. He was seven months old, still little and pink and adorable but alert, he could sit up. I'd dressed him in a little white cotton knit suit and wrapped him in a blanket I'd embroidered with scallops all around the edges.

"And Father took him sort of awkwardly, he didn't know how to hold a baby. And I said, I whispered really, I guess I stupidly expected him to be moved, well *I* was, so I said, 'His name is Stephen.' And he just thrust him back at me, almost threw him at me, he had a big grin on his face and he said 'So now some little kike has my name,' and then he turned away."

Long silence.

"That's Father," Elizabeth said finally.

"And I . . . I did something so terrible! I threw Stephen in a chair, I just tossed him and ran out of the room, I was so upset but I refused to cry in front of that man, I didn't even want him to know he'd made me cry. I just threw the baby on the chair, I shocked him, he screamed but I kept running until I couldn't hear him anymore. *I threw him away!* As if I felt that if Father didn't value him then neither did I. I can't forgive myself for it. I can't forgive Father for it."

She covered her face with her hands.

Ronnie said, "Your father roared for my mother. She rescued the baby, picked him up and comforted him. If it's any comfort to you, he peed in the chair."

Mary and Elizabeth laughed hard, long, almost hysterically. Gradually, Alex calmed.

"I probably scarred him for life," she moaned, her nose stuffed. She blew it but the thickness remained. "Every time he acts scornful to me — and he does! — I think I'm being punished for that. Ooooh!" She put her hands to her temples. "I thought I'd never come back here. But when you called, I felt I had to. I felt I had to tell Father how he hurt me, demand he apologize to me and to David and Stevie and all the millions of people he discounted disdained scorned in a single breath! I want him to ask forgiveness for it!" She snatched a cigarette from Elizabeth's pack and lighted it.

Elizabeth looked amazed, amused. Mary grimaced. Ronnie grinned at Mary, reached out and patted her hand. "It's those old war movies," she said. "Terrible tense moment, vibrating moment of grief and loss, no words suffice, guy offers the other guy a smoke. We've all been brainwashed. Can't escape it!" she laughed.

Alex coughed out smoke, her voice thickening. "And I want to know why he never came to see me or invited me to come to see him. All these years," she concluded, tamping out the cigarette vengefully.

They were silent for a long time. When Mary spoke, her face was a tragic mask. "It would all be all right, you could deal with it — the way they were, the things they did, parents who broke rocks and made us walk on them as children. Treated us cruelly, violated us. . . . It would all be all right if you just . . ." her voice hardened — "just didn't fucking love them! If you could just hate them and get it over with, just toss them out in the trash, yesterday's newspaper full of fish bones."

She stared at the fire, pale. "Hate is easy. And love is easy — at first, anyway. It's the in-between . . ."

"Some people don't deserve to be loved," Ronnie said grimly.

"No baby doesn't deserve to be loved," Alex said.

"That's true." Rosa's babies, reaching out their arms to her the minute she entered the apartment. "Babies aren't bad, just needy. They have to be loved. But," her voice hardened, "they turn into terrible adults if they're not."

"But then, don't you see? *Everybody* should be loved!" Alex announced as if she had just discovered America. "Because after all, we never stop being babies, do we? We all still go on needing love!"

"Tell it to Hitler," Ronnie growled.

That moan came from Mary's center, the spot just above the Venusian mound, below the swell of belly, where the truth lives. One's own truth, not the truths of the ages if there are any. That wasn't playacting for attention, not self-pity. It's the sound I always imagined a woman makes when she gives birth. What did she say? "Because he had to be the one, not just the center but the only one." How did she know that? Of course it's true, I saw it once she said it, but I never saw it on my own.

But that moan.

Gazing vacantly into the mirror, Elizabeth dried her face, put on flannel pajamas. Cold tonight. She went back into her bedroom and slid into bed, leaned back against the pillows and reached for a cigarette. She lighted it, put the ashtray on her knees, and switched off the lamp. Think better in the dark.

She had opened the drapes but no stars penetrated the overcast gray-black sky. Was it fear? But what a profound fear! Okay, so she needs money, maybe she needs him to help but that wasn't a moan of worry. I mean, how badly off can she be? It isn't as if she were facing destitution. Or is she. My offer may be taken up sooner than I think, hah!

But no, that sound came from the past, from a time when he really was the god he wanted to be. For his children anyway. Power of life and death, power over mind and body. My god, how did he come to terrify her so?

Could he have been the same with me?

Of course. Of course he could. Oh, the poor terrified little thing! Sad little face looking up at me, Lizabit, please play with me?

And I hated her.

Laura so soignée, slim and elegant in a white linen suit, her thin hands always with the right kind of rings on them, her slick dark hair always in place. She was the real thing; Mother could never be more than a flawed copy. Her voice low, her diction remarkably extensive, grammar and pronunciation correct by Upton standards anyway, not like Mother's screeching, her tough street language, her whiskey voice cursing him out. Laura's hands slim, nails never very long painted a pale rose, reaching out to caress Mary's cheek. Mother's fire-engine-red claws. Mary didn't respond much to her mother — I thought she was a spoiled brat. But maybe she knew of course because I knew too all Laura's gestures were for show, acting the mother, not showing love.

I adored Laura but she looked through me. The enemy: firstborn heir to the throne but child of a commoner, as illegitimate as Ronnie. What would Laura have thought of Ronnie? Tried to pretend I didn't exist, ignored me while she pushed Mary forward, dressed her up in white lace, handed her to Father, isn't she adorable, Stephen? Everything for Mary, nannies, piano lessons, dancing lessons, and oh the clothes that child had! And the playhouse.

God, the playhouse.

I refused to go into that part of the garden while they were building it, kept my head averted, high and stiff on my neck when I went out to my spot in the woods with my book. I was above such childishness. Little white clapboard house with a green roof, its own little child-sized toilet and sink, they had to dig lines through the garden around the tennis court careful to avoid the pool. I scorned Mary the whole time, called her "baby," would not no matter what she did how she begged go to look at it with her. And then when it was finished, I made her wait days before I'd go. How she begged, cried, sulked, before I gave in!

But I was dying to see it. Oh, that playhouse. Little four-over-four paned windows with screens for chrissakes, with lace curtains the housekeeper made from old panels from the house, worn in spots but with enough good fabric for those little windows. Hung on rods three quarters of the way up the window. Table, chairs, where did Laura find that little couch? Mary's dolls and Mary's doll carriage, Mary's beautiful dollhouse full of antique furniture, even a doll high chair and all Mary's stuffed animals. Not that I liked stuffed animals. It wasn't that. It was that I didn't have any and she had so many, too many to love, really.

And oh the little tea set. Tiny teapot, cups, saucers, cake plates, French porcelain with pink roses and green leaves and a gold ring around the rims. The housekeeper, who was it then, Mrs. Abbott, yes, Eloise, white hair, bolster-body, gold-rimmed glasses, what housekeepers were supposed to look like, did look like in those days, every afternoon she carried down a thermos of weak tea and a pitcher of milk with a plate of cookies to Mary's playhouse. And Mary poured the tea into her little teapot and the milk into the pitcher — the sugar bowl was always full — and served tea to her dolls.

Delighted she was or would have been if only she had someone to play with. But I scorned it all, baby stuff, baby play, stupid, play with dolls, I never played with dolls, only stupid babies played with dolls, beneath me, I was ten and reading Adam Smith.

I stalked off, left her crying. Lonely little heart.

She tamped out the cigarette, turned on the lamp, pulled another out of the pack and lighted it, turned the lamp off again. Then threw off the covers and turned on the lamp and found her robe and slipped it on, and went out of the room. She walked down the hall, switching on lights as she went, downstairs and into the living room, to the bar against the wall. She poured scotch into a glass, half filling it, switched off the light and retraced her steps.

What am I doing.

She got back in bed, turned off the light, took a long drag on her cigarette. Stay here I'll turn into an alcoholic. Why am I doing this?

I need it.

She stared at the window and the opaque darkness beyond. I am fifty-three years old and I am tormented by the memory of a playhouse built when I was ten? What in hell is the matter with me?

I loved that playhouse, loved the curtains, the stuffed animals, the little couch, the little toilet and sink, even her own little towels embroidered with her name for chrissake . . . ! Most of all I loved the tea set. And I hated Mary for having it all.

She would have shared it with me. But that wasn't what I wanted. No way sharing could ever be enough.

So I took it.

It had to be after Laura killed herself because Mary was in boarding school. Late August or maybe early September, she had to go back before me, a few days earlier, and I was left here with only the servants, a skeleton staff, Mother wouldn't let me come back until just before school started. I was devastated, abandoned. Wouldn't play with Mary when she was here but when I was alone I felt no one cared. And I went down to the playhouse, just sat there picking up putting down her toys, sneering at them. No one brought *me* tea and cookies. And I decided to take the dishes.

I brought something with me the next day, what? Something soft to wrap them in, a bag? Wrapped them up well, all of them, every last one. Put them in the bag, packed them in my suitcase. Took them back to Boston, stuck them on a shelf in my closet. Never looked at them again, never even took them out of the wrappings.

I wonder what happened to them. Maybe they're still there.

Did Mary miss them? Did she even notice?

She might even have given them to me if I'd asked. But I'd have had to ask.

Not her fault.

She tossed the rest of the drink down her throat and stubbed the cigarette out. She scanned the dark sky desperately, as if she were waiting for something huge and neon to light up, a word, a sign.

I could never speak to him. Little Dodo Bird, Mary Mary quite contrary, he called me. Mouth would open, nothing came out but stupidities. "I never could talk to you. / The tongue stuck in my jaw. / It stuck in a barb wire snare." Cunt, he called me, Elizabeth said. Did buy me a car, though, after all — a Jag with a chauffeur. And gave me that wedding. Loves me, loves me not.

Not until she was drifting off to sleep did she remember: Lizzie said I was smart.

Ronnie turned uncomfortably on her lumpy mattress.

That's Father, she said. Just like that. No surprise, no rancor, objective comment, an ornithologist recognizing the characteristics of the creature just described, Yes, that's a golden grebe.

You saw a man locking all the people in the building then turning on gas jets from the outside? That's Father. You saw a man shoot a baby in its mother's arms? That's Father.

She sat up, shivered. Cold tonight. She got out of bed and put on her old flannel robe. She found her soiled socks and put them on, went out into the kitchen and switched on the light. She put water in the kettle, set it on the stove, and turned on the gas.

That's Ronnie.

She set out a tea bag and a cup, and sat down at the table, head in her hand. We're still babies inside, all still basically needy, Alex said. So can she forgive him? Should have asked her that. One thing to talk. Mostly what she does. Another to mean what you say.

It's as if Elizabeth feels, He is what He is. I am that I am: isn't that what god calls himself in the Bible? "That's Father." Wonderful. Men: they are what they are and women have to accept that and try to shift around them. Especially men with power. Money. The upper hand. The raised hand. Momma's philosophy. Here's to you, Momma.

She raised the empty cup.

What's the use of fighting them. What's the use. To struggle, to live in anger takes everything out of you, drains you, makes people hate you and what's the use? You get nothing you want, all you get is tired.

That's Father. Can't beat'm, join'm. At least that way maybe you end up with something you want. But what the fuck do I want?

The kettle whistle startled her and her head fell off her hand. She laughed at herself, stood up, poured boiling water into the cup over the tea bag, jiggling it a few times. She sat down again.

To be happy in life, you have to love, Ronalda.

So say I drop it. Stop pushing feminism, go into the closet, get myself a suit and heels and panty hose and a job guarding a corporation against environmental laws, whatever environmentalists do in corporations, get $20,000, $30,000 a year, maybe even more, my own car, a nice apartment, some furniture. . . .

Okay, so forget that.

But say I stop being so . . . pugnacious. I've been learning to do that a little, haven't I? See Alex as a good kid really, even Mary's a decent soul in some ways. Elizabeth — she's deluded, even dangerous. But there's something tragically brave about her. Most of their bad qualities come from their unhappiness. Mine too? So suppose I just say, like Elizabeth: that's Father. Forgive or at least forget. Look at the bright side. Isn't that what the ads din into us?

She took out the tea bag and sipped her tea. Too hot.

List good things.

1. He didn't throw her out when He found out about me. He could have. *Would* have, even though it was His child, in the nineteenth, eighteenth, or seventeenth centuries. Maybe even in the sixteenth. It was a kindly act, generous, letting her stay here with a squalling kid.

Unless He still desired her.

She sipped tea.

Okay. 2. He was a baby once too. Things pressed on him growing up, terrible pressures: sex class color family tradition. Turned Him into a monster. But if these things are so good, if they are privileges, how do they turn people into monsters? And why don't didn't people see that He is a monster? Why didn't Momma? Why did they all treat Him like a god?

A memory struck the middle of her forehead: a tall slim handsome man wearing white trousers and a V-necked sweater walked around the lawn carrying a croquet mallet. His deep sure rumble carried all the way to the terrace, where Momma was setting the table for tea, little sandwiches and cakes but with a bar as well as coffee and tea. He laughed and joked with the senior senator from Massachusetts and the junior one from New York, and an aide to the president. Of the United States. He kept telling them croquet was really a mean game. I couldn't understand why meanness made it *better,* as He seemed to be implying. Gorgeous, He sat in the cushioned wrought iron chair, leaned back easily, holding a sandwich in one hand, Bloody Mary in the other. So assured, so easy. Easy jokey talk. They, far less glorious, paunchy and balding, laughed with Him, responded to Him, agreed with Him. Everything in sight belonged to Him. He authoritative about everything that mattered about the everything that belonged to Him. He was beautiful: a god, golden, glowing, impervious.

So it was that really, it was myself, Alex thought, sitting utterly still, fully dressed in the armchair in the bedroom she'd been assigned. One of the guest rooms, furnished formally. She'd pulled the chair up to the window, an antique chair with a stiff back and wooden arms. She sat facing out, querying the stars, so brilliant here at night, far from the city, in the middle of woods.

She glanced at the room around her. Not the room I slept in when I lived here. That must be in the wing that's closed up. I remember it as a suite — nursery, playroom, laundry room, toilets, bathroom, nanny's room.

Funny the way the house is arranged — the parents' suite, Father's room, the wife's room, and their sitting room on one side of the house, the children's suite way across on the other side, all these other rooms in between. You'd think parents would want to be near their babies, not clear across on the other side of the house. Take minutes to get to them if they cried. You wouldn't even hear them.

I suppose that was the point, not to hear it. Nanny's job to take care of crying babies. I wouldn't like that. I'd want to pick up my baby, comfort it myself. Otherwise why have children? The only people in life you can ever love unconditionally. The way they love you. At least while they're little. But I think it lasts, maybe buried under a lot of other stuff. Important to have that, don't you think? Sometime in your life? Unconditional love. Like the foundation of a house.

Do I love Father that way?

Maybe you only love the ones who really take care of you. Father was certainly never a caretaker like David.

I should ask them for the key, go look at that wing, maybe remember something.

This isn't the room they gave David and me that time. . . . Not that I remember it very well, just had a glimpse, my eyes full of tears when I flew up to repack our things. Someone had unpacked them, a maid, I guess. Didn't challenge him, didn't protest, just tore out of here without even saying good-bye. He probably thought I was a fool. Don't accomplish anything by running away, don't change anything, ease anything. He didn't care. What does he care about? Not me, that's sure. Does he love Mary? What would have happened if I'd fought back, attacked him for talking that way, blasted him the way Elizabeth would for deserting me. . . .

I ran because I was trying to make him feel sorry for what he'd said without actually confronting him. Coward's trick.

David was sorry for me, saw the tears, but they weren't tears of hurt, they were tears of rage. But the truth, I see it now, I was really enraged because of what *I'd* done, blamed him, he made me do it, but I did it didn't I threw Stevie away like garbage. Heard him howl, that sudden thrust shocked him, frightened him, but I didn't care. He was garbage, Father said he was garbage.

How could I have done that?

How could I?

11

They stood under the portico waiting for Aldo to bring the car around. Mary's gaze concentrated on the pine trees that protected the house from the road, as in an easy, almost musical voice, she suggested, "Do you think we should go in to see him separately?"

Alex and Elizabeth checked each other's eyes; Alex glanced at Ronnie, who stared straight ahead with a tough unfeeling face.

"No," Elizabeth decided tentatively. Alex slid her arm through Ronnie's and pressed it to her side. Ronnie slid her arm away.

In the ICU, Edna Thompson was praising Stephen for moving his left leg. Tubes were still attached to his nose and chest, and he did not respond to her, staring straight ahead with an expression of rage on his face. When his daughters moved into his field of vision, he moved his face away.

Does he see a difference in the way we are standing here, our shoulders slightly touching? United.

The nurse greeted the sisters warmly, especially Elizabeth, then left the room.

Amazing. She used to dislike Elizabeth, you could see it on her face. Disliked her arrogance. What had changed, Mary wondered.

Elizabeth stepped forward, said hello, kissed Stephen's forehead, asked how he was feeling today. Mary also kissed him, and asked if there was anything they could do for him. He glared straight ahead. The other two stood where they were.

"Good morning, Father," Alex said.

"Sir," Ronnie nodded.

Mary chatted to him, asking if the food was all right, if he was comfortable, if he'd like something to read. When he turned his head and looked at them, their voices dwindled away. He lifted his left hand and made a whisking movement toward the door.

"You want us to leave?" Elizabeth asked coldly. "We will."

Dr. Stamp met them as they left and took them to a smoking lounge. Elizabeth immediately lighted up.

He tried to address each of them in turn, but his eyes kept returning to Elizabeth. "We've been doing tests on your father regularly since his stroke. They show he has Broca's aphasia and hemiparesis, which means that he can't talk and he's paralyzed on his right side. We can't predict how much improvement there might be, and you have to be prepared for the possibility that there might not be any. But we have to move him out of the ICU."

"When?"

"As soon as — probably tomorrow."

"As soon as what?"

"We have to be satisfied that he can breathe on his own without a respirator and doesn't require suctioning. If his blood pressure and heart rate are stable, if he doesn't require intensive monitoring. In any case, you need to start thinking about future care."

"Such as?"

"The best bet would be a rehabilitation hospital if they'll accept him. We'll have the social service department contact a rehabilitation hospital — we've found Middlesex Rehab very competent. They'll send a nurse to evaluate him. But if she decides that he's totally disabled, she'll reject him. And he needs chronic custodial care." He turned a more sympathetic gaze at Mary. "I'm sorry the outlook isn't better."

"Is it hopeless?" Mary peered up at him as at a divinity.

"Nooo. He could start to regain some use of his right side, perhaps even speak again. But there's severe damage to a critical part of the left brain. Some of it is probably irrevocable."

He stood up. He was eager to get away from them, Elizabeth thought. Didn't like delivering bad news. She stood too, put her hand out to shake his. They all stood, shook hands, uttered politenesses. He's not the one to talk to. Doesn't know the nitty-gritty.

After he'd left, Elizabeth said, "I'd like to . . . do you mind waiting? I'd like to speak to the nurse."

"We'll all go," Mary said authoritatively.

They found Edna Thompson in the ICU control room. Elizabeth addressed the nurse in a low voice, respectfully.

My God: what's happened to her? where's her usual arrogant manner? Mary wondered.

"Nurse Thompson, we — my sisters and I — have been wondering. Our father seems — somewhat angry. He seems aware we are present but he doesn't respond to us. We're a bit upset about this."

The nurse put her hand on Elizabeth's arm, and looked in her eyes (first time she's done that, Mary thought). "Oh, Ms. Upton, I understand you're upset. But try to imagine what you'd feel like if you woke up and found yourself paralyzed, unable to speak, unable to move on your own. Especially a big important man like that. The poor soul is just bewildered and frustrated. It'll take a few days for him to comprehend and then to accept what's happened to him. And that can be hard on the family — they sometimes mistake that frustration for anger — but believe me, your dad's not angry, he's just confused and frustrated. He'll be better in a few days, you'll see."

But he was not. Moved on Monday to a private room on an upper floor, surrounded by flowers and magazines his daughters provided (others having by now forgotten him), he continued to glare into space.

"Raging at his fate, such a powerful eloquent man, unable to speak, you can understand it." Dr. Stamp shook his head sadly. " 'Do not go gently into that good night,' " he intoned, showing off. " 'Rage, rage at the dying of the light!' "

The nurse from the rehab hospital had indeed rejected him, Dr. Stamp said apologetically. There was an excellent nursing home near Boston, on the North Shore. Expensive, but he presumed that was not a problem. Good because it was not too far from Logan — they could fly in and visit him, fly out again the same day. Would they like to drive up and see it?

"Could we take him home?" Alex asked timidly, darting looks at Elizabeth.

He stopped dead. "And do what?"

"Take care of him ourselves."

"You sure you want to do that?"

"No. What do *you* think?" Elizabeth said.

Amazing. She sounds human, thought Mary.

He shook his head from side to side. "Well." He grimaced. No idea what they were getting themselves into, these girls. Love, affection, duty, admirable of course, but . . . "Well. It would be hard, I have to warn you. You'd have to have a visiting nurse once a day to check his blood pressure, listen to his heart and lungs, make sure he had no congestion in his chest, check his calves to make sure he isn't developing phlebitis. He'd have to be fed — of course he can help feed himself with his left hand. He'd have to void in a bedpan, which would have to be emptied; he'd have to be bathed every day, sponge bath of course. He might get, probably will get bedsores, which need applications of ointment. You'd have to work to keep his bottom dry. He'd need a hospital bed with electric controls and — other stuff — the nurses would know. A foam rubber mattress, a soft sheet of some sort."

"Chamois. And a bed tray," Alex said helpfully.

"Right." He looked at them meaningfully. "It would mean the most basic care, like taking care of a baby. Round-the-clock. Possibly for years."

"Thank you, Doctor, we'll think about what you've said," Elizabeth said crisply.

"He could have another stroke. It might be frightening for you," he warned.

"What are the chances of that?" Mary asked timidly. "Another stroke."

He shrugged, sighed, shook his head. "I can't predict. But most people don't live long in his condition."

The sisters nodded and went home.

*   *   *

As soon as lunch was over, the table cleared, Elizabeth spoke.

"So what do we do?"

"He'd hate being in a nursing home," Alex said.

"He'd like *us* wiping his bottom?" Elizabeth asked.

"He'd loathe it," Mary moaned.

"Don't expect me to do it," Ronnie warned.

"Why? Didn't he take care of you when you were a baby?" Mary said querulously. "Change your nappies and feed you your pabulum? What an ungrateful child!" Ronnie swung around to face her and she laughed, laying her hand over Ronnie's. Ungloved. "We could hire a woman to do it," she said. "A stranger. A practical nurse, if they still exist."

"He'd prefer that. Of all the options. Being in his own house but being tended by a servant. He'd hate us doing it but he'd also hate a nursing home."

"Do we care what he hates?"

"We care what *we* hate."

"If he goes to a nursing home he'll fade and die. We can write him off, we'll never get a word out of him."

They stared at the table, mouths set, silent.

"And we want a word out of him. *I* do, anyway."

"You may not get it anyway."

"But are we prepared to spend months, maybe years here, taking care of him?" Elizabeth asked. "I'm not."

"Nor I. We have our own lives to get on with," Mary agreed. How can I borrow money from a man who can't speak?

"I have unfinished business with him," Alex insisted. "We can send him to a nursing home when we're through with him. Say we found it too much. Dr. Stamp will certainly understand."

"You're really ruthless," Mary said, surprised.

They looked at Alex, at each other.

"Wouldn't you like a few answers from him too?" she asked sharply.

Mary and Elizabeth exchanged a deep look. They glanced at Ronnie, who dropped her eyes.

"It's decided then?"

"I'm in favor. For a while." Elizabeth laid her hand down in the center of the table. Mary put hers over it, Alex added hers. Ronnie hesitated, then added hers. "Is this a pact?" she asked.

They nodded.

She grinned. "Do we mingle blood?"

Elizabeth and Mary didn't know where it might be, but Ronnie looked in the key cabinet and sure enough, there was a key labeled "Nursery Wing." Alex went upstairs and tried it. The key turned but the door stuck. She banged and pushed, but it didn't open until she pressed down on the doorknob with all her weight. Then it swung open; she peered in. No wonder it stuck, hadn't been opened in years, maybe decades from the look of it. Dust webbed the windows, the legs of tables, the angles of walls and ceiling. Cobweb dimmed the light from the windows but the room was still light enough, a large children's playroom, cluttered with sturdy old-fashioned wooden furniture, armchairs covered with bright-colored chintzes, child-sized chairs and tables for drawing and games, shelves along the walls holding dolls, books, stacks of games. Alex moved farther into the room and examined the shelves more closely. Mostly girls' toys, but a few toy trucks and cars, a chemistry set. Must have been Elizabeth's. Or mine? Freezing in here, the radiators turned off, chill dank air that hasn't been disturbed maybe since I was nine years old, the last child to play here. For surely Ronnie was never allowed to. Why not after all. It was too bad.

"It would blur distinctions, which always leads to disaster."

Was that his voice? Do I remember it?

She walked toward the hallway to the right, toward what she remembered as the nanny's room, yes there was the toilet and the bathroom. She stopped, a memory clicking into place: Mommy. Her mother, here. She slept here when I was sick. And when I was having all those nightmares. Terrible nightmares, she still remembered them, horrible monsters pursuing her, pressing her into corners. . . .

She pushed open the nanny's room door — bare and shabby but also bright. The upstairs rooms were lighter than the front rooms downstairs. The ones you were in at night. Seemed topsy-turvy.

The narrow iron bed was covered with a cheap cotton spread; the mirror over the chest of drawers had some old faded photographs stuck in it — Mary, it looked like, about three or four. Left behind by the last nanny?

She went to the window and looked down — a kitchen garden, protected by palings, invisible from the public outdoor spaces.

Don't remember that. I would have loved it, seeing vegetables grow, I would have helped plant, or at least harvest. . . . Pick tomatoes, green beans. Fun. Was it here then? I bet Noradia put it in. Ronnie and her plants. Yes.

She turned, retracing her steps through the playroom and entering the hallway to the left. She stopped in the doorway of a large white functional room. The nursery. A workroom: no lace-skirted pink-bowed bassinets here. Two narrow beds, a large crib and a small one, a changing table, shelves piled with receiving blankets, baby-sized flannel pajamas, tiny undershirts, and hundreds of diapers, yellowed and dusty now. She peered inside an old Bathinette: its rubber basin was cracked and filthy. Her body began to shudder. She glanced at the cribs, asking herself which was hers, glanced at the beds, glanced away. Her body jerked. She could not breathe, breath wouldn't go in or out, the room shivered. She put out a hand to steady herself, touched cobweb climbing up a shelf, cried out, jerked away carrying a sticky trail. . . .

She woke up on the floor in a crumpled heap. She reached out to pull herself up, touched the same sticky goo, whimpered. She staggered out of the room and across the playroom to the bathroom, turned the tap on full force and put her hands under the water. She stood there as the water hit her hands with such force it sprayed out onto her pants, onto the floor. Her pants were soaked, the floor puddled, before she removed her hands and looked for a towel. The towels hanging on the rod were grimy with dust. She rubbed her hands on the sides of her pants, then put them under the water again and cupped them, tossing water onto her face. She turned off the tap and with the edges of her fingers picked up one of the dusty towels and dropped it on the puddle on the floor. Without wiping up the water, she walked as steadily as she could to the door of the nursery wing. When she left it, she locked it again.

Elizabeth swung around in the desk chair. What the fuck am I doing, what am I getting myself into, I could lose my job, this is insane. I'll become a nonserious person in their eyes, lose what edge I have: men don't take leaves to tend their sick fathers. Not even their sick wives or kids. You are truly mad if you do this. You have to be like them if you want to get ahead. Even the doctor thinks it's crazy. Stick him in a nursing home and get it over with. The others will go along with whatever you decide. Your silence has created a power vacuum in which Alex is able to force her will on them. After all, what do you owe him? An education, that's all he ever gave you. And with his money, he didn't feel that at all.

Not doing it for him.

What then. Keep your eye on your priorities, what *you* want, what *you* need. Don't get caught in emotional struggles that don't advance you, the underbrush that booby-traps people, holds them in the past when they think their eyes are on the future.

Everything I've ever done was for him.

Nonsense. You've derived considerable pleasure from your work and certainly from your status.

Didn't help. Couldn't make up for all the rest.

Nothing can. . . . So do what's best for you now.

She threw her glasses down on the desk and stood up, stared out at the darkening sky. Not even four o'clock and starting to get dark. What day was it, November 26, a month yet till the solstice, December 22, shortest day of the year, when all hope seems dead.

Clare died in May, a beautiful spring day, life returning. Weather means nothing.

Nothing means anything.

She kept pressing her lips together. Her heart was heaving like a stomach just before it erupts.

She and Clare drinking in his favorite Oxford pub, the Spread Eagle, sitting outdoors at a rustic table on a May evening, talking, talking. No end to their conversations, they could have gone on forever. She wanted them never to end but of course he always had to go home. They'd dawdle toward his car, then drive back to London, he'd drop her in Hampstead, head home to Ellen. Sometimes he'd take her home with him — lumbering old house in Ladbroke Grove, surrounded by huge shabby old Victorian houses. It always looked uninhabited from the front because it was always dark, but he'd walk straight to the back where Ellen had set up a studio in an old greenhouse, electric heater going full blast in the drafty damp room. She'd look up at him from her easel or sketch pad — oh hello, you came home for tea? Hello, Elizabeth, you here for tea? Leave the room, disappear for twenty minutes, show up in the sitting room with sandwiches with almost no filling, tea, packaged cake on a tray. For Clare the gourmet. Ate little herself, rail-thin, silent, paying no attention to Clare, who went on talking a mile a minute as if Ellen didn't matter, as if he didn't notice her anger or distance or whatever it was, as if he didn't notice how bad the food was, how *dismissive*. Uncomfortable. Didn't like going there. Better when we were off somewhere, in his study at LSE, driving down to Oxford to visit someone. He never came to my room. Did I invite him? Probably not — ashamed of the shabby furniture, gas ring, electric kettle, nosy landlady. Afraid of his reaction to being in my bedroom. . . .

Time he was invited to Paris and took me along: his assistant! God how my heart leapt, was this it, was he going to make love to me now, was I going to find out what love was like? Twenty-two I was, skinny, practically no breasts or hips, a boy's body. People said I looked like Katharine Hepburn. My hair was long and straight, brilliant red then, it drew attention. Before we left I went to a little boutique near Claridge's and spent a month's allowance on satin pajamas and a matching satin robe, deep gray, forgot to buy slippers, would have looked really stupid, all dressed up in satin with bare feet.

Didn't matter.

My complexion must have matched my hair, I was so excited as we checked into the hotel, charming place on the Left Bank, looked like an old farmhouse. The room was furnished with real furniture, old pieces, lovely, big old windows with lace curtains. Gone now. At least I couldn't find it last time I walked the Left Bank. A huge bathtub in the corner of my room, screened by lace-covered panels. Two rooms, of course. Of course. My hands trembled as I unpacked, hung my things in the armoire, I had trouble with the hangers, dresses kept sliding off. Went off to the conference to register, everyone knew him, he introduced me to all of them, all men, the way they looked at me I was sure they knew, they didn't take me seriously. I was embarrassed, I was still innocent, didn't know nooky was standard at conferences, but oh I was proud too — of being his, of loving

him, being loved by him. He loved me. I know he did. But he never said
he did, did he, Elizabeth. Never even hinted it. Not then. Not until it was
too late. Nothing personal in our talk. Oh, he'd asked a little about Father,
my life in the States. I made it sound as if I lived full-time in a mansion in
Lincoln. Concord Academy, Smith College: it all sounded good.

Dinner with a bunch of them in some brasserie, strange food to me
then, *choucroute garnie,* pork hocks, headcheese, escargots, much wine
and talk, late. Peck on the cheek, good night Elizabeth dear, see you at
eight tomorrow morning, be sure to be ready on time.

I walked down the hall to my room just as out of control as I'd been
that morning, not-seeing, not-hearing, heart pounding not leaping anymore: he didn't love me. He wasn't going to. Why? Am I ugly? Lack
charm? Don't play up to a man's great god-self the way Mary does?

I put on the satin pajamas and robe, I sat at the little table facing the
French windows overlooking the street and I poured myself a drink from
the bottle of single-malt whiskey Clare had insisted I buy at the duty-free
shop. I toasted myself: Here's to Elizabeth, so ugly, charmless, ungainly,
awkward, egotistical, superior, arrogant, and nonsexy that even a man
who loves her doesn't want to go to bed with her!

Drank myself silly, had a big head all day next day, went through the
motions at the conference. Of course he didn't really need me there and I
wondered why he'd brought me, and by dinner, when I'd recovered, I
asked him. A little bitterly, maybe.

"Liz, I want you to get exposure. Getting to know a professional
world, getting familiar with faces and names *and* the language, the
manners — these things are everything, believe me. I want you to learn
them. Talk to people, establish a connection with them. In the academic
world, that can make all the difference."

My heart felt like a desert suddenly rained on, I was overcome with
gratitude. How could I have questioned him? So good he was, intent on
educating me, introducing me to the world he hoped I'd be able to enter.
Of course he wouldn't go to bed with me, he was a married man, he was
honorable, respectful of women, even of his bitter indifferent wife, respectful of me.

So we went on and in that understanding my mind blossomed, I
could trust him, trust his mind, his character, his honesty. He loved me as

a protégée, the way men love boys, advance them, further their careers, and if there was any other element in his love, well, that had to be sacrificed to honor. Went on together for years, even after I came back to Washington; we wrote every week, spoke on the phone. I went to England every summer, spent time with him there. We went together to Italy one summer, to the Loire Valley, to Normandy and Brittany — to Mont-Saint-Michel, the fortifications at Saint-Lô, the Bayeux Tapestry, the *chemins cru*, food cooked with apples and cream and calvados. Made me sick one night.

It was 1958 when he left Ellen. Or she left him. Heard she was living with a woman. Who knows? When he called to tell me, all the feelings I'd buried over all those years welled up, I thought, this is it! It *is* happening! Because I hadn't dated much — who could compare to Clare? A few guys I'd met at the institute, intellectuals, they were the only ones attracted to me. But their intellects didn't make them different from other boys I'd dated over the years, they were just like the jocks, needed to have their egos built up every minute, no room for another ego in their universes. All other men a threat, all women nurses offering ear and bandage.

Not me.

So what makes you think you can nurse Father?

She shrugged. Fuck it.

I went to Father and bargained. Blackmailed him really. And he got Clare a job as an economist at State and a chair at the Brookings Institute. And banished me. Finished with me. Because I referred to it: forbidden. Not only that, I used it as a bargaining chip. I've never really regretted it.

Her mouth twisted.

And Clare came. I met him at the airport, he looked terrible, dark rings under his eyes, his face strained. What had she done to him? Poor baby, I wanted to take him home and take care of him, but someone had lent him a place, he wanted to be alone and think and deal with what had happened. And of course I understood, how could I not understand.

We fell back into the old pattern — a midweek movie or play or concert, drinks and dinner Friday nights. He got an apartment in Georgetown, he never invited me there, said it was a shithouse but he liked it, we'd meet at some café or restaurant there, talk talk talk all night, drive home half-cocked at two A.M. Sometimes he'd come up to my apartment and we'd talk talk talk until five. But he always went home. When he started to jog Sunday mornings, he'd stop in after his run, cook brunch for us. Beautifully — unlike Ellen. Omelets, huevos rancheros, pancakes with lingonberries. Or he'd bring something — those wonderful blueberry muffins he got in a little shop down the street.

It was amazing how he knew about my personal life. I never told him. He seemed to have radar, an antenna that followed my body, saw all my actions. He always knew when I was seeing someone. Andy Bocatelli — sharp, good-looking, nice sense of humor, a little on the macho side but careful with me, didn't push. I had status. Upton name. Couldn't figure what he saw in me. Why he liked me. He really seemed to. Clare came to Treasury one day, saw me walking with Andy, laughing in the hall. Asked me about him. Raised an eyebrow. "Little shoe salesman," he said, voice oozing disdain. Could have been Father. "Not your style, Liz. Not in your class. Beneath you."

I broke it off with Andy.

For a long time I didn't see anyone but him. Then I started to go out with some other men, few enough god knows but I was still young, late twenties, still wanted to find out what love was like. But I didn't love anybody but Clare. And he always found out and he always found them beneath me.

And I always accepted his judgment.

It was Jack Johnson I was seeing when I found out. Clean-cut, from the Middle West, ambitious, even then rising fast at Interior, assistant secretary now. Looking for a wife who could help him along, who'd make a difference. Because he worked at Interior, Clare never saw us together. Jack and I were dating pretty steadily, it was getting near summer, I could tell Jack was hoping that I'd invite him to Father's Fourth of July party, which of course was famous in government circles, everyone knew who was invited and who wasn't. It would be a coup for him, advance his career. I was considering it.

How did it happen, what was the sequence?

Clare had asked me for a Treasury report he couldn't get through the usual channels. He was cleared, but they were sitting on this one for some reason. But he said he absolutely had to have it, and I said I'd get a copy for him. Supposed to give it to him Friday night but they called an emergency meeting and I had to work late, didn't get home until past midnight. So next morning early I drove over to his place to drop it off. I knew he got up early. I'd wondered for a long time why he never invited me to his apartment — he said it was grungy, my place was so much nicer — but it seemed fine to me, a nice old building, a pretty George-town street, even an elevator, what did he mean, grungy? Didn't dawn on me even when the boy answered the door, gorgeous boy in his early twenties wearing only a towel around his middle. He apparently didn't know about me either because he smiled, he invited me in, saw the big brown envelope in my hands, probably thought I was a secretary. He called out quite innocently, "Clare, someone's here to deliver something," padded back to the bedroom, pushed open the door. "Clare, are you decent?"

Clare in the bedroom door in pajama bottoms, no top, barefoot, staring at me. I stared at him.

"Sorry," I mumbled. Held out the brown envelope. "Just wanted to drop off that report you wanted."

All grace, then, came forward, took the envelope, drew me in by the arm, come in come in you must have some coffee. Antony, make us some coffee will you like a good boy? But I couldn't wouldn't, have to go a million things to do just wanted to drop this off, another time. Ran out of there.

Drove home, packed my bags and loaded the car, drove straight here. Called the office Monday morning, said I'd been called away on a personal emergency. No one here yet, only the servants, Father not due for a couple of days, Mary and Alberto the day after next but that was fine with me I needed not to be seen. I came here as if it were home.

Only home I ever had. Could hardly go to Mother's, have her peering at me: Elizabeth, what is the matter with you?

Trembling from the inside, as if every molecule in every blood cell every muscle every bone was trembling, jumping around wanting to jump out of my skin. Stared at the gun case in Father's study, even took a couple of the guns out, examined them, looked for bullets. Didn't know which ones went with which gun. All old, from long before Father's time, proba-bly from his great-grandmother's time. Old-fashioned. Confusing. Walked through these woods, stared at the lake, thought about drowning myself.

When Mary came, she insisted we take out a rowboat but then she wanted me to row. She leaned back luxuriously, complacent, full of satisfaction. "I know everything about love," she said.

Was there no bottom to my stupidity? Anyone else any other woman would have known, seen, long before. Maybe I even did — all those evasions over all the years, the unexplained absences, the way Ellen acted. . . . Thirty-one years old and still so stupid. Blind. Blind deaf dumb. I deserved whatever happened to me.

Got through the Fourth of July party somehow — gray-faced, limping, almost dead, a very sick person. Wonder what people thought. Oh they thought nothing, no one pays attention to you Elizabeth you should know that by now.

When I went back I determined I would marry Jack. Called him the minute I got to town, he was elated, I hadn't shown such enthusiasm before. Had dinner that night and I finally let him seduce me. He was high, thought he had his fish on the hook. So disappointing the sex, though. A lot of heavy breathing, a few swipes across my breasts, a few thrusts, whammo. That's what they consider a triumph?

But I thought I could live with it if it didn't happen too often. It wasn't entirely unpleasant.

At work the next day, five messages from Clare. I tore them up. But he kept calling, and finally I agreed to see him. We met at La Scala, the café he liked in Georgetown the only one in those days that served cappuccino. Didn't realize how angry I was with him, thought it was only with myself. But my voice was so bitter.

"So what have *I* been all these years, your beard?"

He reached for my hands across the table, but I snatched them back. "Elizabeth, Liz, please . . . you must know I love you, my dear, I have always loved you."

Then I fucking cried.

"You are the woman of my dreams, my ideal woman — brilliant, beautiful, strong. You're the person I can talk to better than anyone else on earth. You know that. It's just that I can't — I *can't*, darling — be more than your best friend. But I *am* your best friend, I have your interests at heart in a way a man who was sexually involved with you never would. Believe me, I know that, it's true of me too, I'm not a good friend to my lovers, nor they to me. You're my best friend too, and it would kill me, I think literally kill me to lose you."

It made so much sense the way he said it. I almost got lost in it. Again. He could always bring me round. But I found myself again. I wiped my face, sipped my cappuccino, wiped froth from my upper lip.

"Fine. Fine. We'll be best friends. And you'll have Antony — how long have you had him, by the way?"

He didn't want to tell me but I wouldn't stop pressing. Still I got only the briefest picture, phrases, images I had to fill in myself.

Antony was the great passion of his life. After years of dalliances with a long string of students and other young men, he'd met Antony at a party in London, artists, writers, friends of his. Antony a young composer, penniless of course, had come to London with an older man, the painter Harmon Ascelot, know his work? Hung in several museums, very good really. Antony lived with Harmon, Harmon supported him. Had no way to survive without him. Clare was struck dumb with love, had to have Antony. And Antony loved Clare. No way to be together though: there was Ellen, and he didn't have the money to maintain a second establishment. They went to cheap hotels, but Clare was consumed, life didn't matter, all that mattered was love. It mattered so much he was even willing to come out, after all those years of concealment. He asked Ellen for a divorce, knowing she might expose him.

But she didn't. Sat there on the couch across from his chair and looked at him with her pale dead glance, said, "Why not. Why keep up this charade?"

Seeing a chance to keep his cover, Clare took it. Not possible in London, where everyone knew him, knew Antony, knew Ellen or at least knew she existed. He'd come back to the States. In a big city like Washington, it would not be impossible to remain anonymous, undetected.

"Especially with me for cover," I said bitterly.

"That is not what we are about," he said sadly.

This time I let him take my hands.

"You have him," I burbled, started to cry again like a little kid, "but what do I have?"

"You have your work and the best of me."

I pulled my hands away and wiped my face with the napkin. God if

Father saw that! "I'm going to marry Jack Johnson. I'm going to have what you have!"

Jack hadn't even asked me to marry him, but I wanted Clare to see how it felt.

His pale cheeks turned ashen, he turned in his chair, stared off down the street, hot Washington Saturday, waves of heat rising from the asphalt. He lighted a cigarette. The fingers of his right hand drummed on the table. I knew the signs. He was angry.

Good, I thought, a jab of satisfaction plunging through my stomach.

He turned back his distant, superior face, the face he put on at meetings when he was about to destroy someone's argument — or them, personally. He could be brilliantly cruel. I always got a vicious kick out of his cruelties. He never visited them on me, not full force anyway. He signaled the waiter for the check. He said, "I can't, I'm sorry, Elizabeth, I simply can't bear to see you with that little opportunistic social climber. I love you too much to sit about watching you demean yourself, dwindle into a wife." He left the money for the bill and stood up.

I was still sitting. "What does that mean?"

"It would kill me to see your brilliance, your courage, your fine mind ground down into housewifery under the heel of that boor. Because of course that's what will happen. Ground down in the mill of the ordinary like Isabel Archer in that wonderful James novel. You know the one. I love you too much to stand by and watch it." He leaned over the table, kissed my forehead. "Darling. Try to salvage some of yourself from the marriage. I'll be here if you decide against it. I'll always love you, always have your well-being at heart."

He was saying good-bye. For good.

Life without Clare.

And now I have it anyway. And nothing else.

Cursing her hands, Mary closed the lid over the piano keys.

What's the matter with me today, clumsy, awkward. I played that ballade much better yesterday. Often happens though, doesn't it, play better one day, worse the next. Doesn't mean anything.

She stood up and wandered through the rooms, entered Father's study. Papers were strewn across the desk, but no Elizabeth to be seen.

She walked out into the huge foyer, her heels' click on the parquet floor echoing in the high-ceilinged silent space. She tried the drawing room, the dining room, the kitchen. No one about anywhere. She paused, then pushed open the door leading to the little maids' rooms on the first floor, and knocked on Ronnie's door. At Ronnie's call, she pushed it open. Ronnie was lying fully clothed on the made-up bed, a pamphlet open beside her. Her eyes looked full of sleep.

"Oh, sorry. Did I wake you?"

Ronnie shook her head. "S'okay. Nodded off. Stuff can get really boring."

"I wondered. Would you like some tea?"

Ronnie pondered. She sat up. "Actually, yes."

Mary smiled broadly. "I can make it!"

"Oh, you do tea?" Ronnie grinned a little sarcastically. She got up and went into the bathroom and brushed her teeth; Mary went to start the tea ceremony.

As she entered the kitchen, Ronnie asked, "Where's Mrs. Browning?"

"I don't know. What time is it?"

Ronnie looked at her watch. "A little after four. She should be here. It's Monday, right? Not her day off."

"Maybe she's in town. It's nice she's not here," Mary said, carefully measuring spoonsful of tea into the pot. Her hand was trembling. "It's nice to have our kitchen to ourselves."

Ronnie glanced at her, said nothing. *Nice to be without a servant? Our* kitchen?

"You didn't play long today."

"You noticed?"

"It sounds good. I like it, like listening to it. Is that Chopin you play?"

"Today, yes."

"Did you ever think of playing professionally?"

Mary's hand jerked, boiling water spilled on the counter. "Oh no!" she exclaimed laughing, looking around her hopelessly for something to wipe up the spill.

Ronnie found a sponge, swooped it up.

"I was never good enough for that, not by any standard! Father said I had a nice womanly touch, pleasant for after-dinner entertainment. He liked my playing," she added tonelessly.

"I think you have more than that."

Mary, searching the cupboard, peered round at her. "Really?" Shook her head. "No, no, not possible. You know, there are so many really gifted people out there. The really talented ones are concertizing by the age of seven, nine. The sheep and goats get separated very early in the music world."

"And you're a goat?"

Mary laughed. "Afraid so." She was placing little cakes on a dish. "Let's go inside." She nodded her head in the direction of the sun room.

Not quite ready to *sit* in the kitchen.

Ronnie followed her, carrying the teapot. They settled at the glass table.

"Tea is so comforting," Mary said, pouring. Some tea spilled into the saucer. "Oooh!" she exclaimed exasperatedly. "I don't know what's the matter with me today!"

"Well, it's been a traumatic day."

"Traumatic?"

"Sure. We decided to bring the old man back here, committed ourselves to taking care of him. That's a major decision."

Mary clutched her cup. "Yes."

"Maybe you're having second thoughts."

"Are you?"

Ronnie shrugged. "You want the truth? I don't have any money and I don't have anyplace to go. I could probably get some kind of job in Boston but it wouldn't be much, it would just pay the rent and my food and it would keep me from finishing my dissertation — at best, it would delay it. For years, maybe. I have to write it to get the degree, and I need a degree if I want to do the kind of work I love in my field. If I don't do it now I'll probably never do it. I want to do it. So staying here for a few months suits my purposes." She paused to light a cigarette.

Mary shook her head at her. "I can't believe Elizabeth got you to smoke!"

Ronnie smiled, said, "Don't blame her," blew out smoke. "I figure I *can* do my share of tending him and write the dissertation at the same time. *And* I can live here for nothing while I'm doing it. I probably shouldn't tell you that. You think I'm a leech already."

Mary peered at her over her cup, rubbing her lips together. "If you're a leech, what am I? I at least started out with some money," she said bitterly.

"Huh?"

"I'm broke. Totally broke. I can just about manage to pay the mortgage on my apartment, I'm behind on the maintenance. In fact, I'm in debt. If Father hadn't fallen ill, I was going to come up here and ask him for a loan — against my inheritance, of course," she added hastily.

"I thought you married all those millionaires!" Ronnie burst out.

"Oh, that's Elizabeth's way of seeing it. Well I did marry some of course. But Harry's estate was tied up in court for years and then the judge put most of it in a trust for Marty, I only got three million dollars, oh I know that sounds like a lot of money to you Ronnie but it isn't really, believe me. Not when you're keeping up three residences and a car and chauffeur and you have a child to raise and educate — *and* a husband — because Alberto didn't have any money, he was supposed to be so rich but he wasn't, now *he* really *was* a leech, I ended up paying for everything, even his bar bills. . . ." She was whining now and Ronnie turned her head away.

"When he left me, I got this great settlement in court, everybody thinks I have oodles of money, but I never saw a dime of it. Not a dime! I understand what these women go through, the ones in the papers on welfare whose husbands don't support the children after they get divorced, I know all about it!" She shook her head, her lips pressed together angrily. "And Alberto's in Europe, so there's not a damn thing I can do about it, either!"

Ronnie stared at her.

"So I married Paul, and I would have been all right if I'd just stayed with him. But I met Don . . ." Her voice drifted off. So did her gaze.

"Don," Ronnie prompted.

Mary gazed at the garden. "He was a journalist, but a maverick, always on the wrong side of everything. He made barely enough money to support himself. But I was crazy about him, what I felt for him I'd never felt before. It was overwhelming. I'd have given up anything, everything for it. I did," she concluded grimly. "Pretty sorry story, isn't it. Girl raised for one thing and one thing only, to make a good marriage, can't even manage to do that." She gazed down at the table.

Ronnie wanted to say, you could live more cheaply, get a more modest apartment, learn to drive, sell your sables and minks and that ermine cape, your jewels. You could get a job. She stared at her, trying to imagine Mary in a three-room apartment wearing an off-the-rack dress, hopping the subway to a typing job. The picture wouldn't come.

"You could sell something maybe," she managed.

"Oh, I have! All the jewelry Harry gave me. Everything from Paul. All the good stuff. You get nothing for used furs and mine are very out-of-date. I don't keep a car and driver anymore, I sold the house in Vail after Don was killed. The house in Vermont went long before that. There's nothing left. And Marie-Laure's still in college," she sighed.

"And your son . . . ?"

Mary's mouth twisted. "Marty feels I was insane to leave Paul and that I deserve whatever happens to me. He's right, of course."

"Nice kid."

"Not very. I didn't do a very good job with my children. Wasn't cut out to be a mother. I was trained to be a courtesan," she said with deep bitterness, "and I even failed at that."

Ronnie reached her hand across the table and laid it over Mary's. "You'll be all right," she whispered.

"I will," she said with determination. "I have to be." She cocked an eye at Ronnie. "How much do you think doctors make? Do you suppose that Dr. Stamp is married?"

12

Tuesday morning, as the others stood watching, Elizabeth pulled a chair up beside Stephen's bed and sat down. Looking directly in his eyes, speaking slowly, she informed him of his fate.

"Father, the hospital can't keep you any longer. They can't do anything more for you. Your getting better is up to your body now, they can't speed it along. They'll release you, probably Friday. Most patients in your condition go to nursing homes."

Stephen, who had been glaring at the blanket up to this point, suddenly whirled, turning his fierce glare on her.

"They tell us there's a very nice nursing home on the North Shore," she continued.

Stephen pounded his left fist on the bedclothes, noiselessly: pound pound pound pound pound.

"There is another alternative," she said, her glance faltering. She looked up again bravely. "We could take you home and take care of you there."

He stared at her suspiciously.

"A nurse would come every day to check you out, and we would hire a woman to come in days and take care of your basic needs. We feel you would not care for us to do that. The household staff, at least Mrs. Browning and Teresa, will also help take care of you."

He held his wary gaze.

"But we're afraid to leave you entirely in the care of . . . people who are not family, who sometimes take advantage of helpless people — they'd have to cash checks to buy your food, they'd have control of the money. And we all live too far away to supervise how they're treating you."

His forehead furrowed.

"So to make sure you get proper care we're going to be there with you. All of us."

The mouth formed a huge O.

No?

"Unless you'd prefer the nursing home."

Oh that cold voice.

He gave her a look of such malevolent suspicion that Alex drew a sharp breath, Mary winced. Elizabeth remained impassive.

"Will you tell us which you prefer?"

She's enjoying this, Ronnie thought. Tables turned. Their relation was all about power, and she now had the upper hand. Power of youth. For what it's worth. Transitory. If Elizabeth were in the bed — and someday she might be — who'd be sitting beside her? Mary? It would be the nursing home for sure.

"You have to decide," she said calmly. "Since you don't like the idea of raising your hand, I thought you might prefer to write. I found this in the playroom." She handed him a board with a plastic leaf over it and a pointed stick. You could write on the plastic with the stick and someone could read it, but when you lifted the plastic, the writing vanished. "You can write on this with your left hand — if you like — or you can tap out your answer. One for yes, two for no."

She shouldn't be doing this, Alex thought. She's doing it without love, doesn't know how to do it with love, it's horrible. Humiliating. I should do it.

But can I do it with love? Do I love him?

She stepped forward. "Elizabeth? Shall I try?"

Elizabeth stood up. Her face was strained and very pale, she looked old. "Please," she said, moving away from the bed. She retreated to the doorway and leaned against the frame. Maybe she wasn't enjoying it, just didn't know any other way to talk to him.

Alex sat down, put her hand on Stephen's useless one. She smiled at him and spoke in a low kindly voice. "Hello, Father. We know how unpleasant this must feel to you, you must feel you have no control over your life. But you know, we'll be in the same boat someday too, if we live long enough. So we sympathize, empathize. We want things to be as much in your control as possible. We want you to decide the things you *can* decide. At this moment, it's necessary that someone take care of you, but you can get better, you may be able to speak again. We'll try to help you. What you *can* decide is who will take care of you and where."

His face had softened as she spoke, and Ronnie later swore she saw tears in his eyes. Mary scoffed at that; Alex wasn't sure. She saw a shine, whether of tears or malice she could not tell.

"Would you rather be home in your own house than in a nursing home?"

The old man nodded.

"And would you prefer to have a trained nurse — a stranger — taking care of . . . you . . . personally?"

He nodded again.

Alex smiled, patted his hand. "And would you feel better if we were there to oversee that they take proper care of you?"

His eyes glinted, he actually met her gaze. He seemed to nod. Alex decided to take the movement for a yes.

"That's what we'll do then." She smiled, patted his shoulder, and stood up. His eyes went wild, his mouth opened, trembled, tongue strained. He tried to write on the board, but couldn't hold it steady. Turning back, Alex noticed this, and darted forward to hold the board for him. He scrawled huge misshapen letters; they were illegible. He waved his arm toward Mary and Ronnie standing against the back wall as if he were waving them away.

"You don't want Mary or Ronnie taking care of you?" Alex translated. He nodded. "Who then, Elizabeth?"

He shook his head violently.

"None of us?" Alex asked, frowning.

He pointed at her with his good hand.

"Me? Only me?"

He nodded.

She walked toward her sisters, turned back, faced him. Her voice was puzzled, but chilled too. "After all those years you didn't call me, didn't write, had no contact with me at all, you now want me to take care of you?"

He strained violently, shaking the board at her, bobbing his head wildly from side to side. Alex stood fixed. Mary's face was dead white. Ronnie walked to him, held the board. "Can you write it," she ordered.

CUDNT, he scrawled, and held it up askew.

Ronnie examined it. "I think he means *couldn't*."

Alex stepped forward, her face tense and vivid. "Why not?"

He tried to write, dropped the board. Ronnie retrieved it and held it for him. He scrawled wildly. Alex stepped around to read as he wrote. It made no sense. He watched her face, and clumsily pulled up the plastic. He wrote again: AGREED . . . the word dripped off the board.

"Agreed? With whom?"

He laid his head in his left hand.

"You made an agreement? With my mother? Why?"

His head fell back against the pillow. He closed his eyes, nodding yes.

"Why?"

He did not open his eyes or attempt to answer.

Ronnie laid the board and stick on the side table and walked back to her sisters. They stood there together gazing at him.

Alex spoke. "I'm sorry, but I won't stay without them — all of them. We come together. As a unit. Not separately."

He opened his eyes then and gazed at her. The fierceness was gone, he was drained. He dropped his eyes, looked at his useless hand, closed his eyes.

Silently, the sisters left.

Ronnie took a pair of work gloves and went out to the old barn. She pushed the wheelbarrow toward the woods, walking to the spot where she had last left off picking up kindling, and began to fill the barrow. She filled it swiftly, wheeled the load back, dumped it in the kindling basket in the barn, and returned for more. She worked fast, hard, trying to push away thought, work up a sweat. After three trips, she was wet inside her clothes, tiring, and had to slow down. Mind tilting into craziness, images crowding in, unbearable, unbearable, but it was all unbearable, all of it, Elizabeth sitting there like a schoolteacher instructing a child in basic history, but it was the future she was talking about, his future, with no more feeling than if she'd been reciting the names of the battles fought in World War II, Mary standing there trembling and white, as if she were about to be beaten.

All so ugly.

What was it about this family? All this beauty around them, the gardens, the house, the furniture. All the beauty bought in marriage, refining skin and nostril, sheening the hair of each successive generation. Yet everything that happened among them was so ugly. Was that what families were like?

Suppose Enriqué were in bed after a stroke: what would Rosa do? Ronnie imagined her sitting beside him, stroking his useless hand. She'd cover his face with kisses, she'd be crying. He'd probably be crying too, but he'd put his good hand over hers, try to act as if he had things in control. The kids would throng around clumsily, knocking things over, making noise, tears in their eyes. If they told him they were taking him home to take care of him, how would it be? He'd cry, he'd grab Rosa's hand, he'd try to protest he didn't want to be a burden, but he'd be grateful, happy. . . .

Was that because they were poor, because money and power had not been issues in their household?

But money and power *were* issues in their family. In every family. Rosa and Enriqué argued over how to handle the kids, especially Tina, over Raoul's hanging out with a gang, over Enriqué's Friday-night drinking with the guys he worked with: they weren't even really his friends, Rosa complained, and he spent so much money. He couldn't explain it to her, he couldn't make her understand. He was trying to say those guys are all I have that makes me a man, all I have besides you and the kids, and this place, our home, our kids, all this belongs to you. Here I'm not a man but only part of you, it. After Raoul was killed, after Tina went on the street, Rosa hardened. She stopped giving him all her earnings to pay bills with, she was determined to save some to get Téo out of there, send him to college. They had a big fight. He needed her money to make ends meet, he said. She was enraged, said he'd drunk up enough money to save Raoul. That pushed him over the edge, he loved Raoul, probably felt guilty about what had happened to him. He hit her. She told him to get out. He cried.

But that was the only time he ever hit her. Enriqué was pretty good for a man. What did Linsey say that night? When Emily Tedesco said she'd gotten married but was finding it difficult living with a man. "It's a dirty job but somebody's got to do it." Hah! Enriqué loved his family, he was loving to them most of the time.

And suppose Enriqué stayed helpless for months, years, he'd become a terrible burden. Would Rosa still tend him lovingly, would the kids help? Suppose it was Rosa had the stroke. Would Enriqué take care of her?

He would, he would.

I have to believe he would.

Everything reversed, baby grows up, parents grow old, now the baby has to change the parents' diapers, feed them, put powder on their bottoms, carry away their bedpan. . . . Horrible. Most people sent them to old folks' homes. To die.

Natural economy of life. Old people weren't going to get better and become productive, reproduce, raise children again. Elizabeth says life is naturally cruel. No. What did she say? "The natural economy of life is cruel."

Ronnie sat down on a cold damp stone, pulled a cigarette out of the pack in her pocket, and lighted it, taking a deep drag.

It was Monday, yesterday, the day they made their pact. Having drinks in the sitting room last night. Alex was upset, she looked pale and her whole body was shaking, but she wouldn't say why. Come to think of it, it was after she went up to the nursery, after I found the key for her . . . She wanted a fire, I built it. Mary pale and restless, twisting her string belt around her fingers — what a dress she had on, silk, now that really was silk, pale pale bluish green, cut low, sort of drippy, whatever they call that dress style. Looked regal. Long long long pearls. Real? Maybe she could sell them. Elizabeth smoking one cigarette after another, tight, her thin face pale and lined.

She'd been talking about some disaster in the newspaper, was just musing, and she said, "The natural economy of life is cruel." Went on rambling, a long defense of her economic theories it sounded like: wonder who she was defending them against. Survival of the fittest, which she stupidly equates with the physically strongest — only muscles and money in her economy. Fittest elbow the less fit out of the way, take all the food, take all the women — who don't seem to have anything to say about any of this. Went on and on about individual liberty. I said she seemed to me to be defending a few men's liberty to rob and kill all the others.

She didn't even hear me.

Craziness, neo-Darwinism drummed up to support capitalist exploitation of the entire world by a tiny elite. Created a way of life that's insupportable. Can't last, we're all dying, the world being poisoned. Groups need cooperation, adaptation to survive. Individuals don't survive, after all. Aggression destroys the aggressors *and* the victims. People don't realize that. A higher proportion of slave traders than of slaves died on the slave ships. Every militaristic society overextends, goes down in a heap, real sudden. Assyria, Athens, Sparta, Rome, well that took some time I guess, dwindled down by coffee spoons. Is that in a poem? Freshman English? England, Germany, the United States. On our way out. She knows that too. End of an era, she said, end of western civilization as we know it. God knows it deserves to die, with all its hero-killers and their monuments spanning the globe testifying to their triumph over, destruction of brown-yellowredtanblack people, whites too if they were poor. But she was mourning it like it was something glorious and noble. Mourning her father? Defending him, his politics. Defending the devil. That guy she loved, whatshisface, Clarence?

Her politics are her real legacy from Daddy.

Couldn't keep arguing with her, she looked so awful. Like she was the one going to die not him, skin yellowish-gray, hair limp, face somehow twisted. In pain. Alex went over and sat on the arm of her chair and put her arms around her, held her. I hate her politics but I felt like doing the same thing.

Odd, for me.

Elizabeth permitted Alex's arms but her body stiffened a bit. She tried to relax into the embrace. She closed her eyes. A tear trickled down her cheek and Alex wiped it away with the back of her hand. She patted Alex's hand, acknowledging her kindness.

She pulled herself up. "It's been a hard day," she said.

Hard life. Supporting the devil, advancing his cause. Like Momma. But she couldn't recognize the devil. He presented himself tall and slender and gorgeous, wearing white shoes and a tennis sweater, gracious over drinks. He stood by the pool at a garden party on his own estate drinking with the president of the United States, joking, laughing, easy. Manly, eschewing the comfort of the green-and-white-striped tent even though it's starting to rain, then becoming thoughtful, considerate of some people anyway, easing the president toward the tent, holding his elbow, asking if he wouldn't like to go inside. Doesn't notice me running toward the tent carrying that beautiful platter of poached salmon parsley cucumber lemon and radishes laid just so around it Momma sweated over it, getting spattered by rain. Almost walked right into me. It would have been my fault. I swerved, saved it, the salmon shifted on the plate, my heart in my chest, but I saved it. Terror.

Legitimacy is being easy. Anywhere everywhere.

No one is easy anywhere everywhere.

Ergo, no one is legitimate.

Is that good Socratic logic?

Start again.

Legitimacy is having the manner of appearing easy anywhere and everywhere. And avoiding any situation in which you won't. Therefore, legitimacy is constricting — there's so much of the world you have to avoid. So many people, situations, places!

Like Mary. Terrified in my old neighborhood, studying my apartment the way I'd study a Mongolian yurt. Kept her gloves on the whole time. Bet she even flushed the toilet with them on.

She doesn't feel legitimate, she feels stupid, small, timid, frightened. Clutching at her straw of legitimacy makes her mean. But she can pass for legitimate, one of the elite. She's *in* in a way you never can never could be no matter what you did or do Ronalda Velez.

She snapped her fingers. That for you and your Ph.D. you stupid ass.

She ground out the cigarette, tossed a twig in the wheelbarrow and raised her body. It hurt, and she stretched and rubbed her back.

When will you learn you can't think your way out of a paper bag? You think you're so tough. You don't begin to know tough. Now Elizabeth . . . !

Only Ronnie looked normal when they gathered for drinks that evening. She built a fire without being asked, and she was the one who made the drinks.

"Jesus, I feel like I'm tending three zombies. We don't have to do this, you know. We haven't even told the doctor yet."

There was a long silence before anyone spoke. Then Elizabeth said in a dead voice, "No, I want to do it."

Mary's face, usually clear and white as porcelain, was crisscrossed with shadows. "Yes," she said faintly.

"We *have* to do it," Alex said fiercely. She looked the worst, her usual blonde pert sweet prettiness drained and lined.

"What, am I the only one who doesn't know what's going on?" Ronnie asked suspiciously.

"What's going on?" Alex asked angrily.

Elizabeth stirred. "Don't be paranoid."

"Well for chrissake, what is it?"

The sisters looked at each other.

"I can't speak for anyone else," Elizabeth said. "I have my own problems."

"So what are they?"

"Just memories. The past."

"Or lack of memories," Alex exploded. "I called my mother this afternoon. I told her what he said. In the hospital. I asked her what he meant by an agreement. And you know what she said? She said she had no idea what he was talking about, that the stroke must have addled his brain! Do you believe that? My mother! I CAN'T TRUST my own mother!"

"Join the club," Elizabeth grunted.

"I barely knew mine," Mary said sadly.

Momma.

"She's lying to me! I know it! I know it!" Alex cried.

"Maybe you're lucky," Elizabeth said with a mean smile. "The worst things I ever heard were the truths my mother told me."

"My mother never talked to me at all."

My mother loved the devil.

"And you were no help either," Mary whined to Elizabeth.

"I'm not your mother," Elizabeth said between her teeth.

Ronnie held her head. "Jesus, are we back there again? I thought we'd moved beyond that."

"She doesn't care how I'm suffering!" Alex cried. "She doesn't care that I feel as if I'm going crazy. I told her, I told her, I said, I have to know! But she goes on lying!"

"Mothers fuck," Ronnie said with a grim little smile.

"Obviously," Elizabeth murmured, and they all laughed.

A laugh. Good, thought Ronnie.

"Listen," Ronnie said, "it's intolerable, it's going to be unbearable if you all keep on being this way. We can't do this if you're going to be like this. You have to get past whatever it is that makes you all fight all the time or else we can't do this. You know I'd really like to stay here with you for a month or two, but I can't stand this."

"I've told you what's upsetting me," Alex complained.

"We are all upset, aren't we. It's understandable: we've made a life-changing decision. How come you exempt yourself from this conflict?" Elizabeth asked Ronnie.

"Argh!" Ronnie cried. "I'm not fighting with anybody am I? And I'm not as upset as you-all. It isn't that I don't have my own difficulties with it. It's — I mean, he's coming back here in such a different position, I'm in a different position, I'm not here as his servant's daughter, I'm here . . . with you . . . as another . . . daughter. But I am upset by . . . the whole thing seems so ugly, his . . . incapacity and his rage — and our . . . terror, or whatever it is . . . and . . ." She stared hard at the fire, trying to find words. "It's so strange to see the past being turned upside down. We have the power now. Parents treat kids any way they want . . . but now we're the parents. In a way. I feel as if we're sliding down a tunnel into hell. . . ."

"Power corrupts," Alex said, sententiously.

"A tunnel into hell. Yes," Elizabeth said in a low voice. "I feel that too. But I also feel — you know — being here this way — with Father gone, without a houseful of servants and guests — but with you" — she glanced at Mary — "and you" — she glanced at Alex — "it throws me back into past summers when I was a child. That wasn't the happiest time of my life. It hurls me backwards as if in my body and emotions and whole sense of myself I'm still ten and eleven and twelve . . . I *feel* like that child. But I'm not one, I expect more of myself. These feelings are terrifying and terrible. Here I am, fifty-two — well, almost fifty-three years old . . ."

"Oh! That's right!" Mary exclaimed, "your birthday is soon. The thirtieth, isn't it? When is that?"

"Umm, Friday, I think," Elizabeth said indifferently. "Do you remember how you felt as a child? It's horrible! Childhood is the most terrible time of life!" She stopped pulling at her hair and looked up at them. "Wasn't it?"

"Yes," Mary murmured.

"I was happy as a child," Alex said vaguely. "I think. I have a lot of happy memories, mostly about Grandpa and Charlie after he came into our lives. . . . Funny, I don't have really happy memories of my mother — or unhappy ones either. Charlie and Grandpa are the ones I had fun with, they played with me."

Ronnie smiled. "It's ironic — here I am — a *chicana* bastard whose mother was a servant, who didn't have a dime. Of course, we had a place to live and enough food, without which — nothing. But I had a wonderful childhood. I was really happy — outdoors, anyway. Not at school. But I loved coming back here after school and running outdoors. You know, for a while there were horses. . . ."

"From my mother's time," Mary said softly. "I don't remember when he got rid of the last of them. Do you?" she asked Ronnie.

"I remember horses!" Alex cried in excitement. "I gave them sugar! There was a man . . ."

"Mcsomething," Mary said. "He took care of them. McDonough?"

Elizabeth frowned. "McCormick?"

"Yes," Alex said dreamily, and drifted off.

"No," Mary argued. "MacTavish?"

"That's way off! He was Irish. MacTavish is Scottish!"

Mary shrugged. "Whatever. He really knew horses. When did Father sell them, Ronnie?"

"I was little. Don't remember. Just one day, they weren't here anymore. I cried and cried. Momma bought me a little horse made of clay afterward, to try to make me feel better, and I threw it on the floor and smashed it in a fit of temper. I'll never forget her face. Like I'd slapped her. I'll never forget that. Cruel, I was."

"Kids are cruel," said Alex.

"So are parents," Mary said coldly.

"Anyway, I liked parts of my childhood. There were dogs and cats and normal wildlife — birds and butterflies and chipmunks and squirrels and raccoons, but there used to be deer, wild turkeys, foxes, pheasants, quail here too. And the plants! Flowers and the vegetable garden, and trees to climb or swing on. When no one was here, I'd play in the swimming pool . . . And Momma — she always had a lap for me to sit on, cookies and milk, a hand to stroke me. I was happy until I realized he . . ."

"It was beautiful. I wasn't able to see all that," Elizabeth mourned. "Take pleasure in it."

"No," Mary murmured.

"What are you, an echo?"

"I'm just agreeing with you, Lizzie," Mary said in a hurt voice.

"Tell your own story then."

Mary's fingers were twisting her rings. "It's the helplessness I remember most. Feeling little, feeling like a nothing. Knowing I was sad but knowing too that I couldn't do anything to make myself feel better. Because I was a child. I wanted to be grown up, so I could get away from here. . . ."

"Me too. I wanted to take command of things, of my life. And I knew that to do that I had to get away. From him, from my mother. My mother was bad, she didn't mean to be, she was just totally obsessed with the injustice done her. But I tried to be sort of frozen around her, to keep her from getting to me. But when I was here, the things that happened — oh, Father, or the servants, or the aunts and uncles, your mother" — she glanced at Mary — "somebody would say or do something. Maybe not even to me or about me — to or about you, maybe, you were such a golden girl . . . And the difference in the way we were treated was so striking, I couldn't not feel it. I tried. I wouldn't cry or say anything, I was ashamed of my weakness, humiliated that they could hurt me. I'd go out in the woods. I could never cry. Sometimes I even tried, but I couldn't. I'd imagine being grown up and getting away and doing things that would make people love me, acclaim me, think I was wonderful. And now, I'll be out walking in the woods and suddenly feel overwhelmed, just the way I felt back then. . . ."

Mary leaned forward, staring at the floor, her hands clasped loosely in front of her, almost as if in half-prayer. "It was different for me. Everybody paid attention to me, I was always being picked up and kissed and fondled. But then I was always trundled off out of the way with some nanny or other. Some of them were nice. But . . . And then after Mother died . . . Father wasn't around much, you know. . . . And even when he was, he didn't really pay attention to me except . . . He paid attention to me when other people were around. The only other time . . . the only way I could get him to pay attention to me was if I acted a certain way, if I was coy and teased him, flirted with him, really. . . . So . . ."

"Yes," Elizabeth said sadly. "I tried to be brilliant at the dinner table. He mostly laughed at me."

"No he didn't Lizzie! When you were young, he talked to you! He'd laugh at you but in a nice way. He thought you were really smart. He'd mock me when I tried to join in, say, 'What are you doing, trying to be smart like your sister!' And laugh at me for a fool."

"I don't remember him talking to me."

"He did, though. Before you went to London, before you took the job in Washington. Not later. I wondered why. It seemed as if he was frightened of you, the way he sneered, he wouldn't let you get a sentence out. But when we were little, I used to try to talk like a smart person, talk like you. I'd sit out in my playhouse and pretend I was a grown-up lady, but I could never figure out what to say. I'd say things you'd said, but I knew I didn't have them right. And it wasn't much fun because I didn't know what grown-up ladies did besides have tea and chat with other ladies about clothes and the ladies who weren't there. And I was all alone. . . ."

"I stole your dishes," Elizabeth said.

"What?"

"Your little tea set. In the playhouse. After you went back to school one year, I stole it."

Mary sat back. "My dishes!"

"Don't you remember, that little tea set you had, pink roses on white, with a gold band?"

"I remember a tea set . . ." She broke off, stared at Elizabeth. "But why?" she asked in a soft bewildered voice.

Elizabeth burst into tears. "I guess I was trying to steal the love I felt you had."

The three sat appalled. Elizabeth crying? She sobbed in hard dry wrenches, briefly, pulled a hankie from her pocket and blew her nose. She raised her head.

"Sorry," she said stiffly.

"Oh Lizzie, I would have given it to you if I'd known you wanted it. I would have given you anything. . . ."

Elizabeth's eyes shone wet. "I know." She burst into tears again, burying her face in her hands. No one moved.

It was a long time before anyone spoke, and then it was Alex, musing, "God, how important mothers are! I don't think I ever realized. Don't you think it's hard? I mean, I'm a mother, and I know how hard I tried, how hard I worked, but I bet my kids have complaints like this. Can any mother live up to what we need of them? Is motherhood possible?"

"Oh, my mother didn't mean to be rotten," Elizabeth said. "She was so wretched herself. She never got over what Father did to her. What Father did just sank in there with what her father did and her mother did or didn't do and stewed itself up into a poison broth. She wanted things to be better for me. But she had no idea of what it was to be a child. From the time she was five years old she'd had to take care of one baby or another. She had no childhood."

"You're so forgiving," Mary said ruefully. "I can't forgive my mother, and all she did was die. You can't help dying."

Elizabeth looked at her pointedly.

"Well, maybe she could," Mary said defensively, "but only because she was so unhappy that nothing else mattered. But I guess that's why I can't forgive her. Because she never cared about me at all anyway!"

"Excuse me, but are you saying that Elizabeth is a forgiving person?" Ronnie asked incredulously.

They all laughed, even Elizabeth.

"Well, maybe in that one instance," Mary smiled.

"I'm not. I hate her," Elizabeth said. "Oh I guess I love her too. That's the bitching fact about parents and children. But I *had* to try to understand why she acted the way she did. Otherwise, I'd have to think it was me, my . . . awfulness. I mean, *nobody* loved me. Nobody. Not my mother, not my father, not my grandparents, my aunts or uncles . . . no one."

"Poor, poor baby!" Alex breathed.

Elizabeth glared at her but her eyes were glittery.

Ronnie changed the subject. "So we're all feeling thrust back into childhood, babyhood I guess. When you can't control anything, including your emotions."

Elizabeth wiped her eyes. "It is really strange, this visit. Don't know why — all of you, Father, what's happened in my own life. Decisions I made in my life which at the time I was sure were right but now look crazy to me. I feel as if the whole basis of my life, the floor of it, has cracked, and I'm falling through it, falling into a dark basement. . . ."

Mary leaned forward, face suddenly animated. "Oh, Lizzie, that's how I feel too, only I feel as if I'm in a vertical tunnel, falling falling, it's dark and nothing is familiar, not a signpost, not a single thing I can reach out and touch, recognize. Except Father, and Father looms so huge, it's his face at the top, I know I agreed to help take care of him, but I don't know if I can do it, I'm so afraid. . . ."

"Afraid of what?" Ronnie asked.

Mary's fingers twisted each other cruelly. She shook her head back and forth, over and over.

"Last night," she whispered, "I dreamt he was in bed, in a bed like the one he's in in the hospital, but in his room here, upstairs. And I went in with tea on a tray, and I said, 'Look, Father, I made this by myself,' and he sat up and he said, 'You can't do that,' and he got out of bed and he walked over to me and knocked the tray to the floor and pulled out a knife and he killed me. Killed me!" She laid her head in her hand. "They say you never really die in your dreams, but I did. I felt myself fall, I knew I was dying, I hit the floor. That's when I woke up."

"You're not imagining your dream is prophetic," Elizabeth asked, not unkindly.

"I suppose I am," she sniveled.

"Mary!" Elizabeth spoke sharply. "The damage he's suffered is largely irreversible! He *can't* get up, he *can't* walk or use his right hand! He never will again!"

Mary burst into loud sobbing. With one hand holding a handkerchief to her face, she reached out her other one toward Ronnie. "Ronnie! Ronnie!" she cried.

Ronnie went to her, crouched beside her. She touched Mary's hand. "I'm here, Mary."

Mary threw her arm around Ronnie's neck. "You'll protect me, say you will!"

"*Mary*," Ronnie protested.

"You can do it! You can do it! You're like a boy! And he never acted like a father to you, he wasn't your father except by a shudder in the loin. You can do it. You're free of the taint. You're like the virgin in legend, the one who can tame the unicorn, who can bring harmony to society, you know, like in Shakespeare!"

Ronnie stroked Mary's hand. "Free of what taint," she asked coolly.

"Womanhood! You're not really a woman, you're a lesbian, you're like a man. You can do what we can't."

Ronnie shook her head and stood up.

"That's crazy, Mary," Elizabeth said.

"Maybe it is! Maybe it is! But it's what I feel!" She looked up at Ronnie, her face like a child's, wet and swollen and pink, pleading. "Promise me you'll protect me from him."

Ronnie stroked Mary's forehead. "I promise. For whatever it's worth."

Mary calmed. She blew her nose. She leaned her head back against the chair.

Elizabeth was in deep frown, staring at the floor.

"No one is talking to me," Alex said in a near-whine. "No one is asking me, helping me!"

"What do you want us to do?" Elizabeth asked in irritation. "Call up your mother and scold her? What can we do for you?"

"We all carry around our own pain, Alex," Mary said self-righteously.

"None of you seem to understand," Alex said wildly. "I don't understand myself!" She stood up. "I feel as if I'm going crazy! Really! I have blackouts! Sometimes I faint! I fainted yesterday, fell down on the floor!" She plopped back into the chair. "I don't remember anything from my young life! It's all a blank! A void! I need help!" She put her head in her hands.

"What a crew," muttered Ronnie. "And *we're* going to take care of a sick man?"

13

With the nurses' help, the sisters had made a list of what they would need, went home and drew up a rota. For two days, each did a share of the telephoning to arrange to rent a hospital bed and supplies, hire a registered nurse, a practical nurse, and a live-in maid to help Mrs. Browning and Teresa with the extra work. They called a local shop and ordered a television set, a swivel-top table, and a VCR. They called Boston to order a small computer that would allow Stephen to type messages onto the television screen — but that would take a week to arrive. They discussed his diet with Mrs. Browning, held a meeting with the staff to discuss new schedules and duties. Apart from their frequent conferences about these matters, they had almost no conversation with each other. When their chores were done, each retreated to her private space — Elizabeth to the library, Ronnie to her room, Mary to exercise in the playroom (which she had made her own, no longer reading in the sitting or drawing room), and Alex for a walk outdoors.

At night, they gathered for drinks as usual, but on Wednesday for the first time, they used the playroom, a large room in the rear of the house, with sliding glass doors opening onto a terrace and the back garden. It was isolated so that sound would not carry to the formal front rooms, the dining, sitting, and drawing rooms. Unlike the upstairs nursery, it had been created for children past infancy, and had a big stone fireplace, comfortable plump chintz-covered sofas and chairs, a big television set, stereo equipment, and a Ping Pong table pushed against the wall. Its overcrowdedness added to its easy, comfortable air. The sisters sat in front of the television set watching the evening news, sipping Perrier, cola, wine, and vermouth cassis, watching reports on another spurious effort to end the war in El Salvador, another sharp drop in the stock market, Chilean police rounding up citizens in cities across the country.

Funny how long silences always feel angry, whatever their cause, Ronnie thought. How we are now, each one of us burrowing inwards. Except Alex, who's usually the nice one. Now she's jangly, exploding with frustration. She screamed "Shit!" when she dropped her handbag as we waited for the car. Tears in her eyes as she bent to pick up her scattered possessions. I helped her, but she barely thanked me.

Dinner was almost as silent. Mary's suggestion that Father's bed be moved against the north wall so he could face the windows was discussed at length but without passion, as was Elizabeth's worry that the new intercom system was not working properly. They moved from dinner back to the playroom and immediately turned on the television again, sat there through something, watched the eleven o'clock news, and each went off to bed murmuring unfelt good-nights.

The morning of his move, Stephen maintained a stubborn grim silence, looking like a man about to be led to the death chamber. Nurse Thompson, taking his pulse and blood pressure, reproached him gently: "I don't think you realize how fortunate you are, Mr. Upton. I know it's upsetting to be in your condition, but believe me, few people are as lucky as you. I tell you, I see it every day: people ship their parents off to these rest homes without a second thought. And here your wonderful daughters want to take care of you themselves. You're a very lucky man!"

He was the color of parchment as they moved him. Mary watched the stretcher-bearers slide him into the ambulance, returning him to life, real life, not like the hospital, which was just a transit station, but to his house, his home, his own bedroom, in this shape. Forever in this shape. Forever helpless. Unbearable, it must be, she thought.

Alex saw the tears in her eyes. She laid her hand on Mary's arm.

It took a host of helpers and observers to transfer Stephen to his house, to the tender care of his loving daughters. Poor girls, Dr. Stamp thought, they don't know what they're in for. He must be a remarkable man, to have daughters who love him so much. Of course, there may be a lot of money involved. That may be it. He's probably kept them on tenterhooks about their inheritances. That's it, has to be it. Dr. Stamp shook their hands and went back to work. He knew he would hear from them again. This could not last long.

Each segment of the team had its own ideas of proper procedure, so stretcher-bearers argued with nurses, and again with the nurse waiting at the house, who argued with Mrs. Browning and the practical nurse, all on hand to oversee the important event. The daughters stood guard in the hospital corridor, in the courtyard, and again in front of the mansion, saying nothing, although Mary started forward at one moment when she thought the stretcher was tilted too far to one side. But he was delivered safely back to his house, to his old bedroom in the front of the house on the second floor, a room called his for nearly sixty of his eighty-two years, which opened onto a small sitting room shared with a bedroom that had been home to three different wives. Now and forever more empty.

He didn't care.

He doesn't care, Mary thought. Sex is nothing to him now. "A shudder in the loins engenders there / The broken wall, the burning roof and tower / And Agamemnon dead." Is that all I am to him, a shudder in the loins? Is that all fatherhood is? All it was to my kids' fathers. Harry didn't want more kids, another family. Alberto didn't want any at all: he never even laid eyes on Marie-Laure. She saw him at a party last year for the first time: so dissipated-looking she was shocked. *That* was her father? Dancing with some B-movie queen. Wanted to go up and introduce herself and didn't have the nerve. Poor kid, what must that feel like, your own father doesn't even have the interest to lay eyes on you. Like Alex. Maybe we should just write off fathers. Still, I can't blame Alberto for the way she is. I did that myself, harping, carping: posture, grammar, manners, makeup, you *must* be right, you're a girl! Hates me for it. Always critical, she says. Tries to avoid me.

Mary stood watching, silent, beside the door, trying to keep out of the way of the many functionaries restoring Stephen Upton to his family home. Father, she thought, trying to connect the word with the helpless gray broken man in the bed.

Looks like an alien unsure if he can breathe in this air. Old, he is old and frightened, his life no longer in his control, try to remember that, Elizabeth, try to speak to him gently.

Did he ever speak to me gently?

So what are you going to do, beat him up? He never beat you up.

He did worse.

Elizabeth. Try to be a decent human being. Try to be like Alex.

But she could not control her drive for efficiency, and kept interfering with the professionals arranging the man, the oxygen tank that would be kept near him in case of need, the nurse making the bed, arranging the furniture. The nurse's patient long-suffering looks drove Elizabeth back and she went to stand beside Mary. Both of them stood with their hands clasped behind them. Elizabeth jumped suddenly, as something alien, something soft and clammy wormed into her hand. It was Mary's finger. She clasped it. They clasped hands behind their backs like children.

Alex felt a ferocious thrust of rage. She could hardly bear to look at him. A hate she did not name, failed to recognize, never having felt such an emotion before, inflamed her stomach, her esophagus, her throat. Hideous horrible old man, a father who never was one, who abandoned me, who never even sent me a birthday card. What did I ever do to him, how could I have done anything terrible to him, I was only nine years old.

I have a right to feel this way. My father abandoned me, and the truth is, Mother is abandoning me too, always abandoned me, you can abandon someone without leaving. What else is she doing when she refuses to tell me why she left, why she took me away, why she deprived me of my sisters and my daddy? And now he can't speak. This is unbearable. HE CAN'T SPEAK!

Ronnie tried to help. Because she blended in with the variegated skin hues of the working staff, they took her for one of them, and appreciated her efforts. Her Indian face remained impassive. She did not speak.

Sick old man, helpless now. Left to our tender mercies. We'll probably tear him limb from limb.

Do I really want to do that? Do I care about him at all?

A crab clawed her intestines in answer, doubling her over for a
moment.

Throughout the process, Stephen glared. He glared at the workers, and
once the workers had left, glared throughout Alex's recital of the various
comforts they had arranged for him (for the sisters had agreed that Alex
communicated with him best). See, a remote control button on the table
near his hand, to press if he needed someone; a television set directly
opposite him, with a remote control; a bed tray and bedside table with
everything he could possibly want set upon it. And if not, just press the
button. A little computer was coming later in the week, he'd have to learn
to use it, but he would and he could type instructions on it. He showed
his teeth at that. Well, okay, if you don't like that idea, here is the plastic
tablet with its stick, to write on. "Now," she said, sitting on the armchair
pulled permanently up beside his bed, "tell us what you like to eat."

He looked, for the first time, directly at Ronnie. Nodded his head
toward her.

" 'She knows,' he's trying to say," Elizabeth translated.

They all looked at Ronnie. She shrugged. "I wasn't paying attention,"
she told them. She looked at him. "I don't know. I'm not my mother," she
said coldly.

"You know what you've been eating for the last months, Ronnie,"
Mary said with irritation.

"I can't remember. Anglo food all tastes the same to me."

Alex pulled a side chair up beside the armchair, patted it. "Now
Ronnie, you sit here, and I'll sit here, and we'll ask Father what he likes to
eat."

Ronnie stood where she was. "He likes Anglo food. Roast beef, baked
potatoes, steak, pot roast, leg of lamb well done, lobster salad, omelets.
Mrs. Browning knows, not me. Doesn't he have a diet? Didn't the doctor
give you a menu?"

"Yes. I think so." Elizabeth darted across the room to where her bag
was, searched it violently.

Alex leaned toward Stephen. "Okay. Now, Father, suppose I start naming things and you write on the tablet — here, let me lay it on the tray for you — you write — let's see — you write a number when I say the thing, you know, one to five, according to how much you like it. You know? If you like a thing very much, you make a one, and if you don't like it at all, you make a five. We won't give you any fives. Okay? That shouldn't be too hard."

Stephen glared at her. He picked up the stick with his left hand and scrawled on the tablet: LAWYER. He pulled up the plastic and scrawled again: WILL.

"I knew it, I knew it," Elizabeth muttered to Mary.

"If you knew it, why did you let it happen!" Mary's hair, usually flawlessly composed, was in tangles; curls popped up all over her head. Her face was damp with perspiration and she was breathing heavily as if she had been running.

"It's my fault," Alex said, near tears. "I was treating him like a child. But I didn't know what else to do, how else to do it!"

"It's not your fault. It's no one's fault," Elizabeth said anxiously. "Not even mine!" she said, whirling on Mary. "There's no way to be right with him, no way to be kind. . . ."

"What do we do now?" Mary wailed.

"Call the goddamned lawyer, why not?" Ronnie shrugged. "Jesus, you're being a bunch of fucking saints, why do you feel so guilty?"

"Suppose he disinherits us!" Mary cried. "Suppose he's so angry at us for taking care of him that he cuts us all out!"

"Don't you think this lawyer — is his name Hollis? — don't you think he'd see that as insanity? Because it is."

Mary reached out behind her for the arms of the easy chair and let herself down into it slowly. "It is?" she asked shakily.

"Well, of course it is, Mary!" Alex said heartily, reassuringly. "I mean, we're doing a good thing, a kind thing!"

"We are?"

Elizabeth smiled her grim smile and sat down beside Mary. She patted Mary's hand. "Mary always goes by the emotions. And she knows we have subversive intentions. That we're not being kind."

Ronnie was sitting at the glass sun room table gazing out at the dry gray sunlit field behind the house. "What a champion game player he is," she said. "He knew just how to reverse the power arrangement. How to bring you all to your knees." She hooted a laugh.

Elizabeth stared at her. She lighted a cigarette. "Of course, Ronnie's absolutely right, that's what he's doing. Trying to intimidate us. And succeeding. I'm going to call Hollis. And then we're all going up there and tell him we've done it." She stood up and left the room.

Mary still sat trembling, sweating and pale. Ronnie gazed at her, went and sat beside her. She put her hand on Mary's arm.

"Listen, Mare — can you hear this? You can live without a lot of money. You can learn how. Sell what you can, and invest what you get and live on the interest. You can do it, I can show you how."

"You don't understand!" Mary cried. "If I don't live the way I've always lived, I'd lose all my friends! *Who would I be?*"

Ronnie's body jerked against the chair back.

Elizabeth returned. "Okay," she said briskly, "let's go."

Alex stood up, at attention. Ronnie looked up, unwound her legs, stood up. She looked at Mary. "Come on, Mare."

Mary appealed to Elizabeth with eyes like a child about to be fed cod-liver oil. "Do I have to go?"

"Yes. All of us have to go. Up!" Elizabeth ordered.

Ronnie reached out her hand, Mary took it and stood. "I won't be any use. I'm too . . . destroyed."

Elizabeth grabbed her arm, put her hand around it hard.

"Ouch!" Mary whimpered.

"Now listen," Elizabeth whispered. "You are going to behave like a person! He's trying to intimidate us, and we're going to tell him he can't. *Show* him he can't. Understand?"

"But he can!" Mary cried. "He can hurt me! He always could and he still can! Don't you see?"

Elizabeth stood stock-still. She turned to face Mary, who was inches shorter, and moved back a little so she didn't have to look down. "Mary, the only power he has now is money. And I promise you: if he cuts us out of his will, I will buy a house in Virginia. In a good neighborhood. I can afford it. You'll come and live with me. There are society people in those towns, I have a high-level, visible government job, a high-status job. You have old friends there. You will be accepted."

Mary's eyelashes dampened. She bit her lip. She looked up at Elizabeth like a naughty child. "Suppose you lose your job. Suppose the Democrats win in 'eighty-eight. What will you do then?"

Elizabeth smiled. She really isn't a dope. "I'll be fine. I've been saving money all these years, I've never spent all of my salary. I'll get a university appointment, or go to work for a think tank or an investment firm, and make a fortune. I'll be fine and so will you. If you add what you have to what I have, we'll live like queens. We don't need him, Mary. Try to believe me!"

Mary threw her arms around Elizabeth and buried her head in Elizabeth's bosom. Elizabeth stiffened, looked uncomfortable. She put her hand on Mary's back, patted it automatically. "Okay? Ready?"

Mary stood up, wiped her eyes. "Ready."

And upstairs they marched.

The television set in Stephen's room was tuned to a news program on CNN. Stephen's eyes were at half-mast. The practical nurse, Florence, an almond-colored woman with oriental eyes and a northern British accent, looked up from her knitting and smiled as they entered. "He's been just fine," she said reassuringly, putting down her needles. "Watching the telly."

"Thank you, Florence. Perhaps you'd like some tea? Mrs. Browning is in the kitchen, I'm sure she'd be glad to fix it for you. Will you excuse us? We need to talk to our father."

"Of course!" the woman said heartily, put her work down and stood. "I'll be glad of a stretch," she said, arching her back and stretching her arms out behind her substantial body. She smiled apologetically, darting around them to leave the room.

Elizabeth switched off the television set. Only then did Stephen acknowledge them, looking up sharply, angrily.

"Hello Father, how do you feel?" Elizabeth began, walking to the bedside. The others followed her, stood there like sentinels.

He glared at them.

"I called Hollis. He couldn't come this afternoon and he's going sailing this weekend, but he'll drive out to see you Monday around eleven. He knows you want to discuss your will. He wondered if you want him to bring a secretary with him?"

Stephen shook his head heavily. No.

"I'll inform him. Now, about your meals. Mrs. Browning says she knows what you like, and she has the diet the hospital suggested. She'll draw up your menus and we'll stay out of it. If you want any changes, just let us know.

"We'll leave you alone now, but we'll come up and visit with you after dinner. Is there anything you want? Anything we can do?"

He shook his head, and hit the power button on his remote control, turning the television set back on.

When they reached the downstairs foyer, Mary whispered, "Why did we all have to be there for *that?*"

Elizabeth shook her head, put her finger on her lips. She led them through the sitting room to the library and closed the door. Even there, she spoke softly, just above a whisper.

"I want him to know we're united on everything. That he can't divide and conquer. That we're strong. Okay?"

They all nodded.

"I also want the nurse to see a picture of four concerned daughters tending their father with loving care. If he chooses to respond with anger or malignity — well, that's his business. I don't want them to see us in any way divided among ourselves and above all I don't want them to see us as *plotting* against him."

"Are we?" Alex asked.

Ronnie grinned, shook her head, patted Alex's head, and wandered off to the French doors. She stood there looking out through the glass panes at the empty terrace and the graybrown garden and bare trees beyond.

"But why?"

"Alex! You want something from him, don't you?" Mary cried. "With Father, you have to plot to get something. Anything!"

"All I want is some answers," she protested. "I don't care about the money. What's wrong with that?"

"We all want some answers. That's the last thing he'll give us. He'd rather give us money."

"I don't understand," she said plaintively. "I don't like feeling like a conspirator." She threw herself into a chair petulantly.

Ronnie turned and looked at her. "You want to feel innocent, like a good girl. But you want him to give you what you want. You're quite insistent about that. But you can't have both. Don't you see that?"

"No!" Alex wailed. "I don't! What's bad about what I want?"

"It ain't what Daddy wants, you dope!" Ronnie whirled away from her. "Sometimes I wonder how you can be so stupid."

Elizabeth sat down behind the desk. Mary sat on the leather couch, bent over like an old woman.

"It's not as if I'm asking for something terrible!" Alex said.

"You're asking for something he doesn't want to give. That means we have to force him to give it, somehow. Through pressure, through superior power," Elizabeth explained, lighting a cigarette.

Alex considered. "Maybe . . . maybe . . ." — she stared at the floor — "it would be better if we all went away. So he could miss us. Then we could come back one at a time," she said craftily.

"Hah!" Elizabeth cried.

"You think he likes you," Ronnie surmised. "You think he'd tell you if you were alone."

"Well, maybe he would," she whined.

"He'll never trust us again," Mary said from her corner of the couch. "None of us."

"Why?" Indignant.

"Because we're together. Don't you see? He'd have been entirely different if we'd come in — well, first of all, without Ronnie. Her being there was major, I didn't fully realize how major, although I sensed . . . And then, if we'd gone alone, or if we were squabbling with each other, if we weren't so . . . *united*."

"We weren't, at first."

"That's true, we weren't."

"We were by the time he woke up," Elizabeth said.

"Are you sorry, Mary?" Alex asked.

Mary thought. "No. No. With Father . . . I've always been terrified. Nervous. He always makes me feel like a beggar. I always was with him . . . And I am now too. . . . I need money desperately, I guess you all realize that by now. I'm in real trouble, financially. But" — she looked up at them, turning her head to face each in turn — "I feel I have something with you. Something that will last, something that makes me stronger, not weaker. Something that makes him . . . almost irrelevant." She smiled weakly. "Not that I'm not still horribly scared. I don't know what it is exactly, why he scares me so. It makes me feel . . . humiliated. None of you is frightened that way." She turned to Ronnie.

"Ronnie, I've been thinking for quite a while — in all the business of arranging to bring Father home, I kept forgetting to bring it up. But I think you should move upstairs with us. Take one of the guest rooms — one of the big front rooms reserved for special guests, presidents and board chairmen. They each have a big desk, a settee, an easy chair. They have big closets, big bathrooms. You spend so much time in your room. You'd be more comfortable upstairs."

Ronnie stared at her. Her voice, when she spoke, was hoarse. "Thanks, Mare, but I'll stay where I am. I appreciate the offer — really — but there's no way I can ever feel comfortable in any part of this house except my room or Momma's — or the kitchen. I can sit in here or in the sitting room or the playroom — with you — but not by myself." She shrugged. "Strict childhood training," she smiled.

Mary smiled back. "Well. If you change your mind — just do it. Okay?"

Ronnie nodded.

"All right," Elizabeth said, standing up as if she were ending a meeting. "Father has dinner early, at five, so Florence can leave by six. After she goes, during our cocktail hour, we'll go up and start in on him."

Alex sat forward, eyes bright. "Oh, thank you, Elizabeth. Thank you all!"

"Just don't count on anything," Elizabeth warned.

Ronnie lay on her bed, a book open beside her, supposedly working. She turned to stare out at the dimming light of the afternoon sky, laid her head back on the pillow she had propped against the old wooden headboard. Mary's words, Mary's face hung in her mood like a color, a taste, like something sweet, sweet and thick and healing like blood, knitting up a crack in her heart. Easing her stomach, releasing her fingers, her shoulders, from some locked position. She bit her lip: how much she had needed that acceptance, how much it meant when it came. Humiliating. To need that way. From them. From anyone.

I'm as bad as Mary: "*Who would I be?*" Like her, I need the people around me to tell me who I am. As if I can't be anything without them. Maybe you can't. Maybe everything I ever learned was lies. We're told we make ourselves, identity is individual, forged in the mind, what other people think doesn't matter, they can't affect the rational Man, the free Man. Maybe that's only true of men.

Because women know they're women without somebody else telling them. But they don't know *who* they are, we don't know, do we. All of us bound together by that, the jostling and jangling against and with each other that create our identity. Me the vaunted self-made woman, tough girl, streetsmart schoolsmart, had it locked. Nobody could get to me. Just cut Tania off when she talked about stuff like that, cut her off for good when she wouldn't stop, just packed my things. Look on her face like I'd stabbed her. Made me hate her. I've hated her for years. But she was a sweet kid. Just too needy. Clingy. She was. Sarah too, before she took off. Clinging one minute, gone the next. Shows you. And Susan, so jealous, so watchful. Lilah was like me: didn't believe in that stuff. Don't get too close. So we didn't, and that didn't work out too well either. Funny how devastated I was when we split up. With Sarah too. Still an ache.

Love stinks. Whatever Mary says. Holds up that love of hers, that Don, as if she'd had a transcendent experience. Probably the only guy who ever gave her orgasms. A mistake, Mary, taking orgasm for paradise. I should tell her to try a woman: reliable orgasm, on demand.

If anybody'd told me I'd give a flying fuck what any of my so-called sisters thought about me, felt about me, I'd have screamed in scorn. Of course nobody could tell me that because nobody even knows I have sisters.

How much ya wanna bet it'll be a different story when we leave here. Ta-ta Ronnie, nice knowing you. That'll be the test of truth. One thing while we're all together, doing whatever the fuck it is we're doing. But once they go back to their lives, they won't want to know me. Christ, how would they introduce me? I'd like you to meet my *chicana* lesbian bastard sister?

Inviting me to use one of the upstairs bedrooms, what a laugh. Lady Bountiful. Sitting in the kitchen late at night talking about her money problems. Like to see her listen to mine. Can't you see her face if I met her on the streets of New York when she was getting out of a limo with some friend about to lunch at Le Cirque? You are excused from the tea, Ronnie. Or Elizabeth, say I showed up at her office, said say, how about helping me get a job in government. She'd turn to ice, discuss qualifications, parameters. Alex would be nice, just flaky, she'd shed me by distraction.

Not that I'd ever show up in their lives. Why would I? What do I need with them?

Mary sidled into the library, hung in the doorway like a bored child. "Elizabeth."

Elizabeth looked up over the top of her reading glasses.

"May I talk to you?"

"Come in, sit down," Elizabeth said, rising from the desk and moving to a chair beside the leather couch. Mary perched on the end of the couch cushion.

"About Father. I've been thinking. . . ." She hesitated, her face appealing to Elizabeth for help. But Elizabeth said nothing, regarding her steadily.

"We haven't . . . well, most of us haven't given much thought to him, to how he must feel. Alex does, but her manner . . . well, it's so . . . she acts like a kindergarten teacher and that's got to drive him mad."

Elizabeth nodded.

"She's kind, I'm not criticizing her. But she's picked up this manner from the nurses in the hospital where she volunteers — I think. And it doesn't work with Father."

"Yes."

"But I've been thinking about him. While I was practicing today. I couldn't play well because my mind kept reverting to him. . . ."

"I thought you played very well. What was that, Debussy?"

"Yes. *Suite pour le piano.* I used to play it years ago when we were girls."

"I remember. It's gorgeous, and it sounded splendid. You sound professional."

Mary flushed. "Thanks. I thought I . . ." She paused. "Thanks.

"You know it would be terrible for anyone," she continued. "For me, for you. To be in that state. But for him! Well, you know, you understand, you know him the way I do. He never even rang for a servant when my mother was alive — they had bells then. She did it. He was so powerful things just appeared before him when he wanted them, everyone around him made sure of that. And even afterwards — after we were gone, after Alex was gone — I'm sure Noradia did the same for him. I'm sure she gave him everything he wanted. He didn't live in the same world with the rest of us. I'll bet he's never been in a supermarket in his life."

"Have you?" Elizabeth grinned.

"In recent years," Mary smiled ruefully, "often." She stopped smiling. "He never knew what it was to be without — anything — even for a moment. I don't know if he ever knew pain."

"No one doesn't know pain."

"I guess not. But here he is now, deprived utterly — unable to speak or move by himself, can't even walk to the toilet. . . . I can understand that he's in a fury, can't you?"

Elizabeth nodded.

"And we haven't been thinking about that, really. We were so thrown by his . . . by the way he acted . . . when he woke up. As if we were his enemies. . . ."

"That *is* how he looks at us."

"But it could be he was shocked. He probably never imagined the four of us together. Being able to be together."

"It's mainly because of his behavior that we never were," Elizabeth said sharply. "You were the one who saw that."

Mary moved even closer to the end of the cushion, leaning toward Elizabeth. "But that's irrelevant, Lizzie. We need something from him now. I'm not sure what. Alex needs answers, I need money, well, I thought I needed money. But you-all have made me see — oh, I don't know — that I can survive, I guess. Somehow. Even without his money. Ronnie probably wants some sign, some flicker of acknowledgment, poor kid. I don't know what you want . . . but I know you wouldn't be here, none of us would be here, if we didn't want something from him — rather urgently."

Elizabeth stubbed out her cigarette and immediately lighted another. Her face was wreathed with smoke.

"So, what I was thinking was — if we want something, we have to go about things in a way that will dispose him favorably to us. Let me take this business over. The doctor said he can have one small drink a day, that it might even be good for him. I want to have Mrs. Browning set up a bar in his room. Just a small one — with bourbon, brandy, scotch, gin, some wine and port, didn't he use to drink port after dinner? And Perrier and mixers and Coke for us and an ice bucket and glasses. I think it will make him feel more in charge of himself. And we can have our drinks up there with him. And I want to lead the discussion tonight."

"Fine," Elizabeth sighed.

"You're used to being in charge. You won't mind?"

"I only do it because it has to be done and none of the rest of you has seemed able . . . well, Ronnie *could* do it, but she feels. . . ."

"Illegitimate," Mary smiled nastily.

Elizabeth grinned. "Yeah." She stubbed out her cigarette. "I hate talking to him, I don't know how. I never did know how. I know I sound like. . . . I don't know . . . I must sound like a sergeant giving orders . . . fuck it, I sound like him!"

"I'm sure you can do better. If you're not too frightened. You mustn't do it if you're frightened. You'll blow things."

"I'm frightened but not too frightened. I feel I know what to do." She stood up.

Elizabeth stood too. She moved toward Mary uncertainly, put her arms around her tentatively. "I'm sure you do," she lied.

14

Florence kept Stephen's door open except when she was tending to his bodily needs, so Mary lightly tapped on the open door at six o'clock. Her sisters hovered behind her in the doorway. Florence, straightening his bed for the last time before she left, looked up at the knock.

"Well, here are your daughters, Mr. Upton! Up for a visit are you? Isn't that nice? Your lovely daughters, come to visit you!"

Mary stepped forward lightly. "We usually have cocktails at this hour, Father, and we decided it would be fun to have them with you."

"Yes, I *noticed* that," Florence scowled. "A bar in his room? I don't know about that. What does the doctor say about that, now."

"He says a drink will probably be good for him, Florence. Just one. And he'll enjoy it. Father always enjoyed a drink after dinner."

"I guess that'll be all right, then." She gathered up her sweater and knitting bag, took her coat from Stephen's closet. "I'll be going now. He's fine. Ate his dinner like a good boy, ate it all up! Vegetable soup, roast beef and baked potato and string beans and ice cream. He's got a wonderful appetite, I'll say that. Ate it all up!" She got as far as the door, then turned.

"Miss Upton? May I have a word?" she whispered to Elizabeth, who went outside with her.

"Miss Upton!" Florence whispered urgently, "you know that if he has a drink, he may need to . . . void. Someone will have to get him the bedpan and empty it. You do realize that?"

Elizabeth smiled. "I don't think we had, Florence, but it will be taken care of."

Florence sighed. "Well, that's all right, then," she smiled and started for the stairs.

Stephen glared at her back as she left. Mary smiled at him, and when they heard Florence's footsteps on the wooden floor of the downstairs foyer, she whispered, "She must drive you crazy!"

Stephen looked up at her in surprise. His scowl softened. She smiled. "I'm afraid they're all like that, Father. She means well, and she takes good care of you, doesn't she?"

He nodded reluctantly.

"We don't want to keep you up if you want to sleep. I expect that the hospital settles people in right after dinner, but it's awfully early. But maybe you'd rather go to sleep?"

He stared at her warily for a moment, then relaxed. He shook his head no.

"Do you think you'd like a drink?"

He nodded.

Ronnie stood by the bar, ready. "What'll it be, sir?" she asked, his to command.

He looked up surprised then relaxed further.

World returned to its proper order, Ronnie thought.

He wrote on the tablet. Mary bent over to read his nearly illegible, ill-spelled scrawl. "Brandy," she interpreted for Ronnie. "Remy Martin," she directed. "Put it in one of those big bubble glasses." She glanced flirtatiously at Stephen. "Ronnie isn't used to the high life."

His eyes darted quickly to her face, examining it. He took the glass from Ronnie with his left hand.

"Women?" Ronnie turned to them. "The usual?"

"No. Brandy for me too," Mary said.

"Before dinner, Mary?" Elizabeth protested.

She shrugged. "I want to keep Father company."

"I'll have a gin and tonic," Elizabeth said. "Do you need some help?" She went over to the bar. "Ronnie?"

"I'll have what I had the other night. With you. Whatever you had. It was brown. Scotch?"

"Ice?"

Ronnie nodded. She pulled an armchair from the back wall and set it to the right of the bed, then pulled up a small settee from the front window wall. Mary moved to help her drag it in front of the television stand. The rocking chair they had had brought in from the nursery playroom for the nurse stood on the left, diagonally across from the foot of Stephen's bed, which was now surrounded by chairs. Mary sat in the rocker, Elizabeth in the armchair. Ronnie, who had waited until last to sit, sat beside Alex on the settee. She tensed, waiting for Alex to exclaim, "Isn't this nice?" But Alex did not speak.

"How are you feeling, Father?" Mary said with feeling.

His face twisted, fell.

"Are you in pain?"

He shook his head wearily.

"Just the situation."

He raised his eyes to her. The right corner of his mouth drooped and drool constantly dripped from it, beyond his control. The right side of his face drooped too. His right eye was half closed. He opened his mouth, strained to speak, but only a grunt emerged.

How alone he is. Always was, wasn't he, Ronnie thought, scowling. Are we all he has? Didn't protect his future very well, did he. Doesn't he have any friends? Where are they? Jesus, he's eighty-two, they're either dead or in the same shape as him. Even if he was the devil, he's a poor devil now. So powerful all his life . . . But had he felt sorry for her when he was powerful and she was helpless? She hardened her heart. Never forget, he'd hurt you if he could.

"I'm so sorry," Mary said feelingly.

He blinked and a tear appeared. He lifted his left hand a little, let it fall. A gesture of despair.

Pitiful, Mary thought. Poor baby. She wanted to embrace him but something held her back.

"You know, being back here, living here these past weeks, has thrown us all back into the past, Father. To when we were young."

His eyes rose. Wariness entered them.

"We've been talking over old times — my playhouse, the horses,

Mama, the parties you used to give — and my wedding! What a beautiful wedding you gave me, Father! Alex was just a tot then, she was the flower girl, remember?"

His eyes glistened. He gazed at Alex, smiled.

"But do you know, Alex doesn't remember anything after that. Isn't that odd? There's a huge gap in her memory, and it's very upsetting to her. She can't remember whole years of her life. She starts to remember again after she'd been living in Baltimore for a while. But you were gone then, and she . . . missed you. She needs to know what happened. Why you and Amelia split up, why she never heard from you again."

Stephen's distorted face changed utterly; he stared at them as at an army surrounding him, arrayed against him. His face tightened, he set his brandy down on his tray table. A bitter smile twisted his already twisted face: you could see him thinking: betrayed. Shouldn't have let down my guard. He raised his left hand, waved it at them back first, ordering them out.

Alex started, half rose in her chair. "Please, Father, please tell me!" she cried desperately. "It's making me sick. I black out, I faint . . . !"

Stephen sneered, turned his face away from her. He reached for the remote and switched the power on the television set. He turned up the volume to full. The set, which was right behind the settee, blasted them. Alex crouched, holding her hands over her ears. Ronnie stood up and reached over and turned the volume button down, looking at him angrily. His face set hard and sullen, like a raging child's, and he pushed the volume up again.

"We could pull the plug," Elizabeth said to him, but he didn't hear her over the blasting commercial.

Mary stood, looked at Elizabeth. Alex looked at both of them. Ronnie stood quietly, regarding Stephen. His mouth was open, he was straining. At last, he grabbed the tablet and scrawled. He held it up to them, waved it in front of them.

OUT

He dropped it, scrawled again, held it up again.

BITCHS

Misspelled, Mary thought.

* * *

The others slunk downstairs to the playroom, but Elizabeth went into the study and closed the door. She sat at the desk, her chair turned to the windows. Dark out, she could see nothing. What a bust. Hopeless. Mary tried, she did her best. What the fuck are we staying here for? Life is passing. My birthday today. Fifty-three. He wouldn't remember of course, he never did even before he got sick. No one else either. Why should they? I never remember anyone else's birthday, either. Only Clare's, I always made a fuss over that.

I'm going to marry Jack.

In that case, good-bye.

No, what he said was: I'll be here if you decide against it. I'll always love you, always have your well-being at heart. But I cannot stand by and watch it.

Life without Clare.

I had the driver take me back to Washington, then sent him home, walked home. Long walk. Washington not a walking city, sidewalks along the boulevards empty. I must have looked crazy walking alone, my head hanging, decently dressed bag lady, someone beaten. Destroyed. Life over.

Went back and picked up the phone, made a date to see Jack that night, get him to propose. Too high-handed, Clare, too one-sided. Not enough. And not fair. How come you get to have a love life and I don't. Of course, for a man to have a male lover and for a woman to be married are two different things entirely. Marriage. Still means male ownership some-how for a woman. But I'd have a life with Jack, kids maybe.

I'd have sex in my life.

Sex with Jack. Fumbling and fast. Not much in it for me. But maybe I could teach him, tell him what I'd learned on my own. God knows I'd masturbated enough all those years.

I hated sex with Jack.

What was wrong with me?

I knew what was wrong with me. The books were full of it in those days. I was frigid. Funny, how frigidity's disappeared. It was just a euphe-mism for male ignorance of female bodies, but that's what we called it then. Thought then.

* * *

Jack appeared flushed and high, he figured I was ready for him. Took me
to dinner at a French restaurant, fancy for Washington in those days.
Pink-faced, excited. Ordered champagne, said "I've missed you." Did he
love me or just my name? My possible future wealth? I never knew. How
come I didn't know? I knew *Clare* loved me — in the way he could. I sat
there looking at Jack, trying to imagine his mouth on mine, his body
around mine, in mine, imagine it every night or almost every night. No
more getting into cool clean sheets by myself, putting on my glasses, lighting a cigarette, picking up a book. Quiet peaceful nights. Would he expect
me to cook his dinner? Who never cooked my own? Pick up his dirty
socks, do his laundry, become his servant? Wasn't that what men expected
from marriage?

   We went back to my apartment and made love. That's what it's
called, making love. My insides churning. I tried to guide him, show him
what I needed. He couldn't hear, he was full of his own needs, passion. *For
me or the conquest of my name?* He obliterated me in sex, I wasn't there,
only he was there, I didn't matter, would never matter. Marriage would
obliterate me.

   Probably wasn't fair to him: he didn't turn me on, as kids say now.
Clare turned me on. Clare aroused me — yet he was impossible, inviolable, unapproachable, like the lady in a troubadour poem.

   But so was I. Impossible, inviolable, unapproachable.

   It came to me while he was making love to me: Clare and I belonged
together. So when Jack asked me to marry him later that night, sharing a
cigarette and champagne among the pillows, *no* just came out of my
mouth. "I can't," I said. He seemed so crestfallen. Could he really have
cared for me? He married, only a few months later. I thought, *see:* he didn't
care. But that's not necessarily the case: sometimes when you're full of
love, you have to put it somewhere.

   How come I never felt it again then?

   I couldn't call Clare, I was too proud. Go crawling back to him,
when he'd abandoned me, denied me having what he had? I'd live alone, I
decided, without anyone, it was all too much, couldn't hack it, couldn't.
Heartbroke, mindbroke, spiritbroke. Did my job like an automaton. But
he heard. Jack must have been seen with some other woman, maybe the
one he married. Clare called. He acted as if nothing had happened, as if

we'd just had coffee the other day and it was time for our weekly dinner. We just picked up where we left off. Jack was never mentioned again. I loved him for that, for salving my pride. But he could afford to: he had set the terms.

Wouldn't have worked out, marriage to Jack. Whether he loved me or not, I didn't love him. But I'd always thought that if a man really loved me, his passion would be so powerful, it would sweep me up in it and I'd automatically love him back. Why did I think that? Such a reactive way of seeing. . . .

No one's passion ever swept me away. Not even my own. At least Mary let herself feel that kind of passion once. Lucky girl. No. Not luck.

Courage.

But it isn't true you didn't have a life! You had wonderful times with Clare. True meeting of the minds without the complications of sex or domesticity. Lots of couples stop fucking some time in their marriage. So we never fucked at all, so what? Does that mean we didn't love each other?

It would be nice to know what it's like, loving sex.

Just your garden-variety twentieth-century nun, that's me. Mary calls me a frigid cow. Casts aspersions on Clare's male sexuality. She knows. Clever bitch. Maybe she can psych out Father too.

Father.

That's why.

For the past few days Mary had whispered in the kitchen with Mrs. Browning about menu and cake and candles for a birthday dinner for Elizabeth on Friday night. Thursday afternoon while Elizabeth was working, she and Ronnie and Alex sneaked out of the house and went shopping in Concord. They were all a little high: it was a small excitement in their monotonous days, planning a surprise celebration. Mary had intended to remind Stephen to wish Elizabeth a happy birthday before they went down to eat, but his explosion propelled it from her mind, and she left Stephen's room in a hangdog silence.

They had to knock at the study door to get Elizabeth to come to the table, and when she entered the dining room, they all gave it their best effort, trying to joke, talk cheerfully, kissing Elizabeth, wishing her a happy birthday. Mary assured her she looked forty-five; Alex said how happy she was to have her sister after all these years; Ronnie squeezed her hand, said "Me too."

The menu included Elizabeth's favorites — poached salmon, pureed greens, risotto — and Mrs. Browning proudly carried in the birthday cake she had made, a single large candle burning in its center.

"That's to celebrate our first shared birthday," Mary explained. "It's lemon-filled, you used to love that," she said, demanding the ritual of blowing it out and cutting the cake. Then they offered their gifts, and demanded oohs and ahs over each one — a book of Louise Gluck poems from Mary, a record — Debussy's *Suite pour le piano,* clearly Mary-inspired — from Alex, and a pair of knitted wool gloves from Ronnie. "For your walks," she said shyly. "I think wool is warmer than leather."

Elizabeth's pale drained face was twisted, her eyes damp.

"This is the best birthday I ever had," she told them. Not a complete lie. One birthday Clare had flown her to Paris to see an art show; once they'd flown to San Francisco. She'd been in a kind of glory, but all their trips were edged with sadness for her, loving him so much, wanting him, knowing she'd never . . . But there's always pain, she thought, whatever happens to us in life. Nothing ever perfect. Try to learn to focus on the pleasure, the joy, instead of the other: the pain is countable on, you can take it for granted. She tried: this was the best birthday, she said.

She succeeded: they all believed her, believed the damp eyes, the twisted smile, the torn voice. And having given her something, they were full of love for her. They gathered around her as they left the table, embracing her, and Mary and Alex walked with their arms around her into the playroom.

Then they subsided again. Elizabeth lighted a cigarette. Mary was twisting her belt in her fingers. Alex was curled up in a chair looking catatonic.

"I don't understand," Alex said finally in a small voice, "why it made him so angry. Okay, so maybe he did something he shouldn't have — I mean, why would Mom leave him if he hadn't? Or why would he make her leave him? But after all these years — I mean, how bad could it have been, what he did? Have another lover, be unkind to her, never be home, what could he have done that was so terrible?" She raised her hand to her mouth and nibbled at the skin around the nail of her right fore-finger.

Elizabeth bent forward and clasped her hands together near the floor between her legs.

Mary leaned back, raised her head as if she were trying to separate it from her body. She peered upward, breathing hard.

Seeing them, Ronnie suddenly stiffened. She sat absolutely unmov-ing, barely breathing.

"Can you understand it?" Alex went on. She bit her underlip, stopped and raised her hand to her mouth again, nibbled skin.

Elizabeth sat up. "I need a drink."

"We all need a drink," Mary said.

Ronnie got up with a sigh. "What'll it be?"

Elizabeth stood. "I'll help. Orders?"

They all asked for scotch, even Alex.

"Oh good," Alex breathed. "Serious-talk drinking."

"I'm turning into a drunk," Ronnie murmured. She and Elizabeth went into the sitting room, where the bar was set up. They returned carry-ing bottles and glasses; Alex went into the kitchen for ice. When drinks had been passed out, Elizabeth sat down and relighted her cigarette, which had gone out, inhaling it deeply. Then slowly, purposefully, she turned to Ronnie. "Why did you leave home so young, Ronnie? You were only fourteen and your mother was wonderful to you, wasn't she? Not like mine or Mary's. So how come?"

Ronnie looked at the floor. "I couldn't stand it here once I knew . . . I didn't like your father very much but once I realized he was my father, I was furious with my mother, and I couldn't tell her that, I didn't want to hurt her. It made me crazy, living here and watching every day, every night, wondering if she was with him . . ."

"Yes. I can understand that. But was that enough to make a kid who'd always been protected risk dangerous alien streets? A big city?"

"I wasn't so protected . . . I just couldn't stand the situation."

"It must have been terrible to drive you out onto the streets."

"I told you, I went to live with my aunt. Rosa."

"Why are you persecuting the child, Lizzie?" Mary protested. "It's perfectly understandable that she wouldn't want to live here under those conditions."

"Kids endure far worse. They endure terrible things. It takes something *unendurable* to drive them to run away from home."

"What makes you an expert on children?"

"I was one." Elizabeth sat forward like a prosecutor and faced Ronnie. "Why did you run away from this house!"

Ronnie looked up at her in terror, her eyes aflame. "Fuck off, Elizabeth!"

Elizabeth leaned back in the deep soft chair, letting out a sigh that was almost a groan. "So," she breathed. She lighted a fresh cigarette from a half-smoked one. She drank a big gulp of scotch.

Mary's eyes were fixed on Elizabeth with terror, her body immobile. Ronnie, her face twisted into wretchedness, stared at the floor.

"WHAT!" Alex cried. "What is going on! What are you saying?" She leapt up, she poked Elizabeth in the shoulder, she whirled on Mary. "WHAT, WHAT, WHAT?"

Elizabeth laid her hand across her eyes. Her voice was toneless. "I've never talked about this. I've never told anyone. Nobody. Ever. I was too . . ." she choked — "ashamed." She laid her head back as if she were studying the ceiling. "When I was ten years old, here for the summer, Father raped me."

The room froze. No one even breathed.

Her dead glance swept Mary. "You were little, only five or six. You still slept in the nursery with your nanny. Laura was here but she was drinking heavily. The war had started and Father was always working in Washington or flying to England. He only came up for long weekends, and only a couple of times that summer. So Laura and I had dinner alone most nights. She was sloshed by dinner and most nights she passed out right after it. The servants got her to bed. When Father came to Lincoln, she barely spoke to him, and she didn't change her drinking habits. Her form of rebellion, I guess.

"He came into my room late one night. I was sound asleep, I woke up when I felt . . . I felt . . ." — her voice trembled — "something someone pressing touching . . ." — she brought her voice back into control —

"underneath my nightgown." She stopped, inhaled deeply. She sipped her drink. She regarded them dry-eyed. They all stared at her, paralyzed.

"I was still a child. I didn't menstruate until I was fourteen, I didn't have breasts, I'd never masturbated, I hadn't felt sexual desire." She inhaled again, turned her gaze to the ceiling. "I fought him off, I pushed him away, I cried. He put his hand over my mouth, I was terrified. I thought he was trying to kill me. He said he wasn't going to hurt me, just make a woman of me. Said it was time someone did and it was a father's office. I still wriggled, struggled, and he patted my head. He patted my head!" Elizabeth cried. "He said he loved me. Loved me!" She broke into tears. "And this was the way men showed love to women. And I . . . I . . . oh, I so yearned to be loved!" She bowed her head, laying it in her hands, sobbing softly.

The sisters sat frozen until Alex got up and went into the bathroom, came back with a box of tissues and handed it to Elizabeth. Elizabeth wiped her face with a tissue.

"It didn't happen often. He wasn't around often. But whenever he was here, I lay in bed so tense, never knowing . . . I couldn't sleep. And even when he wasn't here, the memory . . . the memory was in that bed somehow, in this house, this town."

"That's why you changed your room!" Mary burst out. "When you came for the Fourth one year, you made such an issue of it, insisting on having a different room. I thought England had made you crazy, that you had some snobbish thing about your old room . . ."

"Why didn't you tell your mother?" Alex asked simply. "Why didn't you say you didn't want to come here?"

"I did tell her! I told her I didn't want to come here," she concluded miserably.

"Why didn't you tell her what he was doing?" Alex continued, in some outrage.

Ronnie stared at the floor.

Elizabeth lighted another cigarette, inhaled deeply, sipped scotch, regained her composure. "I was afraid," she said bitterly.

"I don't understand. You were just a little girl . . ."

"*No,* you don't understand!" Elizabeth whirled on her. "You had a mother who loved you! Who would have consoled you. Who wouldn't have blamed you! I didn't know what my mother would say and I couldn't have borne it if she . . ." Her voice broke, she bent her head.

"How long did he do it," Mary asked in a hard voice.

"Until I was seventeen."

Mary calculated. "When I was twelve."

"Then I stopped him."

"You stopped him!" Mary gasped. "How!"

Elizabeth turned to her slowly. "You didn't?"

"I was afraid!" Mary cried. "He started when I was only eight years old! He said I was his girl, that we were lovers the two of us, Mommy was dead, only he and I left in the whole world. He said he was lonely, that I could make him happy and he would make me happy and that it was all all right. That this was what daddies did with their little girls. But I mustn't tell anybody. That would kill him: if I said anything to anybody, he'd shrivel up and die and I would know I killed him. And that if he died, I'd be sent to a home, an orphanage. I'd be all alone. Then later on, years later, he showed me a gun, he pulled it out of his drawer, he said if I said anything he would shoot himself!"

"He told me that if I told, he wouldn't send Mother any more money," Elizabeth said.

"He usually did it in the Georgetown house, when I was home from school on vacations. But when I got older, he did it here, in the summer when he came up," Mary added. "Probably starting about then, when I was about twelve. When you stopped him." She stared at Elizabeth. "How did you know about me?"

"I didn't. It's just — since we've been back here — some things you said — the way he terrifies you. It was the only thing that made sense."

"I didn't even ever imagine he did it to you! He never seemed to care about you and he was affectionate with me. I thought he loved me, not you. I thought that was the proof. That that was what I had to pay for having him love me. But it was so awful! It hurt, and I didn't want it! That's why I was so devastated when you went to England: I knew I'd be here with him all alone with no one to stop him, and he was here most of the summer then. I couldn't stand it, I tried to get away, I begged him for driving lessons or to let me spend the summer with Aunt Pru. But he absolutely refused. He wouldn't let go of me. That's why I got married! To escape him. And he knew it! He tried to stop me! He was furious! But I couldn't stand it anymore! I figured it couldn't be any worse with a husband!"

No one moved to console her, bent over, weeping.

"That's why I needed you so much!" she cried in a muffled voice from between her hands.

Elizabeth rose, went to Mary and stooped down and put her stiff arms around her and held her. "I'm so sorry," she whispered into the hair over Mary's ear. "So sorry," she kept repeating.

Mary threw her arms around Elizabeth's neck. "You didn't know, you couldn't have known," she sobbed.

"I should have known. I could have guessed. I was so jealous of his love for you. . . ."

"Love! That's love!" Ronnie cried.

"Of course it's love!" Mary cried. "That's why it's so . . . terrible!"

"That's not love, it's exploitation! Oppression! Abuse! What's the matter with you?" Ronnie screamed.

"It takes the form of love," Elizabeth said. "And that is what is so terrible about it. Because it defines love somehow. Like pornography, you know? Defining love as torture. It gets into your brain. And it poisons the rest of your life, your sense of things . . . of sex . . . of love. For me, sexual love in a woman meant obliteration. I believed that women's pleasure consisted entirely of pleasuring a man. I thought there was something missing in me, I wasn't a real woman — because I couldn't bear living that way, couldn't bring myself to do it. I thought I was frigid," she said, turning to face Mary fully. "As you always said."

Mary's mouth trembled. Sorry, she mouthed.

"But anyway," Mary said in a small voice, "you *do* love him. Your daddy." She stared at the wall. "The god descends," she said, "sweeps you up in his arms, offering what you yearned for all those years, what you dwindled without, like a plant without sun or rain. But given in a way that hurts, shames, erases you." She shuddered.

Ronnie cried out as if she had hurt herself suddenly, and Elizabeth swerved to face her.

"Is that how you felt?" Elizabeth prodded.

Ronnie was bent over, her elbows resting on her muscular jean-clad legs, her hands over her face.

"That *is* why you left, isn't it," Elizabeth continued relentlessly.

She nodded.

"Tell us."

Ronnie dropped her hands. "WHY! WHY! Isn't it enough that you know about it? You want me to give you all the salacious details so you can wallow in them, in self-pity, in whining victimization? NO! NO! I don't have your problems. I didn't love him and I knew he didn't love me! End of story. It was pure exploitation!"

She stood up suddenly, went to the table where the bottles stood, and poured herself a tall glass of Perrier. She stood there, muttering. "You really loved him. It's natural, he was your father, of course you did. And you wanted him to love you so in some sense you wanted what happened to happen . . ."

They cried out in protest. She held up her hand. "Whoah, whoah! I'm not saying you wanted him to rape you. Just that you feel complicit in it because you took it for love and you wanted love. It's the sense of complicity that's killing you. That makes you feel so . . . shitty."

She returned to her chair and lighted a cigarette. "Anyway, what I'm trying to say is I don't have that sense of complicity. I was a servant's kid, he never gave one flying fuck about me. I was a little *chicana* servant, nobody, nothing. I never even knew he was my father until I really saw his eyes that time. I had no love for him. So when he did what he did to me, just took me, roughly, like I was a piece of meat. . . . I never confused it with fatherly love."

She sat back with her face set hard, blew out smoke.

"You mean he did it to . . . *all of you!?*" Alex cried. She felt as if her head was locked in a bubble, far away. It took time for their voices to reach her, and they reached her only faintly. Bed. She had to go to bed. She stood up, but wobbled. Ronnie jumped up and grabbed her to keep her from falling.

"Bed. I have to go to bed," she mumbled. She sounded drunk.

Elizabeth gave Mary a warning look. "Maybe you should have a little Perrier," Mary said, standing and taking Alex's glass. "I'll get it for you." But Alex had barely touched her drink: her glass was nearly full; Mary held it up for Elizabeth to see.

"Brandy," Elizabeth said.

Mary went for it.

Ronnie settled Alex back in her chair. She looked old, dead white. Her eyes were sunk into dark pockets. She gazed off into nothing.

"I was lying in my crib. In the nursery," she croaked. "I felt this thing and I woke up and Father was there. His hand was inside my panties. He kept rubbing me. It felt. . . . it felt . . . nice. It hurt. It frightened me. Baby scared," she whimpered. "Mommy, Mommy!"

Mary ran back into the room with the brandy, held it under her nose. "Smell this. Sip this."

Alex smelled, sipped. She sat back. Ronnie was crouched down beside her; Mary knelt down on the other side. Elizabeth stood up. Alex gazed up at her and reached her hands out to her like a baby reaching out to a mother to be lifted from her crib. Elizabeth breathed in a sob, moved to Alex, bent and embraced her.

"I was the oldest. I should have helped! But I didn't save any of you!" Elizabeth cried. "All I cared about was saving myself!"

"We all did," Mary said, her head bent, voice muffled. "Any way we could."

"What else could you do?" Ronnie asked, bewildered. "What could any of us do? We were children!"

Alex held on to Elizabeth. Mary sat on the arm of her chair, and embraced Alex with one arm. Ronnie laid her head on Alex's knees, put her arms around them. Then they all started to move, to sway gently from side to side, moaning, murmuring, keening, like women at a funeral, humming and swaying in unison, a single mourning body of women.

15

When Stephen dozed off around ten the next morning, Florence buzzed Mrs. Browning on the intercom, whispered to her to send someone up, she needed a break. Teresa came tiptoeing into the room smiling. Florence mimicked drinking tea and Teresa nodded, smiled, turned the rocker so she could see the television set, which was showing some sports event.

Florence went downstairs to the kitchen and told Mrs. Browning that she wanted to see Miss Upton. Mrs. Browning frowned and said she'd have to see. She went out, came back and ushered Florence from the kitchen down a long hall past a kind of huge parlor, and a room with a pool table in it, to the library. It had a low ceiling and wooden beams and a huge stone fireplace. Miss Upton sat behind a huge desk.

Florence Douley marched somewhat fiercely up to the desk, but then Miss Upton looked up and smiled.

"Miss Upton: about that little matter we discussed last evening as I was leaving?"

"I'm sorry, Florence. What little matter?"

Florence's mouth twisted. "About the possibility of a need for a bed-pan, Miss Upton."

Elizabeth sat back, took off her glasses. "Right."

"Well, I was wondering if you heard Mr. Upton buzz last night. Because the bed was wet this morning."

Elizabeth stood up. "What!"

"I'm sorry. I didn't mean . . . it was just . . . I wondered if he buzzed or . . . some patients do get angry, like babies, the poor souls, and just . . . wet, you know."

"Father wet the bed?" She seemed incredulous.

"Maybe he buzzed and yez didn't hear it?"

"His intercom is connected to the kitchen, Mrs. Browning's room, to the maid's room, and to my bedroom, too, just in case. I can't imagine no one heard it if he buzzed. Did you ask him?"

"I did, ma'am," Florence confessed. "And I thought he sort of grinned at me. Of course, the way his face is, maybe I was mistaken."

Elizabeth stared at her. "I'm so sorry, Florence. You must have had a mess to clean up."

Words burst out of Florence. "It's not as if he's incontint. The incontint ones they can't help it and I can keep them in diapers. Lucky I thought to put a rubber sheet under the chamois or I would have had a time. As it was, I had to move him to the wheelchair, air the mattress, wipe down the rubber sheet and wait for it to dry, first thing in the morning. He seemed fine though — gobbled up his breakfast."

After her outburst Florence felt placated. "Well, sure it's all part of the job, ma'am. Just thought I'd ask. Because if he is, you know, incontint, we'll need to put diapers on him."

"Yes." Elizabeth sat down again and Florence turned to leave. "Florence?" she called.

"If he does it again . . . tell me, all right?"

"Wetting the bed! Father!" Mary exclaimed. "I can't believe it! Father?"

"Maybe he couldn't help it," Alex said.

Mrs. Browning and Teresa entered carrying bowls of steaming pea soup.

"Another gray day," Elizabeth observed.

"Yes," Mary sighed. "I thought of going to Boston tomorrow. It's Sunday, but the museums will be open. Anyone else want to go?"

"Me." Ronnie held up her hand.

The servants left.

"How can we find out?" Mary asked Elizabeth.

"Ask him," Ronnie said.

Elizabeth snorted. "He'd tell us?"

"We could ask the doctor," offered Alex.

After much discussion, they decided to do both: Elizabeth would call Dr. Stamp, Mary was delegated to speak to Stephen.

Mary knocked on the open door. Florence looked up from her knitting. "Oh, bless you, I'm parched," she said, laying her work down. She nodded her head toward Stephen without a smile. "He's fine," she said, briskly. "Nice and quiet, watching the telly," she explained, as if that were not obvious. He did not glance at her, and she made no effort to fluff his pillow or straighten his cover before she left.

"May I speak to you, Father?" Mary asked from across the room.

Stephen hit the mute button on the remote.

She hesitated, then walked around the bed and sat in the rocker. "Florence was very upset this morning."

He scowled at her.

I know that look. What the hell do I care if she's upset?

"Of course, in her work she often has incontinent patients. She's upset because she believes you have self-control. If you don't, we should know it. So we can . . . make arrangements . . . for you."

His eyes opened in outrage. Even the half-shut eye seemed to widen.

Someone else should have done this, Mary thought, her stomach fluttering. Not me. Please don't be mad at me, Daddy.

Don't. Don't crumble. What would Elizabeth say? How Ronnie would mock you.

Her voice rose. "There's no point in looking at me with outrage, Father! You wet your bed! Like a baby! Out of pure malice! I know it! And if you keep doing it, Florence will put you in diapers! Is that what you want?!"

Stephen paled, his eyes widened, he grabbed his heart. Mary stood, terrified, then darted from the room and down the stairs.

"Elizabeth! Lizzie!"

Ronnie met her in the hall. "What's up?"

"I think he's having a heart attack!"

Alex and Elizabeth converged in the foyer and the four of them ran upstairs. Stephen was sitting in bed watching television.

Mary grimaced. Bastard. Always could scare me.

"I just spoke to the doctor, Father. He says there's no reason for you to be incontinent. If it continues, you'll have to be diapered," Elizabeth said coldly.

A look of utter hatred fixed itself like a death mask on Stephen's face.

Elizabeth stared him down.

He dropped his gaze, pushed the tablet to writing position. BORED, he wrote, with a pitiful look at Elizabeth.

"Yes, of course you must be," Mary said sympathetically.

He wrote again: PAPER.

"You want paper? To write on?" Elizabeth asked.

He shook his head.

"The papers?"

He nodded.

"The *Globe?* The *New York Times?*"

He nodded.

"Both?"

Yes.

"The *Washington Post?*" Elizabeth asked.

Yes.

"The *Christian Science Monitor?* A Chicago paper? The *L.A. Times?* We'll have them delivered. Would you like some magazines too?"

Yes.

"Okay. All the news magazines. Any others?"

He grinned evilly, scrawled: PLAYBOY.

Stephen buzzed seconds after Florence left for the day. Ronnie, who was near the kitchen, heard it and ran up. DRNK, he had written on his tablet. He held it up. She hesitated, then asked him what he wanted. BRAN, he wrote. She poured it, handed it to him, and stood there for a moment. He nodded in dismissal and she left.

"He wanted a brandy," she told the sisters gathering in the playroom, where they had had the bar moved. Mary liked being able to gaze out the large back windows into the garden, even though it was completely dark by six.

"Watch him wet his bed again," Elizabeth snorted.

"Who's going to go if he needs the bedpan?" Ronnie wanted to know.

"Doris. That's why we hired her."

"Good!" Ronnie sighed. "As long as it isn't me."

"Or me," Mary said.

"I'd do it," Alex said.

"What are you, a fucking saint?"

"No. Just used to it. Sometimes, when they're short of nurses, I help out in the hospital. I'm only a volunteer, but I've worked there so many years, they trust me for small things. It's a little hospital. I often help them." Alex's voice was thin and dead, as if her breath came only from her throat, not her lungs. She didn't look at anyone directly.

They gathered again after dinner, chatting desultorily, but Alex remained as silent as she had been during dinner. Ronnie confronted her: "Are you remembering things?"

She started, eyes alarmed, gazed around at them. "Sorry!"

"Has anything come back?"

She nodded, her brow furrowed, glancing at a spot between the wall and the floor. "It all came back. Today, in the woods, while I was walking. I saw it. All at once."

"Do you want to tell us?" Mary asked hesitantly, glancing at Ronnie. "I mean, do you feel like talking about it?"

Alex mused. "I guess so. I need to, I think. So many years I've blotted it out.

"I was in Mommy's room, my mother's room. I was sitting at her makeup table putting powder all over my face. I was nine. She said I could. She said I could use her lipstick too, and her eyebrow pencil. She was lying down, she had a headache. Daddy came in and asked how she was, and she said she didn't feel too well. He told me to let her rest and come and play in his room. I didn't want to, I pulled away but he grabbed my arm and dragged me in there. She called out, sort of weakly, 'Stephen!' as he closed her door and he opened it again and said 'I'll take care of her for you for a while, sweetheart. You rest.' It was in Georgetown. Their rooms weren't connected in that house, they were side by side. He took me into his room and shut the door. He said I looked like a grown-up lady with my powder and lipstick. He picked me up and laid me on the bed, and then he started to . . . do what he did. I was whimpering. I didn't want him to do it but also I was scared, I knew Mommy was just in the next room, I didn't want her to hear. So I didn't whimper loud.

"But she must have suspected something. I don't know why. God knows he'd been doing it for years, but something must have made her suspicious. Maybe that was why she'd been having so many headaches. Anyway, the door opened suddenly very softly, like she was sneaking in, and I looked up and saw her face. He didn't, he was lying on his stomach next to me, facing me with his hands on me. My heart stopped, I felt so bad, so dirty, so wrong. I cried out and Father whirled around and she was standing there looking at him. Then she marched over to the bed and grabbed my arm, she grabbed it so hard it hurt, and she pulled me off the bed and pushed me ahead of her into my room. She said 'I'll be back!' and she locked me in. She locked me in! I was crying, I was cold, I had no underpants on. I wanted to die and be buried and forgotten forever. I heard them yelling outside in the hall, I couldn't tell what they were saying, but I remember her saying 'NEVER NEVER NEVER!' She was crying. After what felt like a long time, she came into my room with a suitcase. She threw my clothes into it, grabbed my coat and jammed my hat on my head, and pushed me out the door. I wondered why she was taking me away if she was going to kill me. She didn't say a word to me. She didn't even notice I had no underpants on.

"A cab came and we got in it. We took a train. We went to Grandma's house. Mommy said the first thing, I had to have a bath. She took me upstairs and put me in the tub. Then she went down and I heard her with Grandma and Grandpa, whispering and yelling and crying. I could hear the way they were talking they were trying to calm her. Grandma came up and got me out of the tub — of course, I was nine, I could get out myself but she helped me anyway. She wrapped a big towel around me and held me close to her, rubbing my body with the towel and hugging me. Then I cried. She kept hugging me. I felt safe then.

"But I never felt safe with my mother after that. Not for a long time. Maybe never. I felt she blamed me. She never mentioned it again, and she was sweet to me, nice to me — always. But I never really trusted her again.

"I realize now she or Grandpa must have made some kind of deal with Father. Maybe she threatened to make it public if he tried to see me again or wrote or called. Maybe that's what he meant when he wrote *agreed.*"

"Did he support you?" Elizabeth wondered.

"I don't know. Probably. Mother earned such a pittance — two or three thousand a year. You know how they paid women in those days. Grandpa earned more, but not a lot and then he retired. But we were always comfortable. Of course, we lived modestly. Even after Mother married Charlie. I could ask her," she added bitterly. "Now that I know, maybe she'll talk to me." She turned to Elizabeth. "Did you ever tell your mother about it? Later, I mean. I mean, does she know now?"

"No," Elizabeth said shortly.

They gazed at her in silence, without judgment.

"I still can't get over the fact that you stopped him!" Mary said.

"Yes. Ironic — after all those years, it was so easy: I just said 'Stop.' I was seventeen, I'd finished high school that June, I was going to college in September, I just couldn't stand it anymore. He was married to Amelia, you" — she looked at Alex — "were a baby. He'd come up for the Fourth and hadn't — touched me — and he left a few days later. Every time he left, my whole body would relax, I would feel my stomach unwind. But I always knew he'd be back. It — consumed me, I walked around feeling . . . evil, as if my body was tainted, contaminated, as if it smelled — because if there weren't something foul about it — it wouldn't make him do those things to me. He always said it was my fault, that it was my body that was making him do it. I remember sitting for hours out in the woods trying to figure out what it was about my body that did that . . ."

"Me too!" cried Mary. "That's what he told me! My body did something that made him do that! I used to stand in front of the mirror naked at night looking at myself, wondering what it *was* about me . . . because I was little, you know, like Alex, I was just past babyhood when he started — I wasn't developed at all. But he always said I was a little tease, that I wanted it." She pondered for a time, then shook her head brusquely and looked up at Elizabeth. "So what did you do?"

"He came back in August. It was a couple of days after he arrived. He was staying the whole month. My heart sank when I heard that, just plunged right into my stomach. I didn't *plan* to stop him, I didn't think about it. It never occurred to me that I could, that I had the power to do anything. At all. One afternoon, you were all in the pool — Amelia and you two, Alex and Mary. I was my usual sullen self, hiding in my room reading. He came in and shut the door. I knew what that meant. I was lying on my stomach on my bed, I remember I had just started reading *The Brothers Karamazov*, about this vile father who gets murdered. Maybe that filtered in, I don't know. I pulled myself up into a sitting position still on the bed and I glared at him. I held the book out in front of me like a shield, like a crucifix against the devil in a vampire movie. And I yelled 'NO! NO! NO! No more! I want you to stop!'

"He said, 'Think again, Elizabeth. You and your mother need my support. Just ask her if that's not true. And as long as I support you, you will do as I say.' I stood up, leapt up, I was tall — thin, but strong, I played hockey at school. And I took this posture — I don't know where I got it — I sort of bent my upper body just a little, and my knees just a little — like a karate posture, you know? But I didn't know karate, I'd never even heard of it. I said, 'You support my mother by law, by contract.' God knows I knew enough about it by then, knew he'd hired detectives to frame her, knew he'd trapped her into divorce. I knew what a louse he was. Still — he was my father. So . . . anyway, I put on a brave face, much braver than I felt. I was icy cold, I talked like a grown woman. I said, 'As for me, I don't need your support, I don't care about it, I can make my way without you. You are never going to touch me again!' When I think about it, I have to laugh at myself but I think I may have looked a little fierce.

"He was furious and cold — you know he couldn't bear to be brooked in anything, especially by us, his kids. But I think he was a little amused at the same time." She lighted a cigarette, cleared her throat. "I started to move toward him, my fists raised, getting ready to sock him. God knows what would have happened if I had. I shouted, 'GET OUT! OUT OF MY ROOM!' And he did.

"He did! He snarled, 'You'll regret this, Elizabeth,' but he turned on his heel and left, slamming the door. *I'd made him leave!* That was the greatest moment of my life. For the first time in my life, I felt I had some power. I wasn't just a Ping Pong ball, a counter in other people's game, something everybody, anybody could toss around. Father, Mother, grandparents, relatives . . . teachers. I had something to say about my life! It was a wonderful feeling. I felt so great I put on a swimsuit and ran down to join you guys. But you'd already left the pool. I dove in anyway and just swam by myself. I must have swum for half an hour. I had so much energy. . . ."

She gazed at the dark window for a long time, then wiped her cheek, damp with perspiration. She laid her hands in her lap quietly. "I knew he'd never trouble me again. And he never did. But he never forgave me, and I did something — almost as bad as what he'd done. I didn't care, you see. I have no . . . had no . . . scruples. Not where he is concerned. I went to him when I needed a job and informed him, simply informed him, that I expected him to help me. He did that time, half smiling at my chutzpah. But then I did it again, when Clare came back to the States. He had a half-assed job at a small college, but he needed and deserved something much more, something prestigious. There was no way he could get it without political pull. So I went to see Father again; I told him it would redound to his credit, that Clare was a brilliant economist, a Republican in sympathy, oh I built it up. I shouldn't have had to do more, that's the way the system works, it's — well, they call it networking now, but it's a buddy system. He should have helped me without question. Helped Clare. But he wouldn't. He sneered at me, asked why he should do one fucking thing on this earth to help *me*. Just as if I weren't his daughter. I guess he thought Clare was my boyfriend. I saw red — literally — the insides of my eyes filled up with red. Actually, a blood vessel did break in my eye that day, I had to go to the doctor. I spat at him: 'Because you owe me.'

"Oh, the look! Well, you can imagine! He picked up his pen, asked me what kind of job I wanted for Clare, wrote down his name and phone number. He said we'd hear from his secretary. Then he put down his pen and stared at me with that malevolent glare, you know, you've all seen it. And he said, 'I never want to see you in this office again. You are never to contact me again.' I stood there for a minute. Do you know," — she turned to them with an anguished expression, — "I felt like crying? Isn't that crazy? Here I'd just blackmailed him, but what I felt was that I'd been thrown out by my father — as if none of the rest had ever happened, as if he were just an ordinary father and I just an ordinary little girl and he'd thrown me out of his life. I thought I'd never see him again. She turned back to the window, her cheeks damp. "I wanted to throw myself at his feet, grab him around the knees, plead, beg, please Daddy, don't throw me away!

"I didn't. I pulled myself up and marched out of there — somehow. And I was still invited to the family parties. By his secretary. But he never spoke to me personally again. Only in front of other people." She sighed with a deep shudder, like someone laying down a huge burden she has carried for many miles. She leaned back her head, gazing at the dark window. "And that enraged me. Deeply. I still can't forgive him. That's why it's so hard for me to talk to him now. I don't think he ever said a kind word to me his whole life, except when he was in my bed. And when he was in my bed he was doing something to me that I didn't want done, that made me feel I had no will, no *self* — that I was just a thing he owned. So for me, to this day, kindness, love, sex — mean annihilation." One by one, tears gathered and spilled over the ledges of her eyes. "He ruined my life," she said in a faint voice.

They were silent together.

"Please don't say that," Alex pleaded. "Please. I can't bear it." She sat very straight in her chair, staring at the wall.

No one spoke.

"He ruined all our lives," Elizabeth insisted. "Look at us — a bunch of miseries."

"I've been having these blackouts," Alex said. "Something triggers them, I guess, some memory or association, and I just go into a — cloud. I don't know what happens while I'm there, I don't faint . . . except once I did. I just come to suddenly and know I've been away." She paused. "I began to think — I was possessed. You know? That I was having visions — religious visions — although I never remembered one afterwards. Then I thought — maybe I was sick. That I had a brain tumor or petit mal or something like that. That terrified me.

"After I came up here, it started to happen almost every day. Blackouts. I'd be walking along, or bicycling . . . it's a wonder I didn't fall off. See, it wasn't just in Georgetown. He started doing it here, in this house, when I was still sleeping in the nursery . . . I don't know how young I was when he started, but I know it started there . . . up there, in that room . . ." She broke off. "How old," she sniffled, "how old are you when they move you out of the nursery?"

Mary frowned. "I moved my children into their own rooms when they were nine, but I left the nursery at seven. But that was because I was sent away to school and didn't have a nanny anymore."

"No, no," Alex moaned. "I was just a baby! Two or three. I was lying in a crib. I'm sure of that!"

The women were silent, picturing this.

"My mother used to say — all the time," Elizabeth recalled, "especially after she'd had a Manhattan or two — she'd yell that no law stopped him from framing her and that all the laws in the world were on the side of the Stephen Uptons of this world. At the time, that really shook me because I thought maybe she knew what he was doing to me and was saying she couldn't stop him, that he had the law on his side. I suppose I wanted to believe that. I wanted to believe she knew because I wanted to think she sympathized with me, felt for me, felt with me — but just couldn't do anything about it. I didn't want to feel that I couldn't tell her because she wouldn't believe me — or because she'd blame me. . . ."

She stopped, lighted a cigarette. "Well, of course she never suspected — as far as I know. But she was right: all the laws are on his side."

"That's not true," Ronnie objected. "Incest is against the law."

"Really," Elizabeth sneered. "Do you think he would have been prosecuted if we'd accused him when we were little? Do you suppose anyone, anyone at all would even have believed us? The great Stephen Upton, a molester of little girls, his own daughters?"

They pondered.

"Even now. If we accused him now, would anybody do anything?"

"Maybe," Alex said.

"A sick old man. We have no proof. We waited all these years. We're afraid he'll disinherit us. Oh forget it!" Mary cried. "They'd see us as monsters, monster daughters, ungrateful malevolent Gonerils and Regans bent on destroying a poor old man in his dotage."

"Who's Goneril and Regan?"

"Oh, characters in a play. Monster daughters called *unnatural*. As if love of parents were built into nature."

"It is, though, isn't it," Alex said faintly.

They all looked at her.

"We do love him, don't we. All of us."

"Not me," Ronnie said fiercely.

"I see the kids at the hospital. The abused ones," Alex went on. "There they are black-and-blue, with welts or burns or broken bones, cracked heads. But if the parent comes to see them, the one who did it — they reach out their arms to them, they're *so happy* to see them! The little ones. Even if they're scared of them. It's heartrending."

"What about the older ones?"

"They shrink a bit, they're more fearful. But they cry when their parents leave. It's so . . . There's no solution."

"And men do most of the abusing," Ronnie muttered.

"Not true," Elizabeth said in a bored voice. "Women do half of it."

"Women are with them ninety percent of the time," Ronnie shouted.

"Listen, Ronnie, dominate or submit is a law of nature. . . ."

"That isn't a law of nature, it's a law of patriarchy!"

Mary moaned, put her head in her hands.

"Oh! So lions are patriarchists when they kill anything smaller than themselves?"

"They kill to eat, not to dominate. Only man kills to dominate."

"Man and woman."

"Rarely woman."

"But you'll admit it happens?"

"Women too have been seduced by power on occasion," Ronnie pronounced.

"Oh, they're not a pure saintly sex, immaculate by virtue of their hormones?"

"They're better than men," Ronnie said stubbornly. "They take the responsibility for children, they sacrifice everything for their children, they put the children first."

"Like your mother?" Elizabeth shot in.

"My mother *did* sacrifice everything for me! She wore the same winter coat for fifteen years, she hardly ever bought herself a new dress, and then it was some cheap rag, and she never bought herself anything more than that! She used every paltry penny your bastard of a father paid her to take care of me! God knows *he* never did. He never paid for a diaper, not even a safety pin! Never paid a doctor bill, never bought me a notebook for school! She had to stay here — it was the best way she could protect me!" Ronnie shook her head, tears springing to her eyes. "What a bitch you are," she muttered. "Just because *your* mother was cruel . . ."

"Why! Why, why why, if you want to argue about politics or whatever it is you're arguing about, do you have to attack each other personally!" Alex screamed.

"She started it," Ronnie protested.

"Can't you just agree to disagree," Mary said sourly.

"Jesus!" Ronnie jumped up. She danced around in fury, as if her toes were on fire. "You two act as if we're arguing about some academic matter, angels on pinheads or whose turn it is to do the dishes! But what we're arguing about is fundamental! It goes to the very heart of everything we believe about life, about people, about how to live! She believes" — she stood still, darting a malevolent look at Elizabeth — "that the urge to dominate is inherent and I'll bet she thinks men have more of it than women. Testosterone poisoning, no doubt," she added viciously.

"I'll thank you not to try to describe my beliefs, Ronnie," Elizabeth said stiffly.

Ronnie ignored her. "So that life is inevitably a constant scramble for power, with men having more to start with than women — probably because women have the babies — right, Elizabeth?" she sneered. "And if that's true, then women can't ever be more than victims, are doomed to scramble for safety from generation to generation, finding protection under the wing of the least rotten man they can find . . . !" She stopped, out of breath.

"Whereas," Elizabeth took it up, "you and your ilk *pretend* that domination is not central to the human psyche, *pretend* that if we all just gave it up for Lent, we could create a sweet little cuddly world where everyone shared, cooperated, nourished everyone else — as if you could wipe out, extirpate violence, rage, greed. . . ."

"It's a better vision than yours! Yours is a counsel from hell!"

"And yours comes straight from heaven?"

Ronnie sighed, calmed, sat down again. "Look. We both know that the nature of human nature isn't decipherable, isn't really knowable. That all definitions of the human are manufactured, that we can't know the truth about ourselves if there even *is* a truth. So why not choose to define ourselves in a way that makes felicity possible, that doesn't set us on an endless course of desperate power seeking? Desperate because it never ends, you never have enough power, you never can. Why not adopt a philosophy that allows alternative ways of living? At least mine makes positive action possible."

"And mine puts women on their guard, prompts them to protect themselves — wisely. In this world, they need to."

In the silence, Mary stirred. "I hate politics," she said airily. "Politics is mundane, transient, doomed to obsolescence. I mean, when you read Shakespeare, do you care who was queen? Art deals with universals — which is all that really matters."

Ronnie glared at her. "If you think art isn't political, you're a fool too!"

Alex looked bewildered. "The way you all talk . . . you sound as if you had no sense of the divine, as if — deity, spirit, whatever you want to call it — didn't hover over you . . . as if you invent *yourselves!* How can you believe that?!"

All three groaned.

16

Everyone knows art is above politics, Mary thought, stiffly avoiding meeting Ronnie's hard set gaze opposite her in the car. How can she say it's political? Certainly the great classics she had read during her brief formal schooling — *The Iliad, The Aeneid,* Shakespeare's plays, *Paradise Lost, The Faerie Queene* — certainly *they* weren't political. But what Ronnie meant by political didn't seem to involve Republicans and Democrats or even communism. . . .

Aldo was driving Mary and Alex to Back Bay to lunch with Eloise, dropping Ronnie at the BU library on the way. Elizabeth had elected to remain at home.

They spoke little during the drive.

Alex's mind was a wounded blur wandering in confusion at how other people saw the world. She could not comprehend how they could laugh at, how they could be ignorant of such a huge dimension of experience. Did they never feel it? That powerful sense of connection with something beyond, eternal, hovering, always present, a dimension essential to her, in which she spent much of her time. What would it be like to live without that sense? How could they not feel it around them, embracing them, uniting them, connecting and embracing all humanity, all creatures, the entire created world? She pressed her mind to try to imagine herself without that sense, but managed to blank out only her surroundings, the Massachusetts landscape as they moved from country to city, the road, the cars, the others in the car vanished and she entered the opaque space familiar to her, in which she felt the air brush against her, sensed objects as motes dancing in space, heard their three hearts beating in unison, felt the rhythm of the dance. . . .

Ronnie, facing two distant, distanced countenances, stubbornly set her mouth. She'd been right to mistrust them, they were exactly what she'd thought in the beginning. How could she have let herself be seduced into caring about them? They were useless, worse than useless. Alex a complete flake, Mary one of those supercilious lightweights who floated on the surface like scum, never touching anything real, seeing only what was fashionable to see. And Elizabeth! Of them all, it was Elizabeth she felt most kinship with, felt most *like*. But god! You couldn't, you just couldn't be friends with someone with politics like hers. If Elizabeth had really accepted Ronnie, had learned to care about her, see her, she would have had to question her fascist ideas. So her friendly behavior had no foundation. But then she was capable of anything, even blackmailing her father to get whatever it was she wanted from him. The only thing the four of them had in common was his . . . abuse.

Maybe that was all women as a sex had in common.

She didn't need them. She'd been beguiled but now she was wary, warned, aware, awake, at war. She'd lived without them all these years and could go on doing so, thank you very much.

She tried to calm the churning in her mind, concentrate on what she had to do today. A good statistics handbook she should buy. Some bookstores were open Sundays, but which ones? She couldn't remember, it seemed years since she'd been a student, another life. Before Momma got sick. Before Momma died.

Aldo dropped Ronnie at the library. Mary had arranged for him to return to Back Bay at two o'clock to drive Mary, Alex, and Eloise to the Isabella Gardner Museum, and wait for them there. Then, around four-thirty, he would pick Ronnie up at the library. They separated in near silence.

But some hours later, as they picked Ronnie up, the other two welcomed her warmly, talking and laughing volubly.

"Of course, I don't know anything about art, but the way she's arranged things seems really comical to me. What do you think, Mary?" Alex laughed. "Giant candelabra next to some wonderful painting next to . . ."

"Some piece of kitsch!" Mary exploded, laughing.

Ronnie, more subdued than earlier, sank deeper into glumness.

But Alex wouldn't permit it. "Did you find what you needed, Ronnie?"

"Oh, you found a bookstore open!" Mary exclaimed, pointing to the brown paper bag Ronnie carried. "What did you buy?"

Both exclaimed in awe over the books with their forbidding titles, joshing Ronnie about their contents. Mary opened one at random, read out " 'Antheridia and Gametes in Mosses?' 'Structures and Adaptations of Bryophytes'?" at which even Ronnie was forced to laugh. By the time they reached Lincoln, the three of them had achieved some harmony again.

"It's nearly cocktail time," Mary announced when they arrived. "Shall we change for dinner and meet in the playroom?" She poked her head into the library. "Hi, Elizabeth! We're back!" she sang. "Had a wonderful time! Want to have drinks?"

"I'm busy," Elizabeth growled. She glanced at her watch. "What time is it anyway. It's only five-thirty!"

"Oh, please join us, Lizzie!" Alex pleaded, standing in the hall behind Mary. "I want to tell you all about this funny museum we went to. We're just changing, we'll be ready in a few minutes."

The three of them were settled in the playroom when Elizabeth dragged in wearing ratty old pants and a blue cotton work shirt.

"Aren't you going to dress for dinner!" Mary exclaimed.

Elizabeth examined herself. "I forgot." She looked at Mary. "Do I have to?"

"Of course! Only Ronnie is allowed to come to the dinner table looking like a plumber's helper," she said, grinning wickedly.

"Right. Ronnie isn't dressed, why should I dress?" Elizabeth sighed, settling in a chair. "I'm exhausted."

"Let me get you a drink," Alex offered, jumping up. "Perrier?"

"No. Gin."

"You seem to have given up Perrier," Ronnie observed.

"It's the company. It drives one to drink."

"Lizzie, you really must change. You'll shock the servants," Mary protested.

"Is that what manners are for? To preserve the servants' sensibilities?"

Ronnie smiled broadly. "Right on! If you want us to treat you as gods, you had goddamned better look the part!"

"Can't you just put on a skirt and comb your hair?"

"Oh, leave her alone, Mary."

"We're disintegrating, descending to the lowest common denominator!"

"Which is me?"

"Obviously."

Alex, standing at the bar, turned a puzzled face to them. She was hearing hostile words but no anger in the voices. "Are you all just teasing?"

"Half," Mary said.

"Why are you so tired?" Ronnie challenged Elizabeth. "Find a logical flaw you couldn't rationalize away?"

Elizabeth grimaced at her. "Economics is not a precise science."

"Despite the fact that economists think like men?"

"Now stop it, stop it this minute!" Alex scolded. "You know it doesn't help anything to squabble!"

"At least," Elizabeth went on cheerfully, "some of us try to face realities. Unlike you feminists living in never-never land."

"Are we going to have to listen to this all over again? It's such a bore!" Mary complained.

"Look, Mary," Elizabeth said in exasperation, "Ronnie and I have a real argument and we need to have it out. I'm sorry if you don't like it."

"Fine!" Mary spat. "Have it out by yourselves! Don't subject us to it! We're not interested in it."

"You should be," Ronnie insisted. "It's essential."

"Yes. Especially as it touches on our common situation," Elizabeth agreed.

"What do you mean?"

"What I mean, Ronnie, is that" — she turned to face her — "and I'm not saying this in anger. I'm over that. But you're young enough to be my daughter, you could be my daughter . . ."

"Hardly," Ronnie drawled sarcastically. "Wrong color. And may I add, I'm grateful I'm not."

"I'm grateful you're not too. Mainly because I'm grateful I was never a mother. But that's irrelevant. What I want to point out is that you have everything invested in a bunch of lies."

Ronnie paled, but her voice stayed strong. "Oh, you know the truth," she charged.

Elizabeth held up her hands. "I don't claim to be in total possession of the truth. I just want to make one small point." She lighted a cigarette. "Lying to oneself can have reverberations. For instance, the other night when we were — when we all discovered — revealed — we'd had the same experience with Father — you — and you were the only one — you lied, Ronnie."

Alex gasped. Mary held her breath. Ronnie sat back in her chair, her face hard and dark.

"You said that it wasn't the same for you as for us with Father because you never loved him. And that's a lie, Ronnie."

Ronnie shot forward, her teeth bared. "How dare you! How dare you assert what I feel, felt? How can you possibly know!"

"Do *I* have to say how it was, had to be, must have been? Big house, big man, man Momma loves . . . he was a good-looking man in those days. Tall, handsome, graceful, beautifully dressed, always in control. I've seen the photographs — Christ! I remember! He was the bossman, he had all the power. He *must* have seemed like a god to your mother and to you too, Ronnie!"

"God! He seemed like the devil!" Ronnie cried.

Elizabeth gazed at her steadily.

Ronnie stood up. "He is a devil," she hissed at Elizabeth. "Your father! A rapist, a child molester, a fascist, a killer! You know what his policies were during the war, after it . . . ! And you too, to the degree you support him! I don't want to know you and I don't want to be in this house anymore!" She whirled around and left the room.

"Really, Elizabeth," Mary murmured. "Did you have to do that?"

Elizabeth hung her head. "I thought I did," she said.

*   *   *

Anything, she'll do anything, she said it herself, she has no scruples, takes after her old man. Ronnie turned in her bed, trying the left side now, coiled around as if she had a stomachache.

It's not true, I never cared about him, how dare she what's that word impact import impose impose her feelings on me, impugn, impugn my word. How does she know what I felt? How could she?

That bitch, that traitor to womanhood, that quisling for the devil's party, miserable woman, no one's more miserable than her, the unhappiest woman I ever met, that's where her ideas get her. When you have hellish ideas, you live in hell.

She turned again.

Apologist for her father, who raped her. No wonder she wants to insist everyone else loves him. She's right, she is a destroyed person, her life is a ruin. A monument to patriarchal thought, that's what she is: like him. Alone, alone, she's totally alone. So okay I haven't found the right person either, one woman I can love forever, but I've loved lots of people and someday I will find the right one, I know I will. I'm still young. I'm young, I'm alive. It's not that I can't have good relationships. I'm not like her.

She turned again but her pillow was soaked and she sat up, switched on the bedside lamp. Sighing, she pulled her body up, sat on the edge of the bed, reached for the package of cigarettes she had opened tonight — and after three days without smoking, too! Shit! — and lighted one. She got out of bed. The floor was cold on her bare feet.

She found her socks and pulled her jeans on, buttoned them over the T-shirt she wore to sleep in and left the room. The house was dark and silent, and she didn't turn on any lights, moving quietly by feel into the kitchen, the hall, the foyer, the sitting room, the hall past the billiards room, and pushed open the half-closed door to the library. Moonlight poured in through the French doors facing the garden across the worn Persian carpet, cutting a sharp swathe in the floor.

She stood there until her eyes were fully accustomed to both the dark and the moonlit swathe. Room I avoid. She studied the French doors, the windows, the desk, the low beamed ceiling, the huge stone fireplace, the walls of books. She moved toward the desk, tapped her cigarette into the large round ashtray Elizabeth used, empty now, cleaned, good servants in this house.

I thought he was out.

He *was* out, he went to Boston for the day, but he must have come back early because of the heat. It was horribly hot. Momma was sweating in the kitchen, it must have been over a hundred in there, she was doing a reduction of a sauce, making *blanquette de veau,* he said he might bring someone back for dinner, some important man in the government. I knew she wouldn't let me so I snuck out to the pool with my bathing suit under my shirt, I didn't dare go in naked, the gardeners were around. They wouldn't have told on me, they didn't care if I used the pool, but they would have leered and teased if I'd gone skinny-dipping. I put on my suit in the bushes, and dove in. Oh god it was wonderful, how lucky they were and here it sat they didn't even come here, they hardly used it, but oh, it was wonderful, that cool water lapping around me, and I dove under and around and got my whole self wet and swam, I'd taught myself to swim sneaking in when no one was here, Momma never even knew or maybe she did but never let on. . . .

Oh, I had such a good time. I must have stayed in that pool for an hour, my fingers were all wrinkled and turning blue by the time I got tired. I got out and snuck into the bushes.

Ronnie walked to the French doors and unlocked them, stepped out on the terrace, stared out at the dark mounds of leafless shrubs — forsythia, orange blossom, lilac. The tips of the bare branches were gilded by moonlight.

Right there. And took off my wet suit and reached for my shorts . . . and . . .

"Girl! Come here!"

Froze. Caught. He was here, he was home, he was standing there in the doorway, right where I'm standing now. Could he see me through the leaves? He must see me, he's calling me, naked I am and now what will he tell Momma, will he throw us out, will she cry, will we starve to death?

I started to put on my shorts.

"Come here immediately! NOW!"

"Yes sir," I whimpered, dropped the shorts but grabbed my shirt. "I'll just put on my . . ."

"NOW!"

God I had breasts I had hair down there I was mature it wasn't as if I was little and unself-conscious I couldn't . . .

"NOW!"

I came out from behind the bushes naked, shivering, terrified, starting to cry, please sir I'm sorry but it was so hot I just wanted to try it it was so hot I'll never do it again I never did it before this was the first time it was just so hot today. . . .

But I didn't say any of it, because He strode out there and grabbed me by the arm, I dropped my clothes, He dragged me into the library, my feet didn't even touch the ground, dragged me in and threw me down on the couch.

Slowly, Ronnie turned and went back inside, locked the door, turned to face the long leather couch. Slowly, she crossed the room and locked the door to the hall. Then she stood looking down on the couch.

Unbuckled his belt, I thought he was going to beat me, I'd heard kids talk at school — Did your father whip you? Yeah, I really got it, with the belt. I was crying, shivering, it was hot but I was cold and then he threw himself on top of me, something terrible and hard shot into me I opened my mouth to scream he put his hand over my mouth he was tearing my insides down there he was ripping me open. . . .

Ronnie stood by the couch, tears pouring down her cheeks.

Then he shuddered and a hot stream of liquid filled me up. He got up, he pulled up his pants, I was lying there, this slimy ooze dripping out of me, he buckled his belt.

He wasn't going to beat me. . . .

"Get up."

I did. The stuff poured out of me all over the leather couch. As if I'd peed. Humiliated, so embarrassed . . .

Stared at me, those icy eyes, my small rounded brown body shivering naked. "If you speak of this to anyone, I will dismiss your mother. You'll be on the street, you understand?"

I nodded.

He motioned to the French doors with his head.

I ran to it, it was locked, I fiddled with it, I was sobbing, it was hard to open, finally I got out of the room, back to the bushes, found my clothes and put them on, shivering, crying, whimpering like a baby, what was that, what did he do to me, why? I ran inside, Momma didn't see me, I ran up the attic stairs to the closed-up maids' rooms, I lay down on a bed, there was a sheet over it all dusty I kept sneezing, I didn't care, I just lay there shivering, crying, keeping my sounds low so no one would hear. . . .

Crept around after that. Never went into the pool again. Never, no matter how hot it was, even if he wasn't here. Still, when Momma was out shopping or in the kitchen preparing some special dinner, he'd find me somehow, summon me, call me like I was a dog, call me "girl," grab me by the arm, drag me in here, throw me on that couch. Always the same, never said anything to me again. How I hate this room.

Slowly, her body hunched over, Ronnie left the library and retraced her way to the kitchen.

She says I loved him. How dare she. Maybe they did, do. He didn't treat them the way he treated me. At least he claimed to be doing it out of love, he caught at their hearts. He used the word, whatever his feeling. He counted on their loving him. But he treated me exactly the way a white plantation owner might have treated his African slave. But I'll bet even some of them claimed to love those slaves too; maybe at least they showed desire. He never even did that, he was cold, except his eyes, something shone in them, was it desire, was that how he showed it, that intensity of gaze that took over my body, surveyed and appropriated it the way a woman looks at a nice cut of meat she's about to buy for dinner. I was high tea, he had Momma for dinner.

Momma knew all about the droit du seigneur, she used to talk about the way the white foremen and farmers simply took the Mexican women. Women were property belonging to the master. All of them knew it — the men, the women, the children. It was the way things were. They tried to hide daughters of ten or eleven whose shabby clothes couldn't hide their swelling breasts, thighs and bellies taut with youth, girls who still thought and felt as children, but the men saw something else, saw what they wanted to see, took what they wanted. It happened to her own mother, she said, herself the product of a union like that, probably why I have blue eyes. And Grandma Maria loved Grandpa Rogelio because he didn't beat her for it, didn't threaten to kill her, he knew she had nothing to say about it, couldn't help what happened. He even loved the baby, Momma, and oh how she loved him.

So if I'd told her, what would she have done? Of course, it's different, he wasn't just the seigneur, he was my father. And he knew it. Titillated him, fucking his daughters, got them all didn't he, was that a private little triumph for him?

Still, suppose I'd told her and she'd shrugged? I'd have hated her forever, I'd never have been able to love her again. As it was I couldn't forgive her for not knowing, for somehow not stopping him.

Ten times he did it over that summer, ten times, I counted, each time leaving me feeling like a piece of meat thumped like those slices of veal Momma sometimes made for him, banged with a mallet until they were limp and saggy and spread out, all the muscle broken down. Kept waiting for him to leave but he didn't. Retired, Momma said. Retired! He was never going to leave again. I lived in a state of dread, couldn't study, my grades fell, the teachers looking at me like I was finally fulfilling my promise, the lazy no-good *chicana* finally come of age. My breasts were big then, even if my mind was still a kid's, I was bigger than any of the white girls, more mature. Felt raped every day at school, had to get out, had to find my own kind.

Like Mary couldn't face coming back here from school. I wonder if I'd ever have had the guts just to tell him to stop like Elizabeth did.

No. I'd have been terrified that he'd throw Momma out. Running away was the only solution. She didn't know where I was either, so he knew she wasn't complicit. She was beside herself. He couldn't take it out on her. She thought I did it to punish her, but I'd thought it all out. It was hard on me, too, not calling her, thinking about her horrible worry. . . .

I was a pretty brave kid, I think.

And all she knew was love. Oh Christ. Well shit, she deserved some, didn't she?

Was it just malice made me do that? What did I think I was doing? Getting revenge for a miserable day, all because of her, couldn't think through problems, couldn't work, tearing my hair just because of her stupid politics? The way Mary and Alex looked at me, you'd think I'd killed a puppy.

What the hell do I care.

I do care. I don't want them to hate me, think ill of me.

Why? Stupid, both stupid, what the hell difference does it make what they think of you? Dictatorship of niceness for women, I won't submit to it, never did never will.

But when we're all getting along . . . it makes the edges of my heart curl, I feel lighter, not so jangly and torn. . . . Ronnie too. In some ways, I like her best, she's most like me. So why did I have to . . .

I don't care about her politics, sentimental feminist garbage can't stand up to the light of day. The whole weight of western philosophy stands behind me, the best minds of the centuries, along with all the economic thinkers except a couple of oddballs, the lunatic fringe. But I'm not trying to convert *her,* why does she insist that I believe what she believes? Dictatorship of the new feminist proletariat, everybody has to dress and act the same, no makeup, no high heels, and above all no dissent — worse than the commies.

I stand for liberty. Individual liberty. That's the basis of my politics, my economics, my life.

Satisfied, Elizabeth turned over and made herself more comfortable among the tangle of sheet and blankets, the punch-drunk pillows. She closed her eyes. She willed herself to sleep. But the mind wouldn't close down shop.

Just wasn't going to let her get away with lies, if she has to lie to herself to be a feminist, okay, but she's not going to lie to us to make herself better, purer than we. I won't permit it. How dare she suggest she's purer than we are! That we colluded in our own . . . and she didn't. He just grabbed her and raped her, is that what she wants us to believe? So why didn't she yell, why didn't she tell her mother? A loving mother, she claims. That wasn't Father's style, that isn't how he'd act, he wasn't like that with any of us, you could hear it when we talked about it, he used our love for him, his . . . love . . . whatever . . . for us. Which is the worst part, the killing part, the thing you can't get past, the thing I can't get past. I loved him, I wanted him to love me even if that meant . . . oh god.

Elizabeth turned again, then, despairing of sleep, sat up. She picked up the clock: ten after four. She felt bedraggled, she could feel the bags growing down her cheeks under her eyes. She sighed, lighted a cigarette, slipped out of bed and pulled on her robe. She walked barefoot on the soft carpet to the window, and pulled open the drapes. The moon was gone, no stars were visible, the sky was completely black. You could barely make out the line where trees ended and sky began. She sat on the chaise, gazing out at nothingness.

Father.

I adored him. All those years. Watching him stride around laughing joking talking with all those important men, they all listened to him as if he were somebody, really somebody, and oh how I wanted longed yearned to have him look at me just once with love, to praise me, praise something about me, approve of me. And when I gave up hope for that, when I grew up, I yearned to be like him. What do you want to be when you grow up, little girl? My daddy.

Then he came to me, said words, said _love_.

How could I love Mother, fucking victim, hopeless bitter angry useless woman, sat on her ass fidgeting waiting for the telephone to ring, daydreaming — revenge? restitution? The only thing she ever did in her whole life was give birth to me. Oh, she took care of me, I suppose that's something, it takes something.

But she'd scorn Ronnie's ideas the same as I do.

You all hate women, Ronnie said.

Maybe we can't bear listening to hope when we have no hope.

Holding the palm of her hand under the cigarette ash, she got up seeking an ashtray. She pressed the cigarette out, then slid back into the tumbled bed, trying vaguely to straighten the covers, and lay on her back, her arms folded behind her head.

She hopes for the same things I do the same things I would if I could hope. Justice, decency, humankindness. The difference between us is I know better.

So you try to dash her illusions, all of them. Twenty-five she is, young enough to be my daughter. The young should be permitted illusions.

She'd probably say that they weren't illusions. That's what she'd say. Wouldn't she?

And what would Clare say?

Her heart paused.

Nothing came.

She always knew what Clare's response to any statement would be, but this time she could not guess at it. She knew he was opposed to feminism, but not really why. She'd simply mocked it with him. And now he'd fallen silent. The ceiling was blank. She stared at it in panic; a profound loneliness filled the room.

Alex sat in the formal chair facing the window gazing at a sky moonless now, degrees of darkness, sky, trees, lawn beneath. Would an artist call those colors? Have names for them — night lawn gray, night tree black, night sky . . . what?

Just as she was pulling herself together, regaining her past, filling in the patches, everything around was falling apart. Terrible past but better to know, have something to put in those awful gaping spaces. Mother, dooming me to mental retardation: did she think she was doing me a favor?

Why, Elizabeth Ronnie what is it what is going on? We were so good, we were learning to love each other, embrace each other, help each other, god knows we need help, we need each other, only we alone with our awful truth, our untellable tale, our histories that no history book will ever recount. Women's lives, untold, unknown, as if a species of creature lived on earth, some exotic form of ant or beetle, busy building their homes getting their food getting young raising them, and no one knew it, no one knew anything about it, everyone looked the other way and said, that isn't there. They aren't there. That isn't happening. That is unthinkable.

Unthinkable.

Father.

How to look at him see him, how to think feel about him unthinkable. Don't know, all mixed up, too crazy, and now he's just a helpless old man dying, one more human victim. Can't.

She leaned back, let her eyes close partway, saw her own eyelashes, dark against darkness. Let her hands fall limply on the wooden chair arms, neck fall back, let it all fall away.

Age upon age of humans on this earth, the pain of birth of life of death of injustice, creatures springing up in glorious bodies then are broken, fall down, oppressed and oppressors dancers and dance, age upon age, held in the palm of the ancient parents, small and brown and wrinkled I see them, hold me in your palm, keep me safe, draw your blanket about me, I am one of the children who walk here briefly who need your soft palm on the side of my face. Birth growth desire the dance I too dance to my death in desire and longing and rage and pain, eternal dance, hold me, end this pain. I pray you.

17

The nurse who examined Mr. Upton every day, Elsie Noonan, came early Monday morning so Florence had plenty of time to get Mr. Upton settled again, elegant in his silk pajamas and robe — a heavy crimson silk thing, must have cost a fortune — sitting up in his wheelchair for the lawyers' visit at eleven. She'd been worried because sometimes Elsie didn't get there until ten or ten-thirty, and he would have been in disarray when his important guest arrived, and that would have shamed her. But today she showed up at nine-thirty so everything was fine, Florence had given him a nice breakfast before Elsie came and all she had to do was bathe and shave him and put him in his robe — which was more of a project than you'd imagine — and comb his hair.

She didn't hear the doorbell, you couldn't hear a thing in this house it was so big, but then suddenly there was Miss Upton in the doorway with these two men in suits and ties, important men, you could tell. So of course, she knew how to behave, she excused herself and tiptoed downstairs for her elevenses, Mrs. Browning had an apple crumble for her today, just scrumptious it was, and she had a little breather.

Sat there for almost an hour, then in comes Miss Upton to ask Mrs. Browning if she could possibly handle two extra for lunch and not to worry if she couldn't because they'd all go out and have lunch at the Lincoln Inn. And Mrs. Browning said she had a lovely mushroom soup and plenty of it and a nice fresh apple crumble, and would omelets do? She had some Swiss cheese and a little ham she could toss in, and some nice French bread delivered just this morning, or maybe they'd rather have a soufflé? And Miss Upton said a soufflé would be wonderful and could they have a green salad with it?

So those men were staying for lunch.

Hollis came down first, alone. He stood for a moment uncertainly in the foyer, then peered into the sitting room. No one. He crossed the foyer and peered into the dining room — what a majestic room! That table must hold fifty guests! — then walked the length of the great front hall and peered into the archway under the stairs.

"Hello?"

No one.

He passed through the archway, turned into another wide hall and walked toward an open door at its end. It was the library, and Elizabeth was sitting at the desk.

"Elizabeth!"

She removed her glasses. "Yes, Hollis. Are you through? Come in."

She's different, he thought as he settled himself on the leather couch. Nicer somehow.

"You and the other lawyer — Mr. Kaplan? — will stay for lunch, I hope."

"Can't speak for him but I'd enjoy that. I think Kaplan intends to see Cab's doctors this afternoon, over at the hospital, so I imagine he'll be grateful for a civilized interlude. And it's a bit of a ride back to Boston, I'd be glad to eat first. Especially with such delightful company!" he added, having long ago learned his manners.

Elizabeth lighted a cigarette.

"Still doing that, eh? I gave it up five years ago. Evelyn kept after me, drove me crazy. But I must say I still enjoy getting a whiff of cigarette smoke." He smiled stiffly. "Elizabeth. . . ."

She looked up sharply at his tone change.

"How's Cab feeling? How's he acting?"

Spurts of adrenalin pumped swiftly through Elizabeth's body. Danger. Watch it now. Careful.

She looked directly at him. He was frowning, his head in his hand, his elbow on the arm of the couch. "I'm afraid . . . he's . . . unhappy, Hollis," she smiled apologetically. "We understand, of course. It must be unendurable for such an active . . . *powerful* man to find himself . . . almost helpless. Having to be done for in the ways he is." She let her voice drop, fade, then drew a long breath and started again. "That's why we decided to put our own lives on hold for a while, to oversee his care at home. The only alternatives were a nursing home or bringing him back here with no family member to make sure he was being cared for properly — the way he should be. . . ."

"Of course," Hollis murmured, his face full of sympathy. "What you girls are doing is — well, it's nothing short of damned wonderful, Elizabeth. We'd all be lucky to be on the receiving end of such devotion when we get old . . . helpless. God knows it's awful."

"Yes," she agreed softly.

Didn't know I had it in me.

"You know, I have to confess, Lizzie, I never thought Cab was much of a father. So many women — excuse me, but you know — well — and he was never around, you know, that sort of thing. But he must have done something right."

She tried to picture Bernini's Saint Teresa when she smiled. "Father is very special to all of us."

"Takes his frustration out on you, does he?" The old man gave her a wise look.

She shook her head gently, dismissing this. "It's understandable. We're family. Better on us than on the help," she added laughing. "They might quit!"

He laughed. "Yey-uh, things ain't what they used to be, are they, Lizzie?"

A desperate voice in the hall cried out "Hello? Hello?" Hollis rose, chuckling. "That's Tom, lost in this maze. Forgot how big this house was. Looked different years ago when it was full of people."

"Hollis, why don't you take — Tom — into the sitting room. I'll join you there in a minute. I'll call the others. We can have drinks."

Elizabeth went to find her sisters. As the lawyers in the sitting room put their heads close together to talk in whispers, she gathered the sisters in Ronnie's room, which offered more privacy than the sun room or playroom, and whispered there.

"I think — I'm not positive but almost — that Father wants Hollis to cut us out of his will. My guess is Hollis thinks Father has lost his wits. What's at question is whether the other lawyer — the guardian *ad litem* — thinks the same thing."

"What is that other lawyer doing here?" Mary whined.

"He's the guardian *ad litem*," Elizabeth repeated. "The court appointed him. His job is to decide whether Father is competent or not. We have to persuade him that Father's not in his right mind."

"Well, he isn't," Mary said.

"Well, he thinks he is. And who knows — maybe he is."

"You mean, he's as sane as he ever was," Ronnie said glumly. "That sounds right."

"But this time he's being held up to judgment," Alex said calmly. They all stared at her.

"Yes," Elizabeth said, sounding surprised. "So we have to play this just right. We have to give these guys the impression that we are devoted long-suffering loving daughters who forgive him for his irrational rage against us." She checked their faces. "If you can't," she warned, "don't show up for lunch. I'll say you've gone out, that I didn't know you had a doctor's appointment. . . ."

Mary and Alex nodded their preparedness. Ronnie turned away from them stiffly, stood at the window.

"Ronnie?" Elizabeth asked. "Are you okay? Can you do it?"

She turned. "I'm invited to lunch?"

"Of course!" Elizabeth snapped, as if it were a stupid question. She led the way, stopping in the kitchen. "Mrs. Browning, Mr. Whitehead and Mr. Kaplan will have drinks with us in the sitting room. Will you send someone to serve us?"

The sisters walked down the front hall and into the sitting room. Both lawyers rose.

"Hollis," Elizabeth said, "you haven't met our half sister Ronalda Velez. We only recently discovered her ourselves." Nodding to Ronnie to

step forward, Elizabeth put her hand lightly on her back. "Hollis Whitehead and . . . Mr. Kaplan . . . ?"

"Tom, please!" said the younger man, smiling.

"I didn't know . . . ," Hollis spluttered, his face shocked. "Another
daughter?"

"Yes, Father seems to have specialized in daughters," Elizabeth
smiled. "As far as we know! Please sit down!"

Hollis stared at Ronnie as he lowered his large body into his chair,
his face working unpleasantly. The six of them sat in a circle around the
empty fireplace. Teresa and Doris bustled in with trays, and set bottles and
ice on the small sideboard.

Alex rose. "Let me get you something to drink," she smiled.

"Oh!" Hollis half rose from his chair. "You sure you don't want me to
do it, little lady?"

Alex smiled shyly. "Well, I may not do it as well as you, but I'd like to
try."

Shee-it, Ronnie thought. You thing. You're as bad as Mary.

As soon as they all had drinks, Hollis said, "You know the judge
appointed Tom here guardian *ad litem* to look into the matter of the conservatorship. He has to determine what state Cab is in, whether he's able
to handle his own affairs. He's going to interview the doctors this afternoon. Who are they, Tom?" He turned to him.

Tom pulled a pad from his breast pocket. "Dr. Stamp — the neurologist who took care of Mr. Upton in the hospital? And Dr. Biddle. He was
the family doctor for years as I understand it."

The sisters nodded. So did Hollis.

"Good men, good men," he pronounced solemnly.

"If I may make a suggestion . . . ," Elizabeth began tentatively.

Elizabeth tentative? Shee-it!

"You might want to talk to Nurse Edna Thompson as well. She probably saw more of Father than the doctors — more hands-on work, you
know," she smiled.

"Excellent idea! Excellent!" Hollis boomed.

Tom scribbled on his pad.

Hollis set his sherry on the side table. "Listen, girls, I've known you,
well, Lizzie and Mary at least, and I remember you as a tiny tot, Alex. . . ."

He glanced uncomfortably at Ronnie, then away. "I'm Cab's lawyer, obliged to realize his wishes, you know that, but . . . well, I'm probably not telling you anything you don't know, you said when you called me that he wanted to talk about his will. The thing is, Cab has some idea . . . about changing his will. The question facing us is whether he's . . . well, quite himself yet. I've had a nice little chat with Elizabeth," he smiled at her benignly, "but I'd like to know what the rest of you think." He glanced from face to face, settling on Mary. "Mary? What do you think, dear?"

Mary dropped her eyes, bit her lower lip, then looked shyly up at Hollis with that appealing upward tilt to her face. "Oh, Hollis, you know it has to be so difficult for him!" she said fervently. "It would be difficult for any of us, but for a man like him! It's . . . it's . . . " — she dropped her eyes again — "sometimes it's hard. You know, he was always such a, well, such a *loving* father." She curled her shoulders, raising her face again to his fascinated gaze. "I always felt I was his favorite, but it seems we all felt that way," she said glancing at her sisters, "at times." She pulled an immaculate hankie from the pocket of her silk dress, dabbed her nose lightly.

Does she really think that in this day and age she can get away with that?

"It is a little hard . . . " — she looked up beseechingly — "it's *very* hard . . . for us when he acts as if we were his enemies, when we brought him back here to care for him out of love. I simply can't understand it, none of us can. . . ." She stopped, raised her head and stared courageously at the fireplace. "But it doesn't matter. We're going to take care of him as long as we can. We know that if we don't, if we send him to a nursing home — well, we might as well — just give up hope for any recovery. You know," she appealed to Hollis, "how people in nursing homes just die." She lowered her gaze again, stared at her hands in a kind of shame, as if she had betrayed something.

Hollis's face was wrenched with emotion.

Ronnie thought, awed, she's masterly. Didn't know she was that good. She's right, it is a profession, a high art to be a woman in their world.

"I want you to know I think you girls are wonderful!" he said thickly, pulling his handkerchief from his pocket and giving his nose a great blow. He turned to the other lawyer. "You hear that, Tom?"

"I heard," Tom said, gazing intelligently at Mary.

Is he seeing through her?

"And what about you, my dear," Hollis said kindly to Alex.

"Well, Mr. Whitehead . . ."

"Hollis, Hollis!"

"Hollis. You know, Hollis, I haven't seen Father in years. He and my mother," she shrugged, "had, well, an unhappy divorce. I was still little."

"These things happen," Hollis nodded solemnly. "Sad — but they happen."

"But I remember a man who played with me, who bought me a puppy . . ." Alex's voice broke.

This has to be real, Ronnie thought. *She* couldn't counterfeit.

"I was so happy to see him again after all these years!" she said in a rising voice. "I thought he'd be happy to see me too! I *wanted* to take care of him, it was my pleasure to tend him! But . . . he acts as if he hates me and I don't know why! He acts as if he hates all of us, when we're trying so hard . . ." Her voice cracked again, she leapt up and ran out of the room with her face hidden in her hands.

Silence.

"Alex," Elizabeth said finally, "is a very . . . spiritual . . . person. Very emotional. She's a dear — with him and with us. This business is especially hard on her."

Hollis nodded solemnly, bending forward in his chair, his hands clasped between his legs. He looked meaningfully at Tom. Tom looked meaningfully at him.

"Yes. Well, I think I have as much as I need . . . ," he said, glancing up at Tom.

"You haven't asked Ronnie what she thinks," Mary said sweetly. "She's been living here for the past six or seven months, tending her mother, so she has more recent knowledge of him than we do . . ."

"Ronnie's mother was Father's housekeeper, and his common-law wife for the last thirty-odd years . . . ," Elizabeth explained.

Hollis looked as if he had just been told that the president was consulting an astrologer to determine national policy.

"Of course, we didn't know this before. We discovered it when we came back, and I can see you're shocked, Hollis, well, it was a shock to us too. But you have to know that Ronnie was a great help to Father while her mother was dying. She kept him going; Noradia's death was a terrible blow to him. In fact, it seems that his grief over her death precipitated his stroke. He had it the day she was buried, right after her funeral. . . ."

The lawyer was trying to keep his mouth shut. A film of shine formed on his forehead, and he pulled out his handkerchief again and wiped it. "I see," he said faintly. "I didn't know." He tried to turn toward Ronnie, but could not seem to get his eyes focused on her.

Alex returned quietly. "Sorry," she mouthed to the room at large. "I'm so sorry," she said to Hollis. "I don't usually act this way. It's just been so . . ."

"Quite all right, quite all right," the lawyer said, standing up as she entered, exploding with geniality. "Perfectly understandable, my dear, perfectly understandable. Eh, Tom?"

"Of course," Tom said.

Whether or not he bought Mary, he's buying Alex, Elizabeth thought. Quite rightly.

"For myself, I don't really think I need to know any more. What I'd like to propose is — if it's not an intrusion, I don't want to cause trouble for you girls — I'd like to come back in a week to ten days, have another chat with Cab, see how he feels then. I told him it would take some time to have the . . . have things prepared, and that I'd return for his signature . . . so he'll understand."

"Of course," Elizabeth murmured.

"No trouble at all," said Mary.

"We'd be happy to see you," Alex put in. "And so will Father."

The lawyer sighed. "Things aren't always what they seem," he declared, "eh, Tom?"

Tom nodded, slipped his notepad back into his pocket.

"So what did you think of the election, Hollis?" Elizabeth asked. "A real triumph, no?"

"It was a crazy idea, Elizabeth," Ronnie snapped at her after the lawyers had left, and they had moved into the playroom. "Really crazy. An unacceptable risk."

"What are you talking about?"

"In the first place, I shouldn't have come into that room! And to introduce me that way! You had to know that would upset him. And that it could turn him against all of *you,* not your father! You made him uncomfortable!"

"Yes," Mary murmured. "Rubbed his face in it."

"In what?" Alex asked.

"In . . . Elizabeth breached what is considered good manners in polite society, Alex," Mary explained.

Ronnie laughed. "Rubbed his face in what lies underneath it!" She turned back to Elizabeth. "Did you really think that would undermine his faith in your father's sanity? More likely to undermine his faith in yours! I mean, you risked your entire future, the future of all of you, your birthright, your legacy!"

"It was necessary," Elizabeth said coldly.

"Why?"

Mary studied Elizabeth's face. "Yes," she agreed, "it was."

"WHY?" Ronnie screamed.

"Hush!" Mary whispered. "You want the servants to hear us?"

"I'm not sure," Elizabeth faltered.

"Come on, Elizabeth, you never do anything without figuring all the angles first. Especially run that little scam. What a bunch of fakes you all are!"

"I'm not a fake," Alex protested.

"Probably not," Ronnie said sardonically, as if she thought Alex would be better off if she were.

"And as if it wasn't hard enough for him when you introduced me, you" — she turned to Mary — "had to compound it."

"Wasn't that fun?" Mary giggled.

"You mean you were trying to provoke him? Don't you realize what's at stake for you?"

Mary shrugged. "I don't know what I was trying to do. What are you, worried about *our* futures? You were there and he hadn't asked you anything. . . ."

"Yes," Elizabeth agreed. "You see, you're here. You exist."

"You didn't introduce me the first time he came."

"That was a long time ago," Mary said.

"Yeah. Four weeks," Ronnie commented dryly.

"So we've changed."

"You're . . . our seal," Elizabeth said. "Our symbol."

"FUCK THAT!" Ronnie shouted. "I'm me, a person, not your mascot, your little goat, your dog . . ."

"No, no, no!" Elizabeth cried impatiently. "Don't you see? You are us, we are you. We're illegitimate. All of us. As women we have no rights, even to our own bodies. We don't even have the right to complain. Underneath all the glitzy surfaces we're all in the same boat. That's why it was necessary. We have to hold together. All of us."

All of them sat in silence.

"Let's go for a walk," Alex said suddenly. "Get away from this house."

This time they took the driveway leading to the road and headed toward town. They had trouble walking four abreast on the grass verge, but they kept trying.

"Okay, I understand what you're saying," Ronnie admitted. "And I guess I even agree with it. And of course, it makes me feel . . . more accepted. But I wish I could believe that Hollis guy would blame your father for his discomfort, instead of you for making him feel it."

"Why do you keep saying *your* father? He's your father too, Ronnie," Alex objected.

Ronnie shrugged. "Doesn't acknowledge it, does he? I don't know what to call him. I can't call him Father and I'll be damned if I'm going to call him Mr. Upton — as he probably thinks I should. Would you prefer my calling him the dirty old prick?"

Silence.

She picked it up again. "I wasn't raised an Upton and I can't claim to be an expert on your class's morality. But I'm willing to bet that in Hollis's morality, your sin was more serious than your father's. His is accepted, you know — men are allowed to do anything, really. It's the person who exposes a wrongdoing who's to blame."

"He thinks we were presented with some upsetting information and are brave girls making the best of it," Mary declared.

"Are you sure? Are you sure he doesn't think you're scandalous girls," Ronnie snapped, "rubbing his nose in shit?"

"No. 'Scandalous' goes with 'women,' not 'girls,'" Elizabeth said thoughtfully. "And he kept calling us girls. So I think we're home free."

Mary's voice grew anxious again. "What's going to happen, though, if Father keeps insisting he wants us out, sooner or later Hollis is going to have to cut us out. . . ."

"We'll know soon. If Kaplan awards me the conservatorship, that means he doesn't think Father can manage his own affairs."

"Poor Father," Mary mourned.

"What!"

"Well, think about how he must feel! He's *not* mad or senile or out of his mind. He's the same as he ever was. But suddenly he's totally impotent! He can't even get his lawyer to do what he wants!"

"I don't think he's the same as before," Alex argued, "not the way I remember him. And he must be a little insane to treat us with such hate when we're trying to be kind to him. . . ." Her eyes filled.

"He doesn't think we mean to be kind to him," Elizabeth muttered. "And he's right."

"Well, I mean to be kind to him," Alex said, a tear running down her cheek. She hastily wiped it away with her hand.

"Well, I don't," Ronnie said in a tough little voice. "He was never anything but a bastard to me. He's not acting any different now than when I was fourteen. Only thing, he's not raping me."

"I came here with so much goodwill. So much . . . longing," Alex said in a thickening voice.

"You don't still feel that way, do you? Now that you realize what he did?" Mary challenged her.

"I can't just *stop* feeling that. I had this longing for my father. I'll always have it. Whether he's there or not, alive or not. For the father I knew before . . . or the father I imagined . . . or the way he was sometimes, other times. . . ." She turned to Ronnie. "Don't you? You grew up without any father at all! Didn't you have a longing . . ."

"NO!" Ronnie erupted.

All of them stopped dead and looked at her.

"STOP! Stop looking at me!" She moved with great agitation, shaking her fisted hands, her eyes darting around. "I don't see why you all keep insisting. . . !" she cried. "It's better not to have a father. They're all bastards in one way or another! I was better off than you!" She ran ahead of them, then stopped and faced them in attack position. "It's you who are all crazy!" she yelled, running off.

The sisters walked in silence.

"I think," Alex said finally, slowly, in a low voice, "that Father has to be made to acknowledge Ronnie. Much as he hurt us, he hurt her worst of all."

"Yes," Mary said, "you're right. But he should be made to acknowledge everything — what he did to us as well. I never would have gotten married at nineteen except for . . . Maybe I wouldn't have thought that marriage . . . sex . . . was all I was good for."

"Oh, you might've," Elizabeth said gloomily. "It's what they taught us in those days."

"Maybe," Mary agreed. "But maybe I would have become a poet."

"A poet!"

Mary stuck out a challenging chin. "I write poetry."

"I didn't know," Elizabeth said in a small voice.

"I've written a poem a day since we've been here," she said proudly. "Of course, they're probably not any good. They're probably awful."

Elizabeth put an arm around Mary. Alex embraced her from the other side. At the crossing where their road met a main road, Ronnie stood waiting, kicking dirt. They all walked back together but without speaking.

Mary came a little late to the dinner table. She'd had a telephone call. "That was Chris, Christina, one of my friends, the ones who came to tea? They want to come to visit Father. I've told them he's home, and they want to pay a call. Tomorrow. Is that all right?" She looked around.

They just looked at her.

"I suppose," Elizabeth said.

"They're planning to come at eleven. I feel we should give them luncheon," she said tentatively.

"Not if it's the big deal the tea was," Elizabeth said. "I can't go through that again."

"I'll be glad to help you, Mary," Alex offered.

"Something like what we had for the men today would be adequate," Mary said. "With, perhaps, a more elegant dessert. They know we weren't expecting them. All right then? I'll speak to Mrs. Browning."

Teresa entered to clear their plates.

"Did you see that they arrested another Sikh for murdering Mrs. Gandhi?" Elizabeth said to the table at large.

They gathered in the playroom and Alex turned on the television set. Elizabeth picked up a book lying on a table — poems by Barbara Greenberg. Must be Mary's, she thought. She began to read. Ronnie was gazing dully out the glass doors to the terrace.

Mary rustled in. "Well, that's settled! A watercress soup and a chicken salad — there's enough left over from the birds we had tonight — and she'll make a wonderful dressing and serve it with dill, black beans, and tomatoes. And she's going to make French pastries in the morning! Isn't that wonderful?"

"That sounds delicious, Mary," Alex said warmly.

"These poems are really wonderful," Elizabeth murmured.

"Yes, aren't they? She's a local poet, I found her book in the Concord bookstore."

"Any poems on incest?" Elizabeth asked.

"No. Not by her. But in Anne Sexton. And I often wonder about Sylvia Plath. . . ."

Ronnie sat tensely and looked portentously at Mary, then Elizabeth, then Alex. They all looked back at her. Elizabeth slowly put down the book. Alex switched off the set.

"I'm sorry," Ronnie said.

"No need," Elizabeth muttered.

"It's nothing," Mary said.

"Oh my dear." Alex reached a hand toward her.

"You're right, of course," she said in a dead voice. "I don't know why it's so hard for me to say. To think. To admit."

She turned her body to face them. "When I was little, I used to lie in bed and imagine that I had a poppa and that he would come one day in an old black car and lift me up crowing with joy at me. Wanting me. And take Momma and me away from here to our own house, where I could run around just as I chose. Momma had wonderful parents, her poppa used to carry her on his shoulders when they all walked out to the fields in the morning. The grass was still covered with dew, it was damp and she had no shoes. She remembered the light coming up, she remembered him with so much love. I wanted a poppa like that, a man who wanted me, wanted me to exist, I mean, not what he . . . your father . . . what he wanted. And with my Poppa would come all these people, grandmothers and grandfathers and cousins and aunts and uncles, and they'd all be happy that I existed. That I was alive. I yearned to feel that, feel them, be surrounded by them. I wanted to be . . . welcomed into the world." She stopped, rose, left the room. They heard the bathroom door slam, then silence.

Only Alex was unaware of her, was elsewhere. "Yes," she sighed, almost to herself. "Lifted! Warmed by body heat, smelling their body smells, seeing the pores on their skin, the gray in their hair, feeling part of them, like them, not perfect but wanted. Then you know what home is!"

Elizabeth studied the Ping Pong table. She carefully avoided rolling her eyes.

Ronnie came back with swollen eyes and a washed face. Even her hair was damp. She sat on the edge of a hassock, staring at the floor.

"Talk to us, Ronnie," Alex pleaded. "It'll make you feel better and us feel wanted."

"Wanted?"

"As if you need us. We want you to need us. We need it."

Ronnie grimaced. She asked Elizabeth for a cigarette. She stared at the floor, smoking.

"Your father," she said in a dead voice, "did seem like a god to me when I was little. He was so tall and handsome and rich and powerful and my mother adored him, and he was so easy with all those important people. . . ."

She stopped. No one spoke.

She looked up at them. "But he treated me like a nigger slave, and I don't want to talk about it," she said firmly.

"We won't mention it again," Elizabeth said after a time.

"Thank you." Dead face, dead voice.

The four of them sat in silence, their faces thoughtful.

"He should be tried for his crimes," Elizabeth said at last.

"Tried?" Alex frowned. "You mean put on trial?" she asked incredulously.

"Yes. Indicted and tried — incest *is* a crime, and we all know he's guilty of it."

"That will never happen," Mary said.

Ronnie said, "Even if we'd been able to tell, even if anyone would have listened to us, even if anyone would have believed us, can you imagine them prosecuting a man who entertained presidents?"

"That's what my mother says: he's above the law," Elizabeth murmured. "But that's unacceptable."

"Yes," Alex said softly. "We have to get Father to acknowledge his acts."

They fell silent.

"He never will and we can't make him," Elizabeth said finally.

"No. No district attorney is going to indict a sick old man like him, even if we were to accuse him. And can you imagine how they'd look at us if we did, especially now? They'd say we were crazy or vindictive or worse! They'd let him change his will!" Mary argued.

"Anyway, he's not able to stand trial. He can't speak."

"Even without being able to speak, he has more control of his life now than I had over mine when I was two or three," Alex said.

They pondered this.

"That's true," Mary agreed.

"We could try him ourselves," Alex said.

They stared at her.

"Hold a trial here. At night, after the servants have gone to bed. He never turns out his light until eleven or eleven-thirty. After the news. We could go up after dinner."

"How do we hold a trial?" Ronnie wondered.

"I don't know. Just present our evidence . . . our memories . . . and see what he says. Does. Writes. How he acts."

"If we're going to do it at all, we should do it right," Elizabeth said. "Someone should accuse, someone defend, someone judge."

"But we're all his victims."

"I like that idea. Elizabeth should be the prosecutor — she's the most articulate in law and things like that," Alex said.

"Mary has the most sympathy for him. She could defend him."

"And Alex could be the judge. She's the kindest of us, and probably the fairest."

"So what about me!" Ronnie protested.

"You suffered the gravest injury. You are the primary complainant," Elizabeth said.

"I suffered the gravest injury? Why? Because I became a lesbian? Is that what you think? That has nothing to do with what he did . . ."

"No, Ronnie!" Mary interrupted. "You suffered the gravest injury because not only did he use you sexually even though you were a child, but he refused to acknowledge you as his child, he did nothing for you, he cast you out into the world with nothing — not just no money, but no love, no help, no — no embrace. And it was clear from the way Hollis acted that he didn't know about you. Which means he didn't acknowledge you even in his will."

Ronnie was placated.

"Okay."

"So. Shall we do it?"

They all agreed.

"What about Wednesday night, when Mrs. Browning is away and only Doris is here. She's new, she doesn't understand the household yet. We'd run less risk of being interrupted," Mary suggested.

"Wednesday night, then. Prepare your cases, women."

18

Ronnie didn't, did not, want to meet the lunch ladies as she called them, did not want to eat with them, make conversation with them, even show herself. But Elizabeth and Mary insisted.

"You are part of us, we've been all through this, you are intrinsic to our — our — sisterhood!" Elizabeth argued.

"You're part of our lives now. What are you going to do, disappear every time someone else from our life appears? You have to have courage, Ronnie. I thought you were so brave!"

The challenge to her machismo worked, and she agreed to appear, but her stomach was twisted, and she had to take a pill to calm it before the women arrived.

Mary's friends arrived a little after eleven in a stretch limo that belonged to Francine. Teresa opened the door to them, but Mary was behind her, waiting in the foyer to welcome them. After Teresa took their coats and they had embraced each other in the tight distant way such women had, she led them upstairs.

"My sisters are up there with him now," she explained. Up there trying to jolly him into being decent to his guests. But in fact, their efforts were unnecessary. Stephen was well schooled in courtesy, and the moment they entered, his strange warped face curled itself into a smile, the first the sisters had seen on him.

"Oh, Mr. Upton, do you remember me, I'm Chrissie, Christine Bidwell I was, my mother used to bring me out to Lincoln sometimes to play with Mary, my mother was a good friend of Laura's, they'd been at school together. You visited my parents a few times, Anne and Walter Bidwell, do you remember, we used to live in Back Bay and on the water in Manchester. . . ." She bent to kiss his cheek and he patted her arm with his good hand, stretched it out then to the next one, "Frankie, Mr. Upton. We played croquet with you once, you taught me the finer points of the game, do you remember?" He opened his mouth in a kind of laugh, stretched out his arm, the old Stephen, full of good humor. Francine kissed his cheek too, then Eloise reintroduced herself, "Lulu, Mr. Upton," all of them talking at once now, reminiscing, "Remember the time up in Manchester when Mary got stuck in a tree and was terrified to come down?" "Remember the party where Willie Lowell got so drunk and fell in the pool?" "I remember riding through your woods on a wonderful bay named Baby!" Remember . . . remember . . . remember. Their reminiscences were highly selective, shot through with tact: they failed utterly to recall Laura falling down drunk, or Francine's father, also very drunk at a party, suddenly smashing her mother in the face, or Elizabeth always hiding out in a corner somewhere away from the action. They recalled no divorces, his, their own parents, or their own. To hear them, Ronnie thought, you'd think life had been one long garden party.

"So glad you're home and better, Mary says you're improving. You'll be talking and up and about in no time, I'll bet." No apparent awareness that Stephen would, whatever else, never be up and about again. They pressed their happy memories upon him, fictional as their happy wishes for the future, convinced that this was the road to well-being. They chatted for fifteen minutes, then noticed he looked tired, they were tiring him out, they should leave but they had so wanted to see him again, to see him home and almost well. . . .

Stephen was indeed tired. So much smiling, twisting his mouth to appear to laugh, so much energy it took, being gracious. He was out of the habit. These days he acted the way he felt. Being honest becomes a habit hard to break.

The women all trooped downstairs. Ronnie came last, still not introduced, but she understood that Stephen's room had not been the place to
do that. Mary waited until they were settled with drinks in the sitting
room, where a fire burned today. "I don't think you've met my half sister
Ronalda," she began and the women looked at her for the first time. At
their looks, Ronnie was ready to dart from the room. Only a fierce desire
not to shame her sisters made her stand her ground.

"Your half sister! How do you do." Gloved hand extended. "I didn't
know you had another sister, Mary."

"Well, I do. We do. Ronnie's an environmentalist, finishing up her
Ph.D. at BU. She specializes in mosses and lichen."

"How fascinating. So nice to meet you."

"A pleasure," murmured Francine.

Bursting with questions they did not dare to ask, they made idle
conversation about Francine's latest acquisition, a David Salle painting,
about Christine's daughter's engagement to a blessedly appropriate boy
from Princeton, about Lulu's last trip to Morocco. Francine tried, once.

"Would we know any of your people, Ronnie? We sometimes stay at
the ranch of some friends of ours in the country near Acapulco — the
D'Honorios, do you know them?"

"They're of Spanish blood, I imagine. I'm Indian — Mayan, actually."
Knew instantly I was Mexican. How come? I could be lots of other things,
Ecuadorian, Puerto Rican. . . .

"A much older aristocracy," Mary put in.

Ronnie rolled her eyes at Mary. "Who says they were aristocrats?"

Alex grinned. "Ronnie keeps us honest," she said. "She punctures
any pretension."

The guests seemed, at this, to shrivel into a paralyzed silence. But
Alex blithely continued. "Doesn't matter what we talk about, she always
sees through false superiority — in life, in politics, in religion. You
know" — she turned to Ronnie — "you're really amazing."

Ronnie, embarrassed, looked away from Alex, but Elizabeth,
amused, picked up the subject. "Yes, she keeps us all on our toes. She's a
feminist, card-carrying. She certainly challenges me."

"You, Elizabeth!" cried Christine. "I always think of you as the intellectual."

"Oh, she is," Mary said fervently. "But Ronnie gives her a run for her money."

"Really."

"So that's what the four of you do all day? Argue about . . . intellectual matters?"

"No, we work," Elizabeth answered. "Ronnie on her dissertation, me on my book, Mary on her poetry, Alex . . . on her soul, I guess," she finished, smiling.

"Oh, that's nice, I like that, Elizabeth." Alex's face was radiant.

"You work."

"I didn't know you wrote poetry, Mary."

"I'm not very good. Not good enough. But I'm working on it."

"You put us to shame," Eloise said, without a shred of shame showing. "I myself do nothing. I just enjoy life. Except of course we all work to help various charities, give luncheons and balls and that sort of thing, which is some sort of contribution I suppose. But mostly," she shrugged at her own irresponsibility like a delightful child, "we have fun."

"So tell me," Francine said to Ronnie, "are you converting them to feminism?"

Ronnie shrugged, unsmiling. "I'm not trying."

"Well, she's set me thinking about things in a different way. Her view of history. . . ." Mary let it hang.

"I don't know if it's feminism . . . ," Alex began tentatively. "A lot of the things Ronnie believes in, I believe in, but I never knew they were feminist ideas."

"Such as?"

"Oh, I don't know. What's really important in life, what matters more than other things. You know, like love and community and well-being. As opposed to, well, power I guess. Worldly power. Which is such an illusion, but people take it for reality, you see. As if it were something you could hold on to forever, that would protect you."

Three pairs of eyes glazed over as Alex continued in this vein until, to the guests' relief, lunch was announced. Mary gracefully steered the conversation back to gossip and acquisitions, trips and parties, and Ronnie crept back into silence, grateful to be ignored for the rest of the lunch.

Still, when it was over and the guests had left, she wandered back to her room feeling a sense of harmony in herself, with her sisters. They had wanted to include her, wanted her to be accepted, had put her forward. She had not, herself, much helped in this effort, and did not regret that. Those women were not her kind, would never be her kind. They would not recognize her, she thought, if she ran into them on a Boston street, or if they did, would not want to linger. But neither would she. Was it necessary, for sisterhood, that all women love and fully accept all other women? If so, sisterhood was impossible. But somewhere, under the surface conversation, they had thought about the serious matters that had been mentioned, and while they were all dependent on rich men — at least to some degree — and accepted the values of that world, they also had sympathy and a kind of guilt for not being, not supporting, something else. And that was something, wasn't it? They weren't enemies. They just weren't quite friends.

She sat down at her computer feeling full of energy and worked well for the rest of the afternoon.

The sisters gathered in the playroom Tuesday night after dinner to discuss strategy. Elizabeth and Mary scrawled lists or outlines on lined yellow pads; Alex stood at the glass doors communing with the stars. Ronnie listened to their ideas, agreed, disagreed. Eventually, after a discussion in which voices were raised, they discarded their original strategy and decided that each sister would be both prosecutor and defender, that Alex would be the final judge but they would each have a voice in the judgment.

Wednesday they were tense and silent, each of them — you could almost see it, Ronnie thought — arguing with herself in her head, preparing her argument with him, the silent man. They picked at the cold dinner Mrs. Browning had left for them, but forced themselves to remain at the table for the usual amount of time. While Doris cleared the table, they went into the playroom and turned on the television set, whose blare and glare passed by them: they barely saw or heard it.

"We have to disconnect the intercom," Elizabeth said.

"Why? That makes it seem as if we're planning a crime!" Alex shuddered. "Like breaking and entering."

"You want him summoning Doris, buzzing constantly while we talk?

He will. It will buzz all over the house. She'll come running, she'll see that something's wrong."

"I'll do it," Ronnie said.

It was nine-thirty when they went up. Stephen's television set was on but his eyes were closed. Ronnie bent and pulled out the plug connecting his intercom. Mary unplugged his telephone. Elizabeth slid the remote control from under his limp left hand, blipped the television set off, and put the remote on a dresser across the room. Alex pushed back the swivel table holding the television set and placed three straight-backed chairs at the foot of the bed and another near the window, facing the bed but at some distance from it.

Stephen's eyes popped open the moment the sound stopped. His left eye widened in alarm and he reached for his remote control. When he saw it was missing, he reached for the intercom. He pressed it wildly, but no one came running up the stairs. Unmoved by the contortions on Stephen's face, his wild hitting of the intercom button, his raised fist, his bared teeth, his rage, the sisters stood and gazed at him. He looks like the villain in a silent movie, Mary thought.

All four of them stood together on one side of the bed. The alarm on Stephen's face was patent, it looked like . . .

I've never seen him afraid, Ronnie thought.

I never imagined Father afraid, Mary thought.

God, Elizabeth thought, he's terrified.

Oh poor man, so frightened, Alex thought. He must think we're going to kill him or something.

Elizabeth began. "Father, you have unfinished business with all of us. You know that, don't you?"

He glared.

"We thought of turning you in," Mary said sadly. "You know, bringing charges, telling the district attorney, or whomever it is one tells in these cases. We understand that there is no statute of limitations in these cases — or that it begins only after the victim remembers what happened."

"Not that *we* ever forgot," Elizabeth said. "But Alex did. She's just remembered."

The left side of his face twisted, the left side of his body writhed in rage, his arm rose, his fist threatened them, his mouth worked, his eye stormed. They stood close together, their shoulders almost touching.

"But it seemed — well, they would hardly indict you now, would they? You can't even speak in your own defense. And years ago, when it was happening, they wouldn't have indicted you then either, would they? They wouldn't have believed us. Such an important man you were. . . ." Elizabeth moved back and walked to one of the straight-backed chairs and sat down. She lighted a cigarette. "My mother — you do remember my mother? — she always said you were above the law. You framed her and got away with it. God knows what else you got away with. We can't have been your only victims." She blew smoke toward the door, crossed her legs, waggled her foot, the only sign of her nervousness.

Was he smiling? Could it be he was smiling?

"I've been reading your papers, you know," she continued. "Sitting down there in your office reading thirty-year-old memos packed away in cardboard cartons. You were a vicious bastard weren't you. Someday someone's going to write quite a nasty biography of you, Father. Of course, someone else will probably write an idolatrous one. The one thing you can count on is"—she turned back to face him — "it won't be one of us."

Insofar as one could read his expression, he seemed to be sneering.

Elizabeth sighed. "I know, I know what you believe: women don't understand Realpolitik. Don't know how the game has to be played to win."

"Let's not get into this, Lizzie," Mary urged. She turned to the old man. "The point is, Father, what you did to us. We have never had any recourse for your terrible crimes against us. We were children. Even if you hadn't been who you are . . . it would have been close to impossible. And we still don't really have legal recourse. But we do have power. Over you. And this gives us moral recourse. We're going to put you on trial ourselves."

One side of his mouth cracked wide, a noise emerged from his throat.

The old bastard is laughing, Ronnie thought. But his left hand was searching for the telephone. It scrabbled around the side table, searched the bedclothes.

"We're going to try you for incest, pass judgment, and enforce that judgment, Father," Mary said.

Alex's light sweet voice intervened. "At first, we thought one of us would act as prosecutor, one as defender, one as accuser, and one as judge. But we couldn't decide who could defend you or who should accuse . . . since we're all your accusers. And since none of us is really impartial enough to be the judge."

She spoke quietly, reasonably, turning her sweet face as if she were arguing a matter of principle with someone who was bound to understand.

His mouth was still cracked in that queer smile.

"So each of us is going to speak against you and for you. Doesn't that seem fair? It's the best solution we could come up with, Father. And we are all going to vote together on the judgment."

"But Alex alone will determine the penalty," Elizabeth put in coldly. "Because she is the kindest of us and because she seems to have some sense of higher things," she explained adding dryly, "At least she believes she does. And since none of the rest of us feels we have such a sense, we're willing to leave that to her."

The crack broadened. He was finding this hilarious.

"Okay," Ronnie said abruptly, "let's get on with it. Elizabeth, you're the oldest. You go first."

Elizabeth sat up erectly. Ronnie and Mary sat down on either side of her. Alex took the chair by the window. She held a pad and pen loosely in her hand.

"If at any time you wish to speak, just . . ." — Elizabeth peered at his hand — "just hold your hand up and I'll stop. Then you can write on your cellophane pad. We'll listen to anything you care to say. Or write."

Elizabeth too had a yellow pad lying on her lap, but she did not glance at it. Nor did she look at Stephen. She looked at her hands, folded loosely over the pad in her lap. She said: "In August 1942, when I was ten years old, you entered my bedroom in this house during the night and raped me. You told me that this was how fathers showed their love for their daughters and that you loved me. I will not detail the acts you performed, made me perform." She turned her head sideways, catching her breath, clearing her throat.

Ronnie stared at him incredulously. Was he smiling?

"Afterwards, you threatened that if I told anyone what you had done, you would cut my mother and me off and leave us penniless. You also said no one would believe me. You raped me again after that, many times, every summer until I was seventeen and stopped you forcibly."

She finally looked at Stephen. "Do you have anything to say? Do you deny any of what I've said?"

Ronnie gasped silently. He *was* staring at her, smiling.

Elizabeth stared back. Ronnie had never seen that expression on her face: numb, helpless, appealing, like a young girl. He did not drop his eye. She dropped hers. This time, she glanced at her pad.

"It wasn't difficult to frame your defense. Because I feel certain — and seeing your expression now, more certain than ever — that you and generations of men before you felt that incest was their prerogative, their right — that fathers own the bodies of their daughters as they do those of their wives and slaves. And that they believe they have the right to own other human beings, to control them, that indeed, they define manhood as the ability to control others. Knowing your heart as I believe I do, I believe this is what you too think. And so I spent all day yesterday and today reading in history and myth and philosophy, trying to frame these charges in a way you would understand and accept."

The lips narrowed; the eye narrowed.

"And I think that to do that, I must discuss the nature of fatherhood itself. But I believe to define fatherhood, we must first define motherhood. Now, traditionally motherhood means carrying a child within one's body to term and giving birth to it. Some mothers feed the baby from their bodies, some take responsibility for its daily care until it is adult. But that responsibility is made impossible by societies in which economic forms are such that mothers cannot carry their children with them while they find or grow the food to feed them, as they do in gathering-hunting and horticultural societies. So motherhood is not a given natural role, but a role partly given by nature, and partly defined by the economics of society."

Elizabeth whispered to Ronnie, who poured a glass of water for her from the pitcher Alex had placed on a side table. Alex glanced at Stephen, offering him one: he merely glared at her. The room was charged with silence as Elizabeth sipped her water. Alex watched solemnly. Ronnie and Mary stared straight ahead. Stephen tried to stare at the wall to his right. Elizabeth cleared her throat and continued.

"And men determine the economics of society. Fathers traditionally have avoided the hands-on responsibility for babies. Mothers have traditionally taken it, but especially after the child is weaned, they bear no special obligation to do so: since both parents are genetically represented equally in the child, both have an equal investment in fostering the child's survival.

"Moreover, it is clear that different acts are required to foster the child in different economies. While in gathering-hunting societies one parent alone can maintain a child — especially if she or he lives in a village society — this is more difficult in horticultural societies unless the maintaining parent, which is usually the mother, owns the right to use of land. In an industrial economy such as ours, two or more parents are necessary to maintain a child. Does that seem clear?" she asked Stephen sharply.

He ignored her. She stood up. She walked around to his right side. She peered at him, moving her face close to his.

"DOES THAT SEEM CLEAR?" she shouted at him. "DOES IT?"

He, startled, nodded.

The sisters too, startled by this interchange, moved slightly in their chairs. Elizabeth returned to her chair.

"What remains to be discussed," she said, turning over a page of her pad, slipping her half-glasses on, examining the page, then removing the glasses and looking up at Stephen again, "is the question of ownership. You" — she pointed a finger at Stephen, who was looking toward the wall — "you, Stephen Upton" — he turned slightly to face her — "have always called yourself a libertarian, a believer in constitutional liberty, in individualism, in the rights of man. Is that correct?" His face, looking at her, was expressionless.

She bent over and picked up a thick notebook. She opened it; it was filled with plastic pages containing newspaper clippings. "I have here one of your scrapbooks, lovingly maintained by your various secretaries over the years, containing clippings of speeches you have given, quotations offered to the press, and reports about your influence on national policy.

Do you wish me to read aloud from these, or can we take it as given that your philosophy has always been one of libertarian individualism?"

He glared.

"Do you want me to read them aloud?"

Oh that cold nasty voice.

His left hand waved her away.

"Very well, then." She put the book back on the floor. "In such a philosophy, the notion that any human can own another human is repugnant. The way such philosophers phrase this belief is that each man has the right to own himself. In many places in legal literature, we are informed that Man is generic and includes also Woman. These writings, however, have neglected children, and it is unclear whether children are believed to own themselves. It appears that, contrary to libertarian thinking, you believe that children do not in fact own themselves, that their fathers own them. Such ownership amounts to the Roman concept of *patria potestas*, which granted the father of the family the right of ownership over wives and children, including the right to punish, sell, or make other use of their bodies, even killing them."

She sipped her water. Stephen looked around at them now, his one alive eye a fiery assault.

Amazing how much expression he can show, Ronnie thought. Contempt, outrage, ridicule, scorn, hatred, belittlement, incredulity — all of that with a single eye and a twisted half-mouth.

"In Roman law, male children were at some age freed from paternal control, but daughters never were until they married, at which point — with certain exceptions — they passed into the control of their husbands. I therefore argue that Stephen Upton had a perfect right to rape his daughter Elizabeth by Roman law which makes her his property and without legal existence of her own. However, the right of *patria potestas* conflicts with libertarian philosophy, and Roman law does not hold in the United States, the country where Stephen Upton resides, and where he built his career as a great defender of libertarianism. Therefore, I charge that according to American law, he must be found guilty of either incest or a hypocrisy so extreme as to negate his entire career. And the penalty I ask for is a signed confession to one or the other of these crimes. I have indeed prepared two confessions" — she pulled some typed pages out from under the yellow pad — "for your signature. If you can make only an X, that will do."

Stephen's head started, his left eye seemed to jump out of his head.

She laid the pages before him and held out a pen. "Will you sign them?"

Stephen swept the pages off his tray with his good hand, looked up at Elizabeth with the defiant frown of a ten-year-old child.

She bent and picked up the pages. She glanced at Alex, who nodded. "I'm finished," Elizabeth said to no one in particular.

"Shall I go?" Mary asked them. Ronnie nodded. Elizabeth returned to her chair and sat utterly immobile, staring down at her lap.

Mary too had a pad, but as she sat up preparing to speak, it slipped from her lap to the floor. She didn't seem to notice. She was wearing something heavy and white, almost like a monk's robe, with a long gold pendant lying beneath the folds of its cowl. She did not look at Stephen at all, but at a crucifix that had long hung on the side wall of the room, a simple gold cross that had belonged to his great-grandmother.

"Yes," she murmured. "All right." She looked at Stephen. "In 1944, when I was eight years old, shortly after my mother died, you came into my bedroom in Georgetown and got in my bed and put your arms around me and told me you loved me and that fathers and daughters who loved each other showed that love this way, and you raped me. You did not at that time use your penis. You told me that if I told anyone it would kill you and I would have no parents at all, I'd be an orphan. You continued to rape me in Georgetown and here in Lincoln, until you married Amelia two years later. I had to look that date up because the horror of what you did to me in bed filled me with terror every time I was in the same house with you, forever afterward. It still does. After Amelia became pregnant, you began again. When I was twelve, you had full intercourse with me, saying you were making a woman of me. Afterwards, you showed me a gun with which you said you would kill yourself if I ever told anyone. You did not stop raping me until I was eighteen and engaged to be married. In 1954."

She turned her head to look at him and her eyes misted. "The problem was I really loved you. Father."

He regarded her warily.

"My accusation, therefore, is that not only did you rape me, which I think is a crime by human law, but you destroyed utterly my ability to discriminate love from power, sex from submission. You ruined my emotional life. Forever." She turned to the crucifix again.

"Elizabeth accused *and* defended you on more or less legalistic grounds. At least, that's what I assume they are, not knowing anything about law — as you well know. Not knowing much about anything, I presume you would say."

She pulled an immaculate hankie from the pocket of her dress and wiped her cheeks under her eyes, careful not to smudge her makeup.

"But I was carefully raised within the bosom of the Episcopal church by my nannies, who felt that religious indoctrination was part of their job. And although I later left the church — religion itself, really — the message was not lost on me as the various priests discussed God the Father, that the Father was god. And indeed, if all fathers are gods to their families, my father was preeminently a deity — Stephen Upton, confidant of presidents, a valued presence among the powers that rule this country, one of the small handful included in books written about 'the Establishment.' Stephen Upton is a god not just to his family but a god among men, who, I believe, sees himself as having divine powers. And we all know that those who make the law consider themselves above the law. He is almost interchangeable with God the Father, to whose will the priests tell us we must submit. I heard this message and always obeyed it. I always deferred to men, especially my father — that is, my God."

She turned away from the crucifix and looked down in her lap, fingering the huge gold pendant she wore. "As I grew older and more thoughtful — I know you think that's ridiculous, Father, but in fact I am a relatively intelligent person, I have even read a few books of philosophy in my time — I discarded the idea of a benevolent god ruling the earth. But not the idea of god the father. And what made father-god so powerful was not goodness but money. Money that can buy things like guns and tanks and planes and soldiers and property and houses and land and oil wells and companies that force other people into obedience one way or another. I never lost my faith in that deity — but for me faith is a belief in his power, a belief that he must be placated or he would punish you — until . . . well, you wouldn't be interested, but once in my life I deserted that god and adopted another, one you'd mock I'm sure, the god of love who gave me an experience more ecstatic than I'm sure any Saint Teresa or whoever Episcopalians venerate ever had . . . well. . . ."

She wiped beneath her eyes again. She looked up, directly at him this time.

"And I *was* punished. Still I wouldn't give it up for anything . . . not even for eternity in heaven if I or you or any of us believed in such a thing. Anyway, you're not interested in that. My defense of you is that you really are a god and that godly power is real even if it is based only in money. Now how the fathers got all the money, that's another question and I can't answer that, I have to leave that to Ronnie, I'm sure she knows. All that matters to me is that they have it and they are not about to give it up.

"So!" She faced him bravely. "My defense of you is based on religious grounds — that this hearing is invalid because no mere human can bring God to judgment. And since the Father is a surrogate for God, his deputy on earth, no child can bring the Father to judgment — especially female children, who are illegitimate and subhuman. Women have no rights at all in the Father's eyes, daughters no more than wives, free women no more than slaves."

Her voice softened, became less formal. "But the way we've arranged this trial, we are each prosecuting, defending, and judging you, Father. So while I accuse you of incest, I defend you on grounds of your godliness. But when I was writing up my notes for this, I noticed I had defined godliness as power. And that, you see, affects my judgment. This father before me, who retains the power of money, and has recently threatened to use it against us, in fact retains few other powers. Indeed, his money right now cannot help him; although he still has his money, he is close to impotent. That means Father no longer equals power; Father is no longer god. At this moment, we, the women without rights, have the physical power to subdue and even kill you if we so choose. At this moment, we, having the power, are the gods and can act with impunity, just as you did when you were a god. At this moment, *we* are above the law. The penalty I recommend is that we should rape you as you raped us — with an instrument, of course, not our bodies — in keeping with the ancient law of an eye for an eye."

Stephen's good eye popped, his mouth grizzled, saliva poured from the right side of it, his left hand clawed up. He stretched it out as if he would could destroy her face with it. But she merely watched him, Mary for once in her life not terrified, Elizabeth thought, watching her almost serene glance around the room, saw her notice the yellow pad on the floor, bend and retrieve it, sit up again, glance at Stephen, then turn calmly to Alex.

"Are you going to speak, Alex?"

Alex licked her lips. "Can I go last?"

The sisters turned to Ronnie. "Okay with you, Ron?"

She shrugged, nodded. She examined the bedclothes at the foot of Stephen's bed. She turned to Elizabeth. "I don't have much to say. I'm not sure I can defend him."

Elizabeth nodded.

Stephen only once or twice turned his eye on her with an extreme wariness, then immediately turned away as if he were unwilling to acknowledge even her presence in the room.

Ronnie looked at him calmly, sadly, as a school director might look at a poor student she was considering expelling from her school.

"I guess what she said — Mary — is right, reflects the way you feel. Felt. Probably would still feel if you were younger, had the power. You had all the rights. So I guess you felt you had the right to screw my mother — she was your servant, I guess to you that meant your property. Anyway, she loved you, I know that. I think you loved her too but I'd be willing to bet you never told her so. But that she knew it. My mother is another matter. Forgiving her is hard.

"Forgiving you is impossible. You took me like a piece of meat, like a slave, an animal. Do you remember it? The day I was swimming in *your* pool?" She leaned toward him, her face fierce.

He drew back, drew in breath — was that a gasp? He glared at her.

"You raped me. You treated me like a thing over which you had complete power, a thing with no feelings of her own, no pride, no dignity, no rights. This left me with a sense of helplessness and inferiority — a sense that I have no existence, don't matter — that I will have to battle as long as I live.

"You are my biological father" — she stopped, her voice thick, then started again — "but you have denied that fatherhood and denied my daughterhood. This will leave me seeking an identity for as long as I live.

"Even though I never harmed you — after all, I have no responsibility for my own existence, my own birth — and never wished you ill,
you have condemned me to eternal shadowhood and pain." She raised her
eyes. Stephen's left eye was looking at her. "I want retribution," she said.

She turned to Elizabeth. "I can't defend him. You'll have to do it."

Elizabeth nodded, gazed at Stephen.

"It is clear that of all the daughters, Ronalda Velez is the most power-
less. She is not just female, but a bastard, not just a bastard but of color,
not of the dominant race, without funds or friends in high places, that is,
with no social standing in this court. Her temerity in bringing these
charges is incredible, and her arrogance requires punishment as an exam-
ple to any others of the inferior classes who might dare to challenge the
superior classes. Challenging the superior class is treason in every state.
The judge should — as many judges in such situations have done — not
only dismiss all her charges but should charge Ronalda Velez with high
treason." She turned to Ronnie, her eyebrows a question.

Ronnie grinned at her with delight.

Stephen gazed at the two of them with a puzzled exhaustion.

Mary intervened. "But there's more to say. Although Ronalda Velez is
your child, you not only never acknowledged her, but you never helped
her financially or emotionally, did not even pay for her education." She
looked meaningfully at Stephen. "The fact that she has completed all the
course requirements for a Ph.D. in environmental science and is presently
working on her dissertation is due entirely to her own efforts. She has not
yet completed that dissertation only because she returned to Lincoln to
nurse her mother through her illness at the demand of Stephen Upton."

Stephen stared at Ronnie.

Ronnie dropped her eyes to her lap. Thanks, Mary. She carefully
avoided looking up at Stephen but the other three sisters stared fixedly at
him. He dropped his eyes.

"Therefore, I have prepared a legal document for you to sign. In
quintuplicate, so each of us has a copy." Elizabeth held out several typed
pages. "It acknowledges your parentage of Ronalda Velez, and entitles her
to a full share in your estate." She stood and placed the pages on his tray
table.

He glared at her with hate. He spit on the pages.

Elizabeth left them where they were. She sat down. She turned to Alex. "Ready?"

"Oh, I guess so," Alex said faintly. She pulled a small, thin gold Star of David from under her blouse and fingered it. She seemed to be in intense comunication with something invisible, something interior. They waited in silence. Finally she looked up at Stephen.

"I forgot everything, you see. It was a gap in my mind. I lost the past. I felt the loss, it was like being without some internal organ that you can live without but not fully — you know something's missing. But coming back here triggered things — I went up to the old nursery. . . ."

Stephen's eye widened.

Tears filled Alex's eyes. "I was only a baby, Father. What was I, two, three years old? Still sleeping in a crib! How could you?"

His mouth widened. He was smiling! He pulled his pad to him and scrawled U LIKD IT.

"I suppose she asked for it," Ronnie said grimly.

Alex studied him. "Father," she began tentatively, "did you — do you — really believe that what you did to us was all right?"

He flung his face away from her.

Alex turned inward again, fingering her star. "The thing is," she murmured, "all of us loved you. Even Ronnie, even though she tries to deny it. Loved you. Love you." Her voice trailed away faintly.

He turned to her grimacing, nearly smiling. He picked up the pad again. CHANGNG WILL. U CANT CHANGE THAT.

Alex snatched the pad away from him, pulled up the plastic, screamed, "FUCK THAT! WHO CARES! Do you acknowledge Ronalda Velez as your daughter? WRITE!" she shrieked, thrusting the spat-upon pages into his left hand.

He hurled them away from him, scrawled on the cellophane. Ronnie stood up, picked it up: BASTD, he'd written.

"Stephen Upton," Alex's voice said wavering, "do you admit you raped your daughters, causing them immeasurable harm and pain for the rest of their natural lives?"

It looked as if he were laughing at her.

"WRITE!" she screamed again.

"FUCK U ALL," he wrote, quite distinctly.

"Oh, Father," Mary sighed palely.

Finally, Alex asked, "Does that mean you're pleading guilty? Admitting you did fuck us all?"

He glared at her, turned his face away from them, stared straight ahead with an expression of great dignity, even nobility. He would not participate. He refused to legitimate these proceedings in any way. He would not plead at all. They had no rights over him. No right. At all.

They watched his face, his body, his left hand. They understood.

Alex stood gazing down on him, her face as still and tragic as a religious painting of a martyr. Thinking: all he has to do is spread out an arm and reach it toward us and all of us — well, Mary and I certainly, maybe Elizabeth too — would enter it, hold him, forgive, sob, pat his face. Well, maybe they wouldn't, but I would. . . . He's my daddy. Yet when a single gesture could win our forgiveness, harmonize us with him whatever his crimes whatever his horrors whatever his scorched and calloused soul spirit psyche might be, Father, our Father, however he was we are doomed to love him forever law of nature, when that's all he has to do, he tells us to fuck off.

Elizabeth stared at the picture that hung over his bed, a nude woman in the style of "September Morn." It had hung there as long as Stephen had occupied the room.

Alex turned away, walked to the window, pulled open the drape and the curtain, gazed out at the moon, brilliant now, low in the sky above the treetops. She leaned her forehead against the windowpane, cold and damp. She was still fingering her star. Did he realize he'd made some terrible mistake? Did he know what he'd given up? Did he care? The sisters watched her; even Stephen glanced at her briefly, uneasily, then swiveled to stare stoically ahead at the dead television set.

Finally, she spoke. "I'm going to give my judgment." She raised her head but did not turn around. "I once saw a movie about a trial and I think that in such cases, the judge is supposed to put a hood over his head. I don't have a hood, so I'll just keep turned away from you.

"I have observed and believe it to be a law of nature that the oppressor hates those he oppresses far more than they hate him. We hate those who harm us, but it is with a lesser fire, because one who is harmed is hurt from the outside but not from his own insides. He does not harm himself. She does not harm herself. Whereas, a person who harms another harms also himself, desperately, wounds his deepest being. So the great haters are those who do the harm, and the people they hate most are the very people they harm.

"So you, Father, hate us with a passion far exceeding any hate we have for you. As you have just shown. But you imagine we hate you equally. That is your worst sin."

She paused.

"Your crimes are of the most serious sort — crimes against your own blood, those you must have loved in some way in some place in your tortured spirit, those you were entrusted to protect and nurture. Such a crime deserves the ultimate penalty — death."

Even Ronnie gasped. The three sisters stared at Alex with absolute intensity. Stephen's left eye glared, flared, seemed to float around in his head. His left hand twitched. He turned his head wildly, looking at them suddenly in terror. Of course they could. They could!

"And death is the verdict of this court," Alex went on.

Stephen pulled himself up, he opened his mouth, a faint sound emerged. . . . Oooooo.

Mary's hand darted to her mouth. "Father . . . !" she cried faintly.

Alex turned to him briefly. "Are you thinking we're going to put a pillow over your face, smother you, kill you before you can change your will?" She laughed grimly and turned away again. "Whatever you think and I know you won't believe this, none of us really came back here for your money. We came for something you scorn, something you will not in any case give — your love, which would enable us to forgive you.

"This court condemns you to die of lack of love. Your inability to give it or feel it. We are going to leave you. And you will die of your own hatred, day by day, alone in this house, your house, your property, the property you begrudge your blood. Keep it, and live with your aloneness, for you have denied us and we now deny you. Tomorrow, we will pack our things and leave this house — and you — forever. We will not return. We will take no responsibility for your caretaking, for the honesty, decency, or kindness of those who tend you. We do not care if they abuse you, rob you, or treat you cruelly. We will not do to you as you did to us: we will not rape your body or your mind or — what is most important to you —

your purse. But we will refuse to acknowledge your humanity as you have refused to acknowledge ours. We will deny your feelings as you have denied ours."

Alex was still talking but Stephen's head was thrown back, his mouth was wide open, he was gasping, his hand clutched at his chest. His eye was rolling in his head, he was falling back, his face had turned blue, his mouth was open, his arm fell. Large, twisted, and bluish, his hand lay still on the sheet. His eyes stared at them.

Alex stopped speaking and turned around. The sisters stared at her in silence, and she walked toward him, put her hand on his wrist, took his pulse, looked up at them, her mouth agape. They looked at her, then all four of them stood around the bed gazing down at his wrenched blue face, his pop eyes staring at them.

He'll have to have a closed casket, Mary thought.

Part III

The Legacy

19

Like criminals, they scurried to replace the telephone, remove the chairs, move back the television set, set the remote control on his tray table, reconnect the buzzer. "It's as if we were cleaning up after a crime," Alex said worriedly. "Well, we are, aren't we," Ronnie said, while Elizabeth called Dr. Stamp's answering service from Stephen's telephone.

She put down the phone and surveyed the room. "Everything in place? Fine. Okay, it's" — she consulted her watch — "eleven-fifteen. Father usually went to sleep around eleven-thirty, after the evening news, so a little before that we came upstairs and looked in on him to say good night and found him like this. Or should it just be one of us? Is one better?" She glanced at their faces. Alex and Mary nodded yes. She considered. "Yes, one is better," she agreed. "She'd try to wake him, she'd call out his name, pat him, touch him, get upset. It would be a few minutes before she called the others, before any action was taken. Okay, which one?"

She examined each of their faces. "Is anybody here going to crack? You can if you have to, but we have to have a story to cover it." Alex looked extremely pale, Mary's face was blotched with tears, Ronnie looked stiff and gray. "How do I look?" she wondered, and ran to Stephen's low chest of drawers and examined herself. Aged and gray, she thought. That's okay. "Which one came up?" She looked from one to the other.

"Not me," Ronnie muttered.

"No."

"Me," Mary said. "I'm considered such a flibbertigibbet anyway. I wouldn't know what to do. I'd flutter around him, call his name, pat his hand, try to bring him to. Only after a while would I think to call the rest of you. Then I'd get hysterical. Which I am." She burst into tears.

"Yes, okay. The rest of us were watching the eleven o'clock news. Did we leave the set on?"

"I'll check," Alex said, running downstairs.

"He would have tried to hit the intercom," Ronnie said.

"Yes. He'd flail out at it, maybe knock it to the floor." ELizabeth walked to the bed, used the sheet to shield her fingers as she picked up the intercom by the wires and dangled it gently down. It fell facedown on the rug beside the bed.

When the phone rang, they all jumped. Elizabeth grabbed it.

"Yes, Dr. Stamp!" She sounded panicked. "I'm not sure. We're not . . . we think he's dead. Alex couldn't get his pulse. We just found him. . . ."

Alex returned breathless. "The set was on. I didn't realize we'd left it on," she whispered to Mary as Elizabeth spoke to the doctor.

She hung up. "He's sending an ambulance." She gazed at Stephen again. "Is there any possibility he's not dead?" she asked Alex.

Alex picked up his wrist again and felt for a pulse; she laid her head against his chest and listened. She shrugged. "I don't think so." She slumped into the armchair and put her head in her hands. "I killed him. I really did kill him. I condemned him to death and he died."

The others sat down too in chairs spread around the room, and gazed at the inert figure of their father.

"If you killed him, we all killed him."

"Oh, what the fuck difference does it make?" Ronnie asked wearily. "He's still alive inside us. Still gnawing away at us from inside."

"Don't you feel you got retribution?" Mary asked, surprised. "I'd think you'd feel . . . I don't know . . . avenged."

"Ronnie didn't want retribution, Mary," Alex said.

"Well, she said she did."

Wanted to be embraced, Alex thought. All of us. All he had to do.

"We should call Aldo. We'll want to go to the hospital with him. And somebody should be downstairs to open the door to the ambulance people," Elizabeth said, rising.

They all rose. As they walked downstairs, they saw the lights of an ambulance flickering in the sky out beyond the trees.

By one-thirty, Dr. Stamp had shaken their hands and left the hospital, mumbling that it was really a blessing, no way to live, a great man like that. Stephen's dead body had been sent for the requisite autopsy. The sisters were completely silent in the limousine driving back to the house. It was nearly two by the time they got home again, and they muttered good-nights and went off to bed immediately, without speaking. It dawned on Elizabeth that Doris would be horribly shocked when she went into Stephen's room to tend him the next morning, so she scribbled a note, took the back stairs up to the third floor and slipped it under Doris's door. Then she threw off her clothes and fell into bed without even washing her face.

Wet anyway, it was, why, why should I cry for him, am I crying for me? I killed tonight. We hounded him to death, we killed him as surely as if we had used that pillow. I killed my father. A person should have some feelings about that. Why don't I? Do I? Grim horse-faced man glaring at me. Gone now. Forever gone. Never again see. Died justly. It was justice. Not mercy, I don't deal in mercy, neither did he. No point in bombing the railroad lines to the camps he said. Waste of ammo, energy, danger to our gallant airmen. Who cares about a few Jews? Who cares about a few daughters? Not him.

We gave him a just trial, not according to the law of course but it was just. We each defended him. By his own lights, his standards. If he defended himself, wasn't that what he would have said? His rights, his prerogatives, his power. And we granted him all of those; we convicted him simply to die of his own values. And he did. Isn't that justice?

Used to hate him, then afterwards when I knew I was safe from him forever, I admired him, so famous, so much power he had, so much *respect* — the people who deferred to him, high-ranking government people when he wasn't even in it anymore! Influence. Esteem. Wanted it for myself. Joke.

The most a woman can ever be in government, Elizabeth, is Eleanor Roosevelt! He burst out laughing, he found her a joke, made fun of the way she talked, her teeth. "My Day," he would say in this simpering voice. Laughed and laughed, my eyes were burning, I asked to be excused from the dinner table, he wouldn't let me go, sat there braying at me. I didn't want to be Eleanor Roosevelt, I didn't want to be a joke. . . .

I wanted to be him.

Maybe I was lucky to be born a woman. If I'd been male, maybe I would have become him.

She shuddered, turned to her side, turned to the other side, sat up, lighted a cigarette.

You hate those you harm, Alex said, more than they hate you, but I don't hate him tonight, for the first time in years I don't hate him.

No hate. Just . . .

A great emptiness had settled inside her, a yawning space like a black sigh, a uterus opened wide to contain life that would never contain life, that would never be filled, never hold anything but space, that would always be open wide, waiting. . . .

She hadn't drawn her drapes and she gazed out at the night sky, dark, the moon already sunk below the trees, no stars.

He will never . . .

Never what? What had I hoped for?

A child's dream, no, a baby's, even by the time I was four or five I knew better, knew he never would. A baby's dream, a baby's demand, pick me up, hold me, keep me warm, keep me safe. . . .

Not just that. He will never acknowledge that I loved him, never allow my love for him to have any meaning.

Her face was soaking now, and she wiped it dry with her sheet, which fell back damp on her naked chest.

Amazing. I managed to find the perfect lover for me: he never touched me beyond a chaste kiss on the forehead, cold it always was, wonder what kind of lover he was with men, so cold his body always, his hands, his lips, did they warm up when he was with them, what did he look like when he felt passion, such cold eyes, only heated up when we argued, ideas made him passionate, conversations, years of conversations, our only form of intercourse. . . .

He was probably the most I could have. That's why I gave in to his blackmail, his coercion. Wonder if somehow he knew how I was, knew what I didn't. . . .

What kind of marriage could I have had, how long before the man I married turned into Father, hot damp hands on my body, me weeping, or later on, just numb, silent, Father's body always so hot, so wet, rubbing against mine, the tortured cry when he came, how I hated it, the hot pulsing liquid I could feel it even though he at least used a condom, impregnating his daughter *would* violate his code.

The opposite of Clare, hot hands, hot eyes, although they could be cold too, as cold as Clare's. Mine too, some people say I have cold eyes. Wide mouth, big teeth Father had: Clare's face was delicate, fine-featured, fine blond hair. . . .

But suppose I'd married . . . whomever. Can't picture myself a mother, couldn't be a mother, don't know how, don't want to be one, I would hate any child of mine. . . . Lucky I never did it, lucky for them, the blessed unborn. . . . Can't picture myself a wife either, why should I be one, what is a wife but an unpaid servant and whore, a breeder of sons to inherit men's property? I was wise, I made the right choices. I made the best choices available to me.

Available.

It isn't that I haven't had a life. News photos of those Ethiopian Jews escaping into Israel, women under twenty wizened and sick, carrying babies that are just a collection of bones, holding them, clutching them, people in Bhopal in the news today, what about their lives, millions and millions of people across the world starving to death, poisoned, tortured, imprisoned, and even they would say: I had a life.

Life's a bitch and then you die. Someone put that on a T-shirt.

If you consider the lives millions of people have, I've been lucky I guess, despite Father. Suppose I'd had a father like my mother's, Grampa Callahan? Would things have been any better for me? Would have been nice to have a mother who knew how to love me, though, that would have made a difference. Have to call her this afternoon, she'll crow, the old bitch, revenge at last, I outlived the bastard, get that bequest.

Her face was wet again, and she turned on her side and rubbed her cheek on the pillowcase. She closed her eyes.

Try to think of one kind thing they did, either of them, either one. Once.

She searched her memory.

He put me on a horse once. Helped me up, told me how to sit, hold the reins. Archangel, the horse was called. Told McCutcheon — that was his name! — to hold the reins, walk me in a circle. Watched. Said "Good, Elizabeth." Smiled. I thought he smiled because the trainer was there, but maybe not. Maybe not.

Bought me a book once. Came back from a trip, handed me this book in a paper bag, said he'd thought I might like it. I was nine. *Arabian Nights*. Funny. Was he already planning . . .

Don't count that one.

She gave up her bridge club to save money to send me to Catholic school, knowing that would force him to pay for private school. And she loved her bridge club. Never rejoined, though. Gambling with those rich women too expensive for her, really, even if she is a super player. She wanted me educated well. Sacrificed for it. Sent me a little allowance the whole time I was in England. Probably ate canned soup to do it.

I remember her holding me, once, when I was little. Once? Must have held me when I was a baby, mustn't she? With love?

There were good things. I just don't tend to hold on to them, I clutch the others, harbor hate.

I condemn you to die of your own hatred. . . .

I had Clare. All in all, Clare was a good thing.

I had my career. Have my career.

Them. I have them now, don't I.

My sisters.

She slept.

Mary went through her entire evening regimen despite the late hour, weeping through her shower, weeping as she creamed her face so that the tears cut through the cream, making her laugh and finally give up. She went straight to her chaise and opened her small cloisonné box of marijuana (should have known Christine would have a supplier, she always had the best junk at Peabrain's) and rolled a joint. She leaned back, inhaled deeply, stared out at darkness against darkness.

A sob burst out of her. She let herself retch sobs for a few moments, then stopped, blew her nose, wiped her face. She got up, dropped the wet handkerchief on the dresser top, and found a clean one in a drawer. She stuck it in her pocket and returned to her chaise. She took another toke, but the sobs returned and she bent her head over in her hands, laying the cigarette in an ashtray.

Oh Daddy.

He'd come into her bed when she was little and alone and frightened because Mommy was gone and he'd snuggled with her and held her and then he did those other things she didn't like but still he would lie there with her, holding her, he was so warm, his body was always hot, hot and wet, and when she was shivering he kept her warm, keeping my little Mary warm, he said, and she'd hold on to him and she would feel safe well kind of safe because she never knew when he'd start the other and sometimes he did it but stayed anyway until she fell asleep. . . .

Later, of course, it was different. When she was grown. Making a woman of you he said. Fussing over her breasts, they were big even then, her ass, he loved her ass he said, so round and shapely. I was numb. Just lay there like a rag doll, same with Harry and Paul, Alberto excited me a bit at first but really all he liked to do was turn me over and ram into me from behind. Just a rag doll, my whole life, porcelain head, rag body. Except with Don.

What Daddy taught me.

Even so, I loved him so much, loved him, loved him. . . . Can't stop loving him.

We killed him tonight, I suppose. Not that he would have lived much longer anyway. In a way, it was a service to him, he probably would have preferred to die than live that way but he never said anything, never even hinted, get me pills. . . . I wonder if he still has that gun he showed me, I wonder where it is. I wouldn't have helped him die. Would have said the hell with you, I'm not going to prison for you you bastard you ruined my life you ruined me for life, I wouldn't do you the favor. . . .

Yet I did it after all. Funny.

The sobs erupted again, deep retching spasms that seemed to come from her stomach, that bent her double in pain, drenched her face. She tried to control them, and they gradually subsided. She used her handkerchief, soaked it, got up, dropped it on the dresser top and reached for a fresh one. Then she gazed at the wet, wrinkled handkerchiefs.

Really miserable for Teresa to have to pick up a hankie full of my snot isn't it.

She collected several wet handkerchiefs from where she had dropped them, carried them into the bathroom, filled the sink basin with hot water and dropped them in. At least that way they won't be snotty.

She returned to the chaise and reached for her joint but it was smoked down, not even a roach left. She rolled a fresh one, leaned back, tried to feel luxurious, pampered, cared for, but she couldn't, she was uncomfortable, the chaise back was not really very comfortable however graceful and lovely it appeared and the cushions wouldn't stay in place. She sat up straight, peered out.

That daddy's been dead for decades. Now Father's dead. He was old, he had a long full life, he had everything he ever wanted, it's okay. Why do I crave, what do I . . . the sobs reached her throat again, but she forced them down.

If he doesn't leave me enough money, I'll just sell the apartment and move in with Lizzie, with what I have left over after the debts are paid I could live a long time if I kept my bills down, I can practice the piano, Lizzie likes it anyway she works all day, and I can write poetry, there are people there to do things with, lunches, museums, it's perfectly acceptable two sisters our age living together, it makes perfect sense, Alex can even come to visit us, she lives near there, we can have get-togethers, we can find some exquisite jewel of a house in Falls Church like the one Alice Willie lived in years ago, huge garden, huge trees, a little Japanese bridge over a brook. . . .

I don't have to have another husband.

The thought shocked her into utter stillness. She held the joint stiffly for so long it went out.

I don't have to do that again. Ever. I don't ever have to act as if I think a man is wonderful when I don't, don't have to pretend to be stupid, don't ever have to lie there in the bed. . . . Unless I meet someone like Don, someone I feel that way about, someone *I* feel that way about oh if only I would. . . .

She stared at the black window.

The image of her daughter's face appeared in the darkness.

My god how I've abandoned her. Like my own mother, with less excuse, I'm still alive if you can call it that. . . .

Lizzie would never want a kid living with us. And Marie-Laure's such a slob, expects the maid to pick up her underclothes even. Never washed a dish in her life, doesn't even help Marguerite when we're at Marty's house at holidays, just goes inside and turns on television or picks up a magazine, doesn't even read books, of course it's true Marguerite has plenty of help in the kitchen but still.

Well, neither did you until a month ago.

Marie-Laure's pale sulky face looked now in her mother's imagination like a face of pain, a face of longing, a silent cry. . . .

Mary got up and went to the bedside table where the telephone lay and dialed her daughter's number. After a long time, a sleepy voice answered.

"Marie-Laure. Dear? Yes, it's Mama. Mom. Your mother. I know, I'm sorry, I know you must have been sound asleep, but I needed to call you, I needed to talk to you. No, of course I haven't gotten married again, what put such an idea in your head? You know I'm at Grandpa's. I wanted to tell you" — Mary's voice broke — "he died tonight." She sobbed, covering the mouthpiece of the telephone.

The young sleepy voice on the other end was silent. After a time, she said, "I'm sorry, Mom."

"Thank you, dear," Mary said feelingly. "I haven't called the boys yet, I'll do that tomorrow. I just wanted to hear your sweet voice."

The silence on the line was shocked. "Will you be all right?" the young voice finally asked falteringly.

"Oh yes, of course, my sisters are here. I want you to meet them all, you should have come here for Thanksgiving, it was just . . . well, you know, he was still in the hospital . . . you've never met Alex or Ronnie. Ronnie's near your age."

"Ronnie? Who's she?"

"Oh. Well, she's another sister."

"I didn't know you had another sister."

"Neither did I," Mary lied.

"REALLY!" The voice grew excited now.

"I'll tell you all about it some other time. Go back to sleep now. I just wanted you to know."

"Did Grandpa leave you lots of money?"

"I don't know. It doesn't matter."

"IT DOESN'T MATTER???? Haven't you been . . ."

"Yes. Yes. But everything's different now. I'm different now."

"Umm," the voice agreed.

"I'm going to come to see you. Soon."

The voice was not overwhelmed with joy. "You are?"

"I am," Mary said firmly.

"Well. Okay. I'm sorry about Grandpa."

"Thanks, dear."

Silence.

"All right. I'm going to be able to sleep now, darling. Will you be able to go back to sleep?"

"Sure."

"Sleep well, baby."

Mary put down the phone, slid into bed, and slept. Like a baby.

Alex was still wearing the dress she had worn earlier in the evening, a heavy jersey she had bought because she had felt it appropriate to the role of a judge. Now she saw it as the dress in which she had killed her father. She was pacing in her bedroom, arms akimbo, head bowed, trying to reach a place where her heart could rest. Talking to it, the spirit, the Shechinah dwelling within her, angry, tearful.

Avenging angel is that what you wanted of me put me here for was that it? What kind of job is that to give a person, without giving her a choice, it is not ever what I wanted to be, wouldn't have been it if I'd known. . . .

She was not speaking aloud but occasionally sounds emerged from her mouth, angry mutterings, gasps, a sob, a hiss. After half an hour, she suddenly stopped, almost ripped the dress off her body, threw it on the floor, threw all her clothes on the floor as she stripped and headed for the shower. She turned the water on as hot as she could bear, stood there soaping herself over and over for as long as she could stand it. Then she rubbed her body with a rough towel hard. She was red from face to toes when she stopped, exhausted, looked at her watch.

Shit I took a shower with my watch on. It read four-fifteen.

It's not waterproof but it's still working. Is that a sign?

Wearily, she walked back to her room, picking up clothes as she went, tossing them onto a chair. She pulled down the spread and climbed into bed naked, something she had never done before.

It had to be me because I was only a baby when he. . . . So he poisoned my entire life, everything touched by that forgotten event. So they reserved me, always they intended me to be an instrument, half alive, without memory, an instrument to be switched on and used when the moment came. Why I always felt I hadn't lived. I don't feel that now.

Is being alive having this terrible guilt? I killed my father. I will never be, can never be, clean of this crime.

Is this what you are, you things, you gods, you Shechinah or whatever else they call you? How dare you, how dare you! Using people to punish other people?

That can't be.

Nature works harmoniously within chaos, works to enable natural processes to survive, works interactively. It is not, cannot be, personally punitive. That's a human imposition on it. Disaster and death are accidents, they have nothing to do with justice, a human concept, yesterday I could have been a woman living in Bhopal, a good woman, a woman of virtue, a good man, a child, and still be dead or dying. . . .

I was only the accidental cause of Father's death.

Why couldn't he see that all he had to do was reach out his arm to us, scrawl SORRY on his pad, and all of us, all of us, well, maybe not Ronnie, but Elizabeth and Mary and I . . . oh, we would have thrown ourselves on him, hugged him, loved him, we all loved him, didn't he know that, couldn't he feel that, we loved him and that had nothing to do with justice either, it is the work of nature that the infant loves the parent. . . .

So he killed himself, he made my verdict come true, the verdict, the words put in my mouth by the Shechinah. The Shechinah worked through me, I am not responsible, I was her instrument, I was a mere working of nature, a hurricane, a spontaneous forest fire, a flash flood, a sunset, a sunrise, a blade of grass that pierces through concrete and the concrete was Father and he cracked. She endowed me finally with my true nature, made me alive, I'm alive now, now I can be who I am, now I am Alexandra. I am a blade of grass. I grow in the world and crack concrete.

Dead dead dead forever never always always for the rest of my life illegitimate bastard by-blow misbegotten baseborn wrong side of the blanket bar sinister but surely only men had those only men had shields come home with it or upon it nice message but you need a shield to have a bar sinister women never have them no defenses not even underpants. And in his eyes a spic nigger wog spade jigaboo coon wetback mulatto half-breed there must be others I probably even know them can't think of them now. How can I respect myself, find any way to stand erect without repudiating half myself, how can I do that, can I cut off my arm, my leg, which one?

Fuck off, Ronnie. You've been repudiating his half all your life.

She lay fully dressed on her made-up bed, stiff as a corpse, hands folded piously on her stomach, staring at the ceiling. Suddenly aware of her posture, she smiled.

Hope my coffin is more comfortable than this mattress.

What a fool he was. Couldn't he see they were dying to forgive him? At least Alex was, and probably Mary too. Killed himself rather than take their love, offer them love, what a person, what makes a person like that?

Terrible, incredible, overwhelming fear.

Jesus H. Christ, one of the richest families in America, one of the most powerful men in the country, you mean he lived in fear?

Fear he didn't deserve it. Fear he'd lose it.

You mean it's true, the poor are happier than the rich? Ronnie laughed out loud, a hard hollow laugh, then stopped suddenly.

Stupid ass.

So it's over. I'm free of him.

You've been free of him for years.

I'll never be free of him. What would I have done if he'd reached out his arm and included me? Huh?

No. Couldn't.

No.

Suppose he'd said he was sorry?

I could have walked toward him. I could have looked at his face without hate.

Taken his hand?

No.

If he'd held it out to you? Specifically to you?

She burst into tears. She let herself weep, no one could hear, wept for a long time into the pillow, heaved, sobbed, then rested, drawing her breath in long deep pulls. Then she sat up and rummaged in her shirt pocket, found a rumpled pack of cigarettes, a few left, lighted one. Have to stop this. Will. As soon as I leave here. She inhaled deeply and got up off the bed, walked into the kitchen, the hall, the playroom, looked out the back windows into the dark garden.

Remember the beautiful things. Once the funeral is over, you'll probably never enter this house again. Or any house like it. Not from the front door, anyway. Have to do something now. Find a job. Haven't made much headway in the thesis, either. A little. Another five six months' work. At least.

Ah, so what. So you don't finish. So what? What difference does it make if you have letters after your name? Will that change anything?

A little, maybe.

Is that what you need to be a person? Letters after your name?

Legitimate, illegitimate, white, black, brown, tan, red, yellow, all that stuff, female, male, all that stuff: why do you let it matter so much.

Because it does.

To them. To them.

And to me.

To you?

She smoked the cigarette down and stubbed it out in an ashtray. She wandered back to her bedroom and began to take off her clothes. She opened her window. She got into bed naked, it was warm tonight, warm for December, maybe they'd forgotten to turn down the hate turn down the heat I mean should I go check the thermostat, the hell with it I'm so tired, tired. She crawled into the lumpy bed and lay there.

I'm not a saint for Christ's sake. I can't pretend what they think doesn't matter to me. It affects me. Every time they look at me, speak to me, don't look at me, don't speak to me, give me a job don't give me a job let me rent an apartment don't let me rent an apartment. . . .

You could go to Mexico. No better there, though: Indian blood,

Spanish blood, mulatto. Maybe they're even worse. Anyway, it's your insides you have to heal.

If they . . . if Elizabeth and Mary and Alex . . .

Forget that.

Forget that. It's over.

It's over.

She turned on her side and closed her eyes and fell into a turbulent sleep.

20

Having all slept past ten, Elizabeth, Alex, and Ronnie were still hanging over their coffee cups at ten-thirty later that morning when Mary came trailing in in a white satin gown and robe and white satin mules. Alex looked up startled.

"No breakfast in bed this morning?"

"Just decided to come down and have my second cup of coffee with you," Mary said airily. She noticed Elizabeth eyeing her robe. "Father's dead. I can come down in my robe now if I want to."

Ronnie got up and went into the kitchen, returning with a clean cup and saucer, which she set before Mary.

"Thanks, Ronnie, that's kind of you."

Alex poured coffee from the carafe and offered cream, which Mary rejected. Alex and Ronnie glanced at her in surprise.

"I'm starting a diet."

Elizabeth folded the newspaper she'd been reading, removed her glasses, sat back and lighted a cigarette.

"Anything about Father?" Mary asked.

"No. Too soon. Tomorrow. It was on the local television news this morning, though, Mrs. Browning said. We may have reporters."

"I suppose there are millions of things to be done," Alex said anxiously. "I have to call David. And my mother. But what else can I do? Are you planning the arrangements?" she asked Elizabeth. "Is there anything I can help with?"

Elizabeth did not seem ready to organize anything. "I guess so. But I imagine — well, I'm guessing the funeral will be taken out of our hands. But we need to call Florence's agency, the home nursing service . . ."

"Right," Mary agreed. "And we have to call Hollis."

Still, they all lingered at the table. Teresa poked her head in to see if she could clean up, grimaced and turned back to face Mrs. Browning pointing to her watch. "It'll be lunchtime before I can clear up the breakfast table," she complained.

"They were up all night, Tess," Mrs. Browning chided. "Why don't you start upstairs? I'll clear the breakfast dishes."

Still the sisters sat on. They remarked on the weather, a hardy sparrow on a bush, their tiredness, Mary's headache, but they all seemed to be waiting for something, their eyes on each other with a certain hunger.

Mary ended it. "Well, I'm going to get dressed. I'll call Hollis. When do you think they'll complete the autopsy?" she asked Elizabeth, who shrugged ignorance.

"Probably tonight or early tomorrow," Alex said, rising too.

"Excuse me," Ronnie interrupted, and they all turned to her. "Do you want me to leave now?"

"Leave?"

"Now?"

"Why?"

"I mean, there are going to be a lot of people coming in here. Public people. There's going to be a funeral. I want to know what you want me to do."

"Oh. I hadn't thought of that," Mary said.

Elizabeth gazed at Ronnie, pondering.

"Why should you do anything?" Alex blurted.

Mary looked hard at Ronnie. "No, well of course, you wouldn't want to be . . ." She turned to Elizabeth. "Lizzie?"

"Ronnie is our sister," Elizabeth said. "Whatever anyone says."

"Yes. They can't shame *us,* only him," Mary said doubtfully.

Ronnie flushed; close to tears, she hardened her face into an angry mask.

Alex gasped. Mary turned to her. "You know what I mean. I'm talking about the world. People don't usually have illegitimate children at their funerals. The press. . . ."

Ronnie fled, made it to her own room before the tears burst out. Give with one hand, take away with the other, she thought, throwing herself on her bed.

"Really, Mary," Elizabeth said.

Mary looked back at her firmly. "Lizzie, I am not being mean! Have you any idea of what the press is going to make of her? Do *to* her?"

Elizabeth fell silent.

"I'm not just thinking about us. I'm not sure she'd want it."

"I don't think she understood that."

"Then I'll explain it," Mary said rising.

She knocked lightly on Ronnie's door. Ronnie mumbled something.

"It's Mary. May I come in?"

"It's your house. Do what you want."

Mary stepped inside the small shabby room, drew a breath at the look of it — not that she hadn't been there before. But somehow, she felt, she hadn't seen it till now. Ronnie stood by the bed. When Mary approached her, she recoiled.

"Oh, Ronnie, don't be angry! When I said they couldn't shame us, I meant that no one of us deserves to be shamed for their behavior except Father. Not us. Not you."

Ronnie watched her warily. When Mary put her hand on Ronnie's arm, Ronnie shook it off.

"But Ronnie, that's not the way the press works. Ron . . . if they know who you are, the press is going to have a field day. With you, with your mother. You know it doesn't matter that the men are the ones who do these things. Whatever men do, it's always the women who are the focus of the . . . attack, really. The persecution. The objects of curiosity. It's mainly women in the photographs. Photographers might follow you, question people who went to school with you, any friends they discover in Boston, people who used to work here about Noradia. I'm not sure you want that. If you want his name, that history, following you around the rest of your life. If you're willing . . . I'll support you. It's up to you."

Mary approached her, put her arms around her. "But whatever you do, however we handle this, we don't want you to leave. I don't want you to leave."

Ronnie buried her head in Mary's shoulder, Mary's arms around her, Mary leaning her head against the top of Ronnie's. "We're sisters," Mary whispered.

Ronnie pulled away gently, wiped her eyes with her shirt sleeve, sat down on the bed and lighted a cigarette, pointing Mary to the only chair, a hard-backed wooden chair at the desk. "We're sisters," Ronnie said in a nasal voice. "Now. But once we leave here . . . your life . . . my life . . . maybe you aren't going to want to know me."

Mary dropped her eyes. No way, no way on this earth could she incorporate Ronnie into her life, her friends, her world. Ronnie would hate it anyway. She looked up.

"Our lives. Well, our lives can never be . . . you know . . . we don't live in the same world. And you wouldn't want to live in mine. Sometimes I don't even want to live in mine but it's the only one I know, the one I'm used to, the one I feel comfortable in. But I don't want to lose you. I want my daughter to meet you, Marie-Laure, I think you could help her, well, I'm not asking you to help her, but she needs help and I can't give it to her, I've wrecked my chance. It would be good for her to meet someone like you."

"You're not afraid I'll seduce her?"

"Maybe that would be good for her," Mary laughed, "if it weren't incest. There's enough incest in this family already."

Ronnie laughed, kept laughing, with an edge of hysterical relief, a threat of tears.

"Do you know what I realized last night?" Mary asked proudly.

Ronnie shook her head.

"I don't need to get married again! I don't need another husband! I never have to sleep with a man again unless *I* want to!"

Ronnie smiled wryly. "Yeah, marriage is a dirty job, but somebody's got to do it."

Mary didn't get it. ". . . And you did that. The three of you. That has

nothing to do with . . . this . . . with Father. . . . But now that Father . . .
well, I can come downstairs in my robe if I want! I can send my poems out
to poetry magazines . . . !" She wore an easy unself-conscious grin that
Ronnie had never seen on her before.

"I wonder," Ronnie said, only dimly understanding the particulars of
Mary's new freedoms but utterly perceiving their essence, "if I'll ever be
able to walk around this house as if I belonged here."

Mary gazed at her. "I hope you will."

"So what do you think I ought to do? I *don't* want the press breathing
down my neck, breathing down Momma's. I *don't* want my picture in the
paper. I don't want to be known as Stephen Upton's bastard. In *my* world,
that would ruin my reputation," she grinned wickedly. Then she dropped
her eyes. "But I don't want to be left out, either, to be hidden someplace
while the three of you . . ." Her eyes glistened. "Makes me feel slimy."

Mary pondered. "Let me speak to Lizzie."

Ronnie nodded.

Mary's glance took in Ronnie's word processor, the hills of books.
"You know, whatever is in Father's will, this house will have to be sold.
And that will take months, maybe years. And meantime, someone has to
live here, we can't leave it completely empty. The estate will have to pay
someone to stay and act as a caretaker. Not a lot but enough to live. And
we need someone trustworthy. So — it might be worth your while — you
could stay here while you finish your dissertation . . . you could move into
Father's study . . ."

"NO!"

Mary shrank, stared, blinked, understood. "Or wherever you
wanted. It's quiet. You could use the Alfa. If you wouldn't be lonely."

"Be an Upton servant again?" Ronnie said tightly.

Mary thought. "Is that what I'm suggesting? Actually, I was thinking
maybe I'd come live here too. Sell my apartment and live up here for a
while. Just until the house is sold. It's closer to Marie-Laure than Lizzie's
place. I have to spend some time with her. She could come here sometimes on weekends, bring her friends. In the nice weather. Maybe I could
save some money living here. You could continue my driving lessons," she
smiled shyly.

"Are you asking me to live with you?" Incredulous.

"I don't know what I'm asking. I'm just having ideas. It's as if the world has just started over again! I feel as if my whole past has been erased and everything is beginning newly."

Ronnie kept her voice steady. "Maybe we could."

The house was full of activity that afternoon as trucks came to pick up the medical equipment rented for Stephen and deliver flowers. The telephone rang — all three telephones, almost constantly — and a few reporters appeared at the front door. But Elizabeth did not manage things. No one did. Somehow, they all knew precisely how to get rid of reporters, how to handle workmen and telephone calls, and to record the senders of flowers for thank-you notes to be written later, and what would keep the servants calm — Teresa especially was distraught, kept wiping her eyes, muttering "Such a kind man." Maybe remembering her own father, Elizabeth thought. But she had spent considerable time sitting with Father. Probably thought he was kind because he never hit her. It would be a kindness to let the woman leave early, Elizabeth thought, then realized it was already nearly four. Couldn't give them tomorrow off, they needed all hands. And after that, Teresa might be let go — the sisters were leaving and would no longer need her. Maybe that was really what the tears were about.

Elizabeth sighed, leaning back in Father's chair, exhaling in deep satisfaction. She had spent the afternoon repacking his papers, labeling the boxes. It would take another two or three days to finish. The boxes would go to an archive somewhere, some college or university, maybe someone would even pay to have them. There were more, a closetful here, perhaps others in New York, Boston, Washington. Let someone else write his life. His disgusting life. Make him out a hero.

Hollis had been cagey, Mary said. Of course he expresssed deep condolences, so sorry my dear, my poor dears, you dear girls, but cagey. Mary laughed, "He isn't coming out to read the will until he's goddamned certain the autopsy shows no sign of foul play!"

Didn't matter. Nothing mattered anymore, nothing that used to matter. Not even if he didn't make me executor. It'll twinge, but no more. Everything changed somehow now. Have to get a new life. Have to get a life. If they pushed her out at Treasury, she'd get a job. Teaching maybe. Maybe near here. Live in this house. No. Too expensive to keep up. Sisters. She had sisters now, people who knew her, who didn't think she was just a coldhearted mean bitch. People willing to put an arm around her. People whose touch she could stand. Welcomed even.

She looked at her watch, picked up the telephone for the twentieth time that day, leaned her head on her hand, then slowly hit the numbers.

"Hello, Mother. It's Elizabeth."

"You might have called earlier. I had to hear on the television that my own husband died?"

"You wanted me to call you at two in the morning? Because that's when I got back here last night."

"You might have called me this morning."

"I slept late."

"It's four o'clock. You just got up?"

"No. I just worked up the energy to call you. It's not pleasant calling you, and I have to steel myself."

"That's a fine thing to say."

"Do you want any information from me? If not, I'll hang up."

"Have you seen the will?"

"No."

"Why not?"

"The lawyer won't read it until after the autopsy."

"Why is there an autopsy?"

"To determine the precise cause of death."

"And what was it?"

"How do I know?"

"What did you do — kill him or something?"

"I think he had another stroke."

Elizabeth could hear a match strike, an exhalation.

"Well at least I outlived him."

"Yes. You were determined to do that."

"He had to leave me twenty-five thousand dollars. Of course, that sounded like a lot more in 1934 than it does now."

"No, Mother, he had to put twenty-five thousand dollars in a trust for you. It's probably up to millions now."

"REALLY!"

"Really."

"I'll have money of my own! I'll be the only one of my sisters with money of my own."

"You will be."

Catherine was silent. Finally she said briskly, "Let me know when you know about the will. And about the funeral. I want to go."

"I'll make sure you're included."

"All right. Will I be seeing you?"

After a silence, Elizabeth said, "I suppose I could drive in one day."

"I'd like to see you, Elizabeth. I never see you."

"Then I'll come."

Glide into it over tea: and by the way, Mother, did you know Father fucked me, regularly, for years and years? And that when I used to cry and beg you not to send me out there, it was because he was fucking me, fucking me, fucking me, did you know that, Mother? Mother?

What would she say? I haven't the slightest idea, no inkling at all, not even a hint of an idea. I don't know her at all I guess.

Suppose she said: Yes, I thought so. Could I bear it? Suppose she said: Better you than me. Or, Why didn't you tell me? Or, I don't believe you. Couldn't bear it. Couldn't. So don't tell her. What else could she say? She could cry out, hug me, say she was sorry she didn't listen to me.

Elizabeth pondered.

Better not tell her.

Alex was busy all day, arranging flowers in vases, answering the telephone, going to the door and getting rid of reporters, patting Teresa on the back, praising Mrs. Browning for her fortitude. But between chores she seemed to vanish, and Mary, Elizabeth, and Ronnie, who were also involved in the practical work of the household, kept noticing her absence. Still, the next time the doorbell rang, she would be there, so no one questioned her.

When they gathered at six for cocktails, she was especially silent, and Ronnie touched her hand.

"Are you okay? You seem — absent. Withdrawn."

She smiled gloriously. "I'm fine."

"What have you been doing all day? Apart from all the shit work?"

"Making telephone calls." She sipped her wine.

Alex terse?

"One thing," she said suddenly. "I'd like to be called Alexandra. Not Alex. If you can remember," she added apologetically.

They stared at her.

"Who did you call?" Ronnie blurted.

"Oh, David and the kids of course. And my mother. I had a long conversation with my mother." She smiled and sipped again. They all leaned toward her.

"Did you tell her?"

"Not exactly. I just said my memory had returned. Let her stew that over for a while. I don't want to tell her over the telephone. I want to see her face."

"What did she say?"

Alex laughed. "She ummed and hummed. She said 'Really? Your memory of what?' " She laughed again, a dark harsh laugh, and all three of them stared at her in surprise. "My mother," she concluded bitterly.

"Our mothers weren't much help to us, were they," Elizabeth said.

They all sat pensively for a time.

"I wonder. If my mother had lived. If she hadn't killed herself . . . ," Mary began, "would she have been any help? Would he still have . . ."

"He did it to me when my mother was alive," Alex exploded. "A woman you say he loved."

"I wonder what it was. Why he had to do it."

"Like a male dog peeing on a tree," Ronnie said. "Marking out his territory."

"You think?"

"He probably really didn't see anything wrong with it. He probably really did see us as his possessions."

"And our mothers? Did they think the same way?"

Silence.

"My mother," Elizabeth said finally, "is very pleased to have outlived him. Get her trust fund. I swear if she'd had a terminal disease, she would have managed to stay alive that long."

"What happened to it if she died before him?" Ronnie asked.

"It died too. Reverted to his estate."

"So you wouldn't have gotten it."

She shook her head.

"I keep being shocked by him. By his . . ." Ronnie shook her head hard, as if she were trying to toss water out of her ears.

"Yes. So foreign to the way we think. Are. Feel. I wonder if all men are foreign to all women that way," Mary mused.

"Are you going to tell her?" Ronnie continued, facing Elizabeth. "Your mother?"

"I don't think so. No."

"Afraid, huh," Ronnie said knowingly. Elizabeth turned to her sharply but Ronnie was not smirking. She seemed thoughtful.

"Yes," Elizabeth said.

"But suppose you had a daughter," Mary said to Elizabeth. "Would you feel that way — that she was his property, that he could do whatever he wanted — her father?"

"Absolutely not!"

"Me either!" Alex announced.

"Nor do I," Mary agreed.

"I'd kill him!" Elizabeth cried.

Ronnie turned to Elizabeth. "Of all the things your mother could say if you told her, which would hurt you the most?"

Elizabeth thought. "If she didn't believe me."

"Would that be worse than if she said — however she said it, however implicitly because she'd probably never say it straight out — that he had the right?"

Elizabeth nodded. "Is that what your mother would have said?"

"I don't know. I suspect it's what she felt, but I'm not sure. I think she would have cried, sort of helplessly, hugged me, but that's all. She wouldn't have tried to stop it. That's what I think."

"So why were our mothers that way and we're not?" Alex asked. "How come they didn't help us?"

"Feminism," all three chorused, then burst into laughter.

Alex smiled, dropped her eyes, raised them again looking like a naughty child. "I made another phone call today. I called the Dominican sisters at St. Cecilia's. A convent school near Newark," she added.

"You're Catholic?" Mary, aghast.

"No. I'm Jewish. Remember I converted when I married David."

"The nuns," Elizabeth reminded her.

"Yes. Well, I first met them at the hospital where I volunteer, and they're so great, so full of life and cheerful and happy, I'm drawn to them. So I go over and give them a hand once in a while. They're great with kids, but they're also very political. They help refugees from El Salvador, they take them in and transport them and hide them if the immigration people try to capture them. And they send nuns and lay medical workers down there to help the people. They hate the pope, they pay no attention to him. They love their lives, they are always so . . . so gay, really. I thought maybe if I lived like them, I could be that way too."

"Dangerous, doing religious work in El Salvador," Elizabeth said.

"Yes. One of the nuns killed there — you remember? — was from their house. But even just medical work is dangerous. Just helping the peasants is dangerous. The government is so terrible, a really cruel regime."

Ronnie leaned forward. "So Alex — Alexandra — why did you call them? Are you thinking of joining them?"

"Oh, I couldn't do that! I'm Jewish!"

Ronnie kept staring at her, but Alex refused to meet Ronnie's eyes. "No. I just wanted to see how they are. I've missed them. See what they're doing now."

"And what are they doing now?" Elizabeth asked, slightly amused, lighting a cigarette.

"They're preparing to send another team down there. After Christmas probably, maybe early spring. As soon as they raise enough money. Some nuns — a doctor, a nurse, and some assistants. And an administrator, probably." Unable to look at any of them, she got up and poured another glass of wine for herself without even asking if they wanted anything.

"Alex! Alexandra! What's going on?" Elizabeth demanded.

Her face flushed painfully, there was a red line on her neck dividing her flaming face from the rest of her body. She bit her lip. She stared at the wall. "Well. Of course, I don't even know if I'm in it, if he remembered me, I mean he never did before. But I thought . . . if Father did leave me any money . . . you see, they always need money for these things of course." She turned to them apologetically, her face eager, begging forgiveness. "So I wanted to know if, if he did, if there *was* anything, if I can do anything if there was anything to do. You see?"

They smiled, embraced her with their eyes.

"Do you think I'm being greedy?"

They shook their heads.

She sighed. She returned to her chair and took a great gulp of wine. "Well, that's what I was doing!"

Dinner was quiet that evening, but a great peace hovered around them, even Mrs. Browning noticed it, although she read it as sorrow. Even though the old man was dead now, they still left the head of the table empty and sat in their usual places, two on one side, two on the other facing each other at one end of the long table.

Elizabeth sighed. "Jesus, there'll be so much to do once they release the body. A million phone calls. We'll have to pick out a casket. All that. That's how you get through these things when you really are in grief, I suppose."

"Are we not?" Mary wanted to know.

"Are we?" Elizabeth challenged her.

"People always have mixed feelings, don't they?" Mary said.

"I suppose," Alex mused.

"Well, certainly we don't miss him," Elizabeth said in a very low voice.

No one responded.

"Do we?" she asked in surprise.

Three heads shook no.

"But when a person dies — a lot of things die with him. Or her. What he used to be. What you hoped for from him. What you wanted him to be," Alex said. "And you know those things were dreams, are illusions, will never happen, and you have to put them away. Forever. And you grieve. For them. For yourself."

They sat in silence.

Mrs. Browning heard it as she cleared the soup bowls and served the chops, the vegetables. Poor girls, she thought. They cared so much about him.

"I was telling Ronnie," Mary began as they started to eat, "that whoever inherits this house will sell it. I mean, if it's us, or a foundation, I can't imagine anyone will keep it. And the estate will have to have a caretaker until it's sold. A *paid* caretaker. And I thought maybe Ronnie would want to stay on here and do that for a while. Until she finishes her dissertation."

Elizabeth, mouth full of food, nodded. "Good idea."

"I thought I might stay here with her. Go back and put my apartment on the market, then come up and keep her company."

Elizabeth put down her fork.

"I thought you were coming to live with me."

"I am. I will. After the house is sold and my apartment, and I have some money and Marie-Laure is . . . after I get to know her a little better. Then I thought we could buy a house together in Virginia. There are some gorgeous little places in Falls Church, or even Arlington. What do you think?"

"Great!" Elizabeth cried, picking up her fork again. "I'd love a house after all these years in an apartment. Maybe we could find one with a little garden. Or even a pool. I used to love to swim." She turned suddenly to Ronnie. "Maybe you'll get a job with the government and come and live with us! Alex is only over near Wilmington! We could have dinner together every week!"

Ronnie stared at her. Her throat full of tears, she could only growl, "I wouldn't work for the fucking federal government in a million years, and you know that perfectly well, Elizabeth!" But once she had swallowed her emotion, she added, "However, I am sure that working in my field, I'll have lots of reasons to travel to Washington and scream at somebody in the government."

"No, Ronnie, that isn't the way it's done. If you want to get things done in Washington, you don't scream at anybody, you make friends!" Elizabeth said tutorially.

"How did you get ahead then," Ronnie snapped. "You're about as friendly as a guard dog."

Mary and Alex burst into laughter; Alex hid hers behind her napkin. Even Elizabeth grimaced a smile.

"If you can get ahead in government, so can I, Elizabeth," Ronnie argued.

"I got ahead partly on Father's name," Elizabeth said.

"Aha!" Ronnie grinned. "Well, I'll be coming down there for one reason or another, and I insist you have a guest room with my name over the door in that house of yours."

"Okay. How do you want it decorated?" Mary asked.

"Decorated?"

"Yes. What style of furniture do you like? What colors?"

Ronnie seemed to shrivel in her chair, and Mary suddenly realized she had never in her life had the luxury of deciding on the look of her own environment.

"Well," Ronnie said finally. "You know that old pine table I use as a desk? In my room? I'd like that to be in it."

"Oh that!" Mary exclaimed. "It's old and probably valuable, but it isn't — well, I wouldn't have it in my house! Take it with you when you leave if you want it. But that's a good clue — you like Early American. I can see that. Maybe with Indian throw rugs on the floor — Navaho rugs — do you like them, Elizabeth? I think they're gorgeous. A room in earth colors, that would suit Ronnie."

Ronnie's emotions swooped from resentment at patronization to resentment of charity to resentment of Mary's taking over her life, until she began to laugh inside, and after a moment the laughter burst out.

Alex smiled at them benignly, as if from a great distance. "How good! How good to have found my sisters!" she exclaimed softly. Then stretched out her hands to Ronnie beside her, and Elizabeth across the table from her, and they did the same to Mary, and the four of them sat in smiling silence for a long minute.

21

By Friday morning, the autopsy had been completed. The cause of death having been found to be natural, Stephen's body would be released to them for burial. The few reporters who had lingered around the hospital left, and Dr. Stamp called and asked if he could stop in and see the Upton sisters around eleven on his way from the hospital to his office.

All four of them were waiting for him in the front sitting room, where the tea table was already set with coffee and little cakes. Entering, he stared in awe at the huge foyer, its tapestries and sculptures, and walked solemnly into the sitting room like a man entering a museum or a shrine to a revered scientist. Mary wore a dark wool dress with pearls, only the little pleats of the lower skirt lightening its mood, but the others wore sweaters and pants — jeans in Ronnie's case — and low-heeled shoes. They served him coffee. The doctor sought out Mary, but this time she did not seem to be waiting for his gaze. She acted as if, today, *he* were there for her consideration. He felt the difference, but could not have expressed it in words. Disconcerted, he wondered if she blamed him for her father's death.

He wiped his mouth, set down his cup.

"I want you all to know that everything that could have been done was done . . . ," he said.

They assured him of their belief in this.

"I know you've heard by now that your father died of a pulmonary embolism. This is something that happens very often to bedridden people, and I don't want you girls to feel in any way responsible. You did everything you could for him. His time on earth was limited — after all, he was eighty-two. Nothing could have saved him. You have nothing to reproach yourselves with."

"Yes, we believe that," Elizabeth said. But there was such a strange look on her face that he felt he was taking part in some drama without knowing his role. He glanced at the others: they had it too. He searched for a way to erase his discomfort. "You girls were really wonderful!" he declared.

"We're hardly girls, Dr. Stamp," Ronnie said.

His mouth opened.

"I'm the youngest, and I'm twenty-five. Elizabeth's fifty. Would you call a fifty-year-old man a boy?"

He squirmed in his chair. "Sorry, of course, I wasn't thinking. What I meant was you are truly wonderful ladies."

Ronnie opened her mouth again, then shut it.

He launched into an explanation of pulmonary embolism, explained that their father had died swiftly, in minimal pain, and that in the end it was a mercy, given the state in which he was living and his unhappiness with it. The doctor wanted to leave, but did not know how to do so quickly, so rambled on and on. The sisters attended politely, nodding their heads occasionally, but asking no questions.

Finally, he felt he could lay down his napkin and make his departure. "I just want to say it was a privilege to attend your father. I'm sorry the outcome wasn't happier."

Elizabeth smiled politely, but Dr. Stamp's glance yearned toward Mary, seeking that sweet turned-up look she usually gave him. But she barely glanced at him. Grief, probably.

He left hastily, in deep disappointment and discomfort. Strange women, he thought.

*   *   *

No, Mary decided when he'd gone, he's completely unsuitable: insufficient chin and no idea at all of how to dress. And he'd require constant bolstering. Not worth it unless he were a trillionaire. Not even then.

She turned to Elizabeth. "Do you think we should call Hollis and tell him that Father has been found to have died of natural causes?" she asked with a conspiratorial smile.

"I imagine he already knows. Channels," Elizabeth said dryly.

And indeed, Hollis soon called to say he would drive out late that afternoon to read them the will.

Others called as well: the president and the secretary of state and the governor of Massachusetts, as well as hundreds of other men of high rank in government, bankers, diplomats, corporate presidents, university presidents, foundation heads. Elizabeth and Mary handled the phones. The governor wanted the funeral to be held in Boston, in St. Paul's Cathedral, where generations of Uptons had worshiped. He argued that the bishop would want to eulogize this great man and that the church, although shabby and old, was a revered monument. And it would be easier for the president to get to Boston than to Lincoln.

Elizabeth and Mary were grateful to relinquish control of the ceremony. Besides, Stephen never went to church in Lincoln, never went to church at all except for weddings and funerals. A formal ceremony in the 1830s Boston church, which despite its crumbling state still glowed with the bishop's prestige, the president and governor in attendance, with a small reception afterward for a hundred and fifty chosen figures to be held in Worth Jr.'s house in Louisburg Square, absolved them of the need to devise a more personal farewell. Still, there were a million details to be seen to. Their time was completely given over to the practicalities of death. Mary thought, if you were really shot through with grief, if it was pouring like boiling blood screaming through your veins, arms, legs, fingers, the way it had when Don died, then all this busyness helped. How had Emily Dickinson put it?

> The bustle in a house
> The Morning after Death
> Is solemnest of industries
> Enacted upon Earth —

The Sweeping up the Heart
And putting Love away
We shall not want to use again
Until Eternity.

And maybe she was. Maybe that sick feeling running through her veins, as
if her blood had turned watery, depleting her strength, so that even walking was an effort, and her voice came out in a croak, maybe that was grief?
How could she be grieving for him, for such a man? Yet Elizabeth too
looked pale and stiff and spoke in a surly terse manner, the way she had
when they'd first arrived here, tense and mean. Even Ronnie seemed subdued and withdrawn, she hid out in her room almost all day. She helped
with nothing, involved herself in no arrangements; she refused to pick up
the telephone even when she was standing beside it when it rang. Only
Alex seemed serene, liberated, well of course she had her memories back.
But *what* memories! How could such a replacement ease a mind?

Although Hollis arrived during their usual cocktail hour, Ronnie did not
join them in the sitting room where they waited to greet him. He scanned
them quickly, his genial self, expansive, a man bringing good news, Elizabeth thought with some relief. He made a great fuss opening his briefcase
and pulling out papers, setting his half-glasses on his nose. He asked if it
might be better to do this in Stephen's study, but Elizabeth objected. She
did not want him sitting at Father's desk. It was a mess, she lied, papers all
over everything, and he did not insist, he was pleased with himself, with
them, and with the timing of the event, which had saved him a painful
decision. Sorry as he was about Cab, he'd had a long life, a good life, had
accomplished much, was one of the prominent men of his generation. . . .

He happily accepted the Manhattan Mary mixed for him. The sisters
held decorous glasses of wine.

The will was long and involved, with bequests to many institu-
tions — schools and churches and conservative foundations. There was a
trust for Catherine Callahan Upton, and, Alex was surprised to hear, one
for Amelia Upton Massey; there were substantial trusts for Albert and
Marie-Laure di Cenci and a small one for Martin Burnside, whose own

father had left him a great deal. The remainder — and it was substantial — went to his daughters Elizabeth, Mary, and Alexandra.

"You should each have between ten and fifteen in investments at today's prices, I'd estimate. He was a very canny investor. And maybe four or five more apiece from the real estate. His properties have increased in value tremendously. Of course, the real estate market is at an all-time high."

"Ten to fifteen . . . thousand dollars?" Alex asked innocently.

He looked at her over his glasses.

"Ten and fifteen million, my dear," he said haughtily, sounding insulted.

And he had made Elizabeth executor.

Something in her heart gave a great pang, then rested.

"I'm real glad we didn't change anything. He clearly wasn't himself at the end," he concluded. "This thing must have been coming on even then. Tom Kaplan had decided to award you conservatorship," he told Elizabeth. "I have to tell you, he wasn't himself even with us. I've never seen Cab act that way — well, it's water over the dam now, but his condition just seemed to make him hate everybody. . . ."

Having brought good news, he was happy to lean back and talk genially to these lovely ladies, beloved daughters of a multi-millionaire, a great man who entrusted them with the bulk of his estate. Too bad he had no son, but they were worthy heirs. Great ladies. A shadow crossed his face. He set his drink down, leaned forward and lowered his voice.

"I know . . . you girls are . . . you're really special, I am certainly aware of that. The way you gave up your own lives to care for Cab, the way you took his . . . confusion . . . everything you've done. And accepting his bas— . . . illegitimate daughter, that was the act of true Christians, of kind generous ladies. You behaved like saints, if you ask me.

"And she too may be a perfectly fine person for all I know, a good woman. But" — he glanced warily toward the hall — "she could also present you with a problem. He didn't acknowledge her, didn't mention her but" — he leaned back and held his hand loosely in front of his mouth — "if she can produce any proof . . . of her parentage . . . she could . . . well, she could make trouble for you. Even without any proof, she can make trouble. Probably not shake the will, but hold it up in the courts for a while, years even. . . . "

Elizabeth stood up. "I can't permit you to discuss Ronnie unless she is present. I'll get her."

Hollis started forward in his chair, appalled. "No! The whole point is to . . . Listen, Elizabeth, sit down!"

She stopped.

"What I was going to suggest is that you girls each kick in a little sum, say a hundred, a hundred fifty, two hundred apiece, and we'll have her sign a paper promising to make no claims against the will. She'll be happy, you'll be safe."

"A hundred and fifty dollars?" a dismayed Alex whispered to Mary.

Mary smiled patronizingly at her. "Thousand, dear."

"Say what you have to say in her presence and see what she says," Elizabeth said brusquely and left the room.

Hollis sat back, glancing uneasily at Mary and Alex. What was the matter with Elizabeth? And the others, just sitting there, not even trying to stop her. Never heard of such a thing. Ridiculous. Improper. Insane. Old man crazy at the end, maybe it ran in the family, maybe they're all nuts, maybe he always was crazy, all those wives, all those women, god, I remember a few of them, a real swordsman he was, why couldn't he just have stayed married to whichever one it was, oh yes, the Irish secretary, well of course he was just a kid then, and then the next one died, suicide they said, still a gentleman should just stay married and keep his sex life discreet, the rest of us managed it, you don't have to keep getting married, and you damned well don't have to produce bastards. . . .

Elizabeth was gone a long time, and while she was gone, no one spoke. At least fifteen minutes passed before she returned, rather pink in the face, leading a reluctant Ronnie. "Had to go out to the woods to find her," she announced, a little out of breath. She dropped into a chair, motioned Ronnie to do the same. Ronnie slid out of her heavy jacket, threw it on a chair, and sat down next to Elizabeth.

"Now will you please repeat what you told us, Hollis?" Elizabeth asked formally, politely.

His face was patched with pink and he seemed for a moment unable to speak. Alex took pity on him. She stood and took his glass from his hand. "Another Manhattan, Hollis?"

He nodded.

"You know you can't make a Manhattan, Alex — andra," Mary said, rising to do it. Hollis surrendered to them and did not speak until he had sipped his fresh cocktail and Mary had seated herself again.

"Miss . . . Velez. I know these ladies believe you to be their half sister, their father's illegitimate daughter . . ."

"Believe her! Look at her eyes, Hollis! Look at her chin!" Elizabeth interrupted.

"Ummmm," he mumbled, fiddling with some papers. "Nevertheless, he has not acknowledged you in his will, which gives you no legal right to any claim on his estate. What I'm saying is that unfortunately, your father left you nothing. Now what these ladies are willing to do . . ."

"NO!" Elizabeth said sharply. "We have indicated no such willingness! What you are proposing we do, Hollis."

He flushed and his voice changed into that of a lawyer dealing with an opponent, a tough negotiator, an enemy.

Our enemy, Mary thought.

"What I propose is that these ladies compensate for your father's neglect, and share part of their inheritances with you. I have mentioned a certain figure, but of course that would be negotiable. But it seems to me receiving some hundreds of thousands of dollars would go a long way toward making you feel you'd received some justice, and it should certainly help make your life easier."

Ronnie's face was expressionless. "And in return?" she asked.

"In return, you sign a paper relinquishing any claim to his estate."

"Don't do it, Ronnie," Mary advised. "You never know. Maybe some old letter will turn up admitting something. You've never gone through your mother's things. Maybe she had something . . ."

"My dear!" Hollis exploded.

"Anyway, we'll share with you without your signing anything, Ronnie," Alex said. "He left so *much!*" She looked at Mary. "Well, *I'll* share with you anyway. You can have half of my share."

Ronnie looked at Elizabeth. Elizabeth shrugged. "We're not asking you, *he* is."

Hollis's heart was palpitating, he put his hand over it. "Ladies, ladies," he protested weakly, "as your attorney, as your father's attorney, I cannot countenance such promises, such . . ."

"I won't sign a fucking thing," Ronnie said savagely. "He never ac-knowledged me, I'm not acknowledging him. But I'll tell you this, old man: I don't want his money. I don't want half of Alex — andra's inheri-tance, or half of anybody else's. The only things I ever might have wanted from him he didn't have to give." She stood up, reached for her jacket. "If that's all, I'll go back outside. The air is better out there."

She left. The sisters watched Hollis's face. He stared after Ronnie, stared at them.

Finally he spoke, stiffly, formally. "Perhaps you'd like to get someone else to probate this will for you. I have all the files, I can easily transfer them to another attorney."

"No, Hollis, we're quite content with you handling it. You just don't understand Ronnie. But we want you to set things in motion. How long will it take, do you think?"

"Six, eight months. At least."

"This house is left to us?"

He nodded and began to return his papers to his briefcase. He never looked directly at any of them again until Mary sidled up to him as he was leaving and asked about the chances of receiving an advance — perhaps a quarter-million — within the next month. Now *that* he understood. He smiled benignly. "With an estate of this size, Mary my dear, I don't think that should be a problem. I'll see to it first thing next week."

He left feeling something of himself had been salvaged.

Ten to fifteen million dollars. Ten to fifteen million dollars. At the least. Pay off all the debts, hire a full staff of servants again, get a car and driver, pick up my old life. Lunch at Le Cirque, go to the designer shows, the charity balls and lunches, travel, maybe even buy a little place somewhere wonderful. Capri.

Mary undressed slowly, her wonder affecting the way she saw her body, which seemed to shimmer in the shower like the white silk under-garments she had removed, the white silk nightgown she put on after-ward. She moved toward the chaise like a queen walking in state, in slow dignity, her head erect. Ten to fifteen million dollars. I wouldn't have to lift a finger to find another husband, they'd be clustering around me, it would be like the old days when I was young, only this time the bait wouldn't be me but my money, I could pick and choose. I could hold out for the real thing, for another Don. If there can ever be another Don . . .

Will I ever feel that way about anyone again?

She lighted her joint and gazed benignly out at the darkness as if in it she saw the winding stone lanes of Capri, the bougainvillea, the sky the color of periwinkle, the bay below. . . . She remembered being with Don in San Francisco, disappointed, they had planned something, what was it, a picnic? a walk? But they woke to a terrible morning, dark and ominous, the fog rolling over the top of the mountains like clouds, poured over them like lava, wave after wave of it, and rain would ruin everything. But it was only fog pouring over the top of the mountains and by ten it had risen and the sky glistened as if it had just been washed. . . .

It had been one of their perfect days.

That might not come again, but now everything was as it had been years ago, always had been. My birthright returned to me, at least he did that much. If he hadn't died when he did, though . . .

She shook off the thought.

How could Elizabeth and I possibly live together, what can I have been thinking of, all we do is quarrel, we share nothing, not one thing, and a room in the house for Ronnie, what nonsense! How could we introduce her? She might bring her friends, a bunch of Latino dykes, are we supposed to entertain them? Even Alex is a problem, she doesn't fit into my world, even Elizabeth just gets by because she has manners and Father's name and is secretary of the treasury or assistant or whatever it is. . . .

What was I thinking of, staying here with Ronnie, bringing Marie-Laure here on her school vacation, I must have been out of my mind.

Ten to fifteen million dollars.

Marie-Laure will start to get money from her trust immediately, luckily I have control of it, I'll have her pay her own expenses, school fees, her clothes, get that car she's been nagging me for. . . . Must make sure she makes a will too, don't want Alberto ever to get his hands on her money. Bertie too, well he's a lawyer with a wife, he surely has a will and there's no way he'd include Alberto in it. I won't have to worry about her anymore, she'll be able to marry well, it's not a huge amount, but it's enough, enough to attract someone from a good family. . . . If there are any left, so many scandals, everyone seems corrupt these days.

Maybe they always were but we didn't know about it. Were people more honest years ago? Who was it during the Revolution who bought and sold imported goods after vowing not to, signing a boycott, John Hancock, I think, and now there's a building named for him. And Paul Revere making an engraving about an incident with violence on both sides but changing it into soldiers massacring a crowd of poor peaceful citizens so it was called the Boston Massacre, wasn't it? And who was it herded poor immigrants off the boats and loaded them onto railroad cars that ran straight inside his factories to break strikes, and the poor men didn't know what was happening to them, when was that, who was that? Andrew Carnegie? Maybe Elizabeth would know.

That's how they made all that money.

I wonder how the Uptons made theirs. I wonder how Father . . .

Don't think about that.

Surely he was always honest in business at least, he was a lawyer, how could he not be, he'd know he'd get into trouble. But lawyers on the inside track always hear about deals. . . .

Harry cheated, I know he did. Something came out after he died, I sensed at the time that he was under some pressure, he was so irritable, drinking so heavily, that's what killed him, not screwing around, he knew some government agency was breathing down his neck, selling parts to the air force at inflated prices, something like that, I didn't really read the stories. . . .

Don't think this way.

Besides, *I've* never done anything evil.

She took a long drag on her joint and put it out. The darkness outside the window was almost total now, only a faint line divided sky from treetops. There were no stars.

Ten to fifteen million dollars, times three is thirty to forty-five million, not counting the real estate and all those other bequests, all told he must have had a hundred million or more, god he was rich, how did he get so rich, how can anyone get that rich? You're supposed to be an economist, Elizabeth, you should know.

Word will get out without my lifting a finger. It will make me. Whatever cachet I had before will be multiplied infinitely, just the smell of money, as potent in Washington as in L.A. or New York, anyplace, anyplace at all, just the hint of it makes you a magnet, draws them all, the lowly and the powerful, the wanna-bes and the haves. If Mary comes to live with me we could buy a house in Georgetown, she could decorate it, we could hold small dinner parties, invite only the very powerful, they'd come, all that money, she's a wonderful hostess, she has charm and I could talk politics with the men, we could be like Gertrude Stein and Alice Toklas except not lovers. Maybe I could even make the Council, be the first woman on it.

Elizabeth was still sitting fully dressed on the chaise in her bedroom, smoking. She put out her cigarette and stood, feeling enormously tall, commanding, as commanding as . . . Father. She walked toward the bathroom and began to undress slowly, imagining how people would treat her now, the little marks of deference she would receive, not that she didn't receive deference as it was, but it would be multiplied exponentially. . . .

They could keep a car and driver for Mary, she of course had her official car, they could afford anything, everything, how could you possibly spend that much money, they'd each have ten to fifteen million, invested even conservatively they'd have a million or two to spend every year, when even on her salary, which was a fraction of that, she saved money now. No, the money was too much, couldn't imagine spending it, maybe I should look around for some worthy foundation to endow, I have no kids.

What can you do with ten to fifteen million dollars that's worth doing, that's as wonderful as the idea of it, that's as wonderful as the sound of it, that can make you as happy as the sound, the promise of it? Mother's going to have a few million, Hollis said. Really did get her revenge. What on earth do I want, can I want, that's as good as that?

Maybe something Ronnie cares about, something environmental, one thing about us Republicans, we aren't too good on the environment. But it's important. Maybe set up a foundation and have Ronnie run it, no she wouldn't like that. Want to make sure she has an income, she won't take anything from us, I know that. Have to take care of her somehow. Everything stacked against her kind, people not exactly like us. Nothing about her matters as much as that . . . she could be a bastard, who would know or care? Or a lesbian, well of course she'd have to hide that. But she can't hide her golden skin. . . .

And he made me executor, she thought, a smile crossing her face as she stepped into her shower, feeling tall, commanding, as if she'd grown a few inches today. He gave me that responsibility, didn't treat me like a woman, treated me like a son, of course, he would have left a son the major part of the estate, and left the daughters smaller trusts, but he didn't have a son, hah hah. Still, he made me executor.

She was smiling as she stepped out of the shower, as she dried her body, and when she glanced at herself in the mirror while brushing her teeth, she saw herself smiling still.

Ten to fifteen million dollars, she thought. I won't ever be lonely again.

Good heavens. I can't even picture ten to fifteen million dollars. What would that much money look like? What on earth can a person possibly do with it?

Alex undressed uneasily, feeling somehow unlike herself, and stepped into the shower. Unthinkingly, she turned on only the cold water and was blasted with a freezing rain. She stepped back and slipped, almost fell. God. She adjusted the temperature, holding her hand under the water until it was warm enough, then stepped gingerly back under the waterfall.

David will want to invest it, put it away for the kids' future, but there's too much, they don't need that much, that much money isn't good for people. Especially for kids. No. I can't let him do that. Some of it, yes, but not all. But I've never opposed David about anything. How can I do it now? This damned money is going to wreck my marriage, this inheritance, why did he have to do that to me?

What I'd like to do, he probably won't want me to do it, is give it to the nuns — they could use it for something worthwhile. Maybe if I gave him half to help the Ethiopian Jews settling in Israel. He had tears in his throat when we were talking the other night, I could hear them in his voice, so proud of Israel for taking in those poor people, homeless, with nothing. Even though Israel is so small, and has so many problems of its own, it always makes room for Jews in the Jewish homeland, the state as it should be but almost never is, he said, a state that exists not just for the men who rule it but that is concerned with its people. Funny to hear him so emotional. Most of the time he's angry at Israel, thinks it's militaristic. But maybe the tears just meant he misses me more than he says.

Drying her hair with a towel, she walked naked into her bedroom and threw open the window. Cold air blasted in, but she stood there as if she were trying to bring herself back to consciousness.

Drunk, it's as if I'm drunk. Isn't that what they do to drunks? Toss them into cold showers? She wrapped the towel around her shivering body, pulled the window shut and went for her pajamas.

I need to get sober. Drunk on money am I? On the promise of money. On words that mean money. Nothing's really different, is it? I'm still the same person I was this morning, aren't I? Why couldn't I call David and tell him? Sat there for almost an hour but couldn't bring myself to pick up the phone.

That time in Jerusalem, when David attended that conference of chemical engineers. We stayed at that wonderful guesthouse, Mishkenot Sha'ananim. I couldn't sleep the first night and from there I could watch the sun come up over the walls of the Old City. First time I ever heard of the Shechinah, she-who-dwells-among-us, really means the neighbor-woman, but also the spirit indwelling, Esther said, the spirit in us that reaches out to others, who forms community. Esther, a rabbi in spirit but not allowed to be one, she's a woman, spoke like a prophet, a healer, she sold potions, secret teas and herbs. Lived above a potter's shop in the Old City, stone walls, stone streets, voices echoing, quiet in the Jewish Quarter, the Muslim and Christian quarters clamorous like bazaars, brilliant-colored silks hanging across the passageways to cool them from the sun, everyone pulling at you, come, come in, buy buy. But the street the pottery shop was on, Yoel Moshe Salomon, was only a narrow passage like an alley, the sidewalks so narrow you had to walk single file.

The tiny shops opened onto the street, their doors wide open. The potter's shop had a door leading to a courtyard where he kept his wheel. Esther tended the shop when he went for clay or to make a delivery or worked his wheel in the yard. I visited her while David attended the conference, sat and drank tea with her in the cool beautiful shop full of things made of earth, made by a man's hands. I'd like to go back, see if she's still there. She told me to walk around outside the walled city, just walk.

Out the Damascus Gate, brown hills spreading across the visible world, like an entire hemisphere baking under a merciless sun, a few trees dotting the terraced mountains, tall thin shapely cypresses, the olive groves, a few eucalyptus trees. Once long ago, plum trees grew in Jerusalem, she said. Gone now. I blotted out the ugly new buildings, Brigham Young University, the Hyatt, the Hilton. I tried to see it as I remembered it, I knew how it used to be, I knew I'd been there before in another life.

I stood on a mountain like that, the goats were running around my legs. I stood for hours with my arms folded staring out across the red-brown hills, there were more trees then, I remember olive trees and a few domed stucco houses. Only a few then. The sky was the same, the huge blue spread of it, I could see for miles, the dry red hills, the merciless land that everybody fought for, why I wonder? Did I know then? Watching for something, an army maybe, a horde of men, I was planning something, leading something, I had a heart of steel, I was a fighter, a leader of fighters. Hard land, scraping food from the earth with your fingernails, hard life, but I didn't question it, didn't question anything then, just tried to survive, one knew in those days what constituted survival. We all knew.

Tall I was for a woman and very thin, with a hawk face and long thick straggly black hair. The wind blew it around my face. I stood with folded arms, watching. Five thousand years ago maybe. And when I spoke, people listened; I uttered words and people attended to them, acted on them. Maybe I was a prophet.

Dawn rose over city walls ancient as tortoises, gilded and pocked and softened by time, but I remember when they were new. I knew this place better than my own name, yet standing there I didn't know my own name, didn't know my history, my past.

But I knew what I was, what I had been, what I had to do, something I never knew before. But I forgot it when I came home. How could I do that? Blanked out memory. Until now. What does ten million dollars have to do with that? All it will do is cause a breach between David and me, I can't stand that, I hate that. I wish he'd left me out of his will. I wish he'd forgotten me completely. I wish Ronnie would take it. It isn't what I wanted from him, it's not what I can use, what I need.

She pulled down the covers and got into the cold bed, still shivering.

And the worst part is there really isn't anyone I can talk to about this.

Elizabeth and Mary won't understand, I know they won't. David won't understand. The nuns won't understand why I don't just give it to them. But how could I be sure it wouldn't go to pay for some anti-abortion action or something like that. And if I gave it to Israel, how could I be sure they wouldn't use it to buy weapons? And that isn't what I want, not at all. To talk to Ronnie would be insulting: she *was* left out. God: I wonder how that must feel. Even worse than I feel now.

Ronnie lay naked on her bed staring at the ceiling, her arms thrown out to the sides. A bitter taste wouldn't leave her mouth, must have been the strawberries they'd had at dinner, strawberries in December, probably been picked unripe, flown up from California or Costa Rica. Sour, lingering taste. Everything had happened as she had expected. She hadn't expected anything different. What, after all these years he was going to remember something in her that touched him once, some little gleam of eye or run or jump that had caught at his heart? Insert some sweet little clause about my unacknowledged daughter . . . ? He never even looked at me until he raped me, of course he must have, under his eyes, when I wasn't aware, otherwise why would he . . . how would he even have known? No, if he'd been going to do it at all, he'd have done it to my face, in life; he'd never put evidence of his peccadillo on paper, in his will for all the world to know, remember, to be read and stamped and sealed in some court, to go down in the history books, the great statesman Stephen Upton. . . .

I didn't expect acknowledgment for one minute.

Not ever, never, not for one instant.

So why does it seem so bitter?

Money is shit, Freud said didn't he? Most people think money is love. Maybe I do too? Not love exactly, but giving it or not giving it does seem some kind of measure of feeling. Food too, Momma, her face flushed from cooking, laying out our dinner on the kitchen table so pleased, so pleased at there being enough food for us, for me, good food too, so happy that my eyes lit up at the smells, the heat rising, Momma's good food, I was so happy to eat it, made her happy too. Holding a hand, embracing, is sort of like that too. Only money is different, I don't know how, maybe because it's such a weapon. But so is food, look at the Ethiopians, the

Somalians, withholders of food during war . . . the Nazis in their death camps making people work while starving them.

Nothing is pure.

Love he didn't know about but he knew about giving and withholding. Surely he must have been loved once, held by his nanny, probably even his mother and father, rich kid in a house filled with luxury and ease, why not? Not like poor Rosa, grabbing up one kid under the waist while she stirred a pot with the other hand, a screaming toddler grabbing her around the legs. . . .

But he loved Momma. I know he did. She knew it too. Only he didn't know it.

Maybe Mary's right, maybe I should look through her things, maybe there is something, a note, a letter, a valentine. It would have meant so much to her even though she couldn't read it, she'd have known what it was . . . maybe he slipped once and put something on paper, gave it to her.

What crap. Why would he write a note to a woman who couldn't read?

Everything is exactly as I expected. Even them, the way they were different after Hollis left, you could see it, rich women suddenly, withdrawn, already planning how to spend it. Their whole world changed, Mary saved. Didn't I predict that this sisterhood wouldn't last? Is sisterhood possible only in hardship? Does it inevitably fall apart when things get easier, softer? Lilah and I were closer when we were having a hard time, trying to get by on our teaching assistant's pay, living in that awful room in Roxbury, crack addicts on every corner. Living on rice and beans and lettuce, we had such laughs, we made a wonderful joke out of our poverty. But once that damned Professor Witlow we called him Witless discouraged her so cruelly, she fell apart, left school, went and got a job as a secretary and moved out, didn't want me with her, probably resented the idea of supporting me. . . .

Not that the brothers are any better. Brotherhood too seems hard to sustain once one person is coopted, that's the secret, make it better for one and unity dissolves, stratification it's called. Destroys union, community.

They'll each go their own way now, back to the way they were in the beginning. Still, it was nice while it lasted. I liked it.

Her eyes moistened.

So if everything is exactly as I expected, why do I feel so alone suddenly? Alone in this house, in the world, in the universe, like a fragment broken off from a star that long ago whirled eons away, a tiny fragment whirling in orbit, alone in the dark cold silence forever and ever and ever. Or did I feel this way before and just not recognize it?

You are alone. You have neither mother nor father and your half siblings live in different worlds. You have no blood kin that accepts you.

She gazed out her window at the night sky, barely perceptible above the trees, then got up and stood there looking up. Dark tonight dark dark no stars. Sometimes the heavens are peopled with stars, dotted so heavily you imagine stars living on top of each other like street folks looking out the windows, sitting on stoops, standing in the shops, working at their sinks. . . .

Go back where you came from. Better there than here. Why should you stay here as their caretaker? Noradia's daughter, occupation passed down in the family, while they go off to their penthouses and forget they ever knew you.

What about the dissertation?

Fuck it.

Find a job somewhere, any kind of job, something to get you by, live decently, why aim for anything in their kind of world. There is nothing you can do, ever, that will make them recognize you as a full person, will force them to acknowledge you. The most you can ever be is part of a power bloc of the marginal, detested, feared, mocked, one more illegitimate trying to blast open the doors. Concentrate on what will make you happy: find a lovely warm woman, someone kind who will hold you, will understand you, someone you can let yourself cry with. . . .

Cry with?

Jesus, Ronnie. Someone to laugh with is more like it girl!

You're just depressed tonight. Left out. You let yourself come to love them. And believe they loved you.

What a fucking fool you are.

22

"You have to come," Elizabeth said quietly but with an almost threatening edge in her voice. "You must."

Ronnie shook her head.

"We need you," Alex wailed. "I'll feel so alone without you!" Then swiveling toward Elizabeth and Mary, reaching her hand out toward Mary's arm, she added swiftly, "Not *alone* alone. *You* know. But you all know these famous people and you know how to act with them and I don't and" — she turned back to Ronnie — "I need Ronnie to hold my hand."

"On the assumption that I don't know how to act with them either," Ronnie said dryly.

Distant and stiff again, Elizabeth thought. She's changed. She's been different since the will was read, Father's split us again. She garnered all her energy.

"We have to be together," Elizabeth insisted, "all four of us! We're sisters! We need each other! We need you! And you need us! Tell the truth, how will you feel sitting here alone while we go off to Father's funeral? Sitting in your room in front of your computer, you'll be miserable and lonely, you'll feel left out. And so will we!" She stood and put her hands on the sides of her head. "Don't let Father win again!" she cried.

Jesus H. Christ. Is she really that upset? Ronnie's face softened and she spoke quietly. "Look, Lizzie, Mary's right. If I'm with you, the press might make a scandal of it, might ask questions, investigate, write articles, print pictures of my mother, of me. . . . I don't want to be known as his bastard for the rest of my life!"

Elizabeth took her hands away from her head and shook it hard. She turned to Mary in despair. "Say something," she begged.

"We don't *know* they will," Mary mused. "It's possible they won't pay any attention to you. At all. Or to us, for that matter. Especially with the president coming to the funeral."

"Don't act mealymouthed with me!" Ronnie cried. "You know you'll be photographed in the limo, getting out of the limo, sitting in the pew together, shaking the president's hand, all that. You in your fancy black dresses and hats, and I'm supposed to follow you in my grubby jeans."

"Well, we could fix you up a bit, you know," Mary said haughtily. "You could be very attractive if you tried. Unless you consider it a badge of honor to wear nothing but jeans."

"Thanks a lot. I don't own anything else," Ronnie said between her teeth. Three pairs of jeans, some tops, two pairs of high-tops, a raincoat, a jean jacket and a down jacket: that's my wardrobe. I travel light.

"Well, maybe we could cut something down for you. Teresa has a gift with a needle. I have a black silk I don't wear anymore," Mary said, and almost thinking aloud, allowed her glance to travel to Ronnie's feet and legs, imagining them encased in black satin slippers and hose. . . .

Then saw Ronnie's face.

Mary sat back. "Maybe," she said, "you could come separately. You could drive yourself in the Alfa, sit in the back of the church. We'd make special arrangements for you . . ."

"What would that accomplish!" Elizabeth shouted. "That defeats the entire purpose! It's us — the four of us — in the face of him, don't you see?"

Alex stared at her. Ronnie gazed at the ceiling. Mary rearranged her face sympathetically and turned to Ronnie. "I understand how you feel. And I want you there too, I truly do, I feel it will be wrong if you're not." Her voice changed, as if suddenly she was feeling what she was saying. "Without you we feel incomplete, missing a link . . . part of our heart."

Ronnie met her eyes for the first time. She stood up and walked to the bar, set down her Coke glass and poured a scotch. "Anybody else?"

They all stood up, walked to the bar, poured drinks for themselves. Elizabeth put her hand on Ronnie's arm as she stood there; Mary put a hand on her head. Alex embraced her, refusing to let her go for a long minute. Then they all sat down again.

"Ohhh, what a day!" Mary sighed, tossing off her shoes.

"I don't see why you always wear high heels," Elizabeth said in an irritated voice. "Naturally you're exhausted. And they're terrible on your feet."

"I normally have no trouble with my feet, thank you very much, Elizabeth!"

"There must be some way to get around all this," Alex said biting her lip. "Some way to include Ronnie without calling undue attention to her. . . ."

"I could come as the daughter of the longtime family servant. Don't family retainers sometimes get invited to the funerals of their lords and masters? Isn't Aldo invited? And Mrs. Browning? Aren't they slotted into row two hundred or something?"

No one responded.

"Or you could wear a dress with a train, Mary, and I could walk behind you and hold it up off the ground."

She sipped her drink, glanced at their lowered faces, and shame-faced, leaned forward to them. "I'm sorry. I know you didn't create this situation, and I believe you don't like it either."

Three sets of eyes rose, warmed gratefully.

"Look. He never acknowledged me. I'm not going to acknowledge him. To attend his funeral, however I did it, would be to acknowledge him."

"But not acknowledging him is not acknowledging *us*," Alex argued. "We're tied to each other through him."

Ronnie sat back, pondered. "Yeah," she finally decided, "Stephen Upton gave us our biological bond, but he did everything he could to keep us from forming any other kind. Besides, how many sisters get along, care about each other? How many brothers do you know who are compet-itive and jealous of each other? We're tied to each other through ourselves, through our own efforts, our own . . . love." Her face flamed.

I can't believe I used that word.

"And if our tie unravels," she added slowly, deliberately, "it's because that love is insufficient."

They all looked at her.

"He came to *your* mother's funeral," Alex said with a wily look.

"And told me to get her shit out of his house right after it," Ronnie muttered.

They all stared at the rug.

When Ronnie finally looked up, her voice was firm, calm. "If I don't go, you'll feel incomplete — you say — and I'll feel left out. I admit it: I probably will. But if I go, the press may pick me up, pick up my relation to you, may make my life — and maybe yours — miserable. So for me the choice is between two potential miseries. But they're not equal. Say the press doesn't notice me, what are you going to do with me afterwards? Take me to the reception at Louisburg Square and introduce me to the governor? To your father's nephew, the possible next governor of Massachusetts? Or will you ask me to sit in the car with Aldo waiting for you? Or take the train home to Lincoln and walk back from the station? Or go to my friend Rosa's house over in Somerville and wait for you to pick me up? A *limo* in Somerville? She'd never live it down. Or go to Linda's on the T?

"Don't you see: whatever I do, I'm going to feel left out. There is no alternative to that for me."

They all gazed sadly at her. Then Mary got up and walked over and bent over Ronnie and kissed her lightly on the forehead.

Hollis had named himself head usher and was there early, meeting the great men as they stepped out of their limousines, making the appropriate conversation — a great loss, but a life well lived, a long life, needless to grieve unduly, and how are you, Chip, hear you pulled off a real coup with Bonn last week. . . .

But he couldn't breathe easy until he saw the Upton car pull up and *three* sisters get out, god that Mary, exquisite in black chiffon, even though he was getting on these days and couldn't always get it up, even though she was one of his best friends' daughters, he really wouldn't mind . . .

Anyway, the important thing is the wog bastard isn't with them, which is what his stomach had been worrying about all morning, forcing him to down several antacid tablets and finally Evelyn had made him swallow a couple of tablespoons of that disgusting white stuff. . . .

What would I have said to the president? the governor? Bill Benton of the BCLI Bank? How could it have been explained to the press? Claim no knowledge of course, mutter something about an old family retainer, but still . . .

It would have been impossible under any circumstances, the girl stood out so with her color, that short square Mexican body and those Upton eyes blazing in her head, Jesus, and even Cab's chin, so noticeable, so remarkable, remarkable looking girl she was or would be if she ever wore anything but dirty jeans and T-shirts. . . . If her mother looked anything like her, you could understand why Cab . . .

Well, but it was all right, he sighed, his smile properly subdued as he bowed, kissed their hands, three of them erect and dignified in black, all wearing hats, Mary's with a veil, so lovely, up the steps into the church, scandal that it was in such bad shape but it had a great history, it was central to New England history. And with the bishop presiding, it had seedy class, the mark of Boston in a way, not glitzy like New York or L.A.

Everyone else had already arrived except the governor and he'd accompany the president, they'd arrive last, there was their limousine now, Hollis stepped forward, prepared himself, the door opened, he stood erect, put out his hand, Mr. President, Mrs. Reagan, Governor, led them into the already full church, led them to the front row alongside former president Nixon and Helmut Schmidt and Richard von Weizsäcker, the president of West Germany, and the British ambassador. Jim Baker in the second row with the vice president and the widows . . . the daughters that is . . . and most of the Council on Foreign Relations. In the row behind them, in the Upton pew (marked with a discreet plaque), Mary's children sat with the nieces and nephews, most prominently Worth Upton IV, who was probably going to be the next governor of Massachusetts, and might even someday make president.

With grave approval, Hollis noted Peter Highland, the Texas oil billionaire, Arnold M. Richards, chairman of Calloosa, and dozens more chairmen of the richest corporations and foundations in the country. He counted three former secretaries of state, Elizabeth's boss at Treasury, lawyers from the most important firms in New York, Boston, and Washing-

ton. Looking around, he spotted the CEOs of every major insurance company in America. In the first row on the left-hand side, Henry Kissinger sat
beside a Rockefeller and the heads of the World Bank, the International
Monetary Fund, the former chairman of the Federal Reserve Board, the
present national security adviser. Every high-ranking Republican in the
country was there.

It was the funeral of the decade, and he, Hollis Whitehead, had
arranged the whole thing — with the assistance of the secretaries in the
office of the governor and some presidential aides, of course. He, Hollis
Whitehead, could count himself attorney for and trusted confidant of the
greatest men in the United States. With a solemn self-consciousness of the
weighty place in history borne by these great men, he took his place as
one — if only a minor one — among them, at the end of the row where
Evelyn waited for him beside the Upton nephews. And when he took his
wife's hand with bowed head and a humble heart, there were tears in his
eyes. Dear old Cab.

Ronnie sat at the computer for two hours, but barely saw the screen. She
was merely moving words about. She decided to clear her head by taking
a walk, and set out toward town, a longer walk than the one through the
back woods. Everything seemed gray — earth, trees, sky. Her face was
shadowed by the hood of her down jacket, but she was grateful for her
Indian face, which she knew seemed impassive, concealed any tumult
inside her. My face has built-in privacy, she thought.

They hadn't acted the way she thought they would last night, she
had been being her old negative self. They hadn't totally abandoned her,
they cared about her, cared to some degree anyway, no, they cared a lot,
they had the same feeling of connection she had, they too seemed to feel
that their connection mattered profoundly, that it kept each of them from
feeling like a fragment, the terrible feeling of being like a discarded hand
or eye floating in space, eternally in search of the arm or head it belonged
to. Blood ties were not like friendship, friendship could be changed, blood
couldn't, not ever — a family was something you were irrevocably tied to.
It survived disagreements, conflict, even hatred. Even if the connection
were severed, it went on living, it had a life of its own. People who hated
their parents or siblings might avoid them for decades yet if they were

reconnected with them, symbolically or really, they could rise into a tornado of ferocity, explode, even kill. Blood ties were stronger than marriage by far — husbands and wives could divorce and completely forget about the existence of the other. Look how little impression any of Mary's marriages made on her — all except the last one, Don. . . .

But blood ties . . . ! Look at Mary yearning for Elizabeth's love, approval, all these years; and Alex all these years gnawing her heart out for her sisters. And Elizabeth denying it, pretending she didn't need anybody, but she was the loneliest of all of them, longed most for . . . something. No one ever longed for me of course. Oh, Momma did, what am I thinking? But here I was, completely unaware of wanting them, yet all the while wanting to be recognized as their sister, as his child, wanting it almost more than I wanted to breathe or eat or walk and I didn't even know it.

To live, you must love, Ronnie.
Is that what she meant?

Okay, so they feel it, but strongly enough to counter the effect of all those millions of dollars they're inheriting? Strongly enough that when they leave here I'll be anything to them but an embarrassment, a sister remembered but left behind, like some half-wit half sister who married years ago and is now an alcoholic slob living in a trailer camp out west somewhere.

Too many differences among us. Even the surface ones are amazing really. Lizzie and Mary were at least raised Episcopalian and I guess they consider me Catholic and Alex seems to consider herself Jewish.

But even if we were all the same everything, we'd have trouble understanding each other. Our take on things isn't the same. We don't inhabit the same mindspace, and we certainly don't share the same . . . heartspace. Share enough feeling that we can reach across all the extremes of what we don't share.

It's like the problem all the women's movements have faced — women come from different classes, religions, colors. . . . No movement has ever been able to unify for very long, or in large numbers, can't get past all the differences. Rich women need maids, need other women to be poor. Hatred among white, black, brown, yellow, red, all the variations, all the religions and splinter religions, how clever they are, the ones who made up, set up this system. Keeps us at each other's throats while they sit safely in luxury raking in all the moolah. Start wars, send us off to kill each other while they stay home, make laws and weapons.

We all join in wholeheartedly, men hate women, whites blacks, straights hate gays, religions hate religions. . . .

And you're so pure? Jesus, I do the same thing, participate in this. All my life I've been part of it. Who don't I hate? Rich white bitches looking down on a little *chicana,* straights who act homophobic, whites who treat people of color like a servant class, women who spend more on a dress than a working woman earns in a month, men who buy two three-thousand-dollar suits, exorbitantly expensive cars, stereos, airplanes, all the male toys, men who treat women like a servant class, men who look at women as if they were things to buy, who whistle at them on the streets, men who rape, murder, beat women, men who pay women like me too little to live on, men who pass laws that harm women, men who think they own women's bodies, men who vote themselves more and more power, men who build armaments then make us pay for them out of our taxes, men who poison the entire earth, men who rule, men like him. . . .

Him.

But how can I not hate him? How can I not hate his kind? How can I not hate the system that gives them this power?

And if I give up my hate, how do I hold myself together?

She stood still on the grass under an old oak, thinking. Then she walked on, hands in her pockets, head bowed, tiredly, like a weary old woman.

Alex, Mary, and Ronnie were drinking wine in the playroom. "Not that I need any more," Alex sighed. "Good heavens, there was so much food and drink at that man's house — what was his name?"

"Worth, idiot!"

"Yes." Alex's voice rose indignantly. "Worth a lot!" she giggled a little tipsily. "People were drinking so much! I never saw people drink so much. Heavens, that President Nixon! And that big tall man everyone seemed to like so much, who joked about being in enemy territory, why did he say that?"

"He's a Democrat," Mary said dryly.

"Oh. Well, his face was the color of a watermelon. But all of them really . . . and they are the people who run this country? It's shocking!"

Elizabeth had not returned with the others. She had had Aldo drop her at her mother's apartment in the Prudential Center ("Horrible place," Mary bristled), where she would spend the night "and maybe even part of tomorrow!" Mary announced in shock. "I can't believe she'd spend time with that bitch."

Alex glanced at her. "Do you know Elizabeth's mother?"

Mary raised her eyebrows. "I met her once or twice. Years ago, in Boston, when Lizzie lived with her."

"So how do you know she's a bitch?"

"Well, listen to how Lizzie talks about her!"

Alex looked at her penetratingly, unsmiling.

Mary raised her shoulders haughtily and turned her face away.

Alex sipped her wine, gazing at Mary over the rim of her glass.

"Really, Alexandra, you act as if you were our . . . priest . . . or something. What makes you so superior?"

Alex looked surprised. "Is that how I'm acting? I'm sorry. It's hard to know how to act when there are things you want to say and you feel you can't say them. I always used to feel — too — embarrassed — ashamed — to say what I thought, and I decided I wouldn't do that anymore. It's hard to change your whole self."

"Why do you need to?" Ronnie wondered.

"Because I'm a different person now. I'm . . . well, Alexandra."

"So, *Alexandra,* what is it you're dying to say?" Mary asked sarcastically.

Alex looked at her fingers. "Just that it's so easy for us to call each other bitches, cows, all the things women call women — you know. Especially our mothers. Maybe Elizabeth's mother is a decent woman. We don't know. I think about how angry I am with my mother, how I — I actually hate her at moments, for lying to me, for not telling me, for letting me walk around feeling hollow where . . . something important — my heart, or my stomach or my courage — was supposed to be. But I *know* my mother is a good woman, a kind person, I know she meant the best for me. I have so much . . . bitterness, I guess it is . . . because I needed her to do something she didn't do. Because I'm her daughter."

Mary studied her rings. "Okay. So you're saying I'm just jealous that Elizabeth *has* a mother to visit and I don't."

"That *isn't* what I was saying!"

"Well, but maybe it's true."

Alex sighed.

Ronnie was gazing at the two of them still dressed in their black dresses and hose and heels, Mary in a chiffon with a full skirt in layered panels, Alex in a silk and wool sheath that showed off her slender graceful figure. Ronnie was wearing dirty jeans and a torn sweatshirt. Especially for the occasion, she pronounced formally — but silently.

"So how was the funeral?" she asked finally.

"Oh, splendid," Mary sneered. "Totally splendid. Eulogies by the bishop, the president, the governor, the former president, the former secretary of state, the senior partner in his old law firm, oh, and much much more . . . ! They all found him the most distinguished man of his generation, of course that was easy for them to grant him, he's not part of *their* generation. They called him brilliant, a great political strategist, god we probably wouldn't have won World War II without him, a great sense of humor — he must've reserved it for men, at least I never saw it — a man who could keep secrets — well, that part's true — confidant of the heads of state of half the western world, along with the heads of their secret service agencies, their banks, their military forces . . ."

"I didn't hear that, Mary!" Alex protested.

Mary grimaced and leaned toward Alex. "I know, sweetheart," she said. She reached out and patted her hand.

"Oh, was I being naive again?" she wailed faintly.

"So who was there?" Ronnie asked hungrily.

"I told you!" Mary repeated several dozen names, starting with the president, but the last ten or so were unknown to Ronnie.

"The real rulers of our world, my dear," Mary explained.

"And where did they all sit?"

"Hollis and the governor's protocol officer drew up a list." Mary sketched the seating plan for Ronnie. "Most of the family sat in the Upton pew," she concluded.

"What about Elizabeth's mother?"

"Oh, she was someplace in the back. Way back. I didn't see where."

"And was there a servants' row?" Ronnie asked with a nasty smirk on her face.

Mary bristled. "I don't know. I think Aldo was sitting someplace in the back, but Mrs. Browning said she'd just stay here and do her job, that she'd prefer to mourn in her own way."

"Ummm."

How did the girl manage to make everything she said sound so snippy?

"And how was the reception?"

"Splendid. Overflowing with food, drink, and famous names."

"Did the president come?"

"No, he had to fly to California to give a speech. But Nixon and Vice President Bush stopped in for fifteen minutes. Worth was quietly over-joyed, you could see him counting support as he pumped hands. I'll bet you anything he runs for governor next election. Hollis was so impressed, if he hadn't thought it undignified, he would have knelt to him. . . ." Mary laughed.

"And were you formally presented to all of them?"

"Yeees!" Alex drawled, sprawling back in her chair. "God I was livid with fright. My hands were cold as ice. But they didn't really even see you, you know? Except Mary, they kind of looked at her, didn't they Mare?" She made goo-goo eyes at Mary, who grimaced-grinned. "It didn't matter. Except I wasn't sure if I was supposed to curtsey or not, and I kept wanting to and Lizzie kept hauling me up by my arm." She giggled again.

"What's Worth's house like?"

"Smaller and darker but grander than this one. No comfortable back playrooms or sun rooms. But it has a similar feeling. It smells exactly the same as this one, you know — beeswax and lavender — and every surface shines. Full of old furniture and paintings, some of the windows have nineteenth-century stained glass. Nice. It hasn't been let go like this place."

"And what did people talk about?"

"What people always talk about — gossip about each other: sex, pol-itics, money — only in a disguised way of course, you know, deals."

"I would have hated it, wouldn't I?"

"You probably couldn't have contained yourself. You would have leapt up on a table and begun giving a speech damning all these men to eternal hellfire. You might have livened things up a bit." Mary raised an eyebrow. "So you *did* wish you were with us! You would have liked to be there!" Mary crowed.

"Just wondering what particular kind of obscenity it was," Ronnie said airily, then smiled nastily. "So Mary, didn't you spot a potential husband in that huge crowd?"

She grimaced. "Several. Really makes one wonder about oneself. Ones *old* self." She turned to Alex.

Alex smiled at her radiant with gratitude. "So you *do* understand!"

Ronnie looked at them curiously. Alex was gazing through the sliding doors to the terrace at the dark woods beyond. Her face wore an expression of almost blissful serenity. Mary was staring down at her hands, folded in her lap, as if she were contemplating some profundity. Christ. If these were the new women, give me back the old.

"So Elizabeth's mother did come to the funeral?"

"Yes. In an imitation Chanel suit, can you imagine?" Mary said acidly.

Well, the new Mary's not *that* different from the old.

Alex spoke up petulantly. "We didn't even get to meet her! I was so disappointed, I told Elizabeth I wanted to meet her. She just disappeared afterwards, of course, she wasn't invited to Worth's house. But we could have gone up when we dropped Elizabeth off and had a drink with her! I told Elizabeth that! But she just brushed me off, she just said, 'Some other time, Alex.' She said there wasn't enough time but I don't know what the rush was. She didn't even remember to call me Alexandra. She certainly had time for all those important men. She wasn't too busy to talk to them!" she added in a wounded voice.

I think I liked the old Alex better.

Alex seemed to sulk for a while, then turned brightly to Ronnie. "Oh, it was a horrible day, Ronnie! Horrible! So stiff and boring and . . ."

"Pretentious," Mary put in.

"YES!" Alex cried. "I wish you'd been there, Ronnie! We could have giggled together."

Well, maybe she's not so bad.

"So what did you do today?"

Ronnie shrugged. "Took a walk. Did a little soul-searching."

"You too? I thought you already had everything figured out, had done enough soul-searching for your whole lifetime," Mary said, not maliciously, even, perhaps, with affectionate acceptance.

"You did?"

"Sure. You seem to be the only one of us who has it together in her head. Your generation, I guess."

"But maybe what I have is a headful of garbage. . . ."

Mary looked over at her appraisingly. "Well, if so, it's no worse garbage than we carry around. At least you have a purpose in your life."

"I have a purpose in my life," Alex said dreamily.

"And what is that, pussykins?" Mary asked patronizingly.

"To be a blade of grass and crack concrete," Alex confessed.

A blade of grass to crack concrete. Imagine that. What can she mean by it? But isn't that the ideal, somehow? Supple and green, tender shoots of grass, nourishing earth, animals, giving off the wonderful sweet wet smell of dew in the morning and when it's cut the dew just seems to pour out of it and yet it is so powerful, it can crack concrete, burrow the road, check a marble mausoleum, eat up a city if you give it time, crack through all the life-killing edifices of our effort to prove that we preside over grass, that we are supreme. . . .

Who would have thought of Alex coming up with something like that? Isn't that what I want to be, isn't that what environmental work means to me, don't I study a moss that stops the onslaught of the machines, a moss that stands up and cries out that its place in nature is essential, that we cannot do without it, that each small thing figures as intrinsically in the whole as the large things, and nothing is marginal. . . .

Ronnie was sitting cross-legged on her bed in her underpants and T-shirt, staring at the night sky and smoking.

Where did she ever come up with that ambition? And how does she expect to realize it? With her millions, maybe. What on earth will her husband say? Giving all that money to the starving Armenians? Hey, Alex, how about a little glance closer to home. . . .

Well, that's her problem.

Mine is this hate.

How not be part of it, a hating structure? How escape and still stand for yourself? Can you give up hate and still fight, still stand as hard as you have to?

Can you oppose without hatred?

Hating — that's drawing a line in the sand and saying, okay, across this line is evil, on this side is only murky. Can you understand and oppose without hating?

How.

To live it is necessary to love, Ronnie.

How can I love . . . ?

Try to think of him giving you one kind glance, one touch, performing a single kind act. . . .

Forget it.

Try to think of him giving Momma a kind glance, touch, act. . . .

He probably did, but not in my sight.

Try to think of him ever showing any emotion at all. . . .

Desperate, angry he was all the time, insisting Momma was getting better when she was obviously dying.

When she died. She just put her hand on mine, I was sitting on her bed, and she stopped seeing, just stopped, you could see it, and I cried out, I put my hands over my face, I was crying hard, noisily. He was standing behind me, standing there because I'd told him I thought he should come in . . . and he put his hand on my arm, felt like a steel claw, I pulled away roughly, it reminded me . . . but he wasn't trying to get me, he was shouting in my ear, yelling at me, no, at her, "No! No! No!"

23

It was Ronnie in the Alfa, not Aldo, who met Elizabeth's train from Boston at the Lincoln station Sunday afternoon. It was warm for December, like a day in early autumn, and she had put the top down. Lizzie surprised her by hugging her — a little stiffly — when they met, but then subsided into almost complete silence. She was still wearing her funeral dress, a well-cut black suit with a high stand-up neck, but she was carrying a large unwieldy box in a shopping bag. Elizabeth never even carried a handbag, only a thin wallet in a suit pocket, like a man. At most, she carried an attaché case.

"Never could stand the Thatcher handbag look," Elizabeth had muttered once.

"She's always trying to imitate the dear old Queen," Mary had drawled, adding, "Although such a gift for dowdiness *must* be genetic."

So Ronnie blurted, "What's that you're carrying?"

"Something for Mary," Elizabeth said and closed her lips.

"So how was your visit with your mother?" Ronnie asked more carefully.

Elizabeth took off her small black hat and unloosed the chignon she had tied together at the nape of her neck. She flung her head back and her hair flew out in the wind, loose and straight, a dull brown streaked with silver. She lighted a cigarette.

"Okay," she said. "Better than I could have hoped. Or even imagined."

"What does that mean?"

She was silent for a time. "Something's happened. She's changed. Of course, I haven't seen her in a long time. Over a year. And for years we've had only brief visits — drinks and dinner before I caught a flight to someplace or other. We haven't spent a whole evening together in I don't know how many years. She may have been changing all along and I didn't know it.

"She lives high up, in a boring box of a place but with windows overlooking the whole city, they're almost glass walls. We could see the skyline and the sunset and the lights turn on across the city — it's very splendid, but somehow off-putting, maybe not what I'd like to look at every night, not a view that makes you feel serene, at home. She was still dressed in her fake Chanel, Mary said it was — I wouldn't know the difference — those Nancy Reaganish suits with gold braid and all those cheap-looking chains look equally real and equally ugly to me. . . .

"We were having cocktails. . . . Jesus, she doesn't even drink Manhattans anymore! She was drinking white wine, while I was so anxious, I had a scotch, for god's sake . . . and she began to lecture me on abortion. She kept referring to Catholics for Free Choice. Full of fervor she was, so I said, 'Does that mean if you had it to do now, you'd do it differently?'

"She leaned back and lighted one of these long white cigarettes with a gold tip and blew out smoke and thought. Then she looked away from me. She was staring toward the window, she's thin, her profile had a kind of — tough-bird nobility almost — you know, that some older people get?

"She said, 'You know, you are what you've become, what your life has made you. I could no more wish I'd done differently then than I could wish I didn't exist or that you didn't exist. And I'm very proud that you exist.' "

Elizabeth's voice faltered but Ronnie carefully did not turn her head. Trees whirred past on the curving country road. Elizabeth leaned back and breathed in deeply the cold piney air.

"Then" — Elizabeth gave a deep gurgle of laughter in her throat —

"she became the mother I remember! She said, 'But whatever I am, whatever I've become, I'll tell you one thing — I am fucking glad I'm alive and he's dead, that I lived to get *his* money and use it for *my* purposes! We Callahans never had a pot to pee in — not in the old country and not here. Maybe we would have if some British killers hadn't decided that everything we had was theirs — maybe not. Maybe then it would have been some Irish killers, or some Roman Catholic Italians decided the same thing. But one thing I've learned these last years — killers get the money, the rest of us get *tsuris!*'

" '*Tsuris!*' I burst out laughing. 'Where'd you learn that word!'

" 'Oh, didn't I tell you I have a new friend, well, we've been friends for a few years now. She lives two floors up, Gloria Abzug, she's a widow but she doesn't play cards. She gets involved in community things, she's really helped me a lot, taught me a lot, she gets me out and doing! When I think how for all those years I sat around waiting for some society woman — any society woman — to call me to play bridge, to have tea or cocktails! Gloria ACTS! We help out at the Rape Crisis Center, at the shelter for battered women, and every Sunday we help feed the homeless in the church. I want you to meet her, you'll love her, she's so full of energy.'

"She stopped, then, looked almost wistful, looked in my eyes. 'She has *hope*,' she said, as if that were a staggering fact. 'Hope for the world. It's her word, *tsuris*, it means trouble, pain, it's Yiddish, it's a great word, isn't it?'

"I said I knew the word, but that the Catherine Callahan Upton I knew would have bitten a little piece off her own tongue before she'd use a Yiddish word. She said so much the worse for the little bigot!" Elizabeth crowed. "How do you like that?" She caroled laughter, and Ronnie gave her a little smile.

When her laughter subsided, Elizabeth put her hand on top of Ronnie's, resting on the gearshift. "Ronnie. I don't want us to lose you when this is over. *I* don't want to lose you. I mean that."

Ronnie almost hit a hedge as she turned her head slightly to see Elizabeth's face while cornering fast. Looking away, she corrected swiftly, and by the time she glanced back, Elizabeth had turned away.

When they reached the house, Mary and Alex were standing under the portico waiting for them, and embraced Lizzie as if she'd been away for months.

"How was it, how was it!" Alex cried.

"Oh, Liz, poor baby, was it awful?" Mary embraced her.

Elizabeth had missed lunch and they needed to talk so they decided to have a full if very early tea in the sun room, with sandwiches and cakes.

"Was she awful?" Mary asked sympathetically.

"No, she's changed. She thinks about other people. She's been seeing her family again. She wants to use her inheritance to help them. The Callahans have fallen on hard times. One of her sisters had to go out and clean houses after her husband was laid off. Their daughter was going to have to go to work even though she had a scholarship to Boston College. So Mother is going to buy a garage for her brother-in-law, she thinks she's going to save the family. It's amazing how playing Lady Bountiful enlarges the spirit. I don't imagine it can continue for very long. Resentment is bound to boil up. But at least she's being useful."

"So money heals. Is that the message?" Ronnie asked in a rough voice.

Elizabeth shrugged.

"Did you tell her?" Mary asked.

Elizabeth shook her head. "It was my one merciful gesture."

Ronnie glanced at Elizabeth. "Did you tell them that she supports abortion now?"

Elizabeth lighted a cigarette and sat forward. "She said, 'Nowadays girls had better have abortions.'" Elizabeth minced her mouth, speaking in a tough deep monotone, becoming her mother: "'Because, Elizabeth Catherine, you know as well as I do that what happened to me couldn't happen today. Nowadays, families like the Uptons, if they can't buy a girl off, they have her killed. Look at Teddy Kennedy and Chappaquiddick. Look at the Kennedys and Marilyn Monroe. And Stephen wasn't a married man — these days it isn't considered scandalous for a single man to get a woman pregnant and refuse to marry her. Don't they do it all the time?'

"'Thing was, they were grooming him for a political career, Mother.'

"'Oh, I know, I know, I see it all now, I saw it years ago actually, if not at the time. Then all I could feel was my own broken heart, my wrongedness, all I could see was the injustice. You know I don't go to Mass anymore, I don't feel like a Catholic anymore — any church that would sell a Protestant the annulment he wanted even though it harmed one of their own . . . But I think the Catholics are right about sin. Sin is what you do that hurts yourself. It may or may not hurt others — that's incidental — but mainly, it is a violation of the self. My sin was — well, I don't know what it was. I mean, I don't know what the church would call it. But I know I hurt myself, sinned, by eating away at my own heart for years and years. And I know that hurt you.' Then my mother, queen bitch of the world, leans forward toward me and puts her hand on my knee and says, 'And I am profoundly sorry for that' and bursts into tears."

Elizabeth stood up suddenly. "Got to get out of these clothes!" she announced, disappearing from the room.

In her own room, Elizabeth stood frozen, remembering how, stock still, she had stared at her mother and listened to her sob. Pity scraped its nails across her heart, but she could not move. Her face was gray, stony, eyes dead. The older woman sobbed, her head resting in her hand. When she finished, she raised her head. Her mascara streaked down her face, which had broken out into patches of deep crimson. Mucus rolled down her upper lip, and she wiped it away with her hand. She did not look at Elizabeth. They sat there in silence, neither moving, for a long time. Only now did Elizabeth allow a few tears to trickle down her cheeks.

The packing had begun. Alex walked around the house almost sulkily, picking up the few remnants of herself she had strewn around it — a book on El Salvador (the only book the sisters had seen her read), some mission pamphlets, a hankie stuck in the cushion of a chair, a purse. She piled them on the staircase, a disregard of the rules of the house which Mary noticed with a shudder. Alex's shoulders slumped, her hair hung limp, she looked like a woman heading for jail rather than home. Occasionally, she would gather up a pile and carry it upstairs, where they could hear her clumping around suitcases, dropping piles of shoes.

"I don't know why you don't get Teresa to help you," Mary chided, passing her room. "She came in today — it's her Sunday off — just to help us pack."

Mary herself had strewn her belongings across the house — it would be impossible to pick up all her remains and she didn't even try. Video-tapes, notebooks, 33 rpm records she'd found at a used-book shop in Concord to play on the old stereo, cassettes and many books. She'd sprinkled around a handbag or two, scarves, earrings missing mates, magazines she wanted to keep, magazines she was discarding. She gathered and sighed, dumping the load in Teresa's arms, then fell into an easy chair, sighing "Oh, I can't do any more now!" Teresa dutifully carried the pile up to Mary's room, where she tried to order and pack the even greater disarray of Mary's possessions. Every once in a while she'd creep into the play-room, where Mary lay on the couch listlessly watching a documentary on whales, and ask: "The white satin underwear won't all fit into the satin bags, ma'am. Is it all right if I put some of it into the case without a bag?" or "I've filled up the shoe bag, but there're three pairs left over, ma'am. What should I do with them?"

Finally Teresa announced, "All the dresses don't seem to fit into the dress case, ma'am."

"They don't? Oh, right," Mary recalled. "I have bought a few things in Boston. Just do the best you can, Teresa — I'll come up in a minute. Maybe I'll leave some things here. In fact" — she gathered energy, rising, "I'll come up now and sort things out. Might as well leave some things here. I'll probably be coming back, sometime," she added in an undertone.

Elizabeth, who had spent days repacking her father's papers for the archives for which they were destined, packed her own books and papers efficiently and swiftly, and closed the study door on an immaculate room by five that evening, her word processor packed, her books boxed, her disks secure in a lead container — although she was no longer planning to fly back to Washington. She had decided that with all their gear, it would be easier for the sisters if Aldo drove them all home.

She announced this at six over drinks.

"No, no!" Alex insisted. "I'll take the plane. Wilmington's way out of your way."

Elizabeth looked crestfallen.

"Are you sure?"

"Positive." She sounded it.

"Well, we'll drop you at Logan then."

But Mary was delighted to be driven home and quite cheerfully described the rather extensive wardrobe she was leaving behind. Alex paced the room with her arms wrapped around her body. Her packed bags were already set by the door.

The playroom suddenly looked spartan, although it still held the piles of games and records, the Ping Pong table, the card table, the overstuffed chairs. Once they had all gathered in the room, they were silenced by a sudden sense that the house had cast out their detritus, their droppings, their spoor, had turned its back on them, forgotten their smell and taste and feel, even though they were still physically present. Mary sighed faintly, Ronnie put down her paper, Elizabeth her book. Alex plunked into a chair.

Elizabeth spoke first. "Shall we have champagne tonight?"

"Wonderful, darling," Mary fluttered.

"Sure, why not," Alex muttered.

Ronnie shrugged. She did not want to admit she had never had champagne and as she saw them accept their fluted glasses was careful not to copy the way Mary and Elizabeth held them, but grabbed the goblet like a water glass.

Elizabeth leaned forward, holding out her glass: "To us," she said, and stretched her glass out to clink against theirs.

They followed, sipped, and Mary threw herself back against the cushions of her chair, tossed off her shoes, sighed, and said, "I want you all to know I never expected anything like this! It's the second-best thing that ever happened to me, getting close" — she leaned forward —"finding my sisters."

Alex blew her nose.

"What is the matter with you today, Alexandra," Mary scolded. "You'd think you were being sent to Coventry."

"Coventry?"

"To — punishment, instead of home to your loving family . . ."

Alex burst out in a teary voice, "It isn't the same for me, you know. As for you. You're happy to have that money, you need it, you wanted it, I didn't. All it does is complicate my life, make things hard. I probably will have to fight with David and I don't want to fight with David, I don't want to be angry with him, I don't want to . . ." She lowered her head. Her voice emerged anguished. "I don't want to dislike him."

She raised her head. Her eyes were tormented. "And what about my mother? Do I tell her what I know? I know it would be kinder not to, but I don't think I can stand not to say it, to scream at her, why did she obliterate my memory? Why did she lie? Years of lies!"

She wiped her face with a hankie she held crumpled in her hand and blew her nose. She sipped champagne. She drew a deep breath. "And then I have to tell my family — find the strength to tell my family . . ." She stopped.

"WHAT!"

"What I intend. Want. To do."

"What do you intend to do?" Mary was sitting on the edge of her chair.

"I want . . . to build a clinic. In El Salvador. For the peasants. With the nuns."

Three faces gaped at her. "And do what?" Ronnie gasped.

"Live down there. Part of the year, anyway. Running the clinic. I can do it, I know I can, I've worked in hospitals for years as a volunteer, and I learn fast. I'll have the best help — the nuns are terrific doctors, nurses, administrators — and I have the money. I want to be a blade of grass," she almost wailed, "but I don't know how any of them — David, my kids — they're not going to understand, I know it!"

Ronnie looked at her in awe. "God," she whispered. "Are you serious?"

Alex sat back roughly, threw her sweater off her shoulders, her face set. "Of course I'm serious! I've been mulling things over all these weeks! I know what I need to do, what my life is about now. David — oh, he's sweet, we have a good marriage, the kids are adorable, but they don't need me, not really, not anymore. And maybe the truth is, I don't need them — I need something else now, I need this."

"But you'd sacrifice your life!" Mary cried.

"SHIT, Mary!" Alex exclaimed. "This *isn't* a sacrifice! That's the point! If it were, maybe I could feel easier about it, isn't that what women are supposed to do, sacrifice? This is what I need to do, what my whole being longs to do. What kind of life do you think I have? I get up and make breakfast for my family, I clean up the house, I shower and go off to some volunteer work, I come home, I go marketing, I cook dinner, I talk to my kids and David, I clean up, we watch television . . . that isn't a life! It's — marking time! I want more! I want to use myself!"

She emptied her champagne glass at a swallow, leaned forward, holding it out for more. Elizabeth refilled it.

"I never feel as alive as when I'm working in the hospital, helping people — but what can I do, I'm not a doctor or a nurse or a therapist, there's a limit to what I can do. But with money and medicine and a clinic — I can do so much!"

"So it's a kind of power you want," Elizabeth concluded unjudgmentally.

Alex sat back. "YES! YES! That's it, exactly."

"Well" — Mary still seemed nonplussed — "it's certainly admirable."

"It isn't admirable! It isn't anything! It's just what I need. A kind of power, as Lizzie says. That's in me and needs to come out. It's no more admirable than Lizzie wanting to become secretary of state or Ronnie trying to become an environmental scientist, or you writing poetry. It's just what I need."

"There is some difference in the goals," Elizabeth remarked dryly.

"I don't know," Alex insisted stubbornly. "Don't you think that if you were secretary of state you could make people's lives better? Doesn't Ronnie feel that way . . . ?"

"I can't quite claim that," Elizabeth said with a little smile, "whatever Ronnie can claim."

"It's an eternal question whether poetry ever made anyone's life better," Mary said smiling. "But mine certainly won't, since it isn't even published."

"Oh, Mary! Won't you read us one? Just one of your poems?"

"Oh, everything's packed."

"Surely you remember *one?*"

Mary shook her head. "Not tonight."

"PLEASE! For me! Before my ordeal!"

Mary set down her glass. "All right. I wrote one today, it's still in my head. It's kind of rough. Don't tell me what's wrong with it, all right? It's called 'Father.' "

Father's large warm body pressed against mine
When I was in tears at four.
His encompassing arms

made me know what safe meant.
What is a father?
Safety, warmth, body wholly there, mine and his, always.

Father's large laugh aimed at the others
His talk, his eyes, all for them.
Father's gone.
What is a father?
An absence.
A girl became invisible.

Father's large warm body pressed against mine
When I was near sleep at eight.
His encompassing arms
made me know what fear meant.
What is a father?
Thief in my own bosom, taking
from an invisible child
all she had left: her will.

In the silence, Elizabeth lighted a cigarette. Ronnie gazed at her thumb. Alex looked awed. "Oh, that's wonderful, Mary! Just wonderful! So powerful!"

Mary shrugged. "It's rough."

Elizabeth stood up suddenly. "Oh! I have something for you. Something to return," she added, and walked over to the shelves where there lay a large battered cardboard box in a plastic bag. "It isn't wrapped, but then it isn't a present," Elizabeth said, handing it to Mary.

Mary took her time opening it. She pulled off the cover, and found inside a child's tea set, tiny porcelain cups and saucers and plates, a sugar bowl with a broken top, a chipped pitcher.

She looked up at Elizabeth in total surprise.

"Your tea set. The one I stole. I'm returning it. It's sat all these years on a shelf in my mother's apartment."

"You didn't need to, Lizzie," Mary protested.

"Yes I did."

* * *

Before they parted for the evening, they went over their arrangements. For the time being at least, Ronnie would remain at Lincoln to oversee the house with Mrs. Browning and Teresa and Aldo as a skeleton staff. In the spring, she would supervise the gardeners in restoring the grounds preparatory to selling the house. For this work she would be paid two hundred dollars a week — she would not take more. Elizabeth and Mary promised to remain in constant touch — Alex too, as soon as she had sorted out her life. Their talk had calmed her down — no one had hooted with derision, no one had exploded about her duty to her children, her husband, her husband's family, her mother. . . . And she had clarified her ideas in her own mind, put them in some semisolid form that gave her the strength to go forward. But the other sisters had made no decisions, or if they had, they did not discuss them. Ronnie watched them hedge around their futures, making bets with herself about the chances of Mary's returning to her old life, Elizabeth being able to end her cruel isolation. They hedged around each other too, unwilling to bring up any subject that might stir contention, emphasizing that side of them that Elizabeth always called — with contempt — women's "niceness." They embraced deeply that night before going their separate ways to bed, and rested their heads against each other, standing in a circle.

The car drove off at nine Monday morning. Ronnie waved them out the drive from the portico. She went back to the sun room for another cup of coffee and what she swore was her last cigarette. The house fell into a gloomy silence. Nothing to look forward to, no lunchtime laughter or argument, no cocktails at six, no laughable conversation that tiptoed around the servants at dinner. Gone. Forever.

She felt too empty to work, and took a long walk in the woods behind the house, planning to make plans. It took her some hours, but she eventually got down to work, driven by the haunting silence of the place, its emptiness of sisters. Can't stay here long, too lonely. Have to make progress. She began to work in earnest: she drew up a schedule, she listed references to be obtained, and she scheduled trips to Boston to go to the library and see friends — to keep from going mad. After that, she got down to the collating of her data.

The day passed in a silence more brooding for the memories that hung in the house. She worked on doggedly, but could not muster real concentration. And when she saw that Mrs. Browning had set her place for dinner at the huge dining room table, she blanched.

"Can I just have a small table set up in the playroom?" she almost whined, and Mrs. Browning nodded knowingly. She's thinking breeding tells, Ronnie thought, but didn't care. She turned on the television set while she ate, barely tasting the food.

She woke in the same stuporous state the next day, but it was rainy, cold, and very windy, too miserable for walking outdoors.

I'll clean Momma's room.

The sturdy Teresa was pleased to help. "About time," she muttered, "a regular rat's nest in there." Ronnie dumped the contents of her mother's chest and closet on the bed, then Teresa shoved the two chests into the hall, pushed the bed around and vacuumed under and around it, up the walls, in the closet. She pulled down the shabby curtains, which came to pieces in her hands, and sneezed at the dust, commenting volubly on the filthiness of the room. She washed the windows, the moldings around them, and the doors. With Aldo's help, they carried one chest up to the attic. As Teresa vacuumed and dusted and wiped up soot (see how easy it gets to let other people do the hard work, Ronnie, she told herself), Ronnie folded and sorted her mother's possessions. She counted:

6 pairs cotton underpants, one ragged
6 pairs pantyhose, two ragged
2 bras, 34D, both soiled and torn, pink
1 bra, 34D, black satin, little used
1 pair black satin underpants, slightly torn
6 cotton housedresses in varying states of disrepair
2 black uniforms with white cap and apron
1 pair white nurse's shoes
2 pairs smelly clogs
1 pair shabby black heels
1 black dress, dubious silk, of even more dubious vintage
assorted nightgowns, shabby handbags, a hat with a feather, an old
    black coat, a rough jacket

The clothes were too worn for recycling; any self-respecting home-less person would turn up her nose at them. They would just have to be discarded. She packed the clothes in cartons to be disposed of, but then stood still, puzzled. Noradia had been a respected servant in a proper house. How come she had nothing? It made no sense. She should have at least a few decent outfits, of course there was the purple dress we buried her in, but all of this was dreck. How come? He paid her decently, didn't he?

She pulled at her hair and studied what was left on the bed, the surface of the other chest. More dreck. Some photographs of Ronnie, a sepia portrait of Noradia's family around the 1930s in an old gilt frame, a rosary, some trinkets — jewelry he must have given her, nothing worth much, a little opal ring, a pair of jet earrings. To go with the black bra and pants presumably. A shabby case containing a little makeup — how do you like that? — lipstick and mascara from Woolworth's. And there was an envelope, sealed, addressed "To My Daughter Ronalda." Momma wrote this? It was painstaking, as if she had practiced it over and over.

With trembling fingers she broke it open. Inside a letter:

> I, Algonzada Olguin, friend to Noradia Velez, write this letter for her in Boston, March 15, 1984, to her daughter Ronalda, to be opened after her death:
>
> My Ronalda,
>   I know I die soon. When you little, I decide to take care of you myself forever. Not him, not anybody else, just me. You mine. So I get Murray, you know her, upstairs maid, to go to bank with me and I open account and all I earn go into it. And when you eighteen, I go to bank and tell them to make account yours and mine together. Joint account, they say. Yes. So here is bank book. You don't need them now. Nobody. You momma take care of you always Ronacita. Don't say nothing, don't make no trouble. In their world, it's not no good, no use. Take, go, make happiness for yourself. Love.
> I love you always,
> Your mother,
> Noradia Velez

Also in the envelope were dozens of bankbooks, each full of steady small deposits — $20 and $25 — entered weekly over years. Their size and shape changed over time, and eventually there was simply a computerized sheet. The bankbooks showed the mounting up of interest. The latest computer printout showed that Noradia had saved over $200,000. My god.

Suddenly, Ronnie had energy, drive, concentration. A future, she had a future, she could imagine a future. She realized suddenly that her image of the future had been one of walking down a long dim hall in which all the doors were closed. Now, just as suddenly, one had opened. Does money heal? Is money love? Because it was the discovery of the bankbooks, of her inheritance, that cleared the fog in her head, that opened a path. She worked hard all week, made good progress, and on Sunday drove into Boston to have dinner at her friend Linda's apartment — pasta and salad, cheap wine, many friends, much laughter. She stayed up late and drank more than she was used to, and happily agreed to the suggestion that she spend the night on Linda's couch — although she worried about the car through her dreams, and told herself that next time she'd come by train. But the Alfa was — miraculously — still on the street next morning, and she drove back to Lincoln singing, wishing it were warm enough to put the top down, eager to get back to work.

But something else was working in her stomach, something uneasy, querulous almost. She pushed it away for several days, but by Wednesday morning, body fatigued from steady sitting, the stomach beginning to grind painfully, she decided to go out to the woods to gather kindling — just to do it — she didn't need kindling, she never built a fire just for herself. Taking along a thermos of coffee and a sandwich, she gathered twigs for a couple of hours, wheeling them back to the woodshed, returning for more. She enjoyed the exercise. Around noon, she took a break, wandered to Alex's spot in the woods and sat on the flat-topped stump to eat.

Was it the money? Her mind utterly rejected the thought that money could in fact heal, that it mattered to her, that it could strengthen her sense of her mother's devotion to her, that money, *money*, could make her happy.

Well, it isn't money itself but what it purchases, she told herself, the freedom from worry, the end of anxiety, for she *was*, had been terrified about how she was going to live for the next year or two, until she got a decent job — and when would that be? She hadn't even finished the dissertation much less had it accepted — of course she could probably get a TA appointment at BU but teaching assistants earned only a couple of thousand a year, not really enough to live on, and after this time in Lincoln, living here the way they did, it would be terrible to go back to poor meals, to being cold most of the time, to the many discomforts of student living. One apartment she'd shared had had plaster falling in the bedroom with the bathtub in the kitchen; another had no sink in the bathroom, only the one in the kitchen; none had a really comfortable chair, a television set, or a decent bed. Well, she didn't have a decent bed here either, if truth be told.

So it was that, the sense that she would be able to live in some decency, yet without anxiety about money, that was easing her mind. She could draw a few thousand from the bank to live on. She'd leave most of it there, she wouldn't blow her — matrimony, she wanted to call it — her mother's hardworking life measured out, symbolized, transformed into paper and coin. And since she was saving most of what she earned living here as caretaker, she could even add to it. She'd be fine — she could live, and have enough left to establish herself decently once she found a job. Maybe even buy a car. A car!

And Momma had done that for her, had made this possible by sacrificing everything for her child's future. But Ronnie knew she hadn't felt it as a sacrifice but as a triumph, as power: she was able to guard the future of the person she loved most. She didn't care about clothes, about owning things, or if she did, such desires were buried under layers of knowledge of poverty, of a driving determination that Ronnie should not suffer as she had. She had a clear morality, created in utter hardship and the anguish of losing most of her family, one way or another. Beyond survival, her own and her child's, she cared only about loving, being loved. She was proud of herself, maybe she even took a malicious pleasure in looking poor and shabby for him while putting his money away for the child he refused to acknowledge.

Ronnie's hands were cold and she wrapped them around the thermos cup. A surge of pride in her mother sprouted in her heart. She wasn't just his victim, she had her own agenda. She wasn't a slave to love, a submissive adoring servant of the great man, or at least, not just that. She had a private goal and she had succeeded in it, and she knew it. That serenity on her face as she lay dying proved it: she had had and done what she wanted in life. And if Ronnie had repudiated her for a time, had left her hanging in a tortured vacuum for a year, in the end she had been there, hadn't she, at her mother's side, tending her with the same loving care her mother had given her when she was a baby. And he had been there too, showing his love in his own peculiar way. Who knows what he said or did when they were alone together. Maybe he held her hand, maybe he smoothed her brow. Maybe he even spoke to her, maybe he told her he loved her.

She tried but couldn't picture it somehow. But who knows?

It was too cold to go on sitting. She stood up, walked back to where she'd left the wheelbarrow, and wheeled it toward the woodshed. Leaving the thermos behind after she unloaded the kindling, she went back for one more load. She had collected enough for fires for two weeks. If they ever had a fire again.

On the other hand, why shouldn't she build a fire tonight just for herself? She loved a fire; she had loved sitting there with her sisters drinking her Coke or wine or scotch, watching the fire. She was entitled to have this pleasure alone, why not? She would.

24

About a week and a half after the sisters had left, as Ronnie sat before her fire in the playroom nursing a glass of wine, the telephone rang. It was Elizabeth. Her voice sounded strained, her tone was distant; everything was fine, she said, hard to get back to work somehow, she'd never had so long a period of leisure before, never knew how much she'd enjoy it. Hard to get back to the grind, the bureaucracy, the politics.

"I miss all of you," she said finally.

I'll bet you do. "Me too," Ronnie said.

"I was wondering . . ."

"What?"

"What are your plans for Christmas?"

"Christmas?"

"Yes, Christmas. It's next week."

"Don't have any." Could go see Rosa. Should, probably.

"Well, how would you feel about having some company? For a couple of days? Would it intrude on your work? We could have a tree. I've never had my own Christmas tree. Tell me the truth, though, Ronnie, I won't come if you don't want me."

"I'd love it," Ronnie said in a soft low voice.

Elizabeth's voice cleared. "All right then. I'll come this weekend if that's okay. Sometime Saturday. I'll call you later this week to tell you what flight I'll be on so Aldo can meet me. That will give us time to get the tree up and plan our dinner. Is that all right with you?"

"It's fine," Ronnie said quietly, trying to dismiss the jubilation in her heart.

She set the phone down in a daze. Elizabeth missed her. Elizabeth cared about her. It hadn't been just the contingency of the old man's sickness, the kind of closeness that happens at conferences or crises or vacations, where people meet and come to believe they are best friends, swear eternal friendship, or at least promise to write, but never think about each other again except maybe at Christmas, when they send a card. This wasn't like that: Elizabeth wanted to spend Christmas with her.

Her heart lightened, she sat and gazed out at the garden, although it was dark now by five o'clock and she could see nothing but the reflection of the room in the glass doors. She mulled, she couldn't call it thinking, her mind wandering to the night the old man died, the afternoon her mother died, to her childhood, to what she knew of her mother's. To her mother and Stephen. And her mother's legacy. Love, she had written.

But if she had her own agenda, if she was using him for her own ends, did she love him?

Ronnie knew Noradia had loved Stephen. She could see it.

And I? All my love affairs failed.

She thought about them, the women she had loved. There hadn't been many of them — Tania, Susan, Julieta (but that had been brief), Lilah, Sarah. She recalled her posture with them — a posture she had adopted when she realized — how old was she? fourteen maybe? fifteen? — that it was girls she was drawn to, not boys, the way everything suggested — the movies, the ads, television — it was supposed to be. But it was the sight of a girl's hair lifting in a curl, shining in the sun, a girl's quick walk in the school corridor, a girl's delicate hands clutched around her schoolbooks, that lifted Ronnnie's heart, that twisted her head and made her want to reach out, to touch gently — and sometimes, to grab, not so gently.

She was weird.

She was abnormal.

For months she hid her feelings in a tight withdrawal from girls, palling around with the guys in her class, who could not hurt her because she didn't care about them. She copied them — walked like them, talked like them, cursed like them, showed the same bravado. They had accepted her, seemed to like her, until one evening, hanging out on a street corner with the guys, one of them — Nino — had challenged her, accusing her of not being much of a girl, poking her shoulder, trying to pin her against a telephone pole, to kiss her. She had punched him out — he was only a skinny kid and wasn't expecting that — and stalked off. After that, she determined to live without friends of either sex.

Still, she continued to maintain her masculine posture, and oddly enough, it attracted a number of girls. She became popular, to her own astonishment, sought after; girls were chasing her! And eventually, she began to respond to them with more than grunts, let her face show something more than bland indifference. She began to make friends. The girls adored her: they accepted her as different from them, as the tough girl, one who could defend them, who was unintimidated by boys. But she never kissed a girl, never held a hand or caressed a head. Until she was nineteen, a freshman at BU, and met Susan at a BU party. Susan was older, a psychiatrist who taught part-time at the university but had her own practice. Ronnie was in her course, Intro to Psychology. Susan was grown up: she wore her black hair smoothed back in a knot and dark suits, and she looked at Ronnie with hungry eyes as the girl paraded her boyish ways before her. Amused, delighted, and admiring, Susan invited Ronnie to her apartment for drinks.

What a place! Ronnie had never seen such a place, all chrome and glass and slate, with windows facing the Charles, paintings on the walls (all very modern, Ronnie didn't care for them), a stereo and a huge record collection. She put on some music she said was Mahler, and she made Ronnie sit on the couch next to her and she gave her brandy in a big wide-bowled glass like those Ronnie had seen Stephen hand around to guests. And she asked her how the music made her feel, which was hard to express, it was at once so silly and so dramatic and made her think of death, and then she took her hand, and pressed against Ronnie, leaning her back against the couch, and kissed her so so delicately. Ronnie, having crushed her longings for years, was overwhelmed, responded with fervor, and soon was in Susan's huge bed, lying on satin sheets. Satin sheets!

Susan loved Ronnie's boyishness. She insisted that Ronnie move in with her and gave her a closet and dresser of her own. She had Ronnie drive her car, an antique MG, when they went out in it, and she handed Ronnie her credit card to pay for dinner when they ate in restaurants. And they ate in nice restaurants, places Ronnie had never expected to see the insides of. It was a luxurious life, but Susan liked Ronnie to hurt her in sex, which Ronnie did not enjoy. And there could be no deviation from their roles. Ronnie was the male, Susan the female.

Ronnie began to feel uncomfortable, and the night Susan demanded she handcuff her to the bed and spank her, Ronnie rebelled.

"I don't want to do that."

Susan went white with fury. "Who do you think you are, you little spic! I picked you up off the streets, I support you, keep you in luxury! You do what I want or you get out! Just get out!"

Ronnie packed her few belongings, managed to catch the last T and walked the long blocks to Rosa's at one in the morning, banged on the door asking for a bed.

Still, somehow, her role was set by then. Ronnie was the girl who could change a tire, fix the toaster, who could lift and carry heavy weights, drive the car like a pro, and who never cried, nor showed ever any ache or need for tenderness. She was tough. She could give love but did not need to receive it. Stroking Sarah's back when Sarah was upset had caught at her heart, but when Sarah put her arms around her, tried to console her after she heard the news about her mother, her back and neck stayed stiff, her voice taut. She pulled away, insisting, "I'm okay, it's okay."

Always insisting on giving sexual pleasure first, and then sometimes refusing to receive it. "Seeing you enjoy yourself is enough for me." The crushed look on Lilah's face. Maybe it wasn't that she didn't want to share her new salary with Ronnie that had drawn Lilah away from her: receiving is giving and she had refused to receive, refused to give Lilah the pleasure of pleasuring her, of consoling her, of touching the tenderness hidden beneath all her layers of armor.

How do I know that now?

Momma had been able to love a man she knew was in some sense her enemy, a man who refused to acknowledge her child, his child, who kept her a servant, whose money she took and hid, refusing to spend it on anything that would increase her attractiveness to him. He must have known that, must have seen the rebellion in her. But maybe not. She always wore a uniform when the family was in residence. She wore those cotton housedresses only when they were away. She dressed up for Mass on Sunday, he might have seen her then in one of her rayon things, dresses bought for a few dollars in Filene's basement. And when she took her rare trip to Boston to see her old friends and — although Ronnie did not know it at the time — Rosa.

She stopped to consider this for the first time, the way Momma — once she had heard from Ronnie and knew where she was — had respected her abandonment by leaving her alone, but had visited Rosa from time to time to find out how she was, what she was doing, to make sure she was all right. How did Momma learn such delicacy, how did she know how to juggle things in herself to keep them in balance?

A little awed by her mother's approach to life, she sat feeling her mind gaping open. Then the phone rang again, and she cursed: here she'd built the fire, but was having to leave it every minute. It was Mary, her voice as tense and hollow as Elizabeth's, but far more enthusiastic. Things were fine, wonderful really, she had been able to pay some bills and hire a real maid again, she'd bought some new clothes, she'd been lunching out, going to the theatre. It was wonderful. But — and then she grew tentative — she missed Ronnie, missed the others, and didn't, really didn't want to spend Christmas at Martin's. How would it be if she came up there? Maybe they could even put up a tree together, something she'd never herself personally done, but look, she'd learned to make tea and French toast and even coffee, hadn't she, she'd almost learned to drive, so Ronnie could teach her how to put up a tree.

They all assume I know, Ronnie thought, amused. Actually, I do: every Christmas at Rosa's, it was a major celebration, the putting up of the tree.

"Elizabeth's coming too," Ronnie said.

"Lizzie's coming?" she cried, and sounded near tears. "Oh wonderful! Wonderful!" Her voice was thick. "When?"

"Saturday. I don't know what time."

"All right, I'll call her and find out, so I can get a shuttle that arrives around the same time. That way, it won't be a problem for Aldo."

Mary, worrying about troubling a servant?

"Have you heard from Alex?"

"No. Not a word."

"No. Well, she has a family. Actually, Ronnie, I thought I'd invite Marie-Laure too. She hates to go to Martin's as much as I do, and she was going to a friend's house — but maybe she'll come with me instead."

Is she asking my permission? She owns the fucking house.

"Sure," she said unenthusiastically. Probably a spoiled-brat snob who would complain about everything. Well, she'd better not think she could treat Ronnie like a servant, that was all.

Mary's voice was high and gay. "Wonderful! I'll be in touch then. Soon. Good to talk to you, Ron!"

She was still somewhat in shock from this phone call when the phone rang again. It was Alex, sounding a little wistful.

"How have you been, Ronnie? How's your dissertation going?" She sounded as if she really cared. "Good. I'm glad to hear it. Yes, everything's fine here. It's the first night of Hanukkah tonight, so we're having sort of a party. My in-laws are here and David's uncle and aunt and cousins. But I keep thinking about you — all of you."

"So are the others, it seems. Elizabeth and Mary just called. They're coming up here for Christmas."

"THEY ARE?" Silence. Then a mournful, "Oh, I wish I could be there."

"Why don't you come?"

"Oh, I wish I could. Christmas is the last day of Hanukkah. Well, maybe I can. It's the last day, after all. We don't celebrate Christmas, David doesn't approve of it, even though I think the kids would like to celebrate both . . . but why not? Why shouldn't I be allowed to spend Christmas with my sisters? I'm coming. I may not be able to come until the last minute, probably not until Christmas Eve, but I'm coming, tell them I'll be there. With bells on! I've missed you all so!"

Ronnie could not resist revealing her curiosity. "How have things been at home?"

Alex was silent for a long moment. "Hard," she said finally. "But not cruel. David is really . . . he's a dear man and he understands more than I thought he would. My mother . . . well, it's been hard for her. And the kids don't understand at all. I'll tell you all about it when I see you. I'm so happy I'm coming!"

Ronnie set the phone down with an amazed smile on her face. All of them, all of them, it mattered to all of them. This had nothing to do with money. This was love.

Love!

Presents would be required, and for once she had enough money to buy them, decent presents, presents chosen for people, forgetting price. So on Friday, she asked Aldo for a lift to the station and took the Boston train — it was easier to travel by train than to worry about parking a desirable car that was not her own in the car-theft capital of the world. She got off in Cambridge, walking from Porter Square to Harvard Square, where she wandered from shop to shop, knowing exactly what she wanted for her sisters, feeling she knew exactly what would please them. Then she took the T to Boston and shopped in the department stores for more practical gifts for Rosa, Enriqué, and the kids. She had everything wrapped in gaudy paper. She had called Rosa the night before to make sure the family would be home this evening, and Rosa had ordered her to come to dinner. It was after five when, laden with parcels, she took the T to Somerville, where they lived now. Following Rosa's directions, she walked the long blocks lined with wooden three-deckers. Theirs was on a quiet street with some trees remaining on it and a patch of garden in front. Someone had taken the trouble to plant some roses and chrysanthemums in it, and although everything was brown and dead now, it looked like a garden, not a waste patch like some of the others. Much better than the last place they lived, she thought.

The Torres family had the first floor, and Rosa flung open the door at Ronnie's ring, threw her arms around her neck, talking, crying, almost screaming as she drew her in, and there were Enriqué, Téo, Lidia, and Joey, all waiting in the kitchen, leaping up, beaming, all talking at once, their arms open to her, to little Ronnie, their little love, their sister, the little hurt bird who had healed in their nest.

Wine was poured, even Téo had some, he was sixteen now, a man, and Lidia was allowed to mix some with sparkling water, and Joey had a Coke, and she asked news and they asked news and everyone listened to what the others said. Ronnie was careful not to mention Tina, and Rosa only mentioned Raoul once, tears starting in her eyes immediately she did, but she brushed them away and went on talking. They were fine, they

were good: they *owned* this house! All of it! It was theirs! It was hard
keeping it, good tenants were not always to be found, but they had both
upper floors rented to dependable people now, that made things easier.
Enriqué worked hard keeping it in good condition, he had painted the
house, mended the roof, he had even planted a garden in front and next
spring he was going to put one in back.

"Me too, Papa, right?" Téo interrupted.

"And me too," Lidia yelled. "I want to plant tomatoes."

"*Sí,* we will have tomatoes and corn and beans, and whatever you
want, my children," Enriqué said expansively.

Ronnie noted that although it was a Friday evening, he was home.
His belly was smaller than it had been, he looked fit. Rosa must have won
her battle with him. Ronnie gazed at the small woman with the dark
circles under her eyes, a face that had worn hard folds of worry years ago.
It was fuller now, less tense; she looked almost serene.

Rosa had a real job now, sewing in a sweatshop, hard work but it
paid better than doing piecework at home, and Téo had a job after school
at the supermarket and earned his own spending money, and Lidia took
care of Joey after school — for which her mother (unbelievably in this
family) paid her! And on weekends, she baby-sat for the college professors
who lived down the block. She was saving money, so was Téo.

"They both go to college," Rosa announced in a truculent voice, allowing no contradiction.

Remembering Téo's poor grades, his difficulty learning to read, Ronnie wanted to ask more but didn't dare. Their failure with their two elder
children was a scar across both Rosa and Enriqué, one that had hardened
in such a way as to make further such failures unthinkable. Not to be
allowed. Certainly not to be spoken of.

Every family has its silences, she thought. Silences form over scars.
Even I and I'm not even a family. For she told them nothing about Stephen, nothing about her sisters. She said that since Noradia died, she had
been working as a caretaker at the Lincoln house in order to work on her
dissertation, that she was well into it, thought it would take her six
months, then she would leave.

"He die, you momma's bossman," Rosa said. "I see on TV. Big funeral,
the president come, Nixon come, the Bush, all important Anglo men."

"Yes," Ronnie breathed.

"Right after you momma," she added shrewdly.

Could Noradia have told her?

"Yes."

"Ronnie don't care about that old man," Enriqué said heartily, pouring more wine into her glass. "He was nothing to her!"

But Rosa was looking at her curiously.

"Right," Ronnie said, raising her glass to her lips to drink. Rosa was
still looking at her. She made her voice strong, light, gay. "But you know
what my momma did? — all those years she worked there, she saved all
her money, she put it in the bank. For me! So when I finish my thesis and
get a job, I have enough money for a car, to get an apartment, to get settled
in life!"

Rosa leapt up, threw her arms around Ronnie. "You momma, she
was good woman! More! She was a saint! A saint!" she yelled at Ronnie
ferociously. Tears were streaming down her cheeks.

"I know she was," Ronnie laughed, embracing Rosa back, hugging
her hard enough to satisfy her, so that she could sit down again sighing,
wiping her eyes, smiling broadly at Ronnie.

"You not know how good she was, you run away from home, from
her. She say she understand, she never blame you even though a year you
not tell her where you are. I kill you for that if you mine! She come here
and sit with me while I work, make me coffee, she want to know you okay.
Years and years she did that. A saint!"

Enriqué was uncomfortable with such talk. "How about dinner, huh,
Rosa? You get the girl here to starve her? When we eat?"

Rosa stood up, Lidia too: the bustle of food preparation began, and
the moment passed. The woman and the girl set out the richly flavored
food — a loin of pork roasted overnight with rice and tomatoes and green
peppers and onions and black beans, served with bananas, and for dessert, a gooey cream cake. The family ate with gusto, the children eager to
get on with what they knew was coming, the opening of the presents
Ronnie had brought. In the noisy joyful business ("How did you know I
loved red?" "Oh, just the kind of shirt I love, Ronnie!" "Oh, Ronnie," Rosa
blushed, holding the pink satin nightgown up to her face, "I have always
wanted . . ."), the opening of another bottle of wine, the moment did not

return. But happy as the evening was, warm and embracing, as Ronnie walked back to the T after ten, down past the quiet fronts of the clapboard houses, her steps soundless in her rubber-soled shoes, she felt she could never go back.

Can't come here again. At least not when she's alone. She's too curious. Did Momma get that look on her face when she mentioned him? She probably didn't ask Momma, but she wondered. How could I tell her? Momma and him, what he did to me? She'd blame Momma, she wouldn't understand how she loved him, she'd think Momma sacrificed me to him. The way I felt for a long time. She won't give it up, I can see it in her face, she won't back off, she's determined to find out what happened now that Momma's dead, he's dead.

Good-bye Rosa. Tears formed in the corners of her eyes.

Oh, don't be so dramatic, for god's sake. You can visit them on holidays, birthdays, when the whole family is around. In time she'll accept that you're simply not going to talk about it. You don't have to cut people off. She keeps Tina in her life no matter what Enriqué says, and he knows it. While we did the dishes, I whispered in her ear, "How's Tina?" and she shrugged, "The same, she make lots of money but she look bad. I think maybe she have AIDS." Her eyes filled with tears, I held her, but then Enriqué yelled in asking where Téo had gone, and we broke apart, finished our work. She negotiates silences. I can too.

Ronnie was still laden with packages — her presents from Rosa and Enriqué, her presents for her sisters, and some special items bought with great trepidation that afternoon to surprise them. She smiled imagining their reactions. But she was tired, the packages were heavy, and she still had a long trip ahead of her. Wish Aldo had been waiting just outside the door of Rosa's house.

Spoiled brat you've turned into, she thought, trudging on.

She spent Saturday morning out in the woods examining trees, trying to decide whether they should cut one of their own or buy one in town. She hated to part with a young pine, and she studied them all carefully. Each one seemed to have some special quality that deserved to be retained, and she gave up. Let them decide, she thought, walking back to the house.

And decide they did. They arrived late, around four, long after she expected them, but the car was laden down. They'd stopped in town and purchased a tree, a stand, and Christmas lights. The car also bore their suitcases, their bags of gifts, Mary's two fur coats, Elizabeth's portable computer. They were as excited and almost as talkative as the Torres family, embracing her, laughing, talking at once.

"Well of course Father always had a tree when he was here for Christmas but he always had a giant thing, huge, twenty or more feet high, it stood in the ballroom so you can imagine. . . . It hasn't been used in years, of course. Anyway, we were sure the old stand wouldn't work for the little one we bought, it's only about eight feet high, isn't it darling, Elizabeth was so picky about it, look how sweet it is, so nicely balanced and full. There are tons of ornaments around here somewhere, but we thought the lights might be old and corroded, so we bought new ones, tiny white ones that twinkle, aren't they sweet? and of course we needed fresh tinsel. So we stopped in town to get all this stuff, and it was so quaint, wasn't it, Elizabeth? All the houses had lights or wreaths, all so beautifully decorated, even the stores, and people knew us and greeted us, it was quite lovely, wasn't it?"

Mary was pink and fresh-smelling, she flitted from one set of packages to another, she ordered Aldo to leave the tree on the front steps under the portico — "for now" — and to carry the rest of the things inside — "those things go up to my room, Aldo, yes all of them, make two trips my dear, it's too much to carry all at once," and Aldo, blanching at the "my dear," dropped one of her suitcases and she didn't even scold him, although it was one of her crocodile cases.

Elizabeth was quieter, but she too glowed, hugged Ronnie hard, talked. "We've never done this before, you know? Father always had the gardeners cut a tree from out back, it was a major undertaking, they needed saws and ropes and it took a couple of days to cut it and then put it up. And the servants decorated it, they had to stand on a ladder to do it, then when everything was done, we would be brought into the ballroom all dressed up to ooh and ah, but it was impersonal, it had nothing to do with us, and they always had some sort of ball or party that night, Christmas Eve. And the presents heaped around it, there were enough to stock a small shop I swear . . ." Her voice drifted off. Then she burst out, "Well, this tree will go into the playroom and we'll decorate it ourselves, what a treat!"

When they had changed their clothes, they joined Ronnie in the playroom. She had already started a fire in the old stone fireplace, had already had Mrs. Browning set up a drinks tray for them, and was sitting there in her jeans and sweatshirt holding a wine spritzer, with a big grin on her face. Amazingly, not just Elizabeth but Mary came down in pants and a sweater — granted, both were probably from some designer, but Mary had never dressed so informally before. They went straight to the bar, poured drinks — a scotch for Elizabeth, vermouth cassis for Mary — and threw themselves on the comfortable armchairs with an abandon Ronnie felt certain they never showed elsewhere.

"Oh! This is so good!" Elizabeth sighed.

"Maybe we should hold on to this house," Mary said wistfully. "For things like this — Christmas, Thanksgiving." She turned to Ronnie. "Did Marie-Laure call?"

Ronnie shook her head.

Mary frowned. "Strange. She should have. I think her school let out on Wednesday. I don't even know how to reach her." A little pall settled on her face.

"So tell me what you've been doing," Ronnie urged.

Elizabeth lighted a cigarette. "Mostly cleaning up my desk. This is a slow time in D.C., all the elected officials go home for the holidays, it's not a time for policymaking. Especially since Reagan won with such a huge vote: that tells the guys that people don't want anything to change." She sighed lightly.

"Beyond that, I haven't done much. I did look at a couple of houses in Virginia over the weekend," she said, turning to Mary. "One of them was really beautiful — it had a Japanese garden out back and ten acres of land. It was in Falls Church."

"Ummm. Missy Cambrowe lives in Falls Church," Mary mused.

Elizabeth's face brightened with hope, but Mary changed the subject, turning to Ronnie.

"And what about you? How's the dissertation going?"

"Oh, slowly. But it's going. I've collated most of my research. Now I have to get back to the books. What's left is mostly methodical, painstaking work. The intelligence — if there is any — shows in the way I gathered the research. So it goes slowly. But I'm working."

"Good. This house in Falls Church has four bedrooms, each with its own bath. They're not as big as the bedrooms in this house, but they're a decent size. And enough for all of us!" Elizabeth added, looking at Mary.

Mary met her eyes briefly, then looked away.

"And what about you?" Ronnie asked.

"Oh, I haven't done anything, really. Nothing different." Mary gazed at the fire. "Actually, I just picked up where I left off — only paying the bills this time. Same old life."

"Isn't that what you wanted?"

"Yes. I guess it is."

"You don't sound very happy about it."

"No," Mary admitted slowly. "No. It lacks . . . something."

Elizabeth fixed her eyes on Mary.

"We were all so . . . we could say what we thought to each other. Even if it was vicious, full of venom. We could be ourselves. It was so . . . liberating, so . . . I felt like a real person. I don't think I've ever felt like a real person for any extended period in my life before."

"I've missed you all too," Elizabeth admitted ruefully. "Very much. I'd get home after work, well, after dinner, I usually eat out, and I'd walk around my apartment talking away, telling you all — well, things you wouldn't be interested in, what a bastard Arthur Gilliam is, how sweet Jim Mangdoni doesn't have a chance at Treasury and why, and all the convoluted disgusting politics of the place. They're sending me off on an arm-twisting mission soon after the first of the year. Ten days, six countries, endless cups of tea, tact and diplomacy masking the threat of economic force. My face is tired when I come back from these things. I used to look forward to them, they were such a challenge. But now — I don't know — they seem sort of pointless."

"Would you consider giving up your job?" Mary wondered.

"Give up my job? I'd die!"

"You could teach economics in some nice college. Some pretty school in a pretty town, like Princeton. Get away from all the politics, the infighting."

"No place is more infested with politics than academia. And of the pettiest sort."

"There's no escape, is there," Mary said wistfully. "Listening to my friends this past — what, two weeks? — I keep hearing how petty they are, how ingrown their concerns. And you know, they don't talk much about politics, but under the surface it's their major concern. They always have to be somehow in touch with the people with the power. And they have to let you know they are, that they have an invitation from Helmut or François or Margaret or Nancy. Going back after Father's death — well, everyone knew I was rich again, they just knew it — and the phone rang and rang, and the invitations piled up, and oh! the names that got dropped, all those names. . . .

"Once, that pleased me. I took it as a testimony to my own power. Now . . . I don't know what happened to me here. I feel my stay here ruined me in a way." Her face was sober, thoughtful, not petulant.

No one spoke. The fire crackled, a log fell, and Ronnie got up to fix it. When she finished, she — as usual — wiped her sooty hands on the sides of her jeans and sat down again. She sipped her drink. She gazed at Mary. "Are you sorry?"

Mary flushed, shook her head so her hair flew around. "No. No. I'm not. I'm sorry I can't get pleasure from something that used to give me pleasure, but . . ." — she set down her drink hard on the table beside her — "I just wish I knew what would give me pleasure now!"

"But you do know," Elizabeth said with surprise.

"What?"

"Being with us."

25

When Mary came down for coffee Sunday morning, Ronnie and Elizabeth were still sitting at the breakfast table, and she smiled with delight when Ronnie exclaimed, "I don't believe it! You in jeans?"

"Well, we're going to put up the tree, aren't we? I always dress for the occasion, and jeans seemed right for the occasion. I bought them specially in a place on Second Avenue that sells sportswear, a store where no one knew me. Things there were really cheap. I never knew clothes were that inexpensive." She posed for them, turned around. "Tell me the truth. Am I too broad in the rear for them? What do you think?"

"You've got a great shape," Elizabeth said appraisingly.

"Really, Lizzie? You're not putting me on?"

"No. Shapely is the word."

"Ronnie?"

"The accurate word." She smiled.

"Not *too* shapely?"

"Such distinctions depend on the eye of the beholder," Elizabeth said.

"Yes. Yes. Okay."

She slid into a chair and poured coffee into a cup.

"Did you have breakfast in bed?"

"Yes. Just want a second cup of coffee. I'm dieting anyway, I hardly eat any breakfast now. I just had a slice of that wonderful Italian bread toasted, with a little butter and Mrs. Browning's wonderful raspberry jam."

"You look thinner."

"Really!" She was pleased. "I've lost six pounds. I plan to lose fifteen. I'm not aiming for the anorexic look, just to lose the bulbous one," she laughed.

"You've made a good start."

Cheered, Mary was the organizer this morning. "Okay, first we have to find the Christmas ornaments. Where would they be?" she asked Ronnie. "The attic?"

"Probably. I'll go up with you."

"Why don't we all go? We'll all have to help carry them down," Elizabeth said.

So they all climbed up to the attic, and Ronnie, who had some memory of helping Noradia put the ornaments away, found them in a corner along with a giant tree stand and boxes and boxes of lights.

"So many lights! Shall we put some outside?"

"Why," Elizabeth shrugged. "We're not having guests."

"Just for ourselves! It would look so cheery! I'll ask Aldo to do it."

"The groundsmen usually did it, but they're all off until spring," Ronnie said. "But" — her voice dropped to its boyish register — "I could probably do it."

"I'll help you!" Elizabeth said enthusiastically.

So they spent most of the day in trial-and-error setting up of the tree (whose trunk Ronnie had to saw to fit the holder), attaching lights to the tree and to two tall laurel bushes in front of the house, and then hanging the ornaments, many of them extremely old and delicate. They chatted desultorily throughout their work, easy together, their conversation alternating between affection and sarcasm but never breaking into argument. By the time they hung the tinsel, they were drinking eggnog, and got a little silly, tossing tinsel at each other, into each other's hair. At last they fell laughing into chairs, admiring the tree, the ornaments, their handiwork.

The tree crowded the room, which was crowded already, and Elizabeth decided they should fold up the Ping Pong table, which they never used anyway, and slide it into a closet. This took considerable figuring out and effort, and they were tired when they were through, but all at once the room looked lovely — the great stone fireplace, the tree fronting book-cases in the corner, the overstuffed chairs in a circle that included both. Dim light still glowed through the glass doors to the terrace.

They all sighed at once.

They had given Mrs. Browning and Teresa the day off, deciding to eat out. As the time to dress approached, Mary grew subdued.

"I wonder what happened to Marie-Laure."

Then, later: "Suppose she comes while we're out?"

"We could leave a note and a key for her."

"I did want to be here to welcome her. She hasn't been here in a couple of years. . . ."

"She would have called if she were coming, wouldn't she?" Elizabeth asked impatiently.

"Do you want to stay home? We can rummage in the fridge," Ronnie suggested.

"No, no, we'll go."

They went up to dress for dinner, meeting in the foyer at seven-thirty. Ronnie appeared last, her color high, and her breath short with excitement. Both sisters did a double take; both exclaimed. She was wear-ing black wool pants and a pale blue silk shirt, with a royal blue embroi-dered vest and black low-heeled shoes.

"Ronnie! You look wonderful!" Mary cried.

"Decided to get out of uniform, huh?" Elizabeth commented dryly.

Ronnie just grinned.

Aldo had to drive them; the Alfa would not hold the three of them. As he let them out in front of the restaurant, Ronnie's tension level rose. But there was no trouble in the restaurant. It was a slightly pretentious old inn, homey in appearance but formal in service. Ronnie had never been in such a place before in her life. She'd been to expensive restaurants with Susan, but they were all in Boston, a cosmopolitan place used to varied combinations and colors of people. But this was a countryish place with stained wood beams in the low ceiling, used to catering to the respectable white couples who inhabited this area. Yet the maitre d' did not look startled by her, none of the waiters or customers looked at her strangely.

No one stared at the darkskinned woman eating with the two white ones. It was all right. Could it just be her clothes? Or was the world not what she had thought it?

Their delight at being out together was marred only by Mary's anxiety about Marie-Laure. There wasn't even an argument about the check: Elizabeth insisted on getting it and merely patted Ronnie's hand when she tried to pay her share. Since Mary just said, "Fine, thanks, Lizzie," and Mary had inherited millions, Ronnie decided to let it be.

But as she lay in bed that night staring at the ceiling, she wondered if she had created a totally false picture of the world she lived in. She tried out different scenarios: suppose she had showed up with another dark-skinned woman? She sensed that there would be no problem in that restaurant as long as they were properly dressed. If she'd worn jeans, they might have refused to seat her. Or suppose she'd shown up with someone like Corrinne D'Almay, with her wild hair and flowing clothes, her overwhelming number of necklaces and rings. They might have stared, but they probably would have seated them. But they would balk at a white boy in jeans. What it was was that standards varied greatly in the world: in an expensive restaurant, only dress and money mattered. That would not be the case when she went to find a job. It wasn't that she had built a paranoid vision, it was that she had made it more total than it was. It existed: but it did not encompass her. Somehow, that thought consoled her, and she turned on her side and slept.

Monday was filled with activity — the sisters had offered Mrs. Browning their services as sous-chefs, and while she accepted tentatively, in the end she was glad of their help. They could fetch and carry, they learned to load and unload the dishwasher — Elizabeth did it even better than Browning herself, she admitted; they managed to learn where utensils were kept. They could be trusted to stir a sauce, if not to beat a salad dressing.

They were preparing two meals at once — a buffet dinner for that night, which Doris would set out and clean up, so Mrs. Browning and Teresa could spend Christmas Eve with their families, and a formal dinner for the next day, when Alex would arrive, "and Marie-Laure, I hope," Mary said wistfully. So there was a fresh ham to be baked ("Will Alex eat that?" Ronnie asked; "Oh, I think so," Mary said. "Didn't she eat ham

while we were here?" "Well, there's plenty of other stuff," Elizabeth
pointed out) and a roast beef, with a leg of lamb already larded with garlic
for the next day; there were seviche for tonight and escargots *en croûte* for
tomorrow, nine vegetables (four of them white) and a melted goat cheese
salad with arugula (Elizabeth's one specialty), and a salad of greens and
white beans and red peppers (roasted by Ronnie). Mrs. Browning made
the two pies and finished the torte she had begun days earlier. The work
took all of them the entire day but even Mrs. Browning and Teresa
enjoyed it. These two ladies were shocked when Mary insisted on playing
music, very loudly, on the tape player she had brought with her: they
weren't used to music while they worked, and certainly not to the
dancing that kept breaking out. There was much laughter in the kitchen
that day.

It was after four when the doorbell rang. They stared at each other.
Doorbells did not ring often in this house, certainly not the front doorbell.
Teresa straightened her cap and apron and went to the door, returning to
the women waiting in the kitchen with the news that Miss di Cenci was at
the door.

"Marie-Laure!" Mary cried, and ran out to the foyer without even
removing her heavy white coverall apron.

The sisters stood in the kitchen, uncertain about how long to allow
Mary to welcome her child, how long an absence would appear rude on
their part. Eventually, Elizabeth pushed open the swinging door and
walked toward the foyer. Ronnie followed her.

Mary was talking wildly ("So good to see you, it's been so long, I
didn't know where you were, I called everywhere, where were you? I
wasn't sure you were coming") while embracing a slim stiff figure with
long straight hair, who held one arm loosely around her mother's back; the
other hung down at her side. She stared at the figures gathered behind
Mary, and Mary turned.

"Marie-Laure, you know your aunt Elizabeth, you remember her
from the funeral, and Grandad's eightieth birthday party. And all the
Fourth of July parties."

In fact, the two had barely talked over all those years.

The girl held out her hand, smiled graciously, a learned smile. "Yes,
of course, how good to see you again," she said in rounded formal tones.

Christ, Ronnie thought.

"And this is your aunt Ronnie. You've never met her, but she's our youngest sister."

The girl stared at Ronnie, smiled stiffly, and said, "How do you do."

"I was so worried about you, I didn't know where you were, or when you were coming . . . ," Mary continued. "How did you get here?"

"I didn't know when you were arriving, so I went to Abbie's for a couple of days. She and Duff dropped me off."

"Oh, you should have asked them to stop in for a drink!"

"They have a do tonight, they couldn't stop. They have to get back."

"A do? At their house? Oh, I suppose you would have liked to stay. . . ."

"No, it's at Chip Waylan's. On Charles Street. I didn't particularly want to go," she shrugged. "That crowd's a little raunchy . . . well, not my scene."

Her face was a pale white oval of indifference in which the perfect features were set like marks in a mask. She examined her mother and raised her eyebrows. "You're wearing an apron!" She turned slowly and noticed the aprons on the others, but did not blush or look embarrassed at her remark.

"Oh, we're all cooking Christmas dinner! It's so much fun. Come out into the kitchen . . ."

"The kitchen?"

"Oh, of course, you probably want to freshen up first. Although you look fine." The girl's slim legs were encased in tight jeans and boots and she wore a heavy fur-lined leather jacket. "Teresa will carry your bag upstairs. Your room is all ready!"

Mary's excitement spun around the still center that was her daughter, who simply watched as she ran toward the kitchen calling Teresa.

She's thinking her mother sounds like a fishwife, thought Elizabeth. There goes our Christmas.

The girl turned politely toward her. "How have you been, Aunt Elizabeth."

"Oh for god's sake, call me Lizzie," Elizabeth said sharply, in a tone she had not intended. But the girl did not blink.

"And I've been fine, working hard," Elizabeth said in a softer tone.

"We put up a tree in the playroom, and the lights outside. Did you see them?"

"Oh. I didn't notice." Faintly.

"Actually, they're Ronnie's work," Elizabeth said, trying to include Ronnie in the conversation.

But Marie-Laure merely surveyed Ronnie as she might an article she was thinking of buying.

Then Teresa entered hurriedly, Mary behind her as if she were driving her forward. The maid picked up the girl's bag and packages and led Marie-Laure up the great formal staircase to her bedroom.

"We'll be in the kitchen when you come down," Mary called cheerfully.

As they returned to the kitchen, Ronnie and Elizabeth exchanged looks. But Mary was too excited, distracted, to notice.

"She may be hungry, maybe we should give her tea, oh, I know that would be so much work after all this cooking, I'm so sorry, Mrs. Browning, but could you . . ."

"We don't need a formal tea," Elizabeth said shortly. "She's family, not company. Why not just give her a soft drink and some cookies. We're almost finished here. When we're done, we'll all sit down and have a drink."

"You're right, Lizzie, that's a good idea," Mary said to Mrs. Browning's relief.

"I'll set out the cookies," Ronnie said, as the rest of them returned to the chores they'd been doing. Ronnie found a round cake platter, lined it with a doily, and set out almond crisps, shortbread, some cheese crisps. She carried it into the playroom. But Marie-Laure did not appear.

They finished in the kitchen and debated whether to change before drinks, or after them — "or not at all!" Elizabeth suggested.

"Oh, Lizzie! It's Christmas Eve!"

"Okay," she sighed. "Then let's get it over with first."

Mary took her usual leisured time dressing and working on her face and hair, and by the time she finished, Elizabeth's door was open, her room dark. Marie-Laure's door was still shut. Mary knocked, then opened the door. The girl was sitting at the windows, smoking and staring out at the darkness; the smell of pot was strong in the room. She hurriedly put her joint out.

"Darling?" Mary said, then stopped at the smell. "Do come down. We're about to have drinks."

The girl turned her head indolently. "I'll be down in a while." She was still wearing her jeans, with a heavy white sweater.

"Aren't you going to dress for dinner?"

"For god's sake, it's just your sister, Mom, just a bunch of women. Do I have to? And who is that Ronnie, anyway. She looks foreign, she looks like some wetback or something."

Mary closed the door behind her and approached her daughter. She sat on the chair opposite her. She made no comment on the roach Marie-Laure still clutched.

"Ronnie is your grandfather's illegitimate daughter. She's part Mexican and part Upton, just as you are part Italian and part Upton. You understand? She's very wonderful and I love her and I expect you to treat her with respect."

Marie-Laure looked at her mother as if she were a stranger.

"I can't believe you were working in the kitchen," she whined.

"Yes," Mary laughed lightly. "I've been learning the joys of domesticity! Oh, more than that! Companionship! Sisterhood!"

Marie-Laure stared at her.

"I thought you inherited all that money," she said sullenly.

"Yes. I did."

"So you don't have to be grubbing in the kitchen, do you? You don't have to hang around with *chicana* bastards."

Mary's face hardened. She restrained the hand which rose of its own volition, which wanted to strike out, slap that pale cheek, leave a red mark.

"Marie-Laure, I know I've neglected you. Your education especially. But I've made up my mind to correct that. You've been trained the way I was, to be an unfeeling snob, pervaded by a sense of superiority to which you have no right. Social superiority. But you are not superior. To anyone. You're a callow little girl in training for the marriage market. I was trained the same way. It never made me happy and so I don't imagine it makes you happy. I'm going to try to repair that. But I will ask you, while you're here, to try to act like a human being. If you know how."

She stood up. "I also ask you not to show up stoned at the dinner table. Now get rid of that roach, change your clothes, and come downstairs."

She turned and left the room swiftly, so Marie-Laure could not see her face.

Ronnie was dressed again in the wool pants, but tonight she wore a deep orange sweater very becoming to her golden complexion. She looked — well, they all looked, Mary thought (knowing she did) — very beautiful in the glow of the fire, the Christmas lights, the few lamps on the bookcases. Age did not wither . . . or there were beauties in age that were different from those of youth, different from Marie-Laure's, for instance, who did appear in a silk dress and pumps, her face made up, but as sullen and vapid as before. She grudgingly accepted a cookie, asked for a wine spritzer, contributed nothing to the conversation. The sisters dragged up some funny tales from their cooking orgy, but Marie-Laure barely smiled. Mary asked her about her friends and what she'd been doing the past few days, but she sighed, "Just hanging out, really, it's a bore, Boston, compared to New York," and was unforthcoming.

The sisters' conversation sagged. The girl was a dark hole, gradually sucking them in. Then the doorbell rang again. By now, the servants had left except for Doris, who went tearing out cursing at having to leave the sauce on the stove, but tore back with a broad grin — "It's Miss Alex!" Followed by a voluble, laughing, grinning Alex still in her coat, rushing to them, embracing them. "How do you like that, I got the last plane out of Wilmington!"

"How did you get here? Why didn't you call? We would have sent Aldo!"

"Oh, it's Christmas Eve, why shouldn't he have it off, doesn't he have it off? Yes, you see, so I took a cab, it was just as easy, it carried me right to the door! And who's this? It must be your daughter, Mary, she looks so much like you, Marie-Laure, isn't it, I'm Alex, I'm so happy to meet you, oh, I'm so thrilled to be here, isn't it wonderful? David was so understanding, I think all these years he's felt he was depriving me of my Christian heritage, isn't that a joke, when I never had one, really, my family hardly ever went to church, but I do love Christmas, I don't think about it as the birth of a god, just the solstice, the change in the year, the start of longer days. The worst time of year, the darkest, the shortest days, but it's also the beginning of the change. Don't you feel that?"

By then, Ronnie had taken off her coat, Mary had led her to a chair, and Elizabeth had poured her a glass of white wine. She giggled increasingly over these attentions. A rapt Marie-Laure sat still, observing an alien species.

"Oh, the tree! It's gorgeous! Oh I could weep, I wish I'd been here to put it up with you, maybe next year, I have to check the calendar to see if next year I can get away a little sooner, it all depends on when Hanukkah is, you understand, I have to be home for that. It's so exquisite, just the right size, and those darling ornaments, they must be antique, look at that one with the white snow all over it and that little gold and white one." She leapt up and began fingering the ornaments, oohing and ahing over special beauties. "What are we having for dinner? I'm starving!"

"Alex, I couldn't remember, do you eat pork?"

"Yes, we don't keep kosher. David doesn't believe in it. I do what he wants about these things, you know. I think the real reason is he hated his mother's cooking. They keep kosher, his parents, but they will eat at my house. Just I'm careful what I cook when they come. The rules are very tricky even if you don't keep two sets of dishes and all that. So what are we having?"

"Seviche, baked fresh ham, roast filet of beef, mashed potatoes, yams, white turnips pureed with celeriac and leeks, white onions in cream sauce, applesauce, beet and horseradish sauce, carrots in honey, melted goat cheese salad, and apple pie with ice cream and cheddar cheese: enough for you?"

"God! What a feast! We'll have so many leftovers. We should take them to the homeless!"

"They won't take leftover food," Ronnie said.

"Oh, my! What a waste!"

"Nothing goes to waste in this house," Ronnie said. "What doesn't get recycled and fed to us, the servants will eat."

"Oh! That's all right then! I can eat with an easy conscience!" Alex giggled.

And she did, all of them did except Marie-Laure, who picked and pushed her food about, but managed to drink two glasses of wine and two of champagne, and who then, to their relief, announced her exhaustion, and went up to bed.

Silence followed her.

"You have a problem kid, Mary," Elizabeth said finally.

"I know. I've known for a long time. It's all my fault. I've been avoiding facing it. They were all difficult. They never got any real parenting. They're unlikable. All of them. Even I don't like them."

She frowned. "The way she eats," she began tentatively, anxiously, "or doesn't eat. It's so like me. The way I used to be. Did you notice? Do you think . . ." She searched their faces, mouth trembling.

"Father?" Elizabeth asked, horrified.

"I watched her like a hawk when we were here. I always insisted she sleep in my room. But that man . . . you know, he had such sneaky ways. Do you think it's possible . . . ?"

They exchanged gazes.

"He was so old by then . . . Do you think he still . . . ?"

"He screwed my mother until she was too sick," Ronnie said in a low murmur.

"How do you know that?"

"She told me."

Cabot, he so loving, so sweet. And when I get sick, loving different. With that serene smile. Complacent. Loved.

"What can I do?" Mary was digging her fingernails into her cheeks.

"Nothing right now. You don't even know it happened. She could easily be the way she is without that," Elizabeth said, lighting up.

"Maybe you could ask her," Alex suggested.

Mary was appalled: "Propose that her grandfather raped her? Suppose he didn't?"

"Maybe you should tell her about you," Alex went on, "or we should tell her about us. I'm all for openness now. I really yelled at my mother. It did me a world of good, I don't know about her. She walked around wounded for a few days, but then she went right on being the way she was."

"And how was that?" Elizabeth asked with a sidelong grin. "Indefatigably cheerful?"

"Yes! How did you know?"

"Wild guess."

"Yes. She's always nice. You know? Very nice. Makes it hard to stay angry at her. But I did. All week. She was upset anyway at not having a Christmas tree, so she went off to stay with a friend in the middle of Hanukkah. She didn't even know I was coming up here. And David and the kids are at his mom and dad's tonight, the last night. They'll have a good time. So they won't miss either of us. You see, it's going to work out fine."

"And what about David and the inheritance?" Elizabeth asked.

"Well, he was shaken. He had no idea Father was so rich. He had no idea anyone was so rich, really. Not in reality, only in magazines and newspapers, you know? And he was upset. He felt it was obscene for anyone to have that much money. He didn't want to burden our kids with it either. He thought it would be fun to buy a boat, and the bay's right there, but we don't need a bigger house now the kids are about to go away to college. And he agreed with me, we don't *need* anything, nothing material. He was wonderful. He's my true husband, I married the right man." She sighed, sipped her wine.

"I thought it would be worse when I told him about the nuns, the clinic, all that. But I offered to share the money with him, he could send it to Israel for the Ethiopian Jews. But he said it was my money, and I didn't need to share it with him, I should do what I wanted with it. And I said I wanted to. So he said he'd take some, not half. And he understood about the nuns." She stopped, stretched her glass out for a refill, and Elizabeth poured it in automatically. Her face was gilded by the firelight, shadowed by her golden hair, and she sat far back in her chair, reminiscing.

"We were sitting in our den, it was late, the news had gone off, we usually go up to bed then, but we were talking, sitting on the couch, holding hands. And I tried to explain what I wanted to do, explain it so he wouldn't feel I was abandoning him and the kids, explain it as a force of my passion, but you know me, I'm so inarticulate, I just meandered and blabbed and his face looked so dark to me, shadowed. And he put his hand up over my mouth, very gently, he just said, 'Stop.' "

"And he said, 'For a long time now, I've felt I was losing you. I didn't know what to do. I didn't think it was another man. I didn't even think it was the nuns, or your volunteer work. It was almost — as if you were going into a private world that no one else could enter — almost like madness. You were so shut off. From all of us. We've all felt it. You haven't noticed.'

"I turned in some surprise. 'I have noticed the kids have become — well, more yours than mine. More yours than they used to be.'

" 'I've been worried,' he said. 'Sort of sick about it. I even had a talk with Stan Allen, the shrink at work. Just sort of a general talk. He mentioned menopause. That didn't sound right to me.'

" 'It's a little early for that, David!' I said. 'I'm only thirty-six!'

" 'Yes. I guess. But this sounds right. Some kind of passionate mission you feel inside. There's always been that quality in you. Something interior, buried, profound.'

" 'You've felt that in me! When I didn't myself? That's amazing. Oh, David, I love you so much!'

"Well, we kissed each other and went upstairs and that was the end of that conversation. It was the end of the subject. I just have to make the practical plans, and he's as engaged in it as I am, he wants to help, so it's all wonderful, I'm so happy, all my fears were for nothing, isn't life a miracle?"

If theirs were not, they were full of joy for her, the little one with the mission, the incomprehensible one, the mad one, the golden-haired child who was a blade of grass, and they toasted her, and David, and the blessing of knowing what you want to do in life. So there were embraces, and a few tears on Alex's part, and more drinks all around — champagne this time — and then she wanted to know about them.

And suddenly Ronnie wanted to share her news.

"Well, I've had a kind of surprise," she began shyly. All looked at her attentively. "After you left, I felt somehow out of sorts and I decided to clean my mother's room. She had nothing, of course, just old junk, and I was tossing it all out, she bought herself nothing all those years. And then I found the reason. She had put almost every cent she earned here in a bank account, and as soon as I was old enough, she made it a joint account so it belongs to me now. It's not a lot of money by your standards, but it's a fortune by mine, over two hundred thousand dollars, and it means I'll be able to be self-supporting from the minute I get a job, I'll be able to live with some comfort — which I've never done in my life! Is that great or what!"

"SHE did it," Elizabeth exploded in triumph. "Without him. Without his help! She took care of you! Here's to Noradia, a true heroine!"

"To Noradia!" the others cheered, lifting their glasses, laughing, what a benison, what a blessing, what a great thing for Ronnie.

"It almost consoles me for Father," Elizabeth concluded.

"Oh, Lizzie, how could I have taken his money?" Ronnie asked sadly.

"You're right." Grimly spoken.

"Well, that's sort of how I feel too," Alex said. "As if I don't want the money he left me, not for myself. I've made my own life, I don't want that — opulence — for myself. It's too hard to maintain and too unsatisfying. But oh, I do want to help those poor people in El Salvador."

"Well, let's hope you do. So many charitable efforts backfire. Turn ugly. Watch it, Alex."

"Yes. And be careful of yourself. They don't just shoot their own down there, you know. They even shoot foreigners. Even Americans! Even nuns!" Mary warned.

Alex looked alarmed. "Are you turning against it, now?"

"No, no! But it isn't as simple as it might seem. Not that it seems simple."

"No. I intend to be guided by the nuns — they've done this before, they know all about it. And we're starting small, only spending a couple of million to begin with, a small clinic. Carefully. Working our way in in a nonthreatening way, helping mainly the children at first. I've had a couple of talks with them. They were quite cheerful talks I might add! Great fun! They were of course ecstatic! And quite boozy by the end! It's been the greatest week — well, the greatest month of my life! Meeting you, and then all this! Even though Father died, even though I . . . I never really knew him, after all. Except carnally!" she suddenly burst out in a hysterical giggle.

They all joined in, in a suddenly self-aware discomforted ironic giggle, then the laughter died down into a greater quiet, the crackle of the fire, the aching snap of a pine branch.

"And what about the two of you, then? Have you made plans?"

The easiness tensed. "Not really," Mary said.

"I've looked at some houses in Virginia," Elizabeth said unsurely. "Two really beautiful ones. One with four bedrooms, each with its own bath. Enough for each of us, and a study Marie-Laure could stay in." She looked meaningfully at Mary.

Mary averted her gaze. "She won't want to leave New York."

"If and when she wants to. Or if Ronnie wants to bring a friend to visit" — Ronnie's head snapped up — "or Alex wants to bring one of her kids. It's a big house but not a mansion. For all of us . . ." Her voice dwindled off. Perhaps she heard the plea in it.

Mary gazed at her softly. "It sounds lovely, Lizzie."

She could not contain herself. "And you could write poetry, and we could give parties. There are some sophisticated people in Washington, Mary, some of your old friends . . ."

"And we could be together the way I always wanted when we were little. We could play go fish at night!" she laughed.

"Or I'll teach you chess."

"Actually, I know chess. Paul liked to play. But he always had to win. If he didn't win, he threw, he hurled all the pieces across the room! Then he'd expect me to pick them up. I didn't of course, and the servants always had to scurry around next morning. Once a piece got lost, a knight. Paul was furious, blamed me for it. I said good, without a knight we couldn't play anymore, it wasn't much fun playing with a baby anyway. That was the end of the chess phase. I think that's when he bought a new plane, a bigger one."

"You could have the Bosendorfer moved down there. You could play."

"And what would Ronnie do?" she asked playfully.

"Why, design the garden, of course. There's a gorgeous Japanese garden there now, but it occupies only part of the lot. There are a few acres. Ronnie could design the rest, plant it, whatever. . . ."

Ronnie's eyes glistened. "You're not suggesting we all live together, Lizzie."

"Not unless we want to. If it's convenient. Suppose you got a job in Washington?" She saw the look on Ronnie's face. "You might want just to come for long weekends, or Christmas, or Thanksgiving. Family holidays."

That was imaginable. "Yes."

"And Alex, in between jaunts to El Salvador and trips home might want to wind down. No?"

"Oh, I'll be there every Christmas! Promise!"

"Well, think about it," Elizabeth said, sagging a little. They sat in silence then, as if obeying her. The fire was dying, but it was late, and no one got up to refresh it. A sudden sweep against the window made them sit up.

Ronnie jumped up and looked out the sliding glass door. "It's snowing!" she cried.

They all leapt up and huddled around the window. "Snow!" they announced, and as if they were observing a miracle, they embraced each other, standing there looking out at the soft white drift settling in the pines, the bare gray branches of the dogwoods, on the dry dead ground.

26

Brilliant with snow, the morning did seem to signal a season's difference, a turning from darkness to light. But the sisters discarded its metaphoric baggage to delight in it as they came downstairs in robes and slippers. Each exclaimed on the light, the wonderful light, "like morning in your heart," Alex gushed. Elizabeth murmured almost to herself, "As bright as the sky over Africa, but a different color," making Ronnie think jealously, shit, she's even been to Africa.

Mrs. Browning had set up a tea table in the playroom, and now she loaded it with coffee and juices, a steaming quiche, crunchy French rolls, platters of cakes filled with raisins, apples, nuts, cinnamon. They pulled the drapes as far open as possible, turned on the tree lights, and luxuriated in the food, complacently eyeing the presents heaped up under the tree. No rush. Everything was for pleasure today, they all seemed simultaneously and silently to have decided.

"But where's Marie-Laure?" Mary cried in dismay and ran out of the room and through to the foyer and up the stairs, where she knocked on her daughter's door. No response. She opened the door. Marie-Laure was in a deep sleep, and only vaguely roused at her mother's voice.

"Come down, dear, it's Christmas morning! And it snowed and it's beautiful! You can come down in your robe, we're all in our robes."

The girl moaned and turned over.

Mary shook her shoulder. "Marie-Laure, I want you to get up and come downstairs."

"In a while," she mumbled.

"No, now!"

"Oh, fuck off, Mother," she muttered sullenly, and blood filled Mary's head and she hauled off and smacked the side of Marie-Laure's face. Startled, stung, the girl sat up. Her eyes were wild.

"You hit me!"

"Yes!" Mary shouted. "And will again if you ever speak to me like that again! Now get up and brush your teeth and come downstairs!"

Shocked, the girl got out of bed. Mary watched while she went into her bathroom, waited until she came out again. She was wearing only a T-shirt.

"Do you have a robe?"

Sullen shake of head.

"Wait."

Mary marched out of the room and into her own, found a robe, carried it back. "Put this on. And some socks, or something on your feet."

The girl obeyed.

"Down!"

Marie-Laure started down the stairs, Mary following grimly, but she entered the playroom smiling, crying "Here we are!" As the sisters greeted Marie-Laure, Mary announced, "But we need music! And I brought some!"

She opened a brown paper bag and pulled out tapes of Renaissance and early Italian music, and inserted one in the deck. As it began to play, she sighed, cried, "Isn't that gorgeous!" (thinking, god I sound just like Alex, I wonder if she always feels the way I do now, on the edge of hysteria) and settled herself in an armchair with some coffee and a plate of quiche.

Marie-Laure sipped orange juice and picked at some quiche. The sisters ate leisurely, fully. They barely talked. They wallowed, murmured at a beautiful passage of music, at a waft of snow blown from branch to ground, at a bird's swooping down at some possible breakfast. Ronnie gathered up crumbs from their plates and opened the sliding doors and hurled the crumbs out to the ground, where soon a small bird community gathered. The satiated sisters watched.

"There's enough quiche left for the kitchen," Alex said suddenly, and went inside to tell Mrs. Browning and Teresa to clear the table. "The quiche is still a little warm, you might want to finish it," she added, causing eyebrows to rise in the kitchen. Of course, they had intended to do just that, after a swipe in the microwave.

"No, no more coffee," Elizabeth said lazily, "but you know what I'd like? A beer. Do we have any beer, Mrs. Browning?" She asked, as the woman came in to clear.

"Beer?" She stopped clearing. "Well, we must, the larder here is kept stocked with everything. But you're sure you want a beer at ten-thirty in the morning, Miz Upton?"

"Let's all have beer," Mary decided. "Or a Bloody Mary. Yes, I'd rather have that. I'll make them. I used to make them for Paul, he loved them." She stood up, gazing helplessly at the not-yet-stocked bar.

"All very well to tell us we can eat, but now they want the bar stocked," Mrs. Browning muttered to Teresa in the kitchen as she angrily filled an ice bucket and sliced a lime.

Ronnie waited until they were all settled back with drinks — Marie-Laure also had a beer — to ask like an eager child, "Can we have presents now?"

As Elizabeth handed out the packages ceremoniously, Mary said, "Lizzie, remember when we were little and had Christmas with Father, and sometimes Worth and Harriet and Sam and Pru would be here with their kids, and Worth said that when they were growing up, their father made a rule that the youngest would open a package first, then the next youngest, and so on, and we had to sit there squirming, of course we were the youngest, well, I was, so I went first, but I could only open one package, and then we had to wait until everybody else opened one before we could open another one? And Father said it was good discipline?"

Lizzie smiled, nodding.

"I hated it then, did you?"

"No. It helped to conceal the fact that I got so many fewer presents than all the rest of you. After I'd opened my last box — it was always a bathrobe or a blouse, something I really didn't care about — I could slip away with the presents I loved, the books, and no one would even notice."

"Well, I had lots of presents of course. And I hated it then. But I think we should do it today. Not for discipline — just to draw it out. To exclaim over each thing. To appreciate each thing fully. What do you say?" she asked her sisters.

They liked the idea, so when all the gifts had been distributed, Mary told Marie-Laure to go first. Not knowing she would be there, the sisters had not brought presents for her, but Mary had brought so many that the girl had as high a heap as the others. She pulled languidly at the string on one box, while the others watched. It took her a long time to loosen it, then, using her hands delicately, careful of her long nails, she savagely tore away the beautiful heavy wrapping paper. She pulled out a pair of white silk pajamas.

"Oh, cool. Thanks," she said, dropping the pajamas back in their box, picking up her beer.

Their faces shadowed with disappointment, but Mary said cheerfully, "I'm glad you like them. Ronnie's next!"

She opened a huge box, Elizabeth's gift, a fleece-lined calfskin jacket richer than anything she had ever owned, or even seen close up. She looked up at Elizabeth with glistening eyes.

"When I looked at it, I just felt it was you," Elizabeth said dismissively, feeling banal.

But they all said something similar as each gift was opened, because they had all chosen their gifts with the same deep interest, the same deep sense of who the other was. And except for Marie-Laure, who greeted all her presents listlessly, they paid the same kind of attention to the opening of the gifts, exclaiming over each, discovering in each what made it special, gorgeous, one more item in a treasure heaped at their feet, the marvels the world had to offer, all the beauty and wit of human production, the making of things for the delectation of the senses. So as a chorus, they remarked on the lovely richness of color of the cashmere sweater Mary had chosen for Ronnie, the lovely structure of the lightweight denim jumpsuit Elizabeth gave Alex, its pale soft color, its wonderful weight and texture, its fitness for hard work in a tropical climate. And so it went through the light nylon windbreaker Mary gave her, which would fold into nothing and never wrinkle; and the gorgeous square scarf Elizabeth gave Mary, threaded with gold and purple, that illuminated her eyes, and the tiny velvet purse Alex had discovered for Mary, lined with satin, as beautiful and luxurious as Mary herself. For Elizabeth, Alex had found a globe of the world that came with a set of paste ons that changed borders and country names at will, and Mary had found an antique Mexican silver cigarette case with the Aztec calendar on its face.

Ronnie's eyes burned. They had all also bought small gifts for each other — handkerchiefs, sachets, perfume, potpourri, soaps, chocolates filled with liqueurs and creams. She did not belong in this company; she did not understand gift giving like this. In her world one never bought useless things, things you did not absolutely need. Her small offerings fell to the bottom of the pile, and she dreaded their discovery.

But eventually, of course, they were discovered.

By this time, they had lost track of turns, and Elizabeth opened her small package. "From Ronnie!" she announced tearing the paper, as if she were surprised, as if she had not expected a gift from Ronnie. She stared down at two tapes of Bill Evans and his jazz group in performance. She gazed at Ronnie. Her eyes filled.

"Ronnie!" she said softly. "How did you know I love Bill Evans? And this one has 'I Was Up with the Lark Today'! My absolute favorite!"

Ronnie squirmed, studied a bird pecking at a last crumb. "Yeah. You mentioned it once."

"And you remembered." Elizabeth stood up, crossed the room, embraced her. "Thank you so much! So much! I can't tell you what this means to me. Brings back . . . my old tape is long gone, wrecked . . . I played it so often. And it had so many memories," her voice trailed off wistfully.

Mary watched jealously. "It must be my turn, isn't it? What did I get?" she cried, tearing open her gift. She examined the two books — poems by Sharon Olds and Barbara Greenberg. "Oh, I love Sharon Olds! And Barbara Greenberg! Yes, I bought a book of hers, I was reading it when I was here, but this is a different one, oh, Ronnie, you remembered! Thank you, thank you!"

Alex ripped hers open. She exclaimed "Stein — my name?" and studied the book, read the jacket copy aloud. " 'A biography of Edith Stein, the only Jewish Catholic to become a saint.' " Her eyes raised to Ronnie. And she wept.

*   *   *

So it had worked after all, her gifts were the hit of the day, treasured more than the scented, the luxurious, the luscious, the opulent. They were treasured for the memory in them, for the love required to store up memory. But replete with food of every sort, nourished to their bones, they were all affectionate with each other that day, ardently insistent on saying and doing what would make the others feel loved, valuable. Although dinner was served at three so the servants could get home to their own families and their own Christmases before too late, they all dressed for dinner. And again, Ronnie felt loved, accepted, treasured, as they all exclaimed over her new black velvet smoking suit. Mary wore scarlet satin, low-cut and slim-skirted, and Alex wore a beautifully draped turquoise silk dressier than anything they had ever seen her in. Even Elizabeth conceded to the occasion and wore a dress, a pale blue wool that made her eyes brilliant. Marie-Laure wore a skinny short black skirt over a black leotard and very high black heels.

Determined not to let the girl ruin their day, the sisters ignored her sullen silence to chatter and gossip and praise the food, making the meal another orgy of delight. They were so saturated with good feeling that they sent the servants off (heaped with Christmas gifts, cookies, and bottles of wine) as soon as they had served the dessert — a real gift, since much cleaning up remained to be done. But they said they would do it themselves — after a brisk walk through the woods to burn off some calories. Marie-Laure, who had not eaten enough to need to walk it off, stayed behind. She lay on her bed smoking, wearing earphones and listening to rock tapes, staring at the ceiling. Bundling into heavy coats, the sisters did not mention her, but they were relieved at her absence. They walked for a long time in silence. When they began to speak, their voices seemed to reverberate in the evening light. Serenely they returned to clean up the kitchen with music on the tape deck, a little singing, a little dancing, and some hilariously incompetent tap dancing. And the work went fast enough with four of them, so who can say when it was, what it was that turned things, what exploded a perfect day into fragments that had not even seemed to exist within it.

Maybe there can't be any perfect days, Ronnie thought later.

Maybe it was when they were walking in the woods and Mary began to compare the beauties and pleasures of Islamic art, the Alhambra in particular, with the great Christian cathedrals.

"They were of course brilliant mathematicians, those old Moors, and their craftspeople were superb, but the way they *used* light, drew it in, used shade for coolness, the way they built everything — gardens, fountains, pavilions — to celebrate the sensuous pleasure of the created world, it all seems to me so much more humane and *moral* than the austere straining against created nature that you find in the cathedrals. All those arches struggling to stay erect, straining to hold up a roof that never needed to be so high, that was so high only to daunt, to make people feel insignificant. All that cutting out of light, turning everything into dank dark shadows, into stone, into blue glass. It's cruel and antihuman and denying of pleasure — and after all those poor people had little enough — in the name of some god, some power. The West is really crazy," she concluded.

"But it's precisely that effort," Elizabeth burst out (could that be anger in her voice?) "that makes them so splendid! The struggle to go beyond the mundane, the struggle not to live like sensuous animals, to give life significance — that's what makes the cathedrals great!"

"Well," Mary said easily, "if I had to choose between pleasure and significance in life, I'd take the first any day. Any significance you can come up with you have to invent. At least pleasure is real and it nourishes you. Like us today."

Ronnie braced herself for a nasty "Well *you!*" but Elizabeth tightened her lips and said nothing, and the moment passed.

Or maybe it was when Alex, staring at a leafless tree, suddenly began to talk about the condition of the dispossessed peasants in a town in Brazil, describing hovels and huts built on a hillside, men who worked cutting sugarcane for fifty cents a day, not enough to feed a family, the women working as domestics or laundresses for even less. The women had to come all the way down the hill every day at dawn for water, which was delivered in limited supply. If they were lucky enough to be in the front of the line they got water, then had to carry it back up the steep hillside on their heads. If they didn't get water, they had to use river water, deeply polluted by the chemicals used by the cane growers and filled with parasites. In any case, they had to wash clothes in the river. Most of their babies died, Alex said, of starvation and thirst, but whenever they tried to organize themselves to create a crèche or a clinic, the wealthy cane growers and professional men of the city denounced them as communists and thwarted them. They prevented clean water lines from being put through, or electricity, so huts often burned from spilled kerosene. And they denied that the people were starving.

Alex had learned about these people when she attended a talk at the convent by a Dominican nun who had worked with them, but she spoke innocently, without a real sense of the politics of the situation, her sweet light voice rising in outrage at the monsters who exploited these people and kept them in a state of misery so extreme that mothers rarely mourned when a baby died.

"Once upon a time," she concluded sadly, "these people lived on little plots of land, raised their own food, and lived decently. But they were shoved off the land by the growers, who were greedy for bigger cane plantations, by the rich! It's so cruel!" she explained.

"Don't idealize the way they lived. They were probably little better off than animals," Elizabeth said in a stiff authoritative voice. "Their babies still probably died, they were probably hungry then too."

"No, they grew beans, things that nourished them!" Alex cried. "Now they have to have money to buy food!"

"It's true," Elizabeth conceded in that same authoritative voice, "some people are being destroyed by the shift in the world economic order. That's sad, but it can't be helped. These currents are larger than people, they create the changes we call civilization."

"I'd hardly call what they're doing civilized, Lizzie," Alex objected mildly.

"Alex, you're a political naif, I can't have this discussion with you. But things aren't as black-and-white as you imagine."

Which silenced Alex, and that ended.

But the real trigger was Ronnie herself, when they were back at the house and had finished cleaning the kitchen, and were relaxing in the playroom with drinks. The tape, a Gregorian chant, had run out, but everyone was feeling too lazy to get up and put another one on, and feeling utterly benevolent, Ronnie said, "This was one of the best days of my life."

"Ummm," Mary mumbled. "Me too."

"Oh, me too," Alex said fervently.

"It's so great when women do things together," Ronnie went on. Then she told them about the dinner her friend Linda had had for her. "You know, it was the opposite of this, but it was great too. She's a graduate student, she hasn't got two cents, she lives in a dingy apartment, well, all my friends are poor, they all live like that, but they wanted to celebrate, it's something they do a lot, me too when I lived there. And everybody brings something, you know, pasta or bean soup or rice and beans or a stew, bread, salad, wine, fruit, and we talk and laugh and eat and we all help clean up, and there are no zinging egos flying across the room, no pretenses about manliness to bolster, no lies to defend. We just have a great time."

Elizabeth's chin changed. Was it jealousy at the fact of all those friends? An implicit challenge in Ronnie's saying that dinner had been as fine as this one? The mention of defended lies? The accumulated pleasures of the day lying thick and lardy on an austere heart? Or was it a recognition of some essential difference in her from all the rest of them? Whatever hit her, she was palpably hit. She glared at Ronnie, included the others in the glare, burst into speech.

"You all make me sick with your idealization of femaleness, as if women were morally better than men, as if they had a different nature! What sentimental slop! What a stupid ideal to entertain, some sweet little domestic world, everyone sharing, loving, cooperative, no egos, what a laugh! Who's more competitive than women, I ask you! Weight, shape, clothes, hair, nails, cooking, they work like dogs to vie for men men men! And women have such nasty little ways of getting at each other, all the while smiling, such hypocrites, at least men pull out weapons and kill each other directly!

"Do you really think if there were only women, if we could reproduce ourselves alone, we'd all be living in some communal paradise? We'd all be living in grass huts, that's what!"

When she paused to take a long drag on her cigarette, Ronnie said calmly, "Actually, if you look at the remains of matricentric societies, they lived in considerable luxury and well-being. Without war. And even if we did live in grass huts, if we got along and had enough to eat — and the evidence shows we did when we controlled our own lives and crops, most of the time at least — it might not be so bad. Compare a grass hut to some of the cribs in Roxbury and the South Bronx, and it doesn't look half bad," she laughed lightly.

"Oh, what nonsense!" Elizabeth interrupted. "War broke out eventually, didn't it? When there were enough people, when there was crowding. It was inevitable. It's part of the beast we are! All this feminist nonsense, it's as bad as Marxism, it asserts, simply asserts, that we are kind loving cooperative creatures when every line in every book of history testifies to something else! The commies insisted we were something else, they tried to remake human nature by fiat, look where it's gotten them, they've created the most oppressive society that ever existed — worse than any oriental tyrant, dictator, emperor. The only way you can build a halfway civilized society is by taking into consideration the fact that we are savage, cruel, competitive, aggressive, predatory animals. We're killers, like other large mammals! Haven't you ever heard of survival of the fittest? Well, who do you imagine are the fittest? The most savage, the most efficient killers — and here I'll grant you, men take the prize. And the best you can do is protect yourself against them. But it's inevitable that the weak will be destroyed, they will be exterminated. It's happening clear across the globe right now. Every primitive society, every simple society is being wiped out, there's nothing you can do about that, it's nature, human nature, it's inevitable because it's necessary! And it has a function: it keeps the human race strong!"

"That's terrible!" Alex gasped. "You can't be serious, Lizzie."

"I'm dead serious. You all are a bunch of sentimentalists! You don't know what you're talking about most of the time. Jesus Christ, what kind of world do you think you live in? You think our little idyll in Lincoln is anything but a dream made possible — bought and paid for — by the savagery of our forefathers, who robbed and seized and cheated and bribed and killed sufficiently to realize a little island in the middle of hell?

"What do you think is going on out there! Constantly! The prime minister of India is assassinated, hijackers killed passengers in the airport in Teheran, a chemical factory explodes in Bhopal, hundreds of thousands of people are starving to death in Burkina Faso, and that's just in the last few weeks! And that doesn't count civil wars in hundreds of places across the globe — El Salvador that Alex is so passionate about is hardly the only place, look at what's going on in Ethiopia, Nicaragua, Chile, Afghanistan,

Sri Lanka, Cambodia, Mozambique, Angola, Jesus, even that only skims the surface. And beyond that, look at what people do to each other on the streets of so-called civilized countries, murder and mayhem, even people who love each other or say they do, how many men murder their wives or girlfriends every day, you can't count them, how many if you added them up, beatings, rapes, torture, murders, in all the cities, in the towns, in villages, in the countryside across the world?

"You don't even need to be invaded by hooligans, your own father will do the job right inside that idyllic home! Just like our father! And if he doesn't, your mother may hit you or worse.

"There is no safe place, that's an illusion, there is no security even though people struggle for it their whole lives long as if it existed, as if enough money or power or prestige can insulate you. But we know better, don't we? We are constantly besieged, threatened, life is constant struggle, the best you can do is claw your way to some temporary security, some island like this house or my job or some academic post" — she glanced at Ronnie — "and try for dear life to hold on.

"And beyond that, out there, it's the same: empty space with exploding stars, black holes, planets of methane ice, comets, and now there's a hole in the ozone layer, and acid rain, and god knows what else threatening us.

"It's a struggle to find enough food, to find drinkable water in most parts of the world, and then you have to avoid provoking your fellow man, who may just pull out an Uzi or an AK-47 or whatever the current designer weapon may be. You have to be armed, armed with something, a weapon or money, position, some kind of power, because the name of the game is war, constant war, that's what it is to be alive!"

She fell back, exhausted, her eyes wild, her hands pulling at her hair, her cigarette out. She stared dully at the wall. The others gazed at her, aghast, and remained silent for a long time.

"Oh, poor Lizzie," Alex whispered, finally.

"That's quite a vision, Elizabeth," Ronnie said quietly.

"It's not a vision!" she cried, "it's reality!" She sat up and lighted a fresh cigarette. "Don't you see? Don't you realize?"

"But it's not the only reality," Alex said softly. "It's not all of reality."

"No," Mary murmured. "What about all the beauty, the beauty of days, of light, of nature, of cities, of people? What about all the lovely things we gave each other today, all the wonderful things we ate, the fun we had?"

"And it's not the only truth about us, either, about human beings," Ronnie said stubbornly. "We're not all at war with each other, we help each other. Where I come from, it's a world you don't know, no one would survive if the women didn't watch each other's kids, take each other's kids, sometimes for months, for god's sake. They share food, there's always room for one more at the table even if things are rough, and they lend each other stuff — a blanket, a heavy coat, whatever.

"Listen, I work with nature at the lowest level. Mosses and lichen are called lower plants, they don't have the complexity of larger ones — although some mosses are unisexual and some bisexual," she grinned. "But our entire ecology depends on them, among other such species. And lichen, which is probably one of the first forms of life to appear on earth, which is thus fundamental to other life, is symbiotic, it's made up of two different species that need each other to exist. It survives by cooperating, not conflict. It can live where nothing else can live — in the highest mountains where nothing else grows, at the edges of the oceans, at the very top of the highest tropical trees where the sun blazes too strongly for any other plant. It even lives at the bottom of those trees, where the climate is too dark or wet for other plants. And it's a frontier plant, it makes soil, one of a few species that do. It *creates*.

"And much of nature works this way. If you want to talk about the nature that is in us, and from which we arise, you should think about how the nature outside us works. You know some botanists — guys — the guys are always looking for signs of domination in nature — tried to make out that the fungi are dominant in lichen, because they're more conspicuous and have greater volume. But they concluded that the fungi are utterly dependent on the algae, maybe even more dependent on the algae than the algae are on them. Things are not the way they seem. Consider your father, my mother. There's no comparison between them in terms of power, fame, wealth, you can't even discuss them in the same breath. But I doubt, if your father had died, my mother would have had a stroke — assuming she wasn't already dead. My mother seemed to be completely dependent on your father. But the truth was otherwise. . . ."

She paused, lighted a cigarette, continued in a calmer voice. "Your vision is a male vision, a capitalist vision, well I suppose today's communists have it too, it's the vision that justified the changes in economic structure from feudalism to industrialization. It's taught to us to keep us in line, but it isn't necessarily the truth about human nature. They want us to believe it so we'll go on fighting their wars and dying for them, dying to bolster their power, so they can increase their wealth and only give the dead medals.

"You have to believe this stuff so you can go on working for that administration, go on believing in the economic principles you learned in school. You have to believe it to justify your life. But we don't."

Elizabeth sat erect. "That's nonsense! You are all simply willfully blind. Naive. Well, I don't know why I should expect more from you than other people. Few people are willing to face unpleasant realities. They'd rather console themselves with a hot dog, a beer, and the tube. Like animals!" she snorted.

"Well, we are animals," Alex murmured. "Rather sweet ones, I think, at root."

"Oh, like the torturers of El Salvador?" Elizabeth asked sarcastically. "Or Chile, or Peru, or Argentina, or Algeria, or Vietnam? Do you really think your clinic is going to make a significant difference, is going to affect the problem?"

Alex frowned, considering the question seriously. "I think opening a clinic can ease the pain of some people — maybe hundreds of people. That's all," she concluded.

"And suppose the government decides your clinic is subversive, then what? Suppose they send death squads to shoot you and the nuns, rape you first maybe. Have you considered that that very well may happen, that it happens often where you're going?"

"I do know that," she answered softly.

Elizabeth looked at her, and her eyes filled with tears. "Don't do it, Alex. Don't go! It's asking for trouble! Don't go!"

"Oh, Lizzie." Alex got up and went to her sister and embraced her. Elizabeth sobbed aloud into her cupped hands.

Mary took a deep hit on her joint. What a shock, Lizzie sobbing like that, I can't remember her sobbing ever, ever, even when she dislocated her elbow when she fell out of a tree that time we were climbing in it. Father was so angry, said young ladies don't climb trees, we never did it again, it was so much fun I really loved it, it was too bad.

Was that what it was all about, fear for Alex? I'm afraid for her too, Lizzie's right, she has no idea what she's getting into, I wouldn't go to such a place for anything, not for anything. Not anything. But she . . . who can fathom her?

Such an outburst, is that how she really sees life, how can she bear to go on living? You hear men talk that way, but I always have trouble believing they mean what they say, I always think they're just saying that to justify some particularly vicious business deal, something that harms other people . . . dog-eat-dog world, they say, but only when they've just done the eating. Tough world, they say, you have to be tough, hardheaded, which means not feeling anything. And they do it, I know they do it, but then don't they go home and unbend somehow, ease into a different mode, enjoy their kids, their wife, their dinner? Even Paul, and he was the hardest of my husbands, he could be really tender with me at times. Those were the times when I liked him, when he relaxed and sat in the sun and swam and had a gin and tonic and smiled and let himself enjoy just being alive. . . .

Ronnie's right, she has to believe that stuff to justify her work, which is after all her life. She hasn't had much of a love life I don't think, she has no kids, I don't think she has any friends. . . .

Poor Lizzie. So lonely. I never saw it before. Begging me to move down there, really that's what it amounted to, I never thought I'd hear her beg, when I think how I used to beg her, please please Lizzie, play house with me, swim with me, you want to roller-skate on the terrace?

Truth is, I don't have any friends either, not real friends, not friends like Ronnie has, and Alex with those nuns, the way she talks about Sister Evangeline, nun in a business suit flying all across the country raising money, things have certainly changed, and Sister Bernadette with the freckles and the humor drinking Irish whiskey, she really loves them. . . .

Lizzie and I, we got the worst of it. Alex was removed early, Father never treated Ronnie as part of the family, we got the full blast of his contempt and the manners too, the rules, so many rules. . . .

Mary stubbed out her joint and placed the roach in her little cloisonné case. She rubbed her hands up and down her arms, feeling chilled, alone. The night sky was starless and gray as if a dark dull blanket covered the heavens. She rose heavily and moved toward the bed, not tonight relishing the pleasure of getting into it, sliding her immaculate body between the cool clean white sheets. She didn't, tonight, feel immaculate.

All games I play with myself — white foods, white night clothes, white sheets, white rooms. An illusion I create for myself daily, over and over in rituals, to create the illusion of cleanness, purity, to feel immaculate. But I'm not. Not. I am as corrupted, corrupting, as any other human on earth. Look at what I did to my children. What is wrong with my daughter, my baby? What am I going to do? What can help her? Is it possible that Father . . .

Lizzie is right: we are a cruel selfish predatory race.

Tears squirmed sidewise down her cheeks as she lay there. She didn't wipe them away.

Her poor heart torn up like that, believing such things, well of course she's right to a degree, but the degree makes all the difference. What do I mean by that? Still, I know I'm right.

Alex carefully hung up her dress, smoothing down the silk folds lovingly, such a lovely soft silk, so wonderful to feel. So many wonderful things in life, she leaves all that out of her accounting. Economics she calls it, a science she says, it's a peculiar science if it leaves out half of existence, more than half, but maybe all sciences do that, certainly medicine does, I watch the doctors at St. Mary's, they forget the spirit, they forget how important it is to be held and touched and consoled. Also they forget nutrition, at St. Mary's at least. The terrible food they serve patients, don't they think they would get better faster with healthier food? All they can see is medication and surgery, well my clinic will do a better job, we'll have fresh food there for patients who need that more than they need a pill. Fruit, vegetables, rice and beans, and there will always be a pot of soup cooking in my clinic.

She brushed her teeth and washed her face, barely seeing it in the mirror over the sink, seeing instead a parched plain, the sun beating down on the tin roof of a low white stucco building surrounded by trees and ferns. A canvas canopy extended its shelter all along one side, where people sat in the shade, cups of clean water in their hands, their bodies cooled by the surrounding plants, waiting patiently for a kind, attentive nurse who would know exactly how to help them.

She got into bed and switched off the lamp, but her eyes were wide open. She saw people lying on cots, their faces radiant with the quiet happiness that suffuses the very ill when their pain abates. She heard crying babies quiet down as water and food calmed their agony, saw skin ulcers on thin brown legs cleaned and bandaged, saw faces of people who could not be healed untwist into calm as their pain at least was relieved. Her own face was radiant.

But a frown slowly lined her forehead as another image supplanted this one, an image of men in combat boots and uniforms made of camouflage material carrying automatic guns, invading the harmonious scene. They raised their guns, they spattered shot. The waiting patients fell over, blood spurted like a bouquet of flowers on their pale clothes. The men stormed inside the clinic, dragged out the nuns and Alex in her light blue jumpsuit, threw them on the ground. . . .

No.

Don't think about that. It's unlikely. We'll do everything we can to pacify them, we'll stay miles away from anything political, we won't provoke them. . . .

Of course Lizzie's right, that is the way things are. It's possible it can happen. But not necessarily. There are lots of church clinics where such a thing has never happened. But she's not right about human nature. No. She's blindsided, one-eyed. Look at how she herself, the exemplar of toughness and discipline and she can be harsh, we've all seen it, yet she wept for me, begged me not to go.

Alex's eyes filled.

How sweet, how loving that was, her plea. Lizzie loves me. I love her too. And I don't want to die. But I have to go.

Jesus H. Christ, who would have imagined such fury, such heartbreak in Elizabeth, all that stuff steeping down in her insides while she walks around like a fucking general inspecting the troops. What a way to see life! No wonder she carries herself the way she does. I wonder what her insides feel like. You'd think she'd give up those ideas for the sake of her stomach if nothing else.

Ronnie turned on her side, closed her eyes, but her mind was racing.

So unnecessary. She takes the political philosophers of the last couple of centuries, the males of today because it's always guys who preach this stuff as if they had a handle on absolute truth. When anyone with half a brain can see that this notion that humans or anyway men are innately and utterly aggressive is just a justification for all the power shifts of the last couple of centuries. Anyone who raises little boys knows how sweet and loving they can be, look at Téo, there's nothing necessary about their aggressiveness, they're taught it, taught it means manliness. Like poor Raoul, he was a sweet kid till he joined that gang. And even afterwards, when he was with Rosa or me or his sisters. I remember him combing Lidia's hair, and making tea for Rosa once when she was sick, carrying it to her so tenderly, caressing her forehead, pleading, "You feel better soon, Mama?"

Doesn't she see that? I suppose she hasn't had many models, doesn't seem to know many men very well, I wonder why, Jesus, I'm a dyke and I know tons of sweet men, look at Professor Madrick or Professor Goldie, of course there's also that asshole Reilly, and there are plenty of men like him but they're not all like that.

Of course it's true that men have committed the great sweeping crimes against humanity, Hitler, Stalin, Mussolini, the tsars, Napoleon, Alexander, Genghis Khan, all those millionaires who built American industry, J. Edgar Hoover, whatshisface Palmer, the guys who run the companies that pollute everything. . . . It's true that lots of men are greedy aggressive cruel predatory that all they want is power, money. . . .

She turned on her other side.

But the human race would never have survived if we were all like that. Survival of the fittest, huh! They're not the fittest, they think they are, they grab the best of everything, the most of everything, they leave people to starve. But they die, they destroy their kids, turn them into suicides like Wittgenstein's father, turn them into neurotics. Their sperm doesn't conquer the world. The rest of the human race would go down the tubes if it were left to them. But we don't. Lots of us die young, babies in Ethiopia now, the cane cutters' babies Alex was talking about in the northeast of Brazil, millions and millions do die because of the policies of the very rich. But millions live, and they live because they help each other, they share, they cooperate, they love.

Love.

She sat straight up, stared glumly at the wall, got out of bed and fished for a cigarette on her desk.

You haunting me, Momma? she wondered, exhaling smoke as she climbed back into the bed. She leaned back against the hard headboard of the bed, pulled a pillow behind her, sat there smoking.

Even in the death camps, people cooperated, shared. The women especially. Kept them alive.

Can't tell that to Lizzie, she'd never hear it. Sentimental slop, she'd say. Idealization. Rosa taking Bianca's three kids from two floors up when Bianca was in jail. Nine months they lived with us, and we barely had room ourselves, nine months she fed those kids when feeding her own was a struggle. She took me in, for that matter.

Jesus, what would have happened to me without her?

You didn't think about that, did you, the other night, deciding not to go there again. You can never not go there again, you hear me? No matter what. Rosa saved your life.

Think you're alone, well, you are alone, you and your body and whatever happens to you, no one else can ever know completely, still, there's an eye that sees, a hand reached out, food given, comfort, sympathy. I've been lavished with that all my life, Momma, Rosa, all my friends. Now them. Even Lizzie, despite her beliefs.

Can't live her way. Can't. You must frizzle up inside and turn into a robot, or else you die, really die.

You must love to live, Ronnie.

She stubbed out the cigarette, lay down again, and closed her eyes. A wave of tiredness caught her and she turned sighing, surrendering to it.

Yes, Momma.

27

Marie-Laure was the first to leave. She announced at breakfast that she'd called a friend, who was coming to pick her up and return her to Boston. Mary — who had breakfast downstairs that morning — protested she could stay longer, could leave with them — Aldo would drop her in Boston on the way to the airport that afternoon. But Marie-Laure insisted she couldn't wait until the afternoon, that her friends were going to a movie that afternoon and she wanted to join them.

"We haven't even had time for a heart-to-heart!"

Marie-Laure gimlet-eyed her. "A what?"

"A talk. A long quiet talk together."

Marie-Laure grimaced.

"What time are they coming?"

"Umm. Around eleven?"

"Umm. That means maybe not until twelve. Anyway, they can wait. Put on your coat and boots. We're going for a walk." Mary rose and left the room.

"There's snow on the ground!" Marie-Laure whined after her. But Mary was halfway up the stairs and did not respond.

The girl sighed, dragged herself out of her chair and followed her mother.

Fifteen minutes later, warmly dressed and in fur-lined boots, Mary stood tapping her foot by the front door. "Hurry up, Marie-Laure," she yelled up the stairs, a thing she had never done before, in this house or any other. The girl eventually appeared and sauntered down the stairs.

"We'll walk towards town," Mary said, taking her arm.

Marie-Laure allowed herself to be led, but she was silent as they walked down the long driveway toward the road, silent as they turned onto it and headed toward town. Mary was silent too until finally her daughter burst out, "I don't understand what you're doing. Why this sudden interest? You've never been interested in talking to me before."

"Have I not?" Mary's face was surprised. "I haven't spent time with you shopping for clothes for prep school and college, helping you pack? I've never taken you to dinner, lunch, movies? I've never asked you about your grades, about your classes?"

"Rarely!" Marie-Laure exploded. "I mean, really, I could count the times. You're always off with some *man*." She gave the last word a bitter charge.

Mary did not respond, and they walked awhile in silence again, until Marie-Laure burst out again. "I mean, my whole childhood, you were off somewhere with some man. In Capri or Vail or Virginia or Paris or London or god knows where, while we stayed home alone with a nanny, Bertie and I. Martin was away at school, you were off with some man, my father never even bothered to lay eyes on me, so you'll understand, Mother" — she gave that word a bitter charge too — "that I am not accustomed to parental attention."

"I took you with me! To Capri, to Vail! To Virginia!"

"You took us a few times. Paul didn't like children, remember? And Don . . . well when he was around, we could have dropped dead and you wouldn't have noticed."

Mary mulled that over for a while, then said thoughtfully, "That's the way I was raised too. I was sent away to private school when I was seven. My mother was dead and I rarely saw my father, only on holidays sometimes, and then . . ." She stopped. She waited a bit, then started again. "That's not to excuse it, just to say I didn't know any better. I thought that was the way you raised kids. Most of my friends did the same thing. But I'm sorry now, and I want to change things."

"It's too late."

"It's never too late." Mary hugged Marie-Laure's arm closer as they trudged through the snowy grass verge of the road, faces pink from exertion, breathing deeply. "I'm forty-five, and . . ."

"You're forty-eight, *Mother*."

Mary stopped dead. She looked at her daughter with alarm. "I can't be!" She counted silently. She slumped a bit. "God, I'm almost fifty!"

They set off again, Mary walking a bit slower now, as if age had caught up with her in a sudden sweep.

"Well, anyway," she recovered herself, "I'm not young and yet being here with my sisters while Father was sick has totally changed me, changed my relation with them, created one, really — I had no relation with Alex and Ronnie before. It's been wonderful, it makes me happy. If that can happen at forty- . . . eight, it can happen at twenty."

Marie-Laure was silent now.

"I want us to be close."

No response.

"Wouldn't you like to have a real mother? Someone you could call when you're unhappy or upset, or when you've just aced an exam or when you're having boyfriend problems? Wouldn't that be nice? Wouldn't you like that?"

The girl's face did not change expression, and she did not reply. Mary stopped again, turned to face Marie-Laure directly.

"Wouldn't you?"

The girl would not meet her eyes. "I don't know."

Mary reached out and took Marie-Laure's face between her hands. She turned it toward her.

"Wouldn't you?"

"I guess," she muttered, turning away again. But Mary had seen a glint of tears in her eyes, and was satisfied.

She took Marie-Laure's arm again, held it close, set off walking. "Of course it would. And I would too. It would make me happy."

The girl was silent, but her bodily tone had changed, was less tense.

"So tell me what's going on in your life."

Marie-Laure shrugged. "Nothing much."

"Your grades weren't great this semester, were they?"

"No."

"Don't you like school?"

She shrugged again. "It's okay."

"You don't eat, Marie-Laure. You're too thin."

It was Marie-Laure's turn to stop. She pulled away from Mary. "Is this what you mean by closeness? Picking at me, finding fault?"

"I'm worried about you. I think you're anorectic."

"I eat what I want."

"You eat nothing."

"I eat enough."

Mary gazed at her, then took her arm and began to walk again.

"Do you have a boyfriend?"

She half shrugged. "Sort of. I mean, there's this guy I see. But he lives in Washington and he goes to Yale, so we only get together on weekends, some weekends, not every one."

"What's his name?"

"Ho. We call him Ho. His real name is Howard Hodding McKenzie III. His father is secretary of the interior. He knew Grandpa. His father, I mean, not Ho." Her voice was flat.

"And what's the problem with Ho?"

"How do you know there is one?" Fierce, suddenly.

"Just a mother's intuition," Mary smiled.

Marie-Laure's glance was almost admiring. Surprised. "Oh. He just . . . I never know when he's going to call. He calls when he wants. Weekends go by and I don't hear from him. He doesn't care that I'm sitting there, waiting, doesn't ever think to call just to say hello. I stay in the dorm, I don't go out with my friends, just waiting, but he only calls when he doesn't have anything else to do. That's how it feels. It makes me feel miserable, like some kind of worm."

"Of course, poor baby," Mary said warmly. "Where is he spending Christmas, Washington?"

"No!" she cried. "Aspen, skiing with his parents! And he asked two of his male friends to go along but he didn't ask me!"

"Oh," Mary said sadly. Then, "Why don't you go out with someone else?"

"Because I love him!" Marie-Laure wailed.

"Oh, oh," Mary moaned with her, and removed her arm and put it around her daughter. Tears were streaming down Marie-Laure's face, and she wiped them away with her mittened hands.

They walked in silence. Then Mary said, "I tell you what. Come back to New York with me, or come down tomorrow. We'll go see some plays, visit some museums, I'll take you to some parties. How about it?"

"Maybe," she said unenthusiastically. "Boston's a real bore."

"Everyplace is a bore when you want to be with someone who isn't there. Don't you find that?"

Marie-Laure glanced at her mother again. "I guess."

"So when that happens, we girls just have to cheer ourselves up."

Marie-Laure almost smiled. "Has that happened to you?"

"Oh god yes. I was still married to Paul when I met Don, and couldn't see him very often. And every day I didn't see him, every minute away from him was an agony. That was really the only time I was in love, even though I was married four times. I was infatuated with your father at first, but that didn't last long. I thought it was love, but after I met Don I knew it hadn't been. That's the trouble, you know. Until you really fall in love, you can get confused. Other things seem like love. You know, a man seems appropriate, he's the same class as you, he's rich, he adores you . . . you convince yourself you're in love. But it isn't love. . . ." Her voice wandered off wonderingly.

Marie-Laure pressed her mother's arm against her.

They walked on in an agreeable silence now, hearts pumping, breathing deeply, the steam from their breath warming their faces. They had walked far; they were nearly at the town.

"Marie-Laure? Can I ask you something?" Mary's voice was almost timid.

"Yeah."

"How did you feel about Grandpa?"

"What do you mean?"

"Just that. Did you feel any affection for him, did you like him, did you dislike him, did he frighten you?"

"I didn't feel anything," she answered in a flat voice.

"Nothing at all?" Mary asked incredulously.

"Nothing at all!" Marie-Laure shouted. "Why are you asking me this! He was just a disgusting old man, why should I feel anything for him!"

"What was disgusting about him, why do you say that?" Mary cried.

"Will you stop picking and just leave me alone! Just leave me alone!" She pulled away from her mother and walked swiftly ahead, almost running. Mary's short legs could not keep up, she began to run, calling Marie-Laure's name. But the girl kept up her swift pace, she pulled yards ahead of Mary, farther and farther away. Mary, breathless, stopped running, slowed her pace, but continued. Marie-Laure's figure grew smaller and smaller. But when Mary reached the main road, the girl was standing there, bent like a hoop, waiting.

Mary gazed at her. Marie-Laure's eyes were dropped as if she were staring at the pavement. "Let's have a cup of coffee," Mary said, pulling her across the street and south, toward Lincoln's only coffee shop.

They sat there in silence, sipping coffee. Mary kept glancing at Marie-Laure, who would not return her gaze.

Oh god oh god oh god.

Finally, Mary said, "I'm exhausted. I'm going to call Aldo to come and pick us up, okay?"

Marie-Laure looked up at her. She nodded. Mary gazed into her daughter's face. "Please come to New York," she begged.

"Okay," the girl said faintly.

After breakfast, Alex went upstairs to pack, then nestled in the couch in the playroom reading the biography of Edith Stein. Ronnie, passing her, felt her heart fill with pleasure. Elizabeth, who had said almost nothing during breakfast, locked herself in her father's study.

Ronnie went to her room and sat in front of her computer, intending to work. But she did not even turn on the machine, just sat there, gazing out the window, trying to figure out what she was feeling. No one acted angry with Elizabeth. Mary and Alex seemed if anything newly solicitous of her, Alex as if Elizabeth had suddenly shown signs of illness and needed comfort, Mary as if she had a new distance from her elder sister, a new perspective from which, for the first time, she pitied her. But Ronnie was angry. Elizabeth's attack had left her feeling cold, alone, torn away from a center. By striking out at them, she thought, Elizabeth had ripped the delicate fabric of intimacy they had woven from inside themselves, hurled them out of it into cold space, threads clinging to them like torn tissue. For everything she said was a repudiation of the kind of world they had created over the last two months, a denial of its value, even its reality. Why would she want to do that, Ronnie wondered, when their closeness and affection had so clearly made her happy, warmed and eased her stiff heart? Why had she felt it necessary to renounce what she clearly wanted?

Pondering, Ronnie could not work but hung her head over the keyboard as if she were studying it, lost in some limbo. After a long time, she sat up, her face impassive and still, her eyes dull. She leaned back in her chair, and gazed out at the snowy woods behind the house.

I can live without them, she thought.

But she felt haunted by a question she did not want to bring up to consciousness, but that finally forced itself up: was it irrevocable? Was their sisterhood going now to end, to fragment into bitterness, as if it had never been forged? Was there any way to get it back, to re-bind the connection? Which, she now saw, was precious to her. Where was Elizabeth, her mind and heart, what was going on inside her?

Elizabeth herself hardly knew. She had felt numb since the night before, had gone to bed like a zombie, been unable to sleep, had smoked and drunk until nearly four, sitting up in her bed. Her mind was empty and reeling at the same time; it was full of things racing too fast for her to discern their nature. Nor was she sure why she was going through her father's correspondence files, what she expected to find in them. She had packed only some of his official papers before she left here earlier in the month. There was a closet, really a room, off the study, packed nearly to the door with his files, boxes of files from Washington, New York, Boston. It would take months to go through them all, and for a while she had considered taking a leave of absence to do that, then asked herself why, why, why? But a metal file cabinet in the study itself held correspondence from the last twelve years, since his retirement, and that was accessible. It was that she was going through now, sitting on the floor, pulling out one file after another, reading the letters he received and copies of his replies.

One after another after another, she tore through them, searching, searching. Searching for what? What did she need so desperately? She realized after a time that she was hungry for some personal note, some clue, something that would hook her into what the man had felt, wanted, needed. There were personal notes in many of the letters —

banter about a racquetball or tennis game he'd played with the recipient, compliments on a party or dinner given or attended, gossip about Washington personalities — all of it slightly sarcastic, put-downs, challenges, but with an edge of humor, wit. A great sense of humor, one of the funeral speakers had said. This must be what he meant. This must have been the tone of his conversation with these men too, in fact, she remembered it. Yes.

The personal notes were designed to base the power relation in personal connection, but they ignored the real person, focusing on the image — killer squash player, charmer of the ladies, intimate of the highest and most powerful. She found a few letters to women within the power structure, which had a more flattering tone, but no letters to women friends or lovers. Did he not write them, or did he destroy theirs and not keep copies of his own? Even the letters to his brother or sister were full of business, property matters, or discussion of the proper family stance on a public event. She piled up the files she had already examined, the pile was too high, it fell over. She wanted to weep.

For a long time she sat there, head hanging, eyes damp, her hair wispy and disheveled, gazing at the mess of files spread out on the floor in front of her.

What is the matter with me? What the fuck am I doing?

She pulled herself erect, gathered up the files, straightened them, and without bothering to realphabetize them, slammed them back in the file drawer and pulled out another batch. And started again, desperately.

Mary and Marie-Laure returned subdued and went immediately upstairs to pack. Soon afterward, a little Japanese sports car pulled up in front of the house and a young man jumped out and rang the doorbell. Teresa let him in, led him to the sitting room, and went upstairs to tell Marie-Laure he was there. Mary was sitting on the chaise in her daughter's room, watching her stuff her clothes into her bag.

"Offer him some coffee," Mary told her.

"No!" Marie-Laure cried. "I'm ready. I'm almost ready. Tell him I'll be right down," she told Teresa.

Mary waited until Teresa had left. "What is it, Marie-Laure, you don't want him to meet me?"

"I want to get to Boston. I don't want to miss the movie," she said impatiently.

"Or is it my sisters?"

The girl turned to her mother, stood with her hand on her hip, grimacing. "Everything doesn't have to do with you, you know, Mother."

That *Mother* again.

"Then what does it have to do with?"

"I hate this house, okay? I don't want to be in it any more than I have to!" She was almost screaming, her face pink with rage.

Mary stared at her. "Okay," she said softly. "You don't ever have to come back here again. Okay?"

Marie-Laure's face softened and she looked at her mother almost kindly. "Okay," she whispered, and turned and grabbed her bags, slinging them over her shoulders. "I'm out of here."

Mary rose and followed her downstairs. "You have to say good-bye to the others," she said at the foot of the stairs, as Marie-Laure greeted Duff. She introduced the boy to her mother, then turned. "So where are they?"

"Look in the playroom. Ronnie's probably in her room. Ask them."

The girl disappeared, Mary sat down and spoke easily with Duff, whose mother she knew, and his stepfather, as it turned out, and his grandparents on his mother's side. She'd been to their house at Marblehead, years before.

Marie-Laure was gone only a few minutes. She walked swiftly into the sitting room, gave Duff the high sign, and he rose. After a few politenesses — Marie-Laure suffering her mother's kiss — they were gone.

Mary turned away from the door, shoulders slumped, head down, and went back upstairs. Pack, she would pack. But she didn't. She sank down on the chaise in her room and lighted a joint — something rare for her during the day. She sat there until the gong rang for lunch.

Lunch was soup made of leftover vegetables with leftover roast beef in a salad with leftover roasted peppers and white beans, and the leftover pies. This pleased Alex, who worried about waste — and it was delicious. But conversation was stilted. Mary was sunk inside herself, Elizabeth was vacant. Alex talked and talked and talked, telling them more than they ever wanted to know about Edith Stein. Ronnie watched them all from beneath hooded eyes, her face anxious. Eventually, Alex wound down, her voice simply trailing off.

"I've been looking through Father's correspondence," Elizabeth said suddenly in the silence.

All eyes turned to her. "I've been looking for . . ." — her voice wavered — "something personal. Something that shows him, his feelings. . . ."

Alex was all sympathy. "You feel you don't know him," she said warmly, compassionately. "I know how you feel. I don't know him either, who he was, what he wanted."

"Yet we killed him," Elizabeth said.

They paled, watched her.

"Maybe not with our hands. But with our actions," she continued.

They looked at their empty salad plates.

Teresa came in to clear.

"What time is your plane?" Mary asked Alex.

"Five-ten," Alex replied. "And yours?"

"I can leave at five or five-thirty, there are two shuttles. What time is yours, Lizzie?"

Teresa left the room but they knew she would be returning with dessert.

"Four fifty-nine. So that's convenient. We should leave here about three-thirty, three forty-five, just in case there's traffic."

Teresa entered with the pies, a bowl of whipped cream, a plate of cheddar. She set them on the table and moved among the women, offering them pie. They helped themselves in silence.

"I'll let Aldo know," Elizabeth said after she had taken a piece.

"You have plenty of time to pack," Alex said, looking at her watch.

Teresa left the room.

Silence. All eyes were fixed on Elizabeth.

"I mean, we killed him but we didn't even know him."

"We know what he did to us," Ronnie muttered.

"Yes."

"And maybe Marie-Laure too!" Mary burst out in a tearful voice.

They turned to her. No one spoke.

She wiped tears from her cheeks, looking around at them. "No, I don't know for sure! But the way she acted, the things she said! I don't know what to do!"

"You have to tell her. About you. Us," Alex said softly. "You have to be open. Honest."

"Oh god! How can I tell my daughter that! How? How?" Mary cried.

Their eyes moved uneasily, each considering what that would feel like, how one could do it, how the girl would feel, how she would look at her mother. No one had any advice for her. Shame descended on them like a lowered canopy, muffling them.

Mary stopped sniffling, wiped her face, looked at them. "I guess I'll have to," she said. "I'll think of a way. I may — at some point — need you all to help me. Will you?"

"Oh, of course! I'll come if you need me, Mary, anytime! I'll fly back! Just call me — or maybe," Alex giggled, "you'll have to write or telegraph! I don't know. But I'll come."

Ronnie nodded her head soberly and Mary looked at Elizabeth.

"Yes. Of course," she said.

"Thanks," Mary whispered, and picked up her fork to eat her pie.

Slowly, sadly, Elizabeth folded garments and laid them in her bag. We killed him, and we didn't even know who he was. All we knew was what he'd done to us. We killed him for what? Thousands of little Stephen Uptons springing up around us all the time like the dragon's teeth Cadmus sowed, we can't get rid of all of them so why bother to kill one? Only now *we* have his money. Three of us, anyway. We can't even say we didn't intend to kill him, what had we just done? Condemned him to death. What did Alex say? Can't remember her words, but what she really meant was he'd die from lack of love, from failure to love.

The heart dies first.

His heart must have been near death for a long time. He had only Noradia. Her dying finished him.

So maybe Alex was only confirming what already existed. If we left, he'd have nothing even resembling love, only his hate to carry him. But he lived on hate, it fed him. Might have fed him for more years, for decades maybe.

Unlikely.

And I?

She laid the last item in the suitcase, walked around the room searching for anything forgotten, checked the bathroom, returned and closed the bag. She bent to look in the vanity mirror, ran a comb through her hair. Look like hell.

Suddenly, she bent almost double, and retched a huge sob. What have I done?

Why why why did I do that? Had to attack them, had to attack what we did, what we made, what I loved, what I found I'd needed. Why did I do that?

She lowered herself onto the bench before the vanity table, back to the mirror, and lighted a cigarette.

What happened with them made me happier, made my life better. Was it that I couldn't stand that? I'm not allowed to feel better, I have to keep up the fight, unremittingly, the way he did? But what was he fighting? At the end, us, who were at least partly trying to help him. What do you mean, "at the end," asshole? He treated you like an enemy your whole fucking life!

That was because of Mother.

So he treated Mary better? Well, it seemed so, but look how he undercut her, patronized her, destroyed her confidence in her talents. Is that love?

And Ronnie? She never told us how it happened with her. I can just imagine. Slave girl, come here.

His own children, his own genes, what the sociobiologists say men want to pass on as widely as possible, keep alive. Immortality. Hating your children, abusing them, is not survival of the fittest, it's destruction of the race.

Ronnie's right.

But not all men do that.

Lots do.

It's suicide.

He must have hated himself. Why, I wonder? I don't remember his mother but she was a tough woman, all her kids feared her. Family name and reputation meant everything to her. And wealth. Wonder what his father was like? Like him, maybe. Enough reason to hate yourself maybe.

Who knows. I'll never know. I'll never know you, Father. But — she began to weep silently — I loved you.

Ronnie sat at her computer while the others packed. She was trying to do statistical calculations on some research data, but her eyes kept flickering shut, she felt sleepy. They were all upstairs packing. Then they'd leave, with nothing said, no effort to reestablish connection. It's over. I have no sisters.

You lived without them for twenty-five years, Ronnie, you have lots of other kinds of sisters, you'll survive.

Well, of course I will.

But tiredness overcame her, and she got up and lay down on the bed. Within minutes she was fast asleep.

Alex was wandering through the downstairs rooms. "Where's Ronnie, we have to have a last drink together, don't we Mary, I mean, I know it's early in the day, but we may not see each other again for months, let's have some champagne, shouldn't we, don't you think it's a good idea, oh here you are!" She had pushed open Ronnie's door. "Ronnie, get up, this is no time to be sleeping, come and have a farewell drink with us!"

Ronnie pulled herself out of a heavy dark-dreamed sleep, shook her head, peered up at Alex. "Okay," she mumbled, "be right there."

Alex disappeared but her voice floated back through the rooms, "Now where's Lizzie, why has everyone disappeared at a time like this!"

Ronnie got up and washed her face and teeth, combed her hair. She wandered out toward the playroom, where a bottle of champagne rested in an ice bucket. Mary was standing stiffly at the glass door, stunning in a formal suit, her hair perfectly coiffed, her makeup exquisitely subtle. The old Mary.

She turned, hearing Ronnie, and reached out her arm. Ronnie walked to her, and into the arm. She put her arm around Mary's waist.

Not the old Mary.

"I'm going to miss you," Mary said.

"Me too."

"You still have to finish teaching me to drive."

"Have to come back here for that. I'm not teaching you to drive in Manhattan."

"How about Virginia?"

Ronnie looked at her startled but asked no questions. "That'd probably be okay."

"She's coming," Alex said cheerfully, returning. "We'll wait to open the champagne until she comes, though, shouldn't we? Oh, you-all!" She walked to them and stood at Ronnie's side, her left arm around Ronnie's waist, her right arm around Mary's. They stood this way for a moment, then broke apart. Alex walked to the sliding glass doors, and they both followed.

"Snow's almost gone."

"Yes."

"We should have put some food out for the birds."

"I did. Early this morning. Mrs. Browning bought some suet for them, and I added stale bread."

"Oh, that's good."

"There's still some snow on the pine branches, lying there as if it were in bed. So lovely."

"Beautiful. And the sky is a beautiful blue today."

"Beautiful."

Elizabeth walked in and stopped, seeing them. They all turned, stood facing her.

"Champagne, Lizzie?" Alex asked brightly.

"Sure." She walked into the room, stood there uneasily, while Alex handed Ronnie the champagne to open ("I never can do it, I don't know why I'm so inept!") and Mary walked to an easy chair and sat down. Alex poured the wine and passed it to them. They all sat.

"Shall we have a toast?" Too cheerful, too bright.

"I'd like to do it. May I?" Elizabeth's voice was sober, sad, not peremptory.

They all nodded.

"Last night I attacked you. Attacked a whole lot of things. I don't know why I had to say those things to you, and I can't repudiate what I said, they're things I believe, have believed all my life. But I have been thinking — well, not really thinking — thinking and feeling, I guess — ever since then. And while I still believe . . . I still see truth in what I said . . . but you all are right too, there is more to life than struggle, and unless there is more . . . then the struggle is worth nothing. All you have is a life full of hate. And I don't want to live that way anymore, looking down on the rest of the human race, confined to the company of the one or two people I consider my equals . . . well, there was only one, really . . . and he's dead. Clare was an intellectual snob too, a really cruel one, he would get up noisily in the middle of a concert and walk out if he found the players inadequate, he mocked other people's ideas . . . oh hell, what's the difference. The only other man important in my life was Father, who was a terrible social snob. He never considered me his equal, I didn't make it into his register, I was like Ronnie, illegitimate in his eyes. But then he didn't consider any of us his equals, we were girls, female. And I was raised to make those distinctions — well, we all were, except Ronnie maybe. . . ."

"I wasn't," Alex put in mildly.

"I learned them better than any of you," Ronnie demurred, "from the opposite end."

"You probably did," Elizabeth granted, then turned to Alex. "No, you weren't, sweetheart." She lighted a cigarette but no one spoke or sipped her champagne. "Anyway, I was raised that way, and I was taught or believed or assumed that the distinctions were all important because life was war and they were your armor. But you-all have taught me . . . I've come to see . . . that they *make* life war and they make a person miserable. But I don't know that I'll be able to just drop them. They're habitual now, a lifetime's habit. But I've dropped them with you. And that makes you very precious to me. And so I want to beg you to forgive me for attacking you yesterday and tell you you've convinced me that my . . . morality or whatever it is . . . is, at the least, lacking. And I ask you to let me back in. And I offer this toast to us. Sisters."

They all sat erect, clinked glasses, repeated, "To us, sisters."

Alex fell back in her seat with a broad smile on her face, kept smiling, didn't for once speak. Ronnie, leaning forward holding her glass between her legs, looked at Elizabeth with a warm near-smile. Mary was gazing at the fireplace. She sipped her champagne, then set the glass down.

"Lizzie? When should I come down and visit you to go house hunting?"

"You're going to come!" Elizabeth was stunned. "Really?"

Mary nodded. "Yes. I think it would be nice. I have lots of friends in

Washington. And I could spend time with you instead of going to all these charity dos, of course they have them in Washington too, but it's such a provincial town. . . . I wouldn't be so driven to have lunch with X or Y, I think. I'd stay home and practice and write poetry and I wouldn't be lonely because you'd come home for dinner at night. . . ."

"Well, I do travel a fair amount. . . ."

"Yes, well, I will too. . . ."

"But I'm home a lot too."

"Yes, me too."

"And I'd love your company."

"Finally!" Mary grinned. "It's taken forty years for you to say that!"

They all laughed.

"And it would be a new place, a neutral place for Marie-Laure. Maybe you'll all come visit there when we need to talk to her together. I want to get her away from her New York friends, I don't think they're . . . healthy for her. She loves to ride and there are lots of horses in Virginia. She could come and stay and have two very different mothers. . . ."

"I'd like that," Elizabeth said tremulously.

"Let's toast that," Alex urged, refilling their glasses.

"To Elizabeth and Mary in Virginia, with Marie-Laure," she said with a delighted grin.

Again, they clinked glasses and repeated the words.

"To happiness ever after!" Alex cried.

The others turned and looked at her.

"No? We can't toast that?"

"Not unless we're blind fools."

"Even in hope?"

They were silent, sober.

Ronnie cleared her throat. "Maybe we could say 'To moments of happiness in every day.' Or maybe we could say 'To love and our continuing ability to feel it.'"

"To love," they all said solemnly, clinked their glasses, and drank deep.

Aldo had spent nearly an hour fitting the many suitcases and packages into the trunk and front seat of the car and now the sisters crowded near the doorway of the house saying good-byes, embracing, kissing, holding each other. "Soon," they said. "I love you," they whispered. Then they walked out of the shelter of the portico and got into the car and Ronnie stood there, Mrs. Browning and Teresa behind her, waving them out of the driveway, watching as the car turned into the drive toward the road. The light was fading, and most of the snow had melted, showing again the dismal graybrown landscape of New England winter. She stood there shivering until the car turned on a curve and disappeared into the trees, then went in and closed the door. She stood for a moment leaning against the door.

The thought of living on here alone without them was unendurable.

But I need that two hundred dollars a week, not for long, just till I finish a first draft. What will that take, two more months? Three? Four? It'll be spring then: will I want to work in the garden? No. Not here. Not his gardens. Let the house stand empty or maybe they'll find a buyer who'll turn it into a restaurant or a rest home or an inn. I want to be in Boston with my friends. Maybe I can find a place with a window box. Have *my* life. Momma left me all that money. Maybe for once I don't have to be so careful. Maybe I'll just go now.

Yes. Tomorrow I'll go and look for a share in an apartment. Leave this house forever. My father's mansion, my prison. Go, Ronnie.